DEATH ON WHEELS

Also edited by Peter Haining

DEATH ON WHEELS

Edited by Peter Haining

Souvenir Press

First published 1999 by
Souvenir Press Ltd,
43 Great Russell Street, London WC1B 3PA

ISBN 0 285 63507 7

Typeset by Rowland Phototypesetting Ltd,
Bury St Edmunds, Suffolk

Printed in Great Britain by
Creative Print and Design Group (Wales), Ebbw Vale

CONTENTS

*Either the motor car will drive us all out of our cities,
or the cities will have to drive out the motor car.*

Lewis Mumford (1895–1990)
The Highway and the City (1963)

INTRODUCTION

The fascination and menace of the motor car have been enduring themes in literature almost since the invention of the 'snorting beast'—as it was nicknamed by apprehensive pedestrians—more than a century ago. Subsequently, movie and television producers have found cars an irresistible element in a variety of productions, from high-octane feature films to gritty documentaries about death on wheels. Both literary and film critics have often been divided in their opinions about the reasons for the public's attraction to speed in these media, describing it as suicidal, almost a rush towards disintegration. In a word, Autogeddon.

The mixture of fear and attraction that is so inextricably linked to the motor car has been reflected in many books, especially mystery stories. Indeed, the car as co-hero can be traced back to a series of novels written as early as the first years of the twentieth century by a husband-and-wife team, Charles and Alice Williamson. Charles was a mechanical engineer who turned to journalism and used his fascination with 'autocaring' (as he put it in his entry in *Who's Who*) to create the first full-length fictional works about motor cars. In preparation, he had driven along the tortuous British roads and then over the equally rutted highways of France, Germany and Spain, always accompanied by his intrepid wife, who later co-authored with him such titles as *The Car of Destiny* (1905)—the earliest crime story in which an automobile is used to outwit a threat to a member of the Spanish royal family—*The Lightning Conductor: Strange Adventures of a Motor Car* (1906) and *The Scarlet Runner: The Adventure of the Mysterious Motor Car* (1907). A powerful, imaginary machine, the 'Scarlet Runner' also appeared in several short stories written by the Williamsons for the *Strand* magazine, where they often appeared in the same issues as Sir Arthur Conan Doyle's continuing cases of Sherlock Holmes. All the couple's novels, now rare and very collectable, are notable for their authentic descriptions of the hardships faced by drivers on dreadful roads, the uncertainty of what lay around the corner, and the constant fear of breakdowns at a time when garages, such as they were, were few and far between. Small wonder the Williamsons' books proved so irresistible to thousands of readers, many of whom could only dream of ever possessing a car.

The First World War saw the arrival of another writer whose best-sellers regularly featured automobiles, William Le Queux, described on the dust-jackets of his books as 'The Master of Mystery'. His themes ranged from crime to spying, in fact and fiction. Le Queux had for some years been a special correspondent for several London newspapers, acquiring in the process an insider's knowledge of political machinations and espionage which he used in the books that made his reputation. *The Invasion of 1910*, written in 1906, accurately predicted the First World War, and he also enjoyed considerable success with *The Zeppelin Destroyer* (1916). Le Queux was a dedicated motorist and took part in several eventful journeys—including a marathon ride to Monte Carlo—which proved invaluable in the writing of *The Mystery of the Motor Car* (1906) and *The Lady in the Motor Car* (1908). In both of these, he more than hinted at the problems that lay ahead for drivers and pedestrians with the mounting speed of vehicles and the recklessness of some drivers.

In the Thirties emerged Simon Templar, otherwise known as 'The Saint', who was frequently to be found behind the wheel of a magnificent Hirondel: a car of amazing performance and powerful enough to enable the 'Modern-day Robin Hood' to catch an escaping villain or show a clean pair of wheels to any officers of the law, should the need arise. The pity of it was that the Hirondel—like its predecessor, the 'Scarlet Runner'—was purely an invention of the Saint's creator, Leslie Charteris.

The Aston Martin associated with James Bond is real enough, of course, and Ian Fleming's secret agent is generally regarded as the first hero to have had a car equipped with gadgets intended to kill. However, Bond actually appeared in his debut novel, *Casino Royale* (1953), driving a 1930 Bentley, used it again in the next two stories, and was not given an Aston Martin DB3 until he confronted his most famous adversary, Auric Goldfinger, in the book of the same name (1959). Later he went back to Bentleys again, with a Mark II, for his three run-ins with the arch villain Blofeld which culminated in *You Only Live Twice* (1964). Fleming was himself a Bentley enthusiast—he owned a classic R-type—yet had to bow to pressure from Cubby Broccoli and Harry Saltzman when they began making the Bond movies and decided that an Aston Martin was more in keeping with the spy's image than a vintage motor car. Few readers will need reminding of the highly-dramatic scenes of Bond's car using its forward-firing machine guns, hub-mounted scythes or passenger ejector seat. In more recent versions, 007 has been assisted in his missions to thwart plans for world domination by vehicles able to fly and even travel under water.

Another movie favourite, Batman, has his 'Batmobile' for all crimes and emergencies in and around Gotham City. The sleek, dark, bat-winged car is just one of a whole series of remarkable multi-purpose cars that have been seen on the screen, beginning in *High Treason*, made way back in 1929, which envisaged a car of the year 1950, right through to the recent *Back to the Future* (1985) with its De Lorean sports car specially adapted to function as a time machine.

A look at the motor car in literature—especially in crime and mystery fiction—soon reveals that such apparently modern phenomena as street racing, road rage and ram-raiding are actually not that new, but merely the latest manifestation of old traditions. Edgar Wallace, for one, describes all of these in his novels *The Dark Eyes of London* (1924), *The Flying Squad* (1928) and *When the Gangs Came to London* (1932). The suitability of automobiles to provide criminals with mobility to carry out robbery and then outrun the law became evident in the Twenties and is reflected in the pages of the novels of Raymond Chandler, Dashiell Hammet, W. R. Burnett and the other 'hard-boiled' writers of the time. Indeed, the term 'hit-and-run', often used by such writers, came to typify a whole strategy of mobile murder and terror that was seized upon and developed still further by the organised crime syndicates like the Mafia. Car theft—now considered as big an international problem as drug smuggling—the use of blazing cars to conceal murder and the dangers posed by the ever-growing volume of traffic rushing headlong along the highways have also been mirrored in the work of writers from the past, such as Agatha Christie and J. B. Priestley, and of modern masters like Donald E. Westlake and Arthur Hailey.

It is evident from all this that many authors seem to be sensing the approach of an apocalypse brought about by the motor car. And it is a selection of some of the very best short stories of this kind—from the past, the present and, ominously, the future—that I have brought together in this collection. The writers are from both sides of the Atlantic: some worked in the 'Golden Age' of mystery fiction, others are leading contemporary figures in the science fiction genre who have some very dark ideas about what lies ahead. The car, which has been referred to as 'the world's most lethal weapon', clearly has much about it to inspire the imagination, and quite a few of the contributors to *Death on Wheels* believe it stands at a crucial point in its history. Their stories, especially, are intended as much to make you *think* as to entertain. Autogeddon, you may well decide by the end of this book, could be a lot closer than any of us realise.

Peter Haining
April 1999

ONE

AUTO MANIA

The Machinery of Death

TRUCKS

Stephen King

The automobile is generally acknowledged to be the single most powerful piece of machinery in most people's lives. For this reason, cars often take on personalities and many owners refer to them as 'she' and credit them with all kinds of qualities, some good, some infuriating and, on occasions, some downright evil. The car with a personality has also been one of the most enduring themes in motoring fiction — from as far back as 1908 when the French fantasy writer Maurice Renard wrote Le docteur Lerne, sous-dieu *(translated into English as* New Bodies for Old*), about a dead man's soul which enters a powerful car and causes it to behave spontaneously in the most bizarre ways. Today's most famous novel in this tradition is undoubtedly Stephen King's* Christine *(1983). This story features a 1957 automobile which, ever since its manufacture, has been possessed by an evil spirit that in turn possesses those who own it, causing misery and death. Like so many of King's best-sellers,* Christine *was filmed in 1983 by director John Carpenter starring Keith Gordon. Sinister vehicles have also occasionally appeared in his other stories, most notably in 'Trucks' which provides an ideal opening to this collection. It was adapted for the screen in 1986 as* Maximum Overdrive, *with Emilio Estevez and Pat Hingle.*

Stephen King (1947–) has, since his debut novel Carrie *(1974), grown in stature and sales until today he is probably the most successful English-language author of the century. His novels and short-story collections have sold in uncounted millions all over the world and he has played a major part in the current popularity of horror fiction, as well as inspiring countless tyro writers to follow in his footsteps. 'Trucks' first appeared in print in a men's magazine,* Cavalier, *in April 1971, and was brought to the screen directed by the author himself. The frightening account of a group of people trapped in a truck stop*

*by huge, sentient vehicles which run down anyone who tries to escape
was, however, changed somewhat for the movie, as King explained
at the time. 'The premise became, "What if everything went bullshit?" So in the film not just trucks, but lawn-mowers, electric knives,
everything comes alive.' The film was shot on location close to the
Wilmington and Interstate Highways in North Carolina, and so realistic
was the set of the Dixie Boy Truck Stop that day after day truck drivers
pulled in for fuel and food, seemingly unaware that the wrecked trucks,
lights, reflectors and so on were just the paraphernalia of movie-making!
Maximum Overdrive has been acclaimed as 'a mechanical version of
The Birds', by the US critic Tyson Blue, while 'Trucks' is deservedly
ranked as one of Stephen King's finest stories of 'technofantasy'.*

*   *   *

The guy's name was Snodgrass and I could see him getting ready
to do something crazy. His eyes had got bigger, showing a lot
of the whites, like a dog getting ready to fight. The two kids who
had come skidding into the parking lot in the old Fury were
trying to talk to him, but his head was cocked as though he was
hearing other voices. He had a tight little pot-belly encased in a
good suit that was getting a little shiny in the seat. He was a
salesman and he kept his display bag close to him, like a pet dog
that had gone to sleep.

'Try the radio again,' the truck driver at the counter said.

The short-order cook shrugged and turned it on. He flipped it
across the band and got nothing but static.

'You went too fast,' the trucker protested. 'You might have
missed something.'

'Hell,' the short-order cook said. He was an elderly black man
with a smile of gold and he wasn't looking at the trucker. He
was looking through the diner-length picture window at the
parking lot.

Seven or eight heavy trucks were out there, engines rumbling
in low, idling roars that sounded like big cats purring. There
were a couple of Macks, a Hemingway, and four or five Reos.
Trailer trucks, interstate haulers with a lot of licence plates and
CB whip antennas on the back.

The kids' Fury was lying on its roof at the end of long, looping
skid marks in the loose crushed rock of the parking lot. It had
been battered into senseless junk. At the entrance to the truck

stop's turnaround, there was a blasted Cadillac. Its owner stared out of the star-shattered windshield like a gutted fish. Horn-rimmed glasses hung from one ear.

Halfway across the lot from it lay the body of a girl in a pink dress. She had jumped from the Caddy when she saw it wasn't going to make it. She had hit running but never had a chance. She was the worst, even though she was face down. There were flies around her in clouds.

Across the road an old Ford station wagon had been slammed through the guardrails. That had happened an hour ago. No one had been by since then. You couldn't see the turnpike from the window and the phone was out.

'You went too fast,' the trucker was protesting. 'You oughta—'

That was when Snodgrass bolted. He turned the table over getting up, smashing coffee cups and sending sugar in a wild spray. His eyes were wilder than ever, and his mouth hung loosely and he was blabbering: 'We gotta get outta here we gotta get-outtahere wegottagetouttahere—'

The kid shouted and his girl friend screamed.

I was on the stool closest to the door and I got a handful of his shirt, but he tore loose. He was cranked up all the way. He would have gone through a bank-vault door.

He slammed out the door and then he was sprinting across the gravel towards the drainage ditch on the left. Two of the trucks lunged after him, smokestacks blowing diesel exhaust dark brown against the sky, huge rear wheels machine-gunning gravel up in sprays.

He couldn't have been any more than five or six running steps from the edge of the flat parking lot when he turned back to look, fear scrawled on his face. His feet tangled each other and he faltered and almost fell down. He got his balance again, but it was too late.

One of the trucks gave way and the other charged down, huge front grill glittering savagely in the sun. Snodgrass screamed, the sound high and thin, nearly lost under the Reo's heavy diesel roar.

It didn't drag him under. As things turned out, it would have been better if it had. Instead it drove him up and out, the way a punter kicks a football. For a moment he was silhouetted against the hot afternoon sky like a crippled scarecrow, and then he was gone into the drainage ditch.

The big truck's brakes hissed like dragon's breath, its front wheels locked, digging grooves into the gravel skin of the lot, and it stopped inches from jackknifing in. The bastard.

The girl in the booth screamed. Both hands were clamped into her cheeks, dragging the flesh down, turning it into a witch's mask.

Glass broke. I turned my head and saw that the trucker had squeezed his glass hard enough to break it. I don't think he knew it yet. Milk and a few drops of blood fell onto the counter.

The black counterman was frozen by the radio, a dishcloth in hand, looking amazed. His teeth glittered. For a moment there was no sound but the buzzing Westclox and the rumbling of the Reo's engine as it returned to its fellows. Then the girl began to cry and it was all right—or at least better.

My own car was around the side, also battered to junk. It was a 1971 Camaro and I had still been paying on it, but I didn't suppose that mattered now.

There was no one in the trucks.

The sun glittered and flashed on empty cabs. The wheels turned themselves. You couldn't think about it too much. You'd go insane if you thought about it too much. Like Snodgrass.

Two hours passed. The sun began to go down. Outside, the trucks patrolled in slow circles and figure eights. Their parking lights and running lights had come on.

I walked the length of the counter twice to get the kinks out of my legs and then sat in a booth by the long front window. It was a standard truck stop, close to the major thruway, a complete service facility out back, gas and diesel fuel both. The truckers came here for coffee and pie.

'Mister?' The voice was hesitant.

I looked around. It was the two kids from the Fury. The boy looked about nineteen. He had long hair and a beard that was just starting to take hold. His girl looked younger.

'Yeah?'

'What happened to you?'

I shrugged. 'I was coming up the interstate to Pelson,' I said. 'A truck came up behind me—I could see it in the mirror a long way off—really highballing. You could hear it a mile down the road. It whipped out around a VW Beetle and just snapped it off the road with the whiplash of the trailer, the way you'd snap a ball of paper off a table with your finger. I thought the truck would go, too. No driver could have held it with the trailer whipping that way. But it didn't go. The VW flopped over six or seven times and exploded. And the truck got the next one coming up the same way. It was coming up on me and I took the exit ramp in a hurry.' I laughed but my heart wasn't in it. 'Right into a truck stop, of all places. From the frying pan into the fire.'

The girl swallowed. 'We saw a Greyhound going north in the southbound lane. It was ... ploughing ... through cars. It exploded and burned but before it did ... slaughter.'

A Greyhound bus. That was something new. And bad.

Outside, all the headlights suddenly popped on in unison, bathing the lot in an eerie, depthless glare. Growling, they cruised back and forth. The headlights seemed to give them eyes, and in the growing gloom, the dark trailer boxes looked like the hunched, squared-off shoulders of prehistoric giants.

The counterman said, 'Is it safe to turn on the lights?'

'Do it,' I said, 'and find out.'

He flipped the switches and a series of flyspecked globes overhead came on. At the same time a neon sign out front stuttered into life: 'Conant's Truck Stop & Diner—Good Eats'. Nothing happened. The trucks continued their patrol.

'I can't understand it,' the trucker said. He had got down from his stool and was walking around, his hand wrapped in a red engineer's bandanna. 'I ain't had no problems with my rig. She's a good old girl. I pulled in here a little past one for a spaghetti dinner and this happens.' He waved his arms and the bandanna flapped. 'My own rig's out there right now, the one with the weak left taillight. Been driving her for six years. But if I stepped out that door—'

'It's just starting,' the counterman said. His eyes were hooded and obsidian. 'It must be bad if that radio's gone. It's just starting.'

The girl had drained as pale as milk. 'Never mind that,' I said to the counterman. 'Not yet.'

'What would do it?' The trucker was worrying. 'Electrical storms in the atmosphere? Nuclear testing? What?'

'Maybe they're mad,' I said.

Around seven o'clock I walked over to the counterman. 'How are we fixed here? I mean, if we have to stay a while?'

His brow wrinkled. 'Not so bad. Yest'y was delivery day. We

got two-three hunnert hamburg patties, canned fruit and vege-
tables, dry cereal, aigs . . . no more milk than what's in the cooler,
but the water's from the well. If we had to, the five of us cud
get on for a month or more.'

The trucker came over and blinked at us. 'I'm dead out of
cigarettes. Now that cigarette machine . . .'

'It ain't my machine,' the counterman said. 'No sir.'

The trucker had a steel pinch bar he'd got in the supply room
out back. He went to work on the machine.

The kid went down to where the jukebox glittered and flashed
and plugged in a quarter. John Fogarty began to sing about being
born on the bayou.

I sat down and looked out the window. I saw something I
didn't like right away. A Chevy light pickup had joined the
patrol, like a Shetland pony amid Percherons. I watched it until
it rolled impartially over the body of the girl from the Caddy
and then I looked away.

'We *made* them!' the girl cried out with sudden wretchedness.
'They *can't*!'

Her boy friend told her to hush. The trucker got the cigarette
machine open and helped himself to six or eight packs of Vice-
roys. He put them in different pockets and then ripped one pack
open. From the intent expression on his face, I wasn't sure if he
was going to smoke them or eat them up.

Another record came on the juke. It was eight o'clock.

At eight-thirty the power went off.

When the lights went, the girl screamed, a cry that stopped
suddenly, as if her boy friend had put his hand over her mouth.
The jukebox died with a deepening, unwinding sound.

'What the *Christ*!' the trucker said.

'Counterman!' I called. 'You got any candles?'

'I think so. Wait . . . yeah. Here's a few.'

I got up and took them. We lit them and started placing them
around. 'Be careful,' I said. 'If we burn the place down there's
the devil to pay.'

He chuckled morosely. 'You know it.'

When we were done placing the candles, the kid and his girl
were huddled together and the trucker was by the back door,
watching six more heavy trucks weaving in and out between the
concrete fuel islands. 'This changes things, doesn't it?' I said.

'Damn right, if the power's gone for good.'

'How bad?'

'Hamburg'll go over in three days. Rest of the meat and aigs'll go by about as quick. The cans will be okay, an' the dry stuff. But that ain't the worst. We ain't gonna have no water without the pump.'

'How long?'

'Without no water? A week.'

'Fill every empty jug you've got. Fill them till you can't draw anything but air. Where are the toilets? There's good water in the tanks.'

'Employees' res'room is in the back. But you have to go outside to get to the lady's and gent's.'

'Across to the service building?' I wasn't ready for that. Not yet.

'No. Out the side door an' up a ways.'

'Give me a couple of buckets.'

He found two galvanised pails. The kid strolled up.

'What are you doing?'

'We have to have water. All we can get.'

'Give me a bucket then.'

I handed him one.

'Jerry!' the girl cried. 'You—'

He looked at her and she didn't say anything else, but she picked up a napkin and began to tear at the corners. The trucker was smoking another cigarette and grinning at the floor. He didn't speak up.

We walked over to the side door where I'd come in that afternoon and stood there for a second, watching the shadows wax and wane as the trucks went back and forth.

'Now?' the kid said. His arm brushed mine and the muscles were jumping and humming like wires. If anyone bumped him he'd go straight up to heaven.

'Relax,' I said.

He smiled a little. It was a sick smile, but better than none.

'Okay.'

We slipped out.

The night air had cooled. Crickets chirred in the grass, and frogs thumped and croaked in the drainage ditch. Out here the rumble of the trucks was louder, more menacing, the sound of beasts. From inside it was a movie. Out here it was real, you could get killed.

We slid along the tiled outer wall. A slight overhang gave us some shadow. My Camaro was huddled against the cyclone fence across from us, and faint light from the roadside sign glinted on broken metal and puddles of gas and oil.

'You take the lady's,' I whispered. 'Fill your bucket from the toilet tank and wait.'

Steady diesel rumblings. It was tricky; you thought they were coming, but it was only echoes bouncing off the building's odd corners. It was only twenty feet, but it seemed much farther.

He opened the lady's-room door and went in. I went past and then I was inside the gent's. I could feel my muscles loosen and a breath whistled out of me. I caught a glimpse of myself in the mirror, strained white face with dark eyes.

I got the porcelain tank cover off and dunked the bucket full. I poured a little back to keep from sloshing and went to the door. 'Hey?'

'Yeah,' he breathed.

'You ready?'

'Yeah.'

We went out again. We got maybe six steps before lights blared in our faces. It had crept up, big wheels barely turning on the gravel. It had been lying in wait and now it leaped at us, electric headlamps glowing in savage circles, the huge chrome grill seeming to snarl.

The kid froze, his face stamped with horror, his eyes blank, the pupils dilated down to pinpricks. I gave him a hard shove, spilling half his water.

'Go!'

The thunder of that diesel engine rose to a shriek. I reached over the kid's shoulder to yank the door open, but before I could it was shoved from inside. The kid lunged in and I dodged after him. I looked back to see the truck—a big cab-over Peterbilt— kiss off the tiled outside wall, peeling away jagged hunks of tile. There was an ear-grinding squealing noise, like gigantic fingers scraping a blackboard. Then the right mudguard and the corners of the grill smashed into the still-open door, sending glass in a crystal spray and snapping the door's steel-gauge hinges like tissue paper. The door flew into the night like something out of a Dali painting and the truck accelerated towards the front parking lot, its exhaust racketing like machine-gun fire. It had a disappointed, angry sound.

The kid put his bucket down and collapsed into the girl's arms, shuddering.

My heart was thudding heavily in my chest and my calves felt like water. And speaking of water, we had brought back about a bucket and a quarter between us. It hardly seemed worth it.

'I want to block up that doorway,' I said to the counterman. 'What will do the trick?'

'Well—'

The trucker broke in: 'Why? One of those big trucks couldn't get a wheel in through there.'

'It's not the big trucks I'm worried about.'

The trucker began hunting for a smoke.

'We got some sheet sidin' out in the supply room,' the counterman said. 'Boss was gonna put up a shed to store butane gas.'

'We'll put them across and prop them with a couple of booths.'

'It'll help,' the trucker said.

It took about an hour and by the end we'd all gotten into the act, even the girl. It was fairly solid. Of course, fairly solid wasn't going to be good enough, not if something hit it at full speed. I think they all knew that.

There were still three booths ranged along the big glass picture window and I sat down in one of them. The clock behind the counter had stopped at 8:32, but it felt like ten. Outside the trucks prowled and growled. Some left, hurrying off to unknown missions, and others came. There were three pickup trucks now, circling importantly amid their bigger brothers.

I was starting to doze, and instead of counting sheep I counted trucks. How many in the state, how many in America? Trailer trucks, pickup trucks, flatbeds, day-haulers, three-quarter-tons, army convoy trucks by the tens of thousands, and buses. Nightmare vision of a city bus, two wheels in the gutter and two wheels on the pavement, roaring along and ploughing through screaming pedestrians like ninepins.

I shook it off and fell into a light, troubled sleep.

It must have been early morning when Snodgrass began to scream. A thin new moon had risen and was shining icily through a high scud of cloud. A new clattering note had been added, counterpointing the throaty, idling roar of the big rigs. I looked for it and saw a hay baler circling out by the darkened sign. The moonlight glanced off the sharp, turning spokes of its packer.

The scream came again, unmistakably from the drainage ditch:
'Help ... *meeeee ...*'

'What was that?' It was the girl. In the shadows her eyes were
wide and she looked horribly frightened.

'Nothing,' I said.

'Help ... *meeeee ...*'

'He's alive,' she whispered. 'Oh, God. *Alive.*'

I didn't have to see him. I could imagine it all too well. Snodgrass lying half in and half out of the drainage ditch, back and
legs broken, carefully-pressed suit caked with mud, white, gasping face turned up to the indifferent moon ...

'I don't hear anything,' I said. 'Do you?'

She looked at me. 'How can you? How?'

'Now if you woke him up,' I said, jerking a thumb at the kid,
'he might hear something. He might go out there. Would you
like that?'

Her face began to twitch and pull as if stitched by invisible
needles. 'Nothing,' she whispered. 'Nothing out there.'

She went back to her boy friend and pressed her head against
his chest. His arms came up around her in his sleep.

No one else woke up. Snodgrass cried and wept and screamed
for a long time, and then he stopped.

Dawn.

Another truck had arrived, this one a flatbed with a giant rack
for hauling cars. It was joined by a bulldozer. That scared me.

The trucker came over and twitched my arm. 'Come on back,'
he whispered excitedly. The others were still sleeping. 'Come
look at this.'

I followed him back to the supply room. About ten trucks were
patrolling out there. At first I didn't see anything new.

'See?' he said, and pointed. 'Right there.'

Then I saw. One of the pickups was stopped dead. It was
sitting there like a lump, all of the menace gone out of it.

'Out of gas?'

'That's right, buddy. And *they can't pump their own.* We got it
knocked. All we have to do is wait.' He smiled and fumbled for
a cigarette.

It was about nine o'clock and I was eating a piece of yesterday's
pie for breakfast when the air horn began—long, rolling blasts
that rattled your skull. We went over to the windows and looked

out. The trucks were sitting still, idling. One trailer truck, a huge
Reo with a red cab, had pulled up almost to the narrow verge
of grass between the restaurant and the parking lot. At this distance the square grill was huge and murderous. The tyres would
stand to a man's chest cavity.

The horn began to blare again; hard, hungry blasts that travelled off in straight, flat lines and echoed back. There was a
pattern. Shorts and longs in some kind of rhythm.

'That's Morse!' the kid, Jerry, suddenly exclaimed.

The trucker looked at him. 'How would you know?'

The kid went a little red. 'I learned it in the Boy Scouts.'

'You?' the trucker said. '*You?* Wow.' He shook his head.

'Never mind,' I said. 'Do you remember enough to—'

'Sure. Let me listen. Got a pencil?'

The counterman gave him one, and the kid began to write
letters on a napkin. After a while he stopped. 'It's just saying
"Attention" over and over again. Wait.'

We waited. The air horn beat its longs and shorts into the still
morning air. Then the pattern changed and the kid started to
write again. We hung over his shoulders and watched the message form. 'Someone must pump fuel. Someone will not be
harmed. All fuel must be pumped. This shall be done now. Now
someone will pump fuel.'

The air blasts kept up, but the kid stopped writing. 'It's just
repeating "Attention" again,' he said.

The truck repeated its message again and again. I didn't like
the look of the words, printed on the napkin in block style. They
looked machinelike, ruthless. There would be no compromise
with those words. You did or you didn't.

'Well,' the kid said, 'what do we do?'

'Nothing,' the trucker said. His face was excited and working.
'All we have to do is wait. They must all be low on fuel. One of
the little ones out back has already stopped. All we have to do—'

The air horn stopped. The truck backed up and joined its
fellows. They waited in a semicircle, headlights pointed in
towards us.

'There's a bulldozer out there,' I said.

Jerry looked at me. 'You think they'll rip the place down?'

'Yes.'

He looked at the counterman. 'They couldn't do that, could
they?'

The counterman shrugged.

'We oughta vote,' the trucker said. 'No blackmail, damn it. All we gotta do is wait.' He had repeated it three times now, like a charm.

'Okay,' I said. 'Vote.'

'Wait,' the trucker said immediately.

'I think we ought to fuel them,' I said. 'We can wait for a better chance to get away. Counterman?'

'Stay in here,' he said. 'You want to be their slaves? That's what it'll come to. You want to spend the rest of your life changin' oil filters every time one of those . . . *things* blats its horn? Not me.' He looked darkly out the window. 'Let them starve.'

I looked at the kid and the girl.

'I think he's right,' he said. 'That's the only way to stop them. If someone was going to rescue us, they would have. God knows what's going on in other places.' And the girl, with Snodgrass in her eyes, nodded and stepped closer to him.

'That's it then,' I said.

I went over to the cigarette machine and got a pack without looking at the brand. I'd stopped smoking a year ago, but this seemed like a good time to start again. The smoke rasped harsh in my lungs.

Twenty minutes crawled by. The trucks out front waited. In back, they were lining up at the pumps.

'I think it was all a bluff,' the trucker said. 'Just—'

Then there was a louder, harsher, choppier note, the sound of an engine revving up and falling off, then revving up again. The bulldozer.

It glittered like a yellowjacket in the sun, a Caterpillar with clattering steel treads. Black smoke belched from its short stack as it wheeled around to face us.

'It's going to charge,' the trucker said. There was a look of utter surprise on his face. 'It's going to charge!'

'Get back,' I said. 'Behind the counter.'

The bulldozer was still revving. Gear-shift levers moved themselves. Heat shimmer hung over its smoking stack. Suddenly the dozer blade lifted, a heavy steel curve clotted with dried dirt. Then, with a screaming howl of power, it roared straight at us.

'The *counter*!' I gave the trucker a shove, and that started them.

There was a small concrete verge between the parking lot and the grass. The dozer charged over it, blade lifting for a moment, and then it rammed the front wall head on. Glass exploded inward with a heavy, coughing roar and the wood frame crashed into splinters. One of the overhead light globes fell, splashing more glass. Crockery fell from the shelves. The girl was screaming but the sound was almost lost beneath the steady, pounding roar of the Cat's engine.

It reversed, clanked across the chewed strip of lawn, and lunged forward again, sending the remaining booths crashing and spinning. The pie case fell off the counter, sending pie wedges skidding across the floor.

The counterman was crouching with his eyes shut, and the kid was holding his girl. The trucker was walleyed with fear.

'We gotta stop it,' he gibbered. 'Tell 'em we'll do it, we'll do anything—'

'A little late, isn't it?'

The Cat reversed and got ready for another charge. New nicks in its blade glittered and heliographed in the sun. It lurched forward with a bellowing roar and this time it took down the main support to the left of what had been the window. That section of the roof fell in with a grinding crash. Plaster dust billowed up.

The dozer pulled free. Beyond it I could see the group of trucks, waiting.

I grabbed the counterman. 'Where are the oil drums?' The cookstoves ran on butane gas, but I had seen vents for a warm-air furnace.

'Back of the storage room,' he said.

I grabbed the kid. 'Come on.'

We got up and ran into the storage room. The bulldozer hit again and the building trembled. Two or three more hits and it would be able to come right up to the counter for a cup of coffee.

There were two large fifty-gallon drums with feeds to the furnace and turn spigots. There was a carton of empty ketchup bottles near the back door. 'Get those, Jerry.'

While he did, I pulled off my shirt and yanked it to rags. The dozer hit again and again, and each hit was accompanied by the sound of more breakage.

I filled four of the ketchup bottles from the spigots, and he stuffed rags into them. 'You play football?' I asked him.

'In high school.'

'Okay. Pretend you're going in from the five.'

We went out into the restaurant. The whole front wall was open to the sky. Sprays of glass glittered like diamonds. One heavy beam had fallen diagonally across the opening. The dozer was backing up to take it out and I thought that this time it would keep coming, ripping through the stools and then demolishing the counter itself.

We knelt down and thrust the bottles out. 'Light them up,' I said to the trucker.

He got his matches out, but his hands were shaking too badly and he dropped them. The counterman picked them up, struck one, and the hunks of shirt blazed greasily alight.

'Quick,' I said.

We ran, the kid a little in the lead. Glass crunched and gritted underfoot. There was a hot, oily smell in the air. Everything was very loud, very bright.

The dozer charged.

The kid dodged out under the beam and stood silhouetted in front of that heavy tempered steel blade. I went out to the right. The kid's first throw fell short. His second hit the blade and the flame splashed harmlessly.

He tried to turn and then it was on him, a rolling juggernaut, four tons of steel. His hands flew up and then he was gone, chewed under.

I buttonhooked around and lobbed one bottle into the open cab and the second right into the works. They exploded together in a leaping shout of flame.

For a moment the dozer's engine rose in an almost human squeal of rage and pain. It wheeled in a maddened half-circle, ripping out the left corner of the diner, and rolled drunkenly towards the drainage ditch.

The steel treads were streaked and dotted with gore and where the kid had been there was something that looked like a crumpled towel.

The dozer got almost to the ditch, flames boiling from under its cowling and from the cockpit, and then it exploded in a geyser.

I stumbled backwards and almost fell over a pile of rubble. There was a hot smell that wasn't just oil. It was burning hair. I was on fire.

I grabbed a tablecloth, jammed it on my head, ran behind the counter, and plunged my head into the sink hard enough to crack it on the bottom. The girl was screaming Jerry's name over and over in a shrieking insane litany.

I turned round and saw the huge car-carrier slowly rolling towards the defenceless front of the diner.

The trucker screamed and broke for the side door.

'Don't!' the counterman cried. 'Don't do that—'

But he was out and sprinting for the drainage ditch and the open field beyond.

The truck must have been standing sentry just out of sight of that side door—a small panel job with 'Wong's Cash-and-Carry Laundry' written on the side. It ran him down almost before you could see it happen. Then it was gone and only the trucker was left, twisted into the gravel. He had been knocked out of his shoes.

The car-carrier rolled slowly over the concrete verge, onto the grass, over the kid's remains, and stopped with its huge snout poking into the diner.

Its air horn let out a sudden, shattering honk, followed by another, and another.

'Stop!' the girl whimpered. 'Stop, oh stop, please—'

But the honks went on a long time. It took only a minute to pick up the pattern. It was the same as before. It wanted someone to feed it and the others.

'I'll go,' I said. 'Are the pumps unlocked?'

The counterman nodded. He had aged fifty years.

'No!' the girl screamed. She threw herself at me. 'You've got to stop them! Beat them, burn them, break them—' Her voice wavered and broke into a harsh bray of grief and loss.

The counterman held her. I went round the corner of the counter, picking my way through the rubble, and out through the supply room. My heart was thudding heavily when I stepped out into the warm sun. I wanted another cigarette, but you don't smoke around fuel islands.

The trucks were still lined up. The laundry truck was crouched across the gravel from me like a hound dog, growling and rasping. A funny move and it would cream me. The sun glittered on its blank windshield and I shuddered. It was like looking into the face of an idiot.

I switched the pump to 'on' and pulled out the nozzle; unscrewed the first gas cap and began to pump fuel.

It took me half an hour to pump the first tank dry and then I moved on to the second island. I was alternating between gas and diesel. Trucks marched by endlessly. I was beginning to understand now. I was beginning to see. People were doing this all over the country or they were lying dead like the trucker, knocked out of their boots with heavy treadmarks mashed across their guts.

The second tank was dry then and I went to the third. The sun was like a hammer and my head was starting to ache with the fumes. There were blisters in the soft webbing between thumb and index finger. But they wouldn't know about that. They would know about leaky manifolds and bad gaskets and frozen universal joints, but not about blisters or sunstroke or the need to scream. They needed to know only one thing about their late masters, and they knew it. We bleed.

The last tank was sucked dry and I threw the nozzle on the ground. Still there were more trucks, lined up around the corner. I twisted my head to relieve a crick in my neck and stared. The line went out of the front parking lot and up the road and out of sight, two and three lanes deep. It was like a nightmare of the Los Angeles Freeway at rush hour. The horizon shimmered and danced with their exhaust; the air stank of carburisation.

'No,' I said. 'Out of gas. All gone, fellas.'

And there was a heavier rumble, a bass note that shook the teeth. A huge silvery truck was pulling up, a tanker. Written on the side was: 'Fill Up with Phillips 66—The Jetport Fuel'!

A heavy hose dropped out of the rear.

I went over, took it, flipped up the feeder plate on the first tank, and attached the hose. The truck began to pump. The stench of petroleum sank into me—the same stink that the dinosaurs must have died smelling as they went down into the tar pits. I filled the other two tanks and then went back to work.

Consciousness twinkled away to a point where I lost track of time and trucks. I unscrewed, rammed the nozzle into the hole, pumped until the hot, heavy liquid splurted out, then replaced the cap. My blisters broke, trickling pus down to my wrists. My head was pounding like a rotted tooth and my stomach rolled helplessly with the stench of hydrocarbons.

I was going to faint. I was going to faint and that would be the end of it. I would pump until I dropped.

Then there were hands on my shoulders, the dark hands of

the counterman. 'Go in,' he said. 'Rest yourself. I'll take over till
dark. Try to sleep.'

I handed him the pump.

But I can't sleep.

The girl is sleeping. She's sprawled over in the corner with her
head on a tablecloth and her face won't unknot itself even in
sleep. It's the timeless, ageless face of the warhag. I'm going to
get her up pretty quick. It's twilight, and the counterman has
been out there for five hours.

Still they keep coming. I look out through the wrecked window
and their headlights stretch for a mile or better, twinkling like
yellow sapphires in the growing darkness. They must be backed
up all the way to the turnpike, maybe further.

The girl will have to take her turn. I can show her how. She'll
say she can't, but she will. She wants to live.

You want to be their slaves? the counterman had said. *That's
what it'll come to. You want to spend the rest of your life changin' oil
filters every time one of those things blats its horn?*

We could run, maybe. It would be easy to make the drainage
ditch now, the way they're stacked up. Run through the fields,
through the marshy places where trucks would bog down like
mastodons and go—

—*back to the caves.*

Drawing pictures in charcoal. This is the moon god. This is a
tree. This is a Mack semi overwhelming a hunter.

Not even that. So much of the world is paved now. Even the
playgrounds are paved. And for the fields and marshes and deep
woods there are tanks, half-tracks, flatbeds equipped with lasers,
masers, heat-seeking radar. And little by little, they can make it
into the world they want.

I can get great convoys of trucks filling the Okefenokee Swamp
with sand, the bulldozers ripping through the national parks and
wildlands, grading the earth flat, stamping it into one great flat
plain. And then the hot-top trucks arriving.

But they're machines. No matter what's happened to them,
what mass consciousness we've given them, *they can't reproduce.*
In fifty or sixty years they'll be rusting hulks with all menace
gone out of them, moveless carcasses for free men to stone and
spit at.

And if I close my eyes I can see the production lines in Detroit and Dearborn and Youngstown and Mackinac, new trucks being put together by blue-collars who no longer even punch a clock but only drop and are replaced.

The counterman is staggering a little now. He's an old bastard, too. I've got to wake the girl.

Two planes are leaving silver contrails etched across the darkening eastern horizon.

I wish I could believe there are people in them.

THE DUST-CLOUD

E. F. Benson

Phantom vehicles were a regular theme in fiction long before the advent of the motor car, when ghostly coaches and the like haunted the highways. One of the first 'ghost cars' was reported as early as 1910 on a stretch of road known as Holbeach Marsh between King's Lynn and Boston in East Anglia . . . and strange things have continued to happen there to motorists ever since. A phantom bus with lights blazing has been reported several times since the Fifties on the A21 near Tunbridge Wells in Kent, and there is no more curious story than that of the 'glowing' saloon car complete with a lone driver which has been seen at least three times by eye-witnesses on the Banbury to Bicester road in Oxfordshire.

The first writer to link the motor car with the supernatural was E. F. Benson. 'The Dust-Cloud' was originally published in 1912, when the motor car was still a novelty enjoyed only by the wealthy and privileged classes. It was the era of the big, powerful automobiles like the Rolls Royce, the Bentley and the 25hp Amédée which features in Benson's chilling tale of a reckless driver who causes a fatal accident—and its grim sequel.

Edward Frederic Benson (1867–1940) wrote works of fiction that ranged from humour to romance—including the classic society novel, Dodo (1893)—but he is also acknowledged as one of the twentieth century's finest ghost story writers, on a par with the great M. R. James. Unlike many of his contemporaries, however, Benson wrote his macabre stories to frighten, and there are elements of sexuality and horror in a number of them that undoubtedly shocked the polite society of his time. His tales were often contemporary in their setting, realistic in tone, and involved recent developments in science and technology. Another of his stories, 'The Bus-Conductor', written at the same time as 'The Dust-Cloud', is also about a sinister vehicle that is driven through the streets of London collecting the dead. It was adapted for a cult movie, Dead of Night, *made in Britain in 1945, directed by Basil Dearden and starring Miles Malleson.*

*   *   *

The big French windows were open on to the lawn, and, dinner being over, two or three of the party who were staying for the week at the end of August with the Combe-Martins had strolled out on to the terrace to look at the sea, over which the moon, large and low, was just rising and tracing a path of pale gold from horizon to shore, while others, less lunar of inclination, had gone in search of bridge or billiards. Coffee had come round immediately after dessert, and the end of dinner, according to the delectable custom of the house, was as informal as the end of breakfast. Everyone, that is to say, remained or went away, smoked, drank port or abstained, according to his personal tastes. Thus, on this particular evening it so happened that Harry Combe-Martin and I were very soon left alone in the dining-room, because we were talking unmitigated motor 'shop', and the rest of the party (small wonder) were bored with it, and had left us. The shop was home-shop, so to speak, for it was almost entirely concerned with the manifold perfections of the new six-cylinder Clarence which my host in a moment of extravagance, which he did not in the least regret, had just purchased; in which, too, he proposed to take me over to lunch at a friend's house near Hunstanton on the following day. He observed with legitimate pride that an early start would be unnecessary as the distance was only eighty miles and there were no police traps.

'Queer things these big motors are,' he said, relapsing into generalities as we rose to go. 'Often I can scarcely believe that my new car is merely a machine. It seems to me to possess an independent life of its own. It is really much more like a thoroughbred with a wonderfully fine mouth.'

'And the moods of a thoroughbred?' I asked.

'No; it's got an excellent temper, I'm glad to say. It doesn't mind being checked, or even stopped, when it's going its best. Some of these big cars can't stand that. They get sulky—I assure you it is literally true—if they are checked too often.'

He paused on his way to ring the bell. 'Guy Elphinstone's car, for instance,' he said: 'it was a bad-tempered brute, a violent, vicious beast of a car.'

'What make?' I asked.

'Twenty-five horse-power Amédée. They are a fretful strain of car; too thin, not enough bone—and bone is very good for the nerves. The brute liked running over a chicken or a rabbit, though perhaps it was less the car's ill-temper than Guy's, poor chap. Well, he paid for it—he paid to the uttermost farthing. Did you know him?'

'No; but surely I have heard the name. Ah, yes, he ran over a child, did he not?'

'Yes,' said Harry, 'and then smashed up against his own park gates.'

'Killed, wasn't he?'

'Oh, yes, killed instantly, and the car just a heap of splinters. There's an odd story about it, I'm told, in the village: rather in your line.'

'Ghosts?' I asked.

'Yes, the ghost of his motor-car. Seems almost too up-to-date, doesn't it?'

'And what's the story?' I demanded.

'Why, just this. His place was outside the village of Bircham, ten miles out from Norwich; and there's a long straight bit of road there—that's where he ran over the child—and a couple of hundred yards farther on, a rather awkward turn into the park gates. Well, a month or two ago, soon after the accident, one old gaffer in the village swore he had seen a motor there coming full tilt along the road, but without a sound, and it disappeared at the lodge gates of the park, which were shut. Soon after another said he had heard a motor whirl by him at the same place, followed by a hideous scream, but he saw nothing.'

'The scream is rather horrible,' said I.

'Ah, I see what you mean! I only thought of his siren. Guy had a siren on his exhaust, same as I have. His had a dreadful frightened sort of wail, and always made me feel creepy.'

'And is that all the story?' I asked; 'that one old man thought he saw a noiseless motor, and another thought he heard an invisible one?'

Harry flicked the ash off his cigarette into the grate. 'Oh, dear no!' he said. 'Half-a-dozen of them have seen something or heard something. It is quite a heavily authenticated yarn.'

'Yes, and talked over and edited in the public-house,' I said.

'Well, not a man of them will go there after dark. Also the lodge-keeper gave notice a week or two after the accident. He said he was always hearing a motor stop and hoot outside the lodge, and he was kept running out at all hours of the night to see what it was.'

'And what was it?'

'It wasn't anything. Simply nothing there. He thought it rather uncanny, anyhow, and threw up a good post. Besides, his wife was always hearing a child scream, and while her man toddled out to the gate she would go and see whether the kids were all right. And the kids themselves—'

'Ah, what of them?' I asked.

'They kept coming to their mother, asking who the little girl was who walked up and down the road and would not speak to them or play with them.'

'It's a many-sided story,' I said. 'All the witnesses seem to have heard and seen different things.'

'Yes, that is just what to my mind makes the yarn so good,' he said. 'Personally I don't take much stock in spooks at all. But given that there are such things as spooks, and given that the death of the child and the death of Guy have caused spooks to play about there, it seems to me a very good point that different people should be aware of different phenomena. One hears the car, another sees it, one hears the child scream, another sees the child. How does that strike you?'

This, I am bound to say, was a new view to me, and the more I thought of it the more reasonable it appeared. For the vast majority of mankind have all those occult senses by which is perceived the spiritual world (which, I hold, is thick and populous around us), sealed up, as it were; in other words, the majority of mankind never hear or see a ghost at all. Is it not, then, very probable that of the remainder—those, in fact, to whom occult experiences have happened or can happen—few should have every sense unsealed, but that some should have the unsealed ear, others the unsealed eye—that some should be clairaudient, others clairvoyant?

'Yes, it strikes me as reasonable,' I said. 'Can't you take me over there?'

'Certainly! If you will stop till Friday I'll take you over on

Thursday. The others all go that day, so that we can get there after dark.'

I shook my head. 'I can't stop till Friday, I'm afraid,' I said. 'I must leave on Thursday. But how about tomorrow? Can't we take it on the way to or from Hunstanton?'

'No; it's thirty miles out of our way. Besides, to be at Bircham after dark means that we shouldn't get back here till midnight. And as host to my guests—'

'Ah! things are only heard and seen after dark, are they?' I asked. 'That makes it so much less interesting. It is like a séance where all lights are put out.'

'Well, the accident happened at night,' he said. 'I don't know the rules, but that may have some bearing on it, I should think.'

I had one question more in the back of my mind, but I did not like to ask it. At least, I wanted information on this subject without appearing to ask for it.

'Neither do I know the rules of motors,' I said; 'and I don't understand you when you say that Guy Elphinstone's machine was an irritable, cross-grained brute, that liked running over chickens and rabbits. But I think you subsequently said that the irritability may have been the irritability of its owner. Did he mind being checked?'

'It made him blind-mad if it happened often,' said Harry. 'I shall never forget a drive I had with him once: there were hay-carts and perambulators every hundred yards. It was perfectly ghastly; it was like being with a madman. And when we got inside his gate, his dog came running out to meet him. He did not go an inch out of his course: it was worse than that—he went for it, just grinding his teeth with rage. I never drove with him again.'

He stopped a moment, guessing what might be in my mind. 'I say, you mustn't think—you mustn't think—' he began.

'No, of course not,' said I.

Harry Combe-Martin's house stood close to the weather-eaten, sandy cliffs of the Suffolk shore, which are being incessantly gnawed away by the hunger of the insatiable sea. Fathoms deep below it, and now many hundreds yards out, lies what was once the second port in England; but now of the ancient town of Dunwich, and of its seven great churches, nothing remains but one, and that ruinous and already half destroyed by the falling cliff and the encroachments of the sea. Foot by foot, it too is disappearing, and of the graveyard which surrounded it more than half is gone, so that from the face of the sandy cliff on which it stands there stick out like straws in glass, as Dante says, the bones of those who were once committed there to the kindly and stable earth.

Whether it was the remembrance of this rather grim spectacle as I had seen it that afternoon, or whether Harry's story had caused some trouble in my brain, or whether it was merely that the keen bracing air of this place, to one who had just come from the sleepy languor of the Norfolk Broads, kept me sleepless, I do not know; but anyhow, the moment I put out my light that night and got into bed, I felt that all the footlights and gas-jets in the internal theatre of my mind sprang into flame, and that I was very vividly and alertly awake. It was in vain that I counted a hundred forwards and a hundred backwards, that I pictured to myself a flock of visionary sheep coming singly through a gap in an imaginary hedge, and tried to number their monotonous and uniform countenances, that I played noughts and crosses with myself, that I marked out scores of double lawn-tennis courts—for with each repetition of these supposedly soporific exercises I only became more intensely wakeful. It was not in remote hope of sleep that I continued to repeat these weary performances long after their inefficacy was proved to the hilt, but because I was strangely unwilling in this timeless hour of the night to think about those protruding relics of humanity; also I quite distinctly did not desire to think about that subject with regard to which I had, a few hours ago, promised Harry that I would not make it the subject of reflection. For these reasons I continued during the black hours to practise these narcotic exercises of the mind, knowing well that if I paused on the tedious treadmill my thoughts, like some released spring, would fly back to rather gruesome subjects. I kept my mind, in fact, talking loud to itself, so that it should not hear what other voices were saying.

Then by degrees these absurd mental occupations became impossible; my mind simply refused to occupy itself with them any longer; and next moment I was thinking intently and eagerly, not about the bones protruding from the gnawed section of sand-cliff, but about the subject I had said I would not dwell upon. And like a flash it came upon me why Harry had bidden me not think about it. Surely in order that I should not come to the same conclusion as he had come to.

Now the whole question of 'haunt'—haunted spots, haunted houses, and so forth—has always seemed to me to be utterly unsolved, and to be neither proved nor disproved to a satisfactory degree. From the earliest times, certainly from the earliest known Egyptian records, there has been a belief that the scene of a crime is often revisited, sometimes by the spirit of him who has committed it—seeking rest, we must suppose, and finding none; sometimes, and more inexplicably, by the spirit of his victim, crying perhaps, like the blood of Abel, for vengeance. And though the stories of these village gossips in the alehouse about noiseless visions and invisible noises were all as yet unsifted and unreliable, yet I could not help wondering if they (such as they were) pointed to something authentic and to be classed under this head of appearances. But more striking than the yarns of the gaffers seemed to me the questions of the lodge-keeper's children. How should children have imagined the figure of a child that would not speak to them or play with them? Perhaps it was a real child, a sulky child. Yes—perhaps. But perhaps not. Then after this preliminary skirmish I found myself settling down to the question that I had said I would not think about; in other words, the possible origin of these phenomena interested me more than the phenomena themselves. For what exactly had Guy Elphinstone, that savage driver, done? Had or had not the death of the child been entirely an accident, a thing (given he drove a motor at all) outside his own control? Or had he, irritated beyond endurance at the checks and delays of the day, not pulled up when it was just possible he might have, but had run over the child as he would have run over a rabbit or a hen, or even his own dog? And what, in any case, poor wretched brute, must have been his thoughts in that terrible instant that intervened between the child's death and his own, when a moment later he smashed into the closed gates of his own lodge? Was remorse his—bitter, despairing contrition? That could hardly have been so; or else surely, knowing only for certain that he had knocked a child down, he would have stopped; he would have done his best, whatever that might be, to repair the irreparable harm. But he had not stopped; he had gone on, it seemed, at full speed, for on the collision the car had been smashed into matchwood and steel shavings. Again, with double force, had this dreadful thing been a complete accident, he would have stopped. So then—most terrible question of all—had he, after making murder, rushed on to what proved to be his own death, filled with some hellish glee at what he had done? Indeed, as in the churchyard on the cliff, bones of the buried stuck starkly out into the night.

The pale tired light of earliest morning had turned the window-blinds into glimmering squares before I slept; and when I woke, the servant who called me was already rattling them briskly up on their rollers, and letting the calm serenity of the August day stream into the room. Through the open windows poured in sunlight and sea-wind, the scent of flowers and the song of birds; and each and all were wonderfully reassuring, banishing the hooded forms that had haunted the night, and I thought of the disquietude of the dark hours as a traveller may think of the billows and tempests of the ocean over which he has safely journeyed, unable, now that they belong to the limbo of the past, to recall his qualms and tossings with any vivid uneasiness. Not without a feeling of relief, too, did I dwell on the knowledge that I was definitely not going to visit this equivocal spot. Our drive today, as Harry had said, would not take us within thirty miles of it, and tomorrow I but went to the station and away. Though a thorough-paced seeker after truth might, no doubt, have regret-ted that the laws of time and space did not permit him to visit Bircham after the sinister dark had fallen, and test whether for him there was visible or audible truth in the tales of the village gossips, I was conscious of no such regret. Bircham and its fables had given me a very bad night, and I was perfectly aware that I did not in the least want to go near it, though yesterday I had quite truthfully said I should like to do so. In this brightness, too, of sun and sea-wind I felt none of the *malaise* at my waking moments which a sleepless night usually gives me; I felt particu-larly well, particularly pleased to be alive, and also, as I have said, particularly content not to be going to Bircham. I was quite satisfied to leave my curiosity unsatisfied.

The motor came round about eleven, and we started at once, Harry and Mrs Morrison, a cousin of his, sitting behind in the big back seat, large enough to hold a comfortable three, and I on the left of the driver, in a sort of trance—I am not ashamed to confess it—of expectancy and delight. For this was in the early days of motors, when there was still the sense of romance and adventure round them. I did not want to drive, any more than

Harry wanted to; for driving, so I hold, is too absorbing; it takes
the attention in too firm a grip: the mania of the true motorist is
not consciously enjoyed. For the passion of motors is a taste—I
had almost said a gift—as distinct and as keenly individual as
the passion for music or mathematics. Those who use motors
most (merely as a means of getting rapidly from one place to
another) are often entirely without it, while those whom adverse
circumstances (over which they have no control) compel to use
them least may have it to a supreme degree. To those who have
it, analysis of their passion is perhaps superfluous; to those who
have it not, explanation is almost unintelligible. Pace, however,
and the control of pace, and above all the sensuous consciousness
of pace, is at the root of it; and pleasure in pace is common to
most people, whether it be in the form of a galloping horse, or
the pace of the skate hissing over smooth ice, or the pace of a
free-wheel bicycle humming down-hill, or, more impersonally,
the pace of a smashed ball at lawn-tennis, the driven ball at golf,
or the low boundary hit at cricket. But the sensuous consciousness
of pace, as I have said, is needful: one might experience it seated
in front of the engine of an express train, though not in a wadded,
shut-windowed carriage, where the wind of movement is not
felt. Then add to this rapture of the rush through riven air the
knowledge that huge relentless force is controlled by a little lever,
and directed by a little wheel on which the hands of the driver
seem to lie so negligently. A great untamed devil has there his
bridle, and he answers to it, as Harry had said, like a horse with
a fine mouth. He has hunger and thirst, too, unshakable, and
greedily he laps of his soup of petrol which turns to fire in his
mouth: electricity, the force that rends clouds asunder, and causes
towers to totter, is the spoon with which he feeds himself; and
as he eats he races onward, and the road opens like torn linen
in front of him. Yet how obedient, how amenable is he!—for with
a touch on his snaffle his speed is redoubled, or melts into thin
air, so that before you know you have touched the rein he has
exchanged his swallow-flight for a mere saunter through the
lanes. But he ever loves to run; and knowing this, you will bid
him lift up his voice and tell those who are in his path that he
is coming, so that he will not need the touch that checks. Hoarse
and jovial is his voice, hooting to the wayfarer; and if his hooting
be not heard he has a great guttural falsetto scream that leaps
from octave to octave, and echoes from the hedges that are

passing in blurred lines of hanging green. And, as you go, the romantic isolation of divers in deep seas is yours; masked and hooded companions may be near you also, in their driving-dress for this plunge through the swift tides of air; but you, like them, are alone and isolated, conscious only of the ripped riband of road, the two great lantern-eyes of the wonderful monster that look through drooped eyelids by day, but gleam with fire at night, the two ear-flaps of splash-boards, and the long lean bonnet in front which is the skull and brain-case of that swift, untiring energy that feeds on fire, and whirls its two tons of weight up hill and down dale, as if some new law as everlasting as gravity, and like gravity making it go ever swifter, was its sole control.

For the first hour the essence of these joys, any description of which compared to the real thing is but as a stagnant pond compared to the bright rushing of a mountain stream, was mine. A straight switchback road lay in front of us, and the monster plunged silently down hill, and said below his breath, 'Ha-ha—ha-ha—ha-ha,' as, without diminution of speed, he breasted the opposing slope. In my control were his great vocal cords (for in those days hooter and siren were on the driver's left, and lay convenient to the hand of him who occupied the next seat), and it rejoiced me to let him hoot to a pony-cart, three hundred yards ahead, with a hand on his falsetto scream if his ordinary tones of conversation were unheard or disregarded. Then came a road crossing ours at right angles, and the dear monster seemed to say, 'Yes, yes—see how obedient and careful I am. I stroll with my hands in my pockets.' Then again a puppy from a farmhouse staggered warlike into the road, and the monster said, 'Poor little chap! get home to your mother, or I'll talk to you in earnest.' The poor little chap did not take the hint, so the monster slackened speed and just said, 'Whoof!' Then it chuckled to itself as the puppy scuttled into the hedge, seriously alarmed; and next moment our self-made wind screeched and whistled round us again.

Napoleon, I believe, said that the power of an army lay in its feet: that is true also of the monster. There was a loud bang, and in thirty seconds we were at a standstill. The monster's off fore-foot troubled it, and the chauffeur said, 'Yes, sir—burst.'

So the burst boot was taken off and a new one put on, a boot that had never been on foot before. The foot in question was held up on a jack during this operation, and the new boot laced up with a pump. This took exactly twenty-five minutes. Then the monster got his spoon going again, and said, 'Let me run: oh, let me run!' And for fifteen miles on a straight and empty road it ran. I timed the miles, but shall not produce their chronology for the benefit of a forsworn constabulary.

But there were no more dithrambics that morning. We should have reached Hunstanton in time for lunch. Instead, we waited to repair our fourth puncture at 1.45 p.m., twenty-five miles short of our destination. This fourth puncture was caused by a spicule of flint three-quarters of an inch long—sharp, it is true, but weighing perhaps two pennyweights, while we weighed two tons. It seemed an impertinence. So we lunched at a wayside inn, and during lunch the pundits held a consultation, of which the upshot was this:

We had no more boots for our monster, for his off fore-foot had burst once, and punctured once (thus necessitating two socks and one boot). Similarly, but more so, his off hind-foot had burst twice (thus necessitating two boots and two socks). Now, there was no certain shoemaker's shop at Hunstanton, as far as we knew, but there was a regular universal store at King's Lynn, which was about equidistant.

And, so said the chauffeur, there was something wrong with the monster's spoon (ignition), and he didn't rightly know what, and therefore it seemed the prudent part not to go to Hunstanton (lunch, a thing of the preterite, having been the object), but to the well-supplied King's Lynn. And we all breathed a pious hope that we might get there.

Whizz: hoot: purr! The last boot held, the spoon went busily to the monster's mouth, and we just flowed into King's Lynn. The return journey, so I vaguely gathered, would be made by other roads; but, personally, intoxicated with air and movement, I neither asked nor desired to know what those roads would be. This one small but rather salient fact is necessary to record here, that as we waited at King's Lynn, and as we buzzed homewards afterwards, no thought of Bircham entered my head at all. The subsequent hallucination, if hallucination it was, was not, as far as I know, self-suggested. That we had gone out of our way for the sake of the garage, I knew, and that was all. Harry also told me that he did not know where our road would take us.

The rest that follows is the baldest possible narrative of what actually occurred. But it seems to me, a humble student of the occult, to be curious.

While we waited we had tea in a hotel looking on to a big
empty square of houses, and after tea we waited a very long
time for our monster to pick us up. Then the telephone from the
garage inquired for 'the gentleman on the motor', and since Harry
had strolled out to get a local evening paper with news of the
last Test Match, I applied ear and mouth to that elusive instrument. What I heard was not encouraging: the ignition had gone
very wrong indeed, and 'perhaps' in an hour we should be able
to start. It was then about half-past six, and we were just seventy-
eight miles from Dunwich.

Harry came back soon after this, and I told him what the
message from the garage had been. What he said was this: 'Then
we shan't get back till long after dinner. We might just as well
have camped out to see your ghost.'

As I have already said, no notion of Bircham was in my mind,
and I mention this as evidence that, even if it had been, Harry's
remark would have implied that we were not going through
Bircham.

The hour lengthened itself into an hour and a half, Then the
monster, quite well again, came hooting round the corner, and
we got in.

'Whack her up, Jack,' said Harry to the chauffeur. 'The roads
will be empty. You had better light up at once.'

The monster, with its eyes agleam, was whacked up, and never
in my life have I been carried so cautiously and yet so swiftly.
Jack never took a risk or the possibility of a risk, but when the
road was clear and open he let the monster run just a fast as it
was able. Its eyes made day of the road fifty yards ahead, and
the romance of night was fairyland round us. Hares started from
the roadside, and raced in front of us for a hundred yards, then
just wheeled in time to avoid the ear-flaps of the great triumphant
brute that carried us. Moths flitted across, struck sometimes by
the lenses of its eyes, and the miles peeled over our shoulders.
When It occurred we were going top-speed. And this was It—
quite unsensational, but to us quite inexplicable unless my midnight imaginings happened to be true.

As I have said, I was in command of the hooter and of the
siren. We were flying along on a straight down-grade, as fast as
ever we could go, for the engines were working, though the
decline was considerable. Then quite suddenly I saw in front of
us a thick cloud of dust, and knew instinctively and on the instant,

without thought or reasoning, what that must mean. Evidently something going very fast (or else so large a cloud could not have been raised) was in front of us, and going in the same direction as ourselves. Had it been something on the road coming to meet us, we should of course have seen the vehicle first and run into the dust-cloud afterwards. Had it, again, been something of low speed—a horse and dog-cart, for instance—no such dust could have been raised. But, as it was, I knew at once that there was a motor travelling swiftly just ahead of us, also that it was not going as fast as we were, or we should have run into its dust much more gradually. But we went into it as into a suddenly lowered curtain.

Then I shouted to Jack. 'Slow down, and put on the brake,' I shrieked. 'There's something just ahead of us.'

As I spoke I wrought a wild concerto on the hooter, and with my right hand groped for the siren, but did not find it. Simultaneously I heard a wild, frightened shriek, just as if I had sounded the siren myself. Jack had felt for it too, and our hands fingered each other. Then we entered the dust-cloud.

We slowed down with extraordinary rapidity, and still peering ahead we went dead-slow through it. I had not put on my goggles after leaving King's Lynn, and the dust stung and smarted in my eyes. It was not, therefore, a belt of fog, but real road-dust. And at the moment we crept through it I felt Harry's hands on my shoulder.

'There's something just ahead,' he said. 'Look! don't you see the tail light?'

As a matter of fact, I did not; and, still going very slow, we came out of that dust-cloud. The broad empty road stretched in front of us; a hedge was on each side, and there was no turning either to right or left. Only, on the right, was a lodge, and gates which were closed. The lodge had no lights in any window.

Then we came to a standstill; the air was dead-calm, not a leaf in the hedgerow trees was moving, not a grain of dust was lifted from the road. But, behind, the dust-cloud still hung in the air, and stopped dead-short at the closed lodge-gates. We had moved very slowly for the last hundred yards: it was difficult to suppose that it was of our making. Then Jack spoke, with a curious crack in his voice.

'It must have been a motor, sir,' he said. 'But where is it?'

I had no reply to this, and from behind another voice, Harry's voice, spoke. For the moment I did not recognise it, for it was strained and faltering.

'Did you open the siren?' he asked. 'It didn't sound like your siren. It sounded like, like—'

'I didn't open the siren,' said I.

Then we went on again. Soon we came to scattered lights in houses by the wayside.

'What's this place?' I asked Jack.

'Bircham, sir,' said he.

SECOND CHANCE

Jack Finney

Restoring veteran and vintage cars like those described in their prime in E. F. Benson's story is a passion enjoyed by people all over the world. The narrator of 'Second Chance' is one of this dedicated band, who makes perfect a 'dusty mass of junk' that was once a Jordan Playboy. The car is in this condition as a result of being damaged in a train crash and it takes many hours of hard work and the most painstaking research to locate the missing parts before the Jordan is once again roadworthy. But when the restorer gets behind the wheel the strangest things begin to happen — none stranger than when the bemused man suddenly finds himself back in the past when the Playboy itself was brand new . . .

Jack Finney (1911–95), the pen-name of US writer Walter Braden Finney, was the creator of a number of classic works of science fiction including The Body Snatchers *(1955), filmed no less than three times between 1956 and 1993 — twice as* Invasion of the Body Snatchers, *and the third as* Body Snatchers. *Finney is also regarded as an important writer in modern fantasy for his 'timeslip' stories in which his protagonists (usually) find themselves transported into the past. 'Second Chance' is one of the very best of these tales, with a denouement that is unique among time travel stories.*

*   *   *

I can't tell you, I know, how I got to a time and place no one else in the world even remembers. But maybe I can tell you how I felt the morning I stood in an old barn off the county road, staring down at what was to take me there.

I paid out seventy-five dollars I'd worked hard for after classes last semester—I'm a senior at Poynt College in Hylesburg,

Illinois, my home town—and the middle-aged farmer took it
silently, watching me shrewdly, knowing I must be out of my
mind. Then I stood looking down at the smashed, rusty, rat-
gnawed, dust-covered, old wreck of an automobile lying on the
wood floor where it had been hauled and dumped thirty-three
years before—and that now belonged to me. And if you can
remember the moment, whenever it was, when you finally got
something you wanted so badly you dreamed about it—then
maybe I've told you how I felt staring at the dusty mass of junk
that was a genuine Jordan Playboy.

You've never heard of a Jordan Playboy, if you're younger
than forty, unless you're like I am; one of those people who'd
rather own a 1926 Mercer convertible sedan, or a 1931 Packard
touring car, or a '24 Wills Sainte Claire, or a '31 air-cooled
Franklin convertible—or a Jordan Playboy—than the newest,
two-toned, '57 model made; I was actually half sick with
excitement.

And the excitement lasted; it took me four months to restore
that car, and that's fast. I went to classes till school ended for the
summer, then I worked, clerking at J. C. Penney's; and I had
dates, saw an occasional movie, ate and slept. But all I really
did—all that counted—was work on that car; from six to eight
every morning, for half an hour at lunchtime, and from the
moment I got home, most nights, till I stumbled to bed, worn
out.

My folks live in the big old house my dad was born in; there's
a barn off at the back of the lot, and I've got a chain hoist in
there, a workbench, and a full set of mechanic's tools. I built hot
rods there for three years, one after another; those charcoal-black
mongrels with the rear ends up in the air. But I'm through with
hot rods; I'll leave those to the high-school set. I'm twenty years
old now, and I've been living for the day when I could soak
loose the body bolts with liniment, hoist the body aside, and start
restoring my own classic. That's what they're called; those certain
models of certain cars of certain years which have something
that's lasted, something today's cars don't have for us, and something worth bringing back.

But you don't restore a classic by throwing in a new motor,
hammering out the dents, replacing missing parts with anything
handy, and painting it chartreuse. 'Restore' means what it says,
or ought to. My Jordan had been struck by a train, the man who

sold it to me said—just grazed, but that was enough to flip it over, tumbling it across a field, and the thing was a wreck; the people in it were killed. So the right rear wheel and the spare were hopeless wads of wire spokes and twisted rims, and the body was caved in, with the metal actually split in places. The motor was a mess, though the block was sound. The upholstery was rat-gnawed, and almost gone. All the nickel plating was rusted and flaking off. And exterior parts were gone; nothing but screw holes to show they'd been there. But three of the wheels were intact, or almost, and none of the body was missing.

What you do is write letters, advertise in the magazines people like me read, ask around, prowl garages, junk heaps and barns, and you trade, and you bargain, and one way or another get together the parts you need. I traded a Winton name plate and hub caps, plus a Saxon hood, to a man in Wichita, Kansas, for two Playboy wheels, and they arrived crated in a wooden box— rusty, and some of the spokes bent and loose, but I could fix that. I bought my Jordan running-board mats and spare-wheel mount from a man in New Jersey. I bought two valve pushrods, and had the rest precision-made precisely like the others. And—well, I restored that car, that's all.

The body shell, every dent and bump gone, every tear welded and burnished down, I painted a deep green, precisely matching what was left of the old paint before I sanded it off. Door handles, windshield rim, and every other nickel-plated part, were restored, re-nickelled, and replaced. I wrote eleven letters to leather supply houses all over the country, enclosing sample swatches of the cracked old upholstery, before I found a place that could match it. Then I paid a hundred and twelve dollars to have my Playboy reupholstered, supplying old photographs to show just how it should be done. And at eight-ten one Saturday evening in July, I finally finished; my last missing part, a Jordan radiator cap, for which I'd traded a Duesenberg floor mat, had come from the nickel plater's that afternoon. Just for the fun of it, I put the old plates back on then; Illinois licence 11,206, for 1923. And even the original ignition key, in its old leather case— oiled and worked supple again—was back where I'd found it, and now I switched it on, advanced the throttle and spark, got out with the crank, and started it up. And thirty-three years after it had bounced, rolled and crashed off a grade crossing, that Jordan Playboy was alive again.

I had a date, and knew I ought to get dressed; I was wearing stained dungarees and my dad's navy blue, high-necked old sweater. I didn't have any money with me; you lose it out of your pockets, working on a car. I was even out of cigarettes. But I couldn't wait, I had to drive that car, and I just washed up at the old sink in the barn, then started down the cinder driveway in that beautiful car, feeling wonderful. It wouldn't matter how I was dressed anyway, driving around in the Playboy tonight.

My mother waved at me tolerantly from a living-room window, and called out to be careful, and I nodded; then I was out in the street, cruising along, and I wish you could have seen me—seen *it*, I mean. I don't care whether you've ever given a thought to the wonderful old cars or not, you'd have seen why it was worth all I'd done. Draw yourself a mental picture of a simple, straight-lined, two-seater, open automobile with four big wire wheels fully exposed, and its spare on the back in plain sight; don't put in a line that doesn't belong there, and have a purpose. Make the two doors absolutely square; what other shape should a door be? Make the hood perfectly rounded, louvred at the sides because the motor needs that ventilation. But don't add a single unnecessary curve, jiggle, squiggle, or porthole to that car—and picture the radiator, nothing concealing it and pretending it doesn't exist. And now see that Playboy as I did cruising along, the late sun slanting down through the big old trees along the street, glancing off the bright nickel so that it hurt your eyes, the green of the body glowing like a jewel. It was beautiful, I tell you it was beautiful, and you'd think everyone would see that.

But they didn't. On Main Street, I stopped at a light, and a guy slid up beside me in a great big, shining, new '57 car half as long as a football field. He sat there, the top of the door up to his shoulders, his eyes almost level with the bottom of his windshield, looking as much in proportion to his car as a two-year-old in his father's overcoat; he sat there in a car with a pattern of chrome copied directly from an Oriental rug, and with a trunk sticking out past his back wheels you could have landed a helicopter on; he sat there for a moment, then turned, looked out, and smiled at *my* car!

And when I turned to look at him, eyes cold, he had the nerve to smile at *me*, as though I were supposed to nod and grin and agree that any car not made day before yesterday was an automatic side-splitting riot. I just looked away, and when the light changed, he thought he'd show me just how sick his big four-thousand-dollar job could make my pitiful old antique look. The light clicked, and his foot was on the gas, his automatic transmission taking hold, and he'd already started to grin. But I started when he did, feeding the gas in firm and gentle, and we held even till I shot into second faster than any automatic transmission yet invented can do it, and I drew right past him, and when I looked back it was me who was grinning. But still, at the next light, every pedestrian crossing in front of my car treated me to a tolerant understanding smile, and when the light changed, I swung off Main.

That was one thing that happened; the second was that my date wouldn't go out with me. I guess I shouldn't blame her. First she saw how I was dressed, which didn't help me with her. Then I showed her the Jordan at the kerb, and she nodded, not even slightly interested, and said it was very nice; which didn't help her with me. And then—well, she's a good-looking girl, Naomi Weygand, and while she didn't exactly put it in these words, she let me know she meant to be seen tonight, preferably on a dance floor, and not waste her youth and beauty riding around in some old antique. And when I told her I was going out in the Jordan tonight, and if she wanted to come along, fine, and if she didn't—well, she didn't. And eight seconds later she was opening her front door again, while I scorched rubber pulling away from the kerb.

I felt the way you would have by then, and I wanted to get out of town and alone somewhere, and I shoved it into second, gunning the car, heading for the old Cressville road. It used to be the only road to Cressville, a two-lane paved highway just barely wide enough for cars to pass. But there's been a new highway for fifteen years; four lanes, and straight as a ruler except for two long curves you can do ninety on, and you can make the seven miles to Cressville in five minutes or less.

But it's a dozen winding miles on the old road, and half a mile of it, near Cressville, was flooded out once, and the concrete is broken and full of gaps; you have to drive it in low. So nobody uses the old road nowadays, except for four or five farm families who live along it.

When I swung onto the old road—there are a lot of big old trees all along it—I began to feel better. And I just ambled along,

no faster than thirty, maybe, clear up to the broken stretch before
I turned back towards Hylesburg, and it was wonderful. I'm not
a sports-car man myself, but they've got something when they
talk about getting close to the road and into the outdoors again—
the way driving used to be before people shut themselves behind
great sheets of glass and metal, and began rushing along superhighways, their eyes on the white line. I had the windshield
folded down flat against the hood, and the summer air streamed
over my face and through my hair, and I could see the road just
beside and under me flowing past so close I could have touched
it. The air was alive with the heavy fragrances of summer darkness, and the rich nostalgic sounds of summer insects, and I
wasn't even thinking, but just living and enjoying it.

One of the old Playboy advertisements, famous in their day,
calls the Jordan 'this brawny, graceful thing', and says, 'It revels
along with the wandering wind and roars like a Caproni biplane.
It's a car for a man's man—that's certain. Or for a girl who loves
the out of doors.' Rich prose for these days, I guess; we're afraid
of rich prose now, and laugh in defence. But I'll take it over a
stern sales talk on safety belts.

Anyway, I liked just drifting along the old road, a part of the
summer outdoors and evening, and the living country around
me; and I was no more thinking than a collie dog with his nose
thrust out of a car, his eyes half closed against the air stream,
enjoying the feeling human beings so often forget, of simply being
a living creature. '"I left my love in Avalon,"' I was bawling out
at the top of my lungs, hardly knowing when I'd started, '"and
saaailed awaaay!"' Then I was singing 'Alice Blue Gown', very
softly and gently. I sang, 'Just a Japanese Saaandman!', and
'Whispering', and 'Barney Google', the fields and trees and cattle,
and sometimes an occasional car, flowing past in the darkness,
and I was having a wonderful time.

The name 'Dempsey' drifted into my head, I don't know why—
just a vagrant thought floating lazily up into my consciousness.
Now, I saw Jack Dempsey once; six years ago when I was fourteen, my dad, my mother, and I took a vacation trip to New
York. We saw the Empire State Building, Rockefeller Center, took
a ride on the subway, and all the rest of it. And we had dinner
at Jack Dempsey's restaurant on Broadway, and he was there,
and spoke to us, and my dad talked to him for a minute about
his fights. So I saw him; a nice-looking middle-aged man, very

big and broad. But the picture that drifted up into my mind now, driving along the old Cressville road, wasn't that Jack Dempsey. It was the face of a young man not a lot older than I was, black-haired, black-bearded, fierce and scowling. Dempsey, I thought, that snarling young face rising up clear and vivid in my mind, and the thought completed itself: He beat Tom Gibbons last night.

Last night; Dempsey beat Gibbons *last night*—and it was true. I mean it *felt* true somehow, as though the thought were in the very air around me, like the old songs I'd found myself singing, and suddenly several things I'd been half aware of clicked together in my mind. I'd been dreamily and unthinkingly realising that there were more cars on the road than I'd have expected, flowing past me in the darkness. Maybe some of the farm families along here were having some sort of Saturday-night get-together, I thought. But then I knew it wasn't true.

Picture a car's headlights coming towards you; they're two sharp beams slicing ahead into the darkness, an intense blue-white in colour, their edges as defined as a ruler's. But these headlights—two more sets of them were approaching me now—were different. They were entirely orange in colour, the red-orange of the hot filaments that produced them; and they were hardly even beams, but just twin circles of wide, diffused orange light, and they wavered in intensity, illuminating the road only dimly.

The nearer lights were almost upon me, and I half rose from my seat, leaning forward over the hood of the Jordan, staring at the car as it passed me. It was a Moon; a cream-coloured nineteen-twenty-two Moon roadster.

The next car, those two orange circles of wavering light swelling, approached, then passed, as I stared and turned to look after it. It looked something like mine; wire wheels, but with the spare on a side mount, and with step plates instead of running boards. I knew what it was; a Haynes Speedster, and the man at the wheel wore a cloth cap, and the girl beside him wore a large pink hat, coming well down over her head, and with a wide brim all around it.

I sat moving along, a hand on the wheel, in a kind of stunned ecstatic trance. For now, the Saturday-night traffic at its peak, there they all came one after another, all the glorious old cars; a Saxon Six black-bodied touring car with wood-spoke wheels, and the women in that car wore chin-length veils from the edges of

their flowered hats; there passed a grey-bodied black-topped
Wills Sainte Claire with orange disc wheels, and the six kids in
it were singing 'Who's Sorry Now?'; then I saw another Moon,
a light blue open four-seater, its cut-out open, and the kid at the
wheel had black hair slicked back in a varnished pompadour,
and just glancing at him, you could see he was on his way to a
date; now there came an Elcar, two Model T Fords just behind
it; then a hundred yards back, a red Buick roadster with natural-
wood spoke wheels; I saw a Velie, and a roadster that was either
a Noma or a Kissel, I couldn't be sure; and there was a high-
topped blue Dodge sedan with cut flowers in little glass vases
by the rear doors; there was a car I didn't know at all; then
a brand-new Stanley Steamer, and just behind it, a wonderful
low-slung 1921 Pierce-Arrow, and I knew what had happened,
and where I was.

I've read some of the stuff about Time with a capital T, and I
don't say I understand it too well. But I know Einstein or somebody compares Time to a winding river, and says we exist as
though in a boat, drifting along between high banks. All we can
see is the present, immediately around us. We can't see the future
just beyond the next curve, or the past in the many bends in back
of us. But it's all there just the same. There—countless bends
back, in infinite distance—lies the past, as real as the moment
around us.

Well, I'll join Einstein and the others with a notion of my own;
just a feeling, actually, hardly even a thought. I wonder if we
aren't barred from the past by a thousand invisible chains. You
can't drive into the past in a 1957 Buick because there are no
1957 Buicks in 1923; so how could you be there in one? You can't
drive into 1923 in a Jordan Playboy, along a four-lane superhighway; there are no superhighways in 1923. You couldn't even, I'm
certain, drive with a pack of modern filter-tip cigarettes in your
pocket—into a night when no such thing existed. Or with so
much as a coin bearing a modern date, or wearing a charcoal-grey
and pink shirt on your back. All those things, small and large,
are chains keeping you out of a time when they could not exist.

But my car and I—the way I felt about it, anyway—were almost
rejected that night, by the time I lived in. And so there in my
Jordan, just as it was the year it was new, with nothing about
me from another time, the old '23 tags on my car, and moving
along a highway whose very oil spots belonged to that year—

well, I think that for a few moments, all the chains hanging slack, we were free on the surface of Time. And that, moving along that old highway through the summer evening, we simply *drifted*—into the time my Jordan belonged in.

That's the best I can do, anyway; it's all that occurs to me. And—well, I wish I could offer you proof. I wish I could tell you that when I drove into Hylesburg again, onto Main Street, that I saw a newspaper headline saying, PRESIDENT HARDING STRICKEN, or something like that. Or that I heard people discussing Babe Ruth's new home-run record, or saw a bunch of cops raiding a speak-easy.

But I saw or heard nothing of the sort, nothing much different from the way it always has been. The street was quiet and nearly empty, as it is once the stores shut down for the weekend. I saw only two people at first; just a couple walking along far down the street. As for the buildings, they've been there, most of them, since the Civil War, or before—Hylesburg's an old town—and in the semidarkness left by the street lamps, they looked the same as always, and the street was paved with brick as it has been since World War I.

No, all I saw driving along Main Street were—just little things. I saw a shoe store, its awning still over the walk, and that awning was striped; broad red and white stripes, and the edges were scalloped. You just don't see awnings like that, outside of old photographs, but there it was, and I pulled over to the kerb, staring across the walk at the window. But all I can tell you is that there were no open-toed shoes among the women's, and the heels looked a little high to me, and a little different in design, somehow. The men's shoes—well, the toes seemed a little more pointed than you usually see now, and there were no suede shoes at all. But the kids' shoes looked the same as always.

I drove on, and passed a little candy and stationery shop, and on the door was a sign that said, *Drink Coca-Cola*, and in some way I can't describe the letters looked different. Not much, but— you've seen old familiar trademarks that have gradually changed, kept up to date through the years, in a gradual evolution. All I can say is that this old familiar sign looked a little different, a little old-fashioned, but I can't really say how.

There were a couple of all-night restaurants open, as I drove along, one of them The New China, the other Gill's, but they've both been in Hylesburg for years. There were a couple of people

in each of them, but I never even thought of going in. It seemed
to me I was here on sufferance, or by accident; that I'd just drifted
into this time, and had no right to actually intrude on it. Both
restaurant signs were lighted, the letters formed by electric-light
bulbs, unfrosted so that you could see the filaments glowing, and
the bulbs ended in sharp glass spikes. There wasn't a neon sign,
lighted or unlighted, the entire length of the street.

On West Main I came to the Orpheum, and though the box
office and marquee were dark, there were a few lights still on,
and a dozen or so cars parked for half a block on each side of
it. I parked mine directly across the street beside a wood telephone pole. Brick pavement is bumpy, and when I shut off the
motor, and reached for the handbrake—I don't know whether
this is important or not, but I'd better tell it—the Jordan rolled
ahead half a foot as its right front wheel settled into a shallow
depression in the pavement. For just a second or so, it rocked a
little in a tiny series of rapidly decreasing arcs, then stopped, its
wheel settled snugly into the depression as though it had found
exactly the spot it had been looking for—like a dog turning round
several times before it lies down in precisely the right place.

Crossing over to the Orph, I saw the big posters in the shallow
glass showcases on each side of the entrance. *Fri, Sat. and Sun.*,
one said, and it showed a man with a long thin face, wearing a
monocle, and his eyes were narrowed, staring at a woman with
long hair who looked sort of frightened. GEORGE ARLISS, said
the poster, in 'The Green Goddess'.

Coming Attraction, said the other poster, *Mon., Tues. and Wed.*
'Ashes of Vengeance', starring NORMA TALMADGE and
CONWAY TEARLE, with WALLACE BEERY. I've never heard of
any of them, except Wallace Beery. In the little open lobby, I
looked at the still pictures in wall cases at each side of the box
office; small, glossy, black and white scenes from the two movies,
and finally recognised Wallace Beery, a thin, handsome, young
man. I've never seen that kind of display before, and didn't know
it was done.

But that's about all I can tell you; nothing big or dramatic, and
nothing significant, like hearing someone say, 'Mark my words,
that boy Lindbergh will fly the Atlantic yet.' All I saw was a
little, shut-down, eleven-o'clock Main Street.

The parked cars, though, were a Dort; a high, straight-lined
Buick sedan with wood wheels; three Model Ts; a blue Hup-

mobile touring car with blue and yellow disc wheels; a Winston;
a four-cylinder Chevrolet roadster; a Stutz; a spoke-wheeled
Cadillac sedan. Not a single car had been made later than the
year 1923. And this is the strange thing: they looked *right* to
me. They looked as though that were the way automobiles were
supposed to look, nothing odd, funny, or old-fashioned about
them. From somewhere in my mind, I know I could have brought
up a mental picture of a glossy, two-toned, chromium-striped
car with power steering. But it would have taken a real effort,
and—I can't really explain this, I know—it was as though modern
cars didn't really exist; not yet. *These* were today's cars, parked
all around me, and I knew it.

I walked on, just strolling down Main Street, glancing at an
occasional store window, enjoying the incredible wonder of being
where I was. Then, half a block or so behind me, I heard a sudden
little babble of voices, and I looked back and the movie was
letting out. A little crowd of people was flowing slowly out onto
the walk to stand, some of them, talking for a moment; while
others crossed the street, or walked on. Motors began starting,
the parked cars pulling out from the kerb, and I heard a girl
laugh.

I walked on three or four steps maybe, and then I heard a
sound, utterly familiar and unmistakable, and stopped dead in
my tracks. My Jordan's motor had caught, roaring up as someone
advanced the spark and throttle, and dying to its chunky,
revving-and-ticking-over idle. Swinging round on the walk, I saw
a figure, a young man's, vague and shadowy down the street,
hop into the front seat, and then—the cut-out open—my Jordan
shot ahead, tyres squealing, down the street towards me.

I was frozen; I just stood there stupidly, staring at my car
shooting towards me, my brain not working; then I came to life.
It's funny; I was more worried about my car, about the way it
was treated, than about the fact that it was being stolen. And I
ran out into the street, directly into its path, my arms waving,
and I yelled, 'Hey! Take it easy!' The brakes slammed on, the
Jordan skidding on the bricks, the rear end sliding sideways a
little, and it slowed almost to a stop, then swerved around me,
picking up speed again, and as I turned, following it with my
eyes, I caught a glimpse of a girl's face staring at me, and a man
my age at the wheel beside her, laughing, his teeth flashing white,
and then they were past, and he yelled back, 'You betcha! Take

it easy; I always do!' For a moment I just stood staring after them, watching the single red tail-light shrinking into the distance; then I turned, and walked back towards the kerb. A little part of the movie crowd was passing, and I heard a woman's voice murmur some question; then a man's voice, gruff and half angry, replied, 'Yeah, of *course* it was Vince; driving like a fool as usual.'

There was nothing I could do. I couldn't report a car theft to the police, trying to explain who I was, and where they could reach me. I hung around for a while, the street deserted once more, hoping they'd bring back my car. But they didn't, and finally I left, and just walked the streets for the rest of the night.

I kept well away from Prairie Avenue. If I was where I knew I was, my grandmother, still alive, was asleep in the big front bedroom of our house, and the thirteen-year-old in my room was the boy who would become my father. I didn't belong there now, and I kept away, up in the north end of town. It looked about as always; Hylesburg, as I've said, is old, and most of the new construction has been on the outskirts. Once in a while I passed a vacant lot where I knew there no longer was one; and when I passed the Dorsets' house where I played as a kid with Ray Dorset, it was only half built now, the wood of the framework looking fresh and new in the dark.

Once I passed a party, the windows all lighted, and they were having a time, noisy and happy, and with a lot of laughing and shrieks from the women. I stopped for a minute, across the street, watching; and I saw figures passing the lighted windows, and one of them was a girl with her hair slicked close to her head, and curving down onto her cheeks in sort of J-shaped hooks. There was a phonograph going, and the music—it was 'China Boy'—sounded sort of distant, the orchestration tinny, and . . . different, I can't explain how. Once it slowed down, the tones deepening, and someone yelled, and then I heard the pitch rising higher again as it picked up speed, and knew someone was winding the phonograph. Then I walked on.

At daylight, the sky whitening in the east, the leaves of the big old trees around me beginning to stir, I was on Cherry Street. I heard a door open across the street, and saw a man in overalls walk down his steps, cut silently across the lawn, and open the garage doors beside his house. He walked in, I heard the motor start, and a cream and green '56 Oldsmobile backed out—and I turned round then, and walked on towards Prairie Avenue and home, and was in bed a couple of hours before my folks woke up Sunday morning.

I didn't tell anyone my Jordan was gone; there was no way to explain it. Ed Smiley, and a couple of other guys, asked me about it, and I said I was working on it in my garage. My folks didn't ask; they were long since used to my working on a car for weeks, then discovering I'd sold or traded it for something else to work on.

But I wanted—I simply had to have—another Playboy, and it took a long time to find one. I heard of one in Davenport, and borrowed Jim Clark's Hudson, and drove over, but it wasn't a Playboy, just a Jordan, and in miserable shape anyway.

It was a girl who found me a Playboy; after school started up in September. She was in my Economics IV class, a sophomore I learned, though I didn't remember seeing her around before. She wasn't actually a girl you'd turn and look at again, and remember, I suppose; she wasn't actually pretty, I guess you'd have to say. But after I'd talked to her a few times, and had a Coke date once, when I ran into her downtown—then she was pretty. And I got to liking her; quite a lot. It's like this; I'm a guy who's going to want to get married pretty early. I've been dating girls since I was sixteen, and it's fun, and exciting, and I like it fine. But I've just about had my share of that, and I'd been looking at girls in a different way lately; a lot more interested in what they were like than in just how good-looking they were. And I knew pretty soon that this was a girl I could fall in love with, and marry, and be happy with. I won't be fooling around with old cars all my life; it's just a hobby, and I know it, and I wouldn't expect a girl to get all interested in exactly how the motor of an old Marmon works. But I would expect her to take some interest in how I feel about old cars. And she did—Helen McCauley, her name is. She really did; she understood what I was talking about, and it wasn't faked either, I could tell.

So one night—we were going to the dance at the Roof Garden, and I'd called for her a little early, and we were sitting out on her lawn in deck chairs killing time—I told her how I wanted one certain kind of old car, and why it had to be just that car. And when I mentioned its name, she sat up, and said, 'Why, good heavens, I've heard about the Playboy from Dad all my life; we've got one out in the barn; it's a beat-up old mess, though.

Dad!' she called, turning to look up at the porch where her folks were sitting. 'Here's a man you've been looking for!'

Well, I'll cut it short. Her dad came down, and when he heard what it was all about, Helen and I never did get to the dance. We were out in that barn, the old tarpaulin pulled off his Jordan, and we were looking at it, touching it, sitting in it, talking about it, and quoting Playboy ads to each other for the next three hours.

It wasn't in bad shape at all. The upholstery was gone; only wads of horsehair and strips of brittle old leather left. The body was dented, but not torn. A few parts, including one headlight and part of the windshield mounting, were gone, and the motor was a long way from running, but nothing serious. And all the wheels were there, and in good shape, though they needed renickelling.

Mr McCauley gave me the car; wouldn't take a nickel for it. He'd owned that Jordan when he was young, had had it ever since, and loved it; he'd always meant, he said, to get it in running order again sometime, but knew he never would now. And once he understood what I meant about restoring a classic, he said that to see it and drive it again as it once was, was all the payment he wanted.

I don't know just when I guessed, or why; but the feeling had been growing on me. Partly, I suppose, it was the colour; the faded-out remains of the deep green this old car had once been. And partly it was something else, I don't know just what. But suddenly—standing in that old barn with Helen, and her mother and dad—suddenly I knew, and I glanced around the barn, and found them; the old plates nailed up on a wall, 1923 through 1931. And when I walked over to look at them, I found what I knew I would find; 1923 Illinois tag 11,206.

'Your old Jordan plates?' I said, and when he nodded, I said as casually as I could, 'What's your first name, Mr McCauley?'

I suppose he thought I was crazy, but he said, 'Vincent. Why?'

'Just wondered. I was picturing you driving around when the Jordan was new; it's a fast car, and it must have been a temptation to open it up.'

'Oh, yeah.' He laughed. 'I did that, all right; those were wild times.'

'Racing trains; all that sort of thing, I suppose?'

'That's right,' he said, and Helen's mother glanced at me curiously. 'That was one of the things to do in those days. We almost

got it one night, too; scared me to death. Remember?' he said to
his wife.

'I certainly do.'

'What happened?' I said.

'Oh'—he shrugged—'I was racing a train, out west of town
one night; where the road parallels the Q tracks. I passed it,
heading for the crossroad—you know where it is—that cuts over
the tracks. We got there, my arms started to move, to swing the
wheel and shoot over the tracks in front of that engine—when I
knew I couldn't make it.' He shook his head. 'Two three seconds
more; if we'd gotten there just two seconds earlier, I'd have risked
it, I'm certain, and we'd have been killed, I know. But we were
just those couple seconds too late, and I swung that wheel straight
again, and shot on down the road beside that train, and when I
took my foot off the gas, and the engine rushed past us, the
fireman was leaning out of the cab shaking his fist, and shouting
something, I couldn't hear what, but it wasn't complimentary.'
He grinned.

'Did anything delay you that night,' I said softly, 'just long
enough to keep you from getting killed?' I was actually holding
my breath, waiting for his answer.

But he only shook his head. 'I don't know,' he said without
interest. 'I can't remember.' And his wife said, 'I don't even
remember where we'd been.'

I don't believe—I really don't—that my Jordan Playboy is anything more than metal, glass, rubber and paint formed into a
machine. It isn't alive; it can't think or feel; it's only a car. But I
think it's an especial tragedy when a young couple's lives are
cut off for no other reason than the sheer exuberance nature put
into them. And I can't stop myself from feeling, true or not true,
that when that old Jordan was restored—returned to precisely
the way it had been just before young Vince McCauley and his
girl had raced a train in it back in 1923—when it had been given
a second chance, it went back to the time and place, back to the
same evening in 1923, that would give them a second chance,
too. And so again, there on that warm July evening, actually
there in the year 1923, they got into that Jordan, standing just
where they'd parked it, to drive on and race that train. But trivial
events can affect important ones following them—how often
we've all said: If only this or that had happened, everything
would have turned out so differently. And this time it did, for

now something was changed. This time on that 1923 July evening, someone dashed in front of their car, delaying them only two or three seconds. But Vince McCauley, then, driving on to race along beside those tracks, changed his mind about trying to cross them; and lived to marry the girl beside him. And to have a daughter.

I haven't asked Helen to marry me, but she knows I will; after I've graduated, and got a job, I expect. And she knows that I know she'll say yes. We'll be married, and have children, and I'm sure we'll be driving a modern hard-top car like everyone else, with safety catches on the doors so the kids won't fall out. But one thing for sure—just as her folks did thirty-two years before—we'll leave on our honeymoon in the Jordan Playboy.

USED CAR

H. Russell Wakefield

The Highway Straight Eight which London solicitor Arthur Canning buys in the story of the 'Used Car' is quite obviously a vehicle with a sinister past. There is a suggestion that it once belonged to a dangerous character in Chicago before being shipped over to London. There is also the little matter of the unpleasant stain on the back seat that no amount of cleaning will remove. But it is such a bargain that Canning is prepared to ignore such nagging suspicions . . . until he and his family start to use the car and experience the most terrifying illusions. Or are they, in fact, more than just figments of the imagination?

Herbert Russell Wakefield (1888–1964) was for a number of years private secretary to the English press baron, Lord Northcliffe, who owned a formidable collection of cars. Later he worked as a civil servant and publisher, but a very unpleasant experience in a haunted Queen Anne house, where five previous tenants had committed suicide, changed his life. This event inspired the classic story of 'The Red Lodge' (1928) which, along with his subsequent tales, varying in themes from a haunted golf course to an insidious parody of the 'Great Beast' Aleister Crowley, earned him his place in the supernatural genre beside M. R. James and E. F. Benson. His ingenious mind and gifts as a story-teller are equally evident in 'Used Car', first published in 1932.

*   *   *

Mr Arthur Canning, senior partner in the prosperous firm of solicitors which bore his name, was convinced—for the purposes of family debate—that he neither required nor could afford another car. But his daughter Angela, aged nineteen, derided the former objection, while his wife Joan pooh-poohed the second. A shabby five-year-old which couldn't do fifty with the wind behind outraged Angela's sense of social decency, and her mother knew all about how good business had been lately. So their sire and husband, like a good democrat, bowed to the will of the majority and took a walk one afternoon down Great Portland Street, where are rehearsed the fables of the car-changers and situated the seats of those who sell pups. No new car for him if he could get what he wanted second-hand.

Presently he halted outside a shop and began to examine with apparent interest an impressive saloon which was thrusting its comely bonnet to the edge of the pavement, and which announced by a card slung from its radiator cap that it was a Highway Straight Eight and a superb bargain at £350. This was in the halcyon middle-twenties before the investing public had been initiated into the arcana of high finance through the agency of juries, coroner's and otherwise, and could still contemplate a box of matches without bursting into tears. In those days one could not buy a magnificent used car for five pounds down and a few small weekly instalments; so the Highway *did* look like good value to Mr Canning.

A trim and sprightly young salesman came out from the interior and wished Mr Canning a good afternoon. 'I'm rather interested in this Highway,' said the latter. 'I frequently drove in one in America, but I can't remember ever having seen one over here.'

The young man had been discreetly diagnosing Mr Canning's shrewd and determined countenance, and had already decided that he was a foeman worthy of his steel. (Sometimes it was merely a pleasure to serve a customer!) But this person was clearly not one whom he could easily persuade that £350 was an irreducible minimum. 'No, sir,' he replied, 'they're very fine cars, but their output is small and they're too expensive for the British market.'

'How did this one come into your hands?'

'An American gentleman brought it over with him and disposed of it to us. It's a 1924 model and a *marvellous* bargain.'

'Of course that remains to be seen,' replied Mr Canning with a sophisticated smile, and in the tone of one who had enjoyed, more or less, a higher automobile education. Whereupon he made a thorough superficial examination of the car, and then made up his mind.

'I shall want it vetted by my expert,' he said, 'and if his verdict is favourable, I will make you an offer.'

'I'm afraid—' began the young man.

'Here's his address,' continued Mr Canning imperturbably. 'Deliver it there tomorrow, and I'll let him know it's coming. Good afternoon.'

In the course of the next few days Mrs and Miss Canning inspected the Highway and pronounced a qualified approval of its appearance and appointments, and the expert gave its mechanical doings an A1 certificate, with the result that a cheque for £270 changed hands and Tonks, Mr Canning's chauffeur, drove it down to Grey Lodge, near Guildford, Surrey. The expert drew Mr Canning's attention to a rather large dark stain on the fawn corduroy behind the back seat, saying that he hoped none of his men were responsible. Mr Canning reassured him by declaring that it had been there all the time. He had noticed it in the shop, he said.

Mr Canning, on attaining a certain affluence, had built himself a very comfortable and aesthetically satisfying house in West Surrey. Like everything else about him and his, it suggested super-tax but not death duties. His social standing was well established in the neighbourhood, for Mrs C., a handsome well-upholstered matron, had a shrewd Scottish flair for entertainment, and a flexible faculty for making the right people feel at home; while Angela was lively and decorative and hit balls about with superior skill. On reaching home the next evening he found these ladies had already taken a trip in the car. Their verdict was favourable. Mrs Canning liked the springing and the back seat, though one of the windows rattled, while Angela was satisfied that it would do seventy. 'But,' she added, 'Jumbo loathes it.'

'How do you mean?' asked her father.

'Oh, all the time we were out he was whining and fussing, and when we got home he dashed into the garden with his tail between his legs.'

'Well, he'll have to get used to it,' said Mr Canning in a firm tone, which implied that he would stand no nonsense from that pampered and good-for-nothing liver spaniel. 'Has Tonks got that stain off the cloth?'

'He's working at it this evening,' replied Angela, 'it only wants rubbing with petrol.'

After dinner, while they were sitting round the fire in the

drawing-room, Jumbo with his paws in the grate, Mr Canning tried an experiment by giving his celebrated imitation of a motor-horn, which usually aroused anticipatory ecstasies in Jumbo. This time, however, he stared up uncertainly at his master and the motions of his tail suggested no more than mere politeness. 'You see,' said Angela, who possessed a deep insight into the animal, 'he doesn't know whether you mean the old car or the new.'

'Or rot!' said her father, 'he's sleepy.' But he was half convinced. 'Anyhow,' he presently continued, 'I'll take him with me to South Hill on Saturday. I've always said he was a perfect half-wit.'

'He's a perfect *darling!*' said Mrs Canning indignantly. 'Come here my sweet.' Jumbo lurched reluctantly over to her, his demeanour suggesting that, while affectionate appreciation of his charms was gratifying, when a fellow was sleeping peacefully with his paws in the grate it was a bit thick to keep on disturbing him. 'We're going over to the Talbots tomorrow,' Mrs Canning went on, 'but we'll be back in time to send the car to the station if it's raining.' Her husband grunted drowsily and returned to his perusal of *Country Life*.

'Hullo, William,' said Angela at three o'clock the next afternoon, 'I see you haven't done anything about that stain.' The chauffeur appeared somewhat piqued at this insinuation, his manner implying that, considering he had taught Miss Angela to drive when her hair was still in a pig-tail, she ought to treat him with more deference. 'I did my best, miss,' he replied, 'I gave it a stiff rubbing with petrol, but it didn't seem to make no difference.'

'I wonder what it is,' said Angela.

'I don't know, miss, but last night it felt sticky to the touch.'

'It's quite dry now,' she declared. 'Have another go at it this evening. Ah, here's mother.'

The Talbots lived some twenty miles away. Miss Talbot had been at school with Angela. Bob Talbot had lately taken to blushing heavily when her name was mentioned, much to his chagrin and the delight of the local covey or giggle of flappers. The Talbots were nice people, well-connected, best-quality-county and rather hard up. The Cannings were nice people, only just emerging from the professional-urban chrysalis and on the financial upgrade; so the two families were at once contrasted and complementary. They enjoyed each other's company, and so it was after six when the Cannings started for home in the much admired Highway. After they had covered a short distance Angela said, 'Rather a frowst, mother, shall I open a window?'

'Yes, do, dear. Have you noticed a queer smell, musty and sickly?'

'Yes, it's just frowst,' replied Angela. 'I'll open the one on your side, the wind's blowing hard on mine.' She leaned over and then said sharply, 'Don't, mother. Why did you do that?'

'Do what, dear?'

'Put your hand on my throat.'

'What *are* you talking about! I never did anything of the sort!'

Angela let the window down and then was silent. Why had Mama told that silly lie? She'd caught her throat quite hard. It had almost hurt. It wasn't a bit like her either to do such an idiotic thing nor to pretend she hadn't. Oh well, everyone was a silly ass at times; she'd think about something else. She'd think about that old mutt, Bob; he really had been rather sweet. 'Mrs Robert Talbot,' how did that sound? Not too bad, but she didn't want to be Mrs anybody yet awhile. She mustn't let him get too fond of her till she was sure; but she mustn't choke him off too much. How this judicious via media was to be followed was by no means clear to her; but the feat of having settled the principle of the thing so satisfactorily soothed her and restored her temper, that she now regarded her parent's infelicitous pleasantry with tolerance. When she was getting out of the car she touched the back of it to steady herself. Before following her mother into the house she turned to Tonks, prinking her fingers together.

'That stain's damp,' she said to him. Tonks switched on the light and felt it for himself. 'P'raps it is a bit, Miss,' he said doubtfully, 'I'll work on it again tonight.'

In the hall Angela examined her fingers closely. Then she rubbed them with her handkerchief and scrutinised that. She wrinkled her nose as if puzzled and went up to her room.

The next morning, Saturday, was brilliantly fine, so Mr Canning ordered the car to be round at 9.30. He was awaiting it with Jumbo by his side when it entered the drive from the garage turning. Jumbo gave it one searching glance and was off at a hand-gallop for the garden. 'Jumbo, Jumbo, come here!' cried his master imperiously. There was no response, so Mr Canning, a gleam in his eye, set off in pursuit. There he was, the old devil, peeping round from behind the silver birch. A fruitless and temper-rousing chase ensued, but Jumbo, though obviously alarmed and despondent, was neither to be cajoled nor trapped, so Mr Canning, after reviling him copiously from a distance and promising him prolonged corporal punishment in the near future, went back to the car. He was ruffled, and the sight of that stain irritated him still more. 'Can't you get it out, William?' he asked sharply. The chauffeur had reasons of his own for disliking the subject and replied respectfully but firmly that he'd done his best but could make no impression on it. 'Humph,' said Mr Canning, 'South Hill,' and lit a cigar.

He defeated his ancient rival, Bob Pelham, both rounds, lunched well, perspired satisfactorily and had a large whisky and soda just before leaving for home. So he was feeling full of good cheer, but inclined for repose when he came out from the club-house to drive home. He noticed Pelham emerge from the locker-room, go to the car and look in at the window. A moment later he was by his side. 'Hullo, *there* you are,' said Pelham. 'Funny thing I could have sworn I saw you inside.'

'Then don't have another drink,' said Mr Canning.

'Must be that,' replied the other, 'all the same I could have sworn it. Well, safe home and ten-thirty today week if it's a decent day. I'll have cured that blasted hook by then, so don't forget your note-case.'

'If you prefer to slice, that's your business,' replied Mr Canning. 'So long. I think I'll sit with you, William,' he continued, 'it smells stuffy inside there.'

It was too dark to see more than was disclosed in the head-lights' beam, so he soon closed his eyes. And then of a sudden it seemed to him that the speed of the car increased violently. He opened his eyes with the intention of speaking to Tonks and found he couldn't move, nor could he speak, and there was something pressing hard into his back. What was the matter? What had happened? Where were they? This wasn't the Guild-ford road! They were tearing madly across a plain, a region dim and hazy, and as they flashed past a cross-roads there was a sign-post of strange shape on which he thought he could just read the letters 'Chica'. And then he heard a vile whisper just behind him: 'Let 'em have it.' For a moment he knew the unique, agonised terror of certain and imminent death. There was a scream, a flame through his head, a crash—and Tonks was saying in a very startled voice, 'What's the matter, sir? What's the matter? Have you cut yourself?' The car pulled up hard on its brakes. For a moment Mr Canning remained trembling and silent, then he said hoarsely, 'What has happened?'

'You've put your elbow bang through the glass, sir. Let me look. It's all right, sir, you're not cut.'

'What was that scream?' asked Mr Canning, vaguely examining the elbow of his coat.

'Scream, sir?'

'Yes, a woman's scream.'

'I 'eard no scream, sir.'

'It's all right,' said Mr Canning after a pause. 'I went to sleep and must have had a dream. Drive on but go slowly. Get a new glass put in on Monday,' he said as he got out of the car half an hour later, 'I'll explain to the ladies.'

'Very good, sir,' replied Tonks, 'are you feeling all right, sir?'

'Quite, quite.'

Jumbo was peering round the banisters on the first landing, his eyes rolling with apprehension. 'Hullo, Jumbo,' said his master. 'Good boy!' Jumbo's ears soared in sheer astonishment and relief, and he lumbered hurriedly down the stairs to consolidate this unexpected armistice. Mr Canning twisted his ears and smacked his rump. 'You deserve a good hiding, you old rascal, but somehow I think I'll let you off this time.'

At dinner he alluded with rather elaborate casualness to his encounter with the glass. 'What a funny position to get your elbow into,' commented his wife.

'Oh, I don't know,' he replied, 'I was asleep and it was jerked up, I suppose.'

'Has Tonks got that stain out?' she asked.

'Oh, damn that stain!' said Angela brusquely. 'I'm fed up with it, and anyhow it doesn't show much.'

'Yes, I think we'll leave it for the present,' agreed Mr Canning. 'The stuff, whatever it is, seems to have soaked right into the cloth.' He felt he didn't want to hear another word about that car for the time being.

Later, as he lay in bed waiting for sleep, he was uneasily wondering if he was going to experience another beastly dream like that other one. Of course it had been a dream, though he'd never had one like it before. That scream! He could still hear it in a fading echoed way, a cry of agony and terror. And that filthy

whisper! He shivered a little. Oh well, it was simply that he
wasn't used to dreaming so vividly. That was all. He began to
play over again in his head his first round. First hole; good drive,
fair brassie to the left of the green, nice pitch over the bunker
and a couple of putts. One up. Second hole. Rather a sliced
tee-shot, a slightly topped number three iron and then—and then
it was eight o'clock on Sunday morning, and Jumbo was scratch-
ing on the door for entry and a biscuit, the just reward of a
blameless, though often misjudged dog.

During the next few days neither the ladies nor Mr Canning
had cause to use the car after dark. Mrs Canning developed a
relaxed throat, and cheery, chatty Dr Gables came to have a look
at it. 'Like to see the new car?' asked Angela as the doctor was
taking his leave.

'All right,' said the doctor. 'If only we'd had a decent 'flu
winter, I'd have invested in another one myself.'

'Cheer up,' replied Angela, 'the mumps and measles season
may be better. You go on. I'll get the garage key and catch you
up.' As she came out of the front door she saw the doctor disappearing round the turning to the garage. A moment later she
was mildly surprised to hear him saying, 'Hullo, good evening.'
When she caught him up he remarked, in rather a puzzled tone,
'What's the matter with Tonks?'

'Tonks?' said Angela. 'He's gone home ages ago.'

'No, he hasn't. I saw him standing at the garage door, but
when I spoke to him he disappeared round the corner. Rude
fellow!'

'I don't think it could have been he,' said Angela, rather shortly.
She unlocked the door, switched on the light and they went in.

'Nice looking bus,' remarked the doctor, 'never seen a Highway
before; looks like a very neat job.' He lifted the bonnet flap and
gazed knowingly at its digestive system. 'Let's see the inside.'
He opened the door, peered in and then sniffed once or twice.
He climbed in, sat down and put his head back. 'Hullo,' he
exclaimed, 'my head's sticking to something.' He turned round
and saw the stain. 'It was sticking to that, what is it?'

'Oh, I don't know,' said Angela, 'it was there when we got the
car. Seen enough?'

'Yes,' replied the doctor getting out. 'Nice bus. And now I must
be off. I've got to assist in increasing the population in an hour,
in these times a thoroughly antisocial act, but a man must live.

Ring me in the morning and tell me how your mother is. Make her keep on at that gargle. Goodnight, my dear.'

As he strolled home he was thinking to himself, 'That car has a very odd reek. When I smelt it I could almost believe I was back at the dressing-station near Bois Grenier. Perhaps that's why I took a mild dislike to the car. I suppose that chap Tonks is OK. Always thought he was a very steady fellow, yet it was queer the way he slipped off just now. Of course it *might* have been someone else. None of my business anyway.'

Saturday morning turned out to be chilly and boisterous with a falling glass and an unmistakable smell of coming rain, so Mr Pelham, who had drunk more port than he'd realised at a Masonic dinner the night before and greeted the dawn with loathing, quite agreed with Mr Canning that it was no day for golf. The latter took a stroll round his domain after breakfast. Eventually he turned in to the garage; Tonks was cleaning the car outside it. Mr Canning greeted him and asked how he was. 'Quite well, thank you, sir,' he replied. However his looks and the tone of his voice somewhat belied him.

Hullo, thought Mr Canning, something wrong. Tonks was a cockney and so was his master; they belonged by origin to much the same class. They therefore, had an instinctive understanding of each other. Between Mr Canning and rustics of all social strata there was a great gulf of misunderstanding fixed, but he knew his Londoner of the Tonks type like the back of his hand, and there was something on his mind.

'Now then, William,' he said gently but firmly, 'what's the matter?'

'Nothing, sir.'

'You've been with me seven years and six months.'

'Yes, sir,' he replied, rather gratified at this accuracy.

'And how many lies have you told me in that time?'

'None deliberate, sir.'

'Then don't begin now, William. What is it; money, a woman, some such trouble?'

'None of 'em, sir.'

'I didn't expect so; then what is it?'

Tonks stared at the ground for a time and then he said, 'It sounds like foolishness, sir.'

'Leave me to judge of that.'

'Well, sir, I get a bit scared.'

'Scared, scared! In what way?' asked Mr Canning, wondering vaguely why he'd somehow expected some such answer.

'That's what I'm not sure about,' replied Tonks, his confidence released now the ice was broken. 'That's why it sounds like foolishness, but it seemed to begin like just as soon as the 'Ighway came in.'

'Came into the garage, d'you mean?'

'Yes, sir.'

'Well, what happened?'

'At first it was just that I had a feeling of someone about, someone watching me. I looked around but couldn't exactly see no one. But somehow it seemed to me there was three of 'em. And it's been like that since, sir. It's always after dark. And I've felt they was coming along be'ind me and then standing and watching.'

'Is that all?' asked Mr Canning after a pause.

'Well, sir, one evening when I was putting her away—I'd just opened the door and was about to switch on the light—it seemed to me there was whispering going on just by me, and I thought someone touched me. And there've been other things, other goings on as it were, whenever I've been 'ere after dark. I never feels alone, sir, always expecting something. Now I 'ad an aunt, sir, who saw things and 'eard things that wasn't really there, and she went out of 'er mind later on, and I've got the wind up that I'm going the same way. I was thinking, p'raps I oughtn't to drive, if I was going that way.'

'Nonsense!' replied Mr Canning sharply. 'Nothing of the kind. You're as sane as anyone else.'

'I certainly feels it, sir, but then why do I think I sees and 'ears and feels things?'

'It's nothing, nothing! Many people have that sort of experience.'

'Do they really, sir?'

'Yes! yes! Think no more about it.'

'All right, I'll try, sir.'

For the next hour Mr Canning walked round and round the garden. An ugly, insinuating notion was knocking for admittance to his mind. Something at which he'd always scoffed; something the possibility of which he'd always eagerly derided. For a moment the echo of a scream rang in his head, and the memory of a look on Angela's face came back to him. Of course it was all ridiculous. Silly fancies! He'd shake his mind of them. It was a depressing day and he'd done a very hard week's work. It was all tommy-rot! He began to whistle a cheerful little tune, and went indoors for a glass of that most excellent new sherry.

On Thursday, Angela drove over to a neighbour's house to play tennis on their hard-court. When she got home again, Walker, the butler, who let her in noticed that she was looking tired and upset. She told him rather brusquely to get her some brandy. She swallowed it at a gulp and her colour began to return. During dinner she was silent and preoccupied. Her father noticed it and suggested she might have caught her mother's cold. She answered irritably that she was perfectly all right; but he observed also that she drank more wine than was her wont and that her nerves had got somewhat the better of her. After dinner she pretended to read, but went early to bed.

By Monday morning, Mrs Canning's throat was better, but Dr Gables refused to allow her out of doors. She was a busy, active person who resented any kind of restraint. What made it worse was that Angela had gone up to Town to shop. She felt lonely and bored. Household chores occupied the morning more or less. After lunch she slept a little, did her nails, and tried to concentrate on a novel which its publishers adroitly insinuated had almost been banned. But she found that its author, a young woman of twenty, had really very little to teach a wife and mother of forty-nine. Sex, she thought with a yawn, was nearly always just the same, however much one stupidly hoped it was going to be different. After tea she felt something had got to be done. Her temper was going; Angela oughtn't to have left her; Jumbo's snores got on her nerves; she wanted to scream; Dr Gables was just an old fusser. Suddenly she made up her mind, rang the bell and told Martha to tell William that she wanted the car round at once. She soothed her conscience by wrapping herself up in many garments and went downstairs. 'Just drive around for an hour or so,' she told Tonks, 'and keep off the main roads.'

For a time she gave herself up to the delight of being on the move again and thinking how lovely the county of Surrey looked in the last rays of the sinking sun. Then she began considering this and that rather lazily. It was very warm in the car. Her thoughts became even less coherent and presently her head nodded. Sometime later she woke up with a start under the vague impression that someone had touched her. It was quite dark, she noticed. Weren't they going very fast? What was the matter with her? She opened and closed her eyes very quickly several times. Then very stealthily she tried to move her elbows. She must keep quite calm and think. She had gone out for a drive with William and must have gone to sleep. Why was William wearing that funny cap? And who was that on the seat beside him? And why couldn't she move her elbows; it was just as if they were gripped by two hands. What had happened? Had she gone mad? Suddenly she lunged forward convulsively and it seemed to her she was wrenched back and a hand went fiercely to her throat. She twisted, writhed and tried to scream. There were flashes of flame before her bursting eyes, and as her head was forced agonisingly back, she felt life choked from her.

She was lying on a grass bank beside the road. Tonks was bending over her and trying to force something in a glass between her lips. Someone else was supporting her head. 'Is she subject to fits?' asked the latter.

'No, sir. I don't think this is a fit. She's coming to.' Mrs Canning's eyes opened and her hands went to her throat. 'Where are they? Who's that?' she screamed.

'It's all right, madam,' said Tonks gently, 'you fainted.' Her head fell back again and her eyes closed.

'We'd better take her into the house,' said the stranger.

'It's very good of you, sir,' said Tonks, 'but I'd rather get her home.'

'As you say,' replied the other. The two men carried her into the car.

'Would you mind driving, sir,' said Tonks. 'I think I'd better be inside with her. It's the first turning on the left about two miles along.'

'She's better,' said Dr Gables, two hours later, 'but she's had a very severe shock of some kind. She seems to imagine she was attacked in the car—not quite herself mentally yet. I've given her a strong sedative and the nurse knows what to do. I'll be along first thing in the morning.'

'Father,' said Angela, when he'd gone, 'there's something vile about that car!' She was very white and still trembling. 'I know it! I know it! I didn't say anything about it at the time, but on Thursday when I was driving home, it got dark just before we entered the drive and I suddenly felt someone beside me. It was only for a moment—till I saw the lights of the house—but there *was* someone there.'

Mr Canning stared past her for a time before replying. Then he said, 'It shall not be used again.'

The next day he made some enquiries, first at the shop in Great Portland Street and then at the American Express Company, with the result that he sent the following letter to an address in Chicago.

Dear Sir,

I understand that you were the previous owner of a Highway car which I recently purchased. It is not easy to put into words what I have to say, but as the result of certain experiences which I and members of my household have had with this car I have decided to dispose of it in some way. At the same time I feel a certain strong reluctance against allowing others to suffer the same experiences, which might happen if I sold it. All this may be incomprehensible to you; if so, please do not trouble to reply. If, however, you can throw any light on the matter it might be very useful as a guide to me.

> Yours faithfully,
> A. T. Canning.

Three weeks later he received the following reply.

> —Michigan Avenue,
> Chicago, Ill.

Dear Mr Canning,

In one way I was very glad to get your letter; in another it made me feel terribly badly. I knew when I did it, and I've known ever since, that I'd no business to turn in that Highway. It was just a case of feeling one way and acting another. Now I can't figure out just what's the hoodoo with that car, but I *do* know I wouldn't take another night ride in it for a thousand dollars. That's why I was dead wrong to turn it in; and I've no alibi. Here's its record. Now, there was a well-known moll in this city, named Blonde Beulah Kratz, who was in with a bunch of tough gangsters—she covered the blackmail and vice angle. And she had a temporary sweetie, a thirty-minute egg, named Snow-Bird

Sordone. And they figured it that they ought to have collected more of the loot from some job. So they tried to double-cross the rest of the gang. Well, they were taken for a trip in the country one night, and their bodies were found in that Highway next day—it ran out of gas, I guess. The blonde was knifed and strangled—that gang took no chances—and the Snow-Bird had some big slugs through his back-parting. Well, our District-Attorney, a friend of mine, took over the car, and then pretty soon didn't feel so crazy about it and passed it on to me just when I was coming to Europe, so I took it with me. Well, after I'd had a few rides in it I turned it in quick, just like that, and I guess you know why.

Now, Mr Canning, what I want you to do is this. First of all to forgive me for letting you in for a dirty deal. And then, just fill in the enclosed check for the amount you paid for the Highway; I shall feel very badly if you don't. And then I want you to take that automobile and tip it into the ocean, or stall it on a level-crossing, or match it with Carnera; anyway do something to it so that no one will ride in it again and get so scared the way I did, and I guess you did. I forgot to say that the birds who bumped the blonde and the Snow-Bird were handed out some electric treatment in a gaol near here.

If I get to Europe again I'll look you up, if I may. Now, please, Mr Canning, fill in that check right away, and then I'll know you've forgiven me and I'll feel a whole heap better.

Yours truly
George A. Camshott.

Mr Canning, with a clear conscience, subsequently carried out all these instructions.

DUEL

Richard Matheson

'Duel' is one of the most gripping stories ever written about the terroris-
ing of one driver by another — a situation not unfamiliar in real life
and used a number of times in fiction. Much of the nail-biting suspense
is undoubtedly due to the fact that it was inspired by a traumatic
experience that actually happened to the author, Richard Matheson: 'I
had been playing golf with a friend when we heard the news that
President Kennedy had been assassinated,' he says. 'We broke off our
game and headed for home. As we were driving, muttering and moaning
about the assassination, a truck started tailgating us on the narrow
pass we were driving through. This went on for miles with us screaming
infuriatedly, until we finally pulled over to the side of the road and let
the son of a bitch pass. While we were stopped, I wrote the idea for
"Duel" down on the back of a piece of mail that my friend had in the
car. I didn't write the story, though, until a few years later.' First
published, like Stephen King's 'Trucks', in a men's magazine, Playboy,
in April 1971, 'Duel' was also scripted by Matheson for a film adapta-
tion starring Dennis Weaver, which now enjoys cult status. The project
was given to a young director named Steven Spielberg who was making
his debut, and the rest, as they say, is history.

  Richard Matheson (1926–) has combined a highly successful career
as a novelist and short-story writer with that of scriptwriter. Several
of his books, such as I Am Legend *(1954),* The Shrinking Man
(1956), Hell House *(1971) and* Somewhere in Time *(1980), have*
been successfully filmed, and Matheson's influence was recently recog-
nised by The Encyclopedia of Science Fiction *(1993) which called*
him 'one of the most significant modern creators of terror and fantasy
in both fiction and film.' A regular theme in his work has been paranoia,
as in the story 'Dying Room Only' in which a woman's husband

*disappears in a motel lavatory but no one will believe her, and in the
nightmare ride that is 'Duel'.*

*   *   *

At 11:32 a.m., Mann passed the truck.

He was heading west, en route to San Francisco. It was Thursday and unseasonably hot for April. He had his suit coat off, his
tie removed and shirt collar opened, his sleeve cuffs folded back.
There was sunlight on his left arm and on part of his lap. He
could feel the heat of it through his dark trousers as he drove
along the two-lane highway. For the past 20 minutes, he had not
seen another vehicle going in either direction.

Then he saw the truck ahead, moving up a curving grade
between two high green hills. He heard the grinding strain of its
motor and saw a double shadow on the road. The truck was
pulling a trailer.

He paid no attention to the details of the truck. As he drew
behind it on the grade, he edged his car towards the opposite
lane. The road ahead had blind curves and he didn't try to pass
until the truck had crossed the ridge. He waited until it started
round a left curve on the downgrade, then, seeing that the way
was clear, pressed down on the accelerator pedal and steered his
car into the eastbound lane. He waited until he could see the
truck front in his rearview mirror before he turned back into the
proper lane.

Mann looked across the countryside ahead. There were ranges
of mountains as far as he could see and, all around him, rolling
green hills. He whistled softly as the car sped down the winding
grade, its tyres making crisp sounds on the pavement.

At the bottom of the hill, he crossed a concrete bridge and,
glancing to the right, saw a dry stream bed strewn with rocks
and gravel. As the car moved off the bridge, he saw a trailer
park set back from the highway to his right. How can anyone
live out here? he thought. His shifting gaze caught sight of a pet
cemetery ahead and he smiled. Maybe those people in the trailers
wanted to be close to the graves of their dogs and cats.

The highway ahead was straight now. Mann drifted into a
reverie, the sunlight on his arm and lap. He wondered what Ruth
was doing. The kids, of course, were in school and would be for
hours yet. Maybe Ruth was shopping; Thursday was the day she

usually went. Mann visualised her in the supermarket, putting various items into the trolley. He wished he were with her instead of starting on another sales trip. Hours of driving yet before he'd reach San Francisco. Three days of hotel sleeping and restaurant eating, hoped-for contacts and likely disappointments. He sighed; then, reaching out impulsively, he switched on the radio. He revolved the tuning knob until he found a station playing soft, innocuous music. He hummed along with it, eyes almost out of focus on the road ahead.

He started as the truck roared past him on the left, causing his car to shudder slightly. He watched the truck and trailer cut in abruptly for the westbound lane and frowned as he had to brake to maintain a safe distance behind it. What's with you? he thought.

He eyed the truck with cursory disapproval. It was a huge gasoline tanker pulling a tank trailer, each of them having six pairs of wheels. He could see that it was not a new rig but was dented and in need of renovation, its tanks painted a cheap-looking silvery colour. Mann wondered if the driver had done the painting himself. His gaze shifted from the word FLAMMABLE printed across the back of the trailer tank, red letters on a white background, to the parallel reflector lines painted in red across the bottom of the tank to the massive rubber flaps swaying behind the rear tyres, then back up again. The reflector lines looked as though they'd been clumsily applied with a stencil. The driver must be an independent trucker, he decided, and not too affluent a one, from the looks of his outfit. He glanced at the trailer's licence plate. It was a California issue.

Mann checked his speedometer. He was holding steady at 55 miles an hour, as he invariably did when he drove without think-ing on the open highway. The truck driver must have done a good 70 to pass him so quickly. That seemed a little odd. Weren't truck drivers supposed to be a cautious lot?

He grimaced at the smell of the truck's exhaust and looked at the vertical pipe to the left of the cab. It was spewing smoke, which clouded darkly back across the trailer. Christ, he thought. With all the furore about air pollution, why do they keep allowing that sort of thing on the highways?

He scowled at the constant fumes. They'd make him nauseated in a little while, he knew. He couldn't lag back here like this. Either he slowed down or he passed the truck again. He didn't have the time to slow down. He'd had a late start. Keeping it at 55 all the way, he'd just about make his afternoon appointment. No, he'd have to pass.

Depressing the gas pedal, he eased his car towards the opposite lane. No sign of anything ahead. Traffic on this route seemed almost nonexistent today. He pushed down harder on the accelerator and steered all the way into the eastbound lane.

As he passed the truck, he glanced at it. The cab was too high for him to see into. All he caught sight of was the back of the truck driver's left hand on the steering wheel. It was darkly tanned and square-looking, with large veins knotted on its surface.

When Mann could see the truck reflected in the rearview mirror, he pulled back over to the proper lane and looked ahead again.

He glanced at the rearview mirror in surprise as the truck driver gave him an extended horn blast. What was that? he wondered; a greeting or a curse? He grunted with amusement, glancing at the mirror as he drove. The front fenders of the truck were a dingy purple colour, the paint faded and chipped; another amateurish job. All he could see was the lower portion of the truck; the rest was cut off by the top of his rear window.

To Mann's right now, was a slope of shalelike earth with patches of scrub grass growing on it. His gaze jumped to the clapboard house on top of the slope. The television aerial on its roof was sagging at an angle or less than 40 degrees. Must give great reception, he thought.

He looked to the front again, glancing aside abruptly at a sign printed in jagged block letters on a piece of plywood: NIGHT CRAWLERS—BAIT. What the hell is a night crawler? he wondered. It sounded like some monster in a low-grade Hollywood thriller.

The unexpected roar of the truck motor made his gaze jump to the rearview mirror. Instantly, his startled look jumped to the side mirror. By God, the guy was passing him *again*. Mann turned his head to scowl at the leviathan form as it drifted by. He tried to see into the cab but couldn't because of its height. What's with him, anyway? he wondered. What the hell are we having here, a contest? See which vehicle can stay ahead the longer?

He thought of speeding up to stay ahead but changed his mind. When the truck and trailer started back into the westbound lane, he let up on the pedal, voicing a newly incredulous sound as he saw that if he hadn't slowed down, he would have been prematurely cut off again. Jesus Christ, he thought. What's *with* this guy?

His scowl deepened as the odour of the truck's exhaust reached his nostrils again. Irritably, he cranked up the window on his left. Damn it, was he going to have to breathe that crap all the way to San Francisco? He couldn't afford to slow down. He had to meet Forbes at a quarter after three and that was that.

He looked ahead. At least there was no traffic complicating matters. Mann pressed down on the accelerator pedal, drawing close behind the truck. When the highway curved enough to the left to give him a completely open view of the route ahead, he jarred down on the pedal, steering out into the opposite lane.

The truck edged over, blocking his way.

For several moments, all Mann could do was stare at it in blank confusion. Then, with a startled noise, he braked, returning to the proper lane. The truck moved back in front of him.

Mann could not allow himself to accept what apparently had taken place. It had to be a coincidence. The truck driver couldn't have blocked his way on purpose. He waited for more than a minute, then flicked down the turn-indicator lever to make his intentions perfectly clear and, depressing the accelerator pedal, steered again into the eastbound lane.

Immediately, the truck shifted, barring his way.

'*Jesus Christ!*' Mann was astounded. This was unbelievable. He'd never seen such a thing in 26 years of driving. He returned to the westbound lane, shaking his head as the truck swung back in front of him.

He eased up on the gas pedal, falling back to avoid the truck's exhaust. Now what? he wondered. He still had to make San Francisco on schedule. Why in God's name hadn't he gone a little out of his way in the beginning, so he could have travelled by freeway? This damned highway was two lane all the way.

Impulsively, he sped into the eastbound lane again. To his surprise, the truck driver did not pull over. Instead, the driver stuck his left arm out and waved him on. Mann started pushing down on the accelerator. Suddenly, he let up on the pedal with a gasp and jerked the steering wheel round, raking back behind the truck so quickly that his car began to fishtail. He was fighting to control its zigzag whipping when a blue convertible shot by him in the opposite lane. Mann caught a momentary vision of the man inside it glaring at him.

The car came under his control again. Mann was sucking breath in through his mouth. His heart was pounding almost painfully. My God! he thought. *He wanted me to hit that car head on.* The realisation stunned him. True, he should have seen to it himself that the road ahead was clear; that was his failure. But to wave him on ... Mann felt appalled and sickened. Boy, oh, boy, oh, boy, he thought. This was really one for the books. That son of a bitch had meant not only him to be killed but a totally uninvolved passer-by as well. The idea seemed beyond his comprehension. On a California highway on a Thursday morning? *Why?*

Mann tried to calm himself and rationalise the incident. Maybe it's the heat, he thought. Maybe the truck driver had a tension headache or an upset stomach; maybe both. Maybe he'd had a fight with his wife. Maybe she'd failed to put out last night. Mann tried in vain to smile. There could be any number of reasons. Reaching out, he twisted off the radio. The cheerful music irritated him.

He drove behind the truck for several minutes, his face a mask of animosity. As the exhaust fumes started putting his stomach on edge, he suddenly forced down the heel of his right hand on the horn bar and held it there. Seeing that the route ahead was clear, he pushed in the accelerator pedal all the way and steered into the opposite lane.

The movement of his car was paralleled immediately by the truck. Mann stayed in place, right hand jammed down on the horn bar. Get out of the way, you son of a bitch! he thought. He felt the muscles of his jaw hardening until they ached. There was a twisting in his stomach.

'Damn!' He pulled back quickly to the proper lane, shuddering with fury. 'You miserable son of a bitch,' he muttered, glaring at the truck as it was shifted back in front of him. What the hell is wrong with you? I pass your goddamn rig a couple of times and you go flying off the deep end? Are you nuts or something? Mann nodded tensely. Yes, he thought; he is. No other explanation.

He wondered what Ruth would think of all this, how she'd react. Probably, she'd start to honk the horn and would keep on honking it, assuming that, eventually, it would attract the attention of a policeman. He looked around with a scowl. Just where in hell *were* the policemen out here, anyway? He made a scoffing noise. What policemen? Here in the boondocks? They probably had a sheriff on horseback, for Christ's sake.

He wondered suddenly if he could fool the truck driver by passing on the right. Edging his car towards the shoulder, he peered ahead. No chance. There wasn't room enough. The truck driver could shove him through that wire fence if he wanted to. Mann shivered. And he'd want to, sure as hell, he thought.

Driving where he was, he grew conscious of the debris lying beside the highway: beer cans, candy wrappers, ice-cream containers, newspaper sections browned and rotted by the weather, a FOR SALE sign torn in half. Keep America beautiful, he thought sardonically. He passed a boulder with the name WILL JASPER painted on it in white. Who the hell is Will Jasper? he wondered. What would he think of this situation?

Unexpectedly, the car began to bounce. For several anxious moments, Mann thought that one of his tyres had gone flat. Then he noticed that the paving along this section of highway consisted of pitted slabs with gaps between them. He saw the truck and trailer jolting up and down and thought: I hope it shakes your brains loose. As the truck veered into a sharp left curve, he caught a fleeting glimpse of the driver's face in the cab's side mirror. There was not enough time to establish his appearance.

'Ah,' he said. A long, steep hill was looming up ahead. The truck would have to climb it slowly. There would doubtless be an opportunity to pass somewhere on the grade. Mann pressed down on the accelerator pedal, drawing as close behind the truck as safety would allow.

Halfway up the slope, Mann saw a turnout for the eastbound lane with no oncoming traffic anywhere in sight. Flooring the accelerator pedal, he shot into the opposite lane. The slow-moving truck began to angle out in front of him. Face stiffening, Mann steered his speeding car across the highway edge and curved it sharply on the turnout. Clouds of dust went billowing up behind his car, making him lose sight of the truck. His tyres buzzed and crackled on the dirt, then, suddenly, were humming on the pavement once again.

He glanced at the rearview mirror and a barking laugh erupted from his throat. He'd only meant to pass. The dust had been an unexpected bonus. Let the bastard get a sniff of something rotten smelling in *his* nose for a change! he thought. He honked the horn elatedly, a mocking rhythm of bleats. Screw you, Jack!

He swept across the summit of the hill. A striking vista lay ahead: sunlit hills and flatland, a corridor of dark trees, quadrangles of cleared-off acreage and bright-green vegetable patches; far off, in the distance, a mammoth water tower. Mann felt stirred by the panoramic sight. Lovely, he thought. Reaching out, he turned the radio back on and started humming cheerfully with the music.

Seven minutes later he passed a billboard advertising CHUCK'S CAFÉ. No thanks, Chuck, he thought. He glanced at a grey house nestled in a hollow. Was that a cemetery in its front yard or a group of plaster statuary for sale?

Hearing the noise behind him, Mann looked at the rearview mirror and felt himself go cold with fear. The truck was hurtling down the hill, pursuing him.

His mouth fell open and he threw a glance at the speedometer. He was doing more than 60! On a curving downgrade, that was not at all a safe speed to be driving. Yet the truck must be exceeding that by a considerable margin, it was closing the distance between them so rapidly. Mann swallowed, leaning to the right as he steered his car round a sharp curve. Is the man *insane*? he thought.

His gaze jumped forward searchingly. He saw a turnoff half a mile ahead and decided that he'd use it. In the rearview mirror, the huge square radiator grille was all he could see now. He stamped down on the gas pedal and his tyres screeched unnervingly as he wheeled round another curve, thinking that, surely, the truck would have to slow down here.

He groaned as it rounded the curve with ease, only the sway of its tanks revealing the outward pressure of the turn. Mann bit trembling lips together as he whipped his car round another curve. A straight descent now. He depressed the pedal farther, glanced at the speedometer. Almost 70 miles an hour! He wasn't used to driving this fast!

In agony, he saw the turnoff shoot by on his right. He couldn't have left the highway at this speed, anyway; he'd have overturned. Goddamn it, what was wrong with that son of a bitch? Mann honked his horn in frightened rage. Cranking down the window suddenly, he shoved his left arm out to wave the truck back. '*Back!*' he yelled. He honked the horn again. 'Get back, you crazy bastard!'

The truck was almost on him now. He's going to kill me! Mann thought, horrified. He honked the horn repeatedly, then had to use both hands to grip the steering wheel as he swept round another curve. He flashed a look at the rearview mirror. He could see only the bottom portion of the truck's radiator grille. He was going to lose control! He felt the rear wheels start to drift and let up on the pedal quickly. The tyre treads bit in, the car leaped on, regaining its momentum.

Mann saw the bottom of the grade ahead, and in the distance there was a building with a sign that read CHUCK'S CAFÉ. The truck was gaining ground again. This is insane! he thought, enraged and terrified at once. The highway straightened out. He floored the pedal: 74 now—75. Mann braced himself, trying to ease the car as far to the right as possible.

Abruptly, he began to brake, then swerved to the right, raking his car into the open area in front of the café. He cried out as the car began to fishtail, then careened into a skid. *Steer with it!'* screamed a voice in his mind. The rear of the car was lashing from side to side, tyres spewing dirt and raising clouds of dust. Mann pressed harder on the brake pedal, turning further into the skid. The car began to straighten out and he braked harder yet, conscious, on the sides of his vision, of the truck and trailer roaring by on the highway. He nearly sideswiped one of the cars parked in front of the café, bounced and skidded by it, going almost straight now. He jammed in the brake pedal as hard as he could. The rear end broke to the right and the car spun half around, sheering sideways to a neck-wrenching halt 30 yards beyond the café.

Mann sat in pulsing silence, eyes closed. His heartbeats felt like club blows in his chest. He couldn't seem to catch his breath. If he were ever going to have a heart attack, it would be now. After a while, he opened his eyes and pressed his right palm against his chest. His heart was still throbbing labouredly. No wonder, he thought. It isn't every day I'm almost murdered by a truck.

He raised the handle and pushed out the door, then started forward, grunting in surprise as the safety belt held him in place. Reaching down with shaking fingers, he depressed the release button and pulled the ends of the belt apart. He glanced at the café. What had its patrons thought of his breakneck appearance? he wondered.

He stumbled as he walked to the front door of the café. TRUCKERS WELCOME, read a sign in the window. It gave Mann a queasy feeling to see it. Shivering, he pulled open the door and went inside, avoiding the sight of its customers. He felt certain they were watching him, but he didn't have the strength to face their looks. Keeping his gaze fixed straight ahead, he moved to the rear of the café and opened the door marked GENTS.

Moving to the sink, he twisted the right-hand tap and leaned over to cup cold water in his palms and splash it on his face. There was a fluttering of his stomach muscles he could not control.

Straightening up, he tugged down several towels from their dispenser and patted them against this face, grimacing at the smell of the paper. Dropping the soggy towels into a wastebasket beside the sink, he regarded himself in the wall mirror. Still with us, Mann, he thought. He nodded, swallowing. Drawing out his metal comb, he neatened his hair. You never know, he thought. You just never know. You drift along, year after year, presuming certain values to be fixed; like being able to drive on a public thoroughfare without somebody trying to murder you. You come to depend on that sort of thing. Then something occurs and all bets are off. One shocking incident and all the years of logic and acceptance are displaced and, suddenly, the jungle is in front of you again. *Man, part animal, part angel.* Where had he come across that phrase? He shivered.

It was entirely an animal in that truck out there.

His breath was almost back to normal now. Mann forced a smile at his reflection. All right, boy, he told himself. It's over now. It was a goddamned nightmare, but it's over. You are on your way to San Francisco. You'll get yourself a nice hotel room, order a bottle of expensive Scotch, soak your body in a hot bath and forget. Damn right, he thought. He turned and walked out of the washroom.

He jolted to a halt, his breath cut off. Standing rooted, heartbeat hammering at his chest, he gaped through the front window of the café.

The truck and trailer were parked outside.

Mann stared at them in unbelieving shock. It wasn't possible. He'd seen them roaring by at top speed. The driver had won: he'd *won*! He'd had the whole damn highway to himself! *Why had he turned back?*

Mann looked around with sudden dread. There were five men

eating, three along the counter, two in booths. He cursed himself for having failed to look at faces when he'd entered. Now there was no way of knowing who it was. Mann felt his legs begin to shake.

Abruptly, he walked to the nearest booth and slid in clumsily behind the table. Now wait, he told himself; just wait. Surely, he could tell which one it was. Masking his face with the menu, he glanced across its top. Was it that one in the khaki work shirt? Mann tried to see the man's hands but couldn't. His gaze flicked nervously across the room. Not that one in the suit, of course. Three remaining. That one in the front booth, square-faced, black-haired? If only he could see the man's hands, it might help. One of the two others at the counter? Mann studied them uneasily. Why hadn't he looked at faces when he'd come in?

Now *wait*, he thought. Goddamn it, *wait*! All right, the truck driver was in here. That didn't automatically signify that he meant to continue the insane duel. Chuck's Café might be the only place to eat for miles around. It *was* lunchtime, wasn't it? The truck driver had probably intended to eat here all the time. He'd just been moving too fast to pull into the parking lot before. So he'd slowed down, turned round and driven back, that was all. Mann forced himself to read the menu. Right, he thought. No point in getting so rattled. Perhaps a beer would help relax him.

The woman behind the counter came over and Mann ordered a ham sandwich on rye toast and a bottle of Coors. As the woman turned away, he wondered, with a sudden twinge of self-reproach, why he hadn't simply left the café, jumped into his car and sped away. He would have known immediately, then, if the truck driver was still out to get him. As it was, he'd have to suffer through an entire meal to find out. He almost groaned at his stupidity.

Still, what if the truck driver *had* followed him out and started after him again? He'd have been right back where he'd started. Even if he'd managed to get a good lead, the truck driver would have overtaken him eventually. It just wasn't in him to drive at 80 and 90 miles an hour in order to stay ahead. True, he might have been intercepted by a California Highway Patrol car. What if he weren't, though?

Mann repressed the plaguing thoughts. He tried to calm himself. He looked deliberately at the four men. Either of two seemed a likely possibility as the driver of the truck: the square-faced one in the front booth and the chunky one in the jump suit sitting at the counter. Mann had an impulse to walk over to them and ask which one it was, tell the man he was sorry he'd irritated him, tell him anything to calm him, since, obviously, he wasn't rational, was a manic-depressive, probably. Maybe buy the man a beer and sit with him a while to try to settle things.

He couldn't move. What if the truck driver were letting the whole thing drop? Mightn't his approach rile the man all over again? Mann felt drained by indecision. He nodded weakly as the waitress set the sandwich and the bottle in front of him. He took a swallow of the beer, which made him cough. Was the truck driver amused by the sound? Mann felt a stirring of resentment deep inside himself. What right did that bastard have to impose this torment on another human being? It was a free country, wasn't it? Damn it, he had every right to pass the son of a bitch on a highway if he wanted to!

'Oh, hell,' he mumbled. He tried to feel amused. He was making entirely too much of this. Wasn't he? He glanced at the pay telephone on the front wall. What was to prevent him from calling the local police and telling them the situation? But, then, he'd have to stay here, lose time, make Forbes angry, probably lose the sale. And what if the truck driver stayed to face them? Naturally, he'd deny the whole thing. What if the police believed him and didn't do anything about it? After they'd gone, the truck driver would undoubtedly take it out on him again, only worse. *God!* Mann thought in agony.

The sandwich tasted flat, the beer unpleasantly sour. Mann stared at the table as he ate. For God's sake, why was he just *sitting* here like this? He was a grown man, wasn't he? Why didn't he settle this damn thing once and for all?

His left hand twitched so unexpectedly, he spilled beer on his trousers. The man in the jump suit had risen from the counter and was strolling towards the front of the café. Mann felt his heartbeat thumping as the man gave money to the waitress, took his change and a toothpick from the dispenser and went outside. Mann watched in anxious silence.

The man did not get into the cab of the tanker truck.

It had to be the one in the front booth, then. His face took form in Mann's remembrance: square, with dark eyes, dark hair; the man who'd tried to kill him.

Mann stood abruptly, letting impulse conquer fear. Eyes fixed ahead, he started towards the entrance. Anything was preferable to sitting in that booth. He stopped by the cash register, conscious of the hitching of his chest as he gulped in air. Was the man observing him? he wondered. He swallowed, pulling out the clip of dollar bills in his right-hand trouser pocket. He glanced towards the waitress. Come *on*, he thought. He looked at his check and, seeing the amount, reached shakily into his trouser pocket for change. He heard a coin fall onto the floor and roll away. Ignoring it, he dropped a dollar and a quarter onto the counter and thrust the clip of bills into his trouser pocket.

As he did, he heard the man in the front booth get up. An icy shudder spasmed up his back. Turning quickly to the door, he shoved it open, seeing, on the edges of his vision, the square-faced man approach the cash register. Lurching from the café, he started towards his car with long strides. His mouth was dry again. The pounding of his heart was painful in his chest.

Suddenly, he started running. He heard the café door bang shut and fought away the urge to look across his shoulder. Was that a sound of other running footsteps now? Reaching his car, Mann yanked open the door and jarred in awkwardly behind the steering wheel. He reached into his trouser pocket for the keys and snatched them out, almost dropping them. His hand was shaking so badly he couldn't get the ignition key into its slot. He whined with mounting dread. Come on! he thought.

The key slid in, he twisted it convulsively. The motor started and he raced it momentarily before jerking the transmission shift to drive. Depressing the accelerator pedal quickly, he raked the car around and steered it towards the highway. From the corners of his eyes, he saw the truck and trailer being backed away from the café.

Reaction burst inside him. 'No!' he raged and slammed his foot down on the brake pedal. This was idiotic! Why the hell should he run away? His car slid sideways to a rocking halt and, shouldering out the door, he lurched to his feet and started towards the truck with angry strides. *All right, Jack*, he thought. He glared at the man inside the truck. You want to punch my nose, OK, but no more goddamn tournament on the highway.

The truck began to pick up speed. Mann raised his right arm. 'Hey!' he yelled. He knew the driver saw him. '*Hey!* He started running as the truck kept moving, engine grinding loudly. It was on the highway now. He sprinted towards it with a sense of martyred outrage. The driver shifted gears, the truck moved faster. 'Stop!' Mann shouted. 'Damn it, *stop!*'

He thudded to a panting halt, staring at the truck as it receded down the highway, moved around a hill and disappeared. 'You son of a bitch,' he muttered. 'You goddamn, miserable son of a bitch.'

He trudged back slowly to his car, trying to believe that the truck driver had fled the hazard of a fistfight. It was possible, of course, but, somehow, he could not believe it.

He got into his car and was about to drive onto the highway when he changed his mind and switched the motor off. That crazy bastard might just be tooling along at 15 miles an hour, waiting for him to catch up. Nuts to that, he thought. So he blew his schedule; screw it. Forbes would have to wait, that was all. And if Forbes didn't care to wait, that was all right, too. He'd sit here for a while and let the nut get out of range, let him think he'd won the day. He grinned. You're the bloody Red Baron, Jack; you've shot me down. Now go to hell with my sincerest compliments. He shook his head. Beyond belief, he thought.

He really should have done this earlier, pulled over, waited. Then the truck driver would have had to let it pass. *Or picked on someone else*, the startling thought occurred to him. Jesus, maybe that was how the crazy bastard whiled away his work hours! Jesus Christ Almighty! was it possible?

He looked at the dashboard clock. It was just past 12:30. Wow, he thought. All that in less than an hour. He shifted on the seat and stretched his legs out. Leaning back against the door, he closed his eyes and mentally perused the things he had to do tomorrow and the following day. Today was shot to hell, as far as he could see.

When he opened his eyes, afraid of drifting into sleep and losing too much time, almost 11 minutes had passed. The nut must be an ample distance off by now, he thought: at least 11 miles and likely more, the way he drove. Good enough. He wasn't going to try to make San Francisco on schedule now, anyway. He'd take it real easy.

Mann adjusted his safety belt, switched on the motor, tapped the transmission pointer into drive position and pulled onto the highway, glancing back across his shoulder. Not a car in sight. Great day for driving. Everybody was staying at home. That nut must have a reputation around here. When Crazy Jack is on the highway, lock your car in the garage. Mann chuckled at the notion as his car began to turn the curve ahead.

Mindless reflex drove his right foot down against the brake pedal. Suddenly, his car had skidded to a halt and he was staring down the highway. The truck and trailer were parked on the shoulder less than 90 yards away.

Mann couldn't seem to function. He knew his car was blocking the westbound lane, knew that he should either make a U-turn or pull off the highway, but all he could do was gape at the truck.

He cried out, legs retracting, as a horn blast sounded behind him. Snapping up his head, he looked at the rearview mirror, gasping as he saw a yellow station wagon bearing down on him at high speed. Suddenly, it veered off towards the eastbound lane, disappearing from the mirror. Mann jerked round and saw it hurtling past his car, its rear end snapping back and forth, its back tyres screeching. He saw the twisted features of the man inside, saw his lips move rapidly with cursing.

Then the station wagon had swerved back into the westbound lane and was speeding off. It gave Mann an odd sensation to see it pass the truck. The man in that station wagon could drive on, unthreatened. Only he'd been singled out. What happened was demented. Yet it was happening.

He drove his car onto the highway shoulder and braked. Putting the transmission into neutral, he leaned back, staring at the truck. His head was aching again. There was a pulsing at his temples like the ticking of a muffled clock.

What was he to do? He knew very well that if he left his car to walk to the truck, the driver would pull away and repark farther down the highway. He may as well face the fact that he was dealing with a madman. He felt the tremor in his stomach muscles starting up again. His heartbeat thudded slowly, striking at his chest wall. Now what?

With a sudden, angry impulse, Mann snapped the transmission into gear and stepped down hard on the accelerator pedal. The tyres of the car spun sizzlingly before they gripped; the car shot out onto the highway. Instantly, the truck began to move. He even had the motor on! Mann thought in raging fear. He floored the pedal, then, abruptly, realised he couldn't make it, that the truck would block his way and he'd collide with its trailer. A vision flashed across his mind, a fiery explosion and a sheet of

flame incinerating him. He started braking fast, trying to decelar-
ate evenly, so he wouldn't lose control.

When he'd slowed down enough to feel that it was safe, he
steered the car onto the shoulder and stopped it again, throwing
the transmission into neutral.

Approximately 80 yards ahead, the truck pulled off the highway and stopped.

Mann tapped his fingers on the steering wheel. *Now* what? he
thought. Turn round and head east until he reached a cutoff that
would take him to San Francisco by another route? How did he
know the truck driver wouldn't follow him even then? His cheeks
twitched as he bit his lips together angrily. No! He wasn't going
to turn round!

His expression hardened suddenly. Well, he wasn't going to
sit here all day, that was certain. Reaching out, he tapped the
gearshift into drive and steered his car onto the highway once
again. He saw the massive truck and trailer start to move but
made no effort to speed up. He tapped at the brakes, taking a
position about 30 yards behind the trailer. He glanced at his
speedometer. Forty miles an hour. The truck driver had his left
arm out the cab window and was waving him on. What did that
mean? Had he changed his mind? Decided, finally, that this thing
had gone too far? Mann couldn't let himself believe it.

He looked ahead. Despite the mountain ranges all around, the
highway was flat as far as he could see. He tapped a fingernail
against the horn bar, trying to make up his mind. Presumably,
he could continue all the way to San Francisco at this speed,
hanging back just far enough to avoid the worst of the exhaust
fumes. It didn't seem likely that the truck driver would stop
directly on the highway to block his way. And if the truck driver
pulled onto the shoulder to let him pass, he could pull off the
highway, too. It would be a draining afternoon but a safe one.

On the other hand, outracing the truck might be worth just
one more try. This was obviously what that son of a bitch wanted.
Yet, surely, a vehicle of such size couldn't be driven with the
same daring as, potentially, his own. The laws of mechanics were
against it, if nothing else. Whatever advantage the truck had in
mass, it had to lose in stability, particularly that of its trailer. If
Mann were to drive at, say, 80 miles an hour and there were a
few steep grades—as he felt sure there were—the truck would
have to fall behind.

The question was, of course, whether he had the nerve to maintain such a speed over a long distance. He'd never done it before. Still, the more he thought about it, the more it appealed to him; far more than the alternative did.

Abruptly, he decided. *Right*, he thought. He checked ahead, then pressed down hard on the accelerator pedal and pulled into the eastbound lane. As he neared the truck, he tensed, anticipating that the driver might block his way. But the truck did not shift from the westbound lane. Mann's car moved along its mammoth side. He glanced at the cab and saw the name KELLER printed on its door. For a shocking instant, he thought it read KILLER and started to slow down. Then, glancing at the name again, he saw what it really was and depressed the pedal sharply. When he saw the truck reflected in the rearview mirror, he steered his car into the westbound lane.

He shuddered, dread and satisfaction mixed together, as he saw that the truck driver was speeding up. It was strangely comforting to know the man's intentions definitely again. That plus the knowledge of his face and name seemed, somehow, to reduce his stature. Before, he had been faceless, nameless, an embodiment of unknown terror. Now, at least, he was an individual. All right, Keller, said his mind, let's see you beat me with that purple-silver relic now. He pressed down harder on the pedal. *Here we go*, he thought.

He looked at the speedometer, scowling as he saw that he was doing only 74 miles an hour. Deliberately, he pressed down on the pedal, alternating his gaze between the highway ahead and the speedometer until the needle turned past 80. He felt a flickering of satisfaction with himself. All right, Keller, you son of a bitch, top that, he thought.

After several moments, he glanced into the rearview mirror again. Was the truck getting closer? Stunned, he checked the speedometer. Damn it! He was down to 76! He forced in the accelerator pedal angrily. *He mustn't go less than 80!* Mann's chest shuddered with convulsive breath.

He glanced aside as he hurtled past a beige sedan parked on the shoulder underneath a tree. A young couple sat inside it, talking. Already they were far behind, their world removed from his. Had they even glanced aside when he'd passed? He doubted it.

He started as the shadow of an overhead bridge whipped

across the hood and windshield. Inhaling raggedly, he glanced
at the speedometer again. He was holding at 81. He checked the
rearview mirror. Was it his imagination that the truck was gaining ground? He looked forward with anxious eyes. There had to
be some kind of town ahead. To hell with time; he'd stop at the
police station and tell them what had happened. They'd have to
believe him. Why would he stop to tell them such a story if it
weren't true? For all he knew, Keller had a police record in these
parts. *Oh, sure, we're on to him,* he heard a faceless officer remark.
That crazy bastard's asked for it before and now he's going to get it.

Mann shook himself and looked at the mirror. The truck *was*
getting closer. Wincing, he glanced at the speedometer. Goddamn
it, pay attention! raged his mind. He was down to 74 again!
Whining with frustration, he depressed the pedal. Eighty!—80!
he demanded of himself. There was a murderer behind him!

His car began to pass a field of flowers; lilacs, Mann saw, white
and purple, stretching out in endless rows. There was a small
shack near the highway, the words FIELD FRESH FLOWERS
painted on it. A brown-cardboard square was propped against
the shack, the word FUNERALS printed crudely on it. Mann saw
himself, abruptly, lying in a casket, painted like some grotesque
mannequin. The overpowering smell of flowers seemed to fill his
nostrils. Ruth and the children sitting in the first row, heads
bowed. All his relatives—

Suddenly, the pavement roughened and the car began to
bounce and shudder, driving bolts of pain into his head. He felt
the steering wheel resisting him and clamped his hands round
it tightly, harsh vibrations running up his arms. He didn't dare
look at the mirror now. He had to force himself to keep the speed
unchanged. Keller wasn't going to slow down; he was sure of
that. *What if he got a flat tyre, though?* All control would vanish in
an instant. He visualised the somersaulting of his car, its grinding,
shrieking jumble, the explosion of its gas tank, his body crushed
and burned and—

The broken span of pavement ended and his gaze jumped
quickly to the rearview mirror. The truck was no closer, but it
hadn't lost ground, either. Mann's eyes shifted. Up ahead were
hills and mountains. He tried to reassure himself that upgrades
were on his side, that he could climb them at the same speed he
was going now. Yet all he could imagine were the downgrades,
the immense truck close behind him, slamming violently into his

car and knocking it across some cliff edge. He had a horrifying vision of dozens of broken, rusted cars lying unseen in the canyons ahead, corpses in every one of them, all flung to shattering deaths by Keller.

Mann's car went rocketing into a corridor of trees. On each side of the highway was a eucalyptus windbreak, each trunk three feet from the next. It was like speeding through a high-walled canyon. Mann gasped, twitching, as a large twig bearing dusty leaves dropped down across the windshield, then slid out of sight. Dear God! he thought. He was getting near the edge himself. If he should lose his nerve at this speed, it was over. Jesus! That would be ideal for Keller! he realised suddenly. He visualised the square-faced driver laughing as he passed the burning wreckage, knowing that he'd killed his prey without so much as touching him.

Mann started as his car shot out into the open. The route ahead was not straight now but winding up into the foothills. Mann willed himself to press down on the pedal even more. Eighty-three now, almost 84.

To his left was a broad terrain of green hills blending into mountains. He saw a black car on a dirt road, moving towards the highway. *Was its side painted white?* Mann's heartbeat lurched. Impulsively, he jammed the heel of his right hand down against the horn bar and held it there. The blast of the horn was shrill and racking to his ears. His heart began to pound. Was it a police car? *Was* it?

He let the horn bar up abruptly. *No*, it *wasn't*. Damn! his mind raged. Keller must have been amused by his pathetic efforts. Doubtless, he was chuckling to himself right now. He heard the truck driver's voice in his mind, coarse and sly. *You think you gonna get a cop to save you, boy? Shee-it. You gonna die.* Mann's heart contorted with savage hatred. *You son of a bitch!* he thought. Jerking his right hand into a fist, he drove it down against the seat. Goddamn you, Keller! I'm going to kill you, if it's the last thing I do!

The hills were closer now. There would be slopes directly, long steep grades. Mann felt a burst of hope within himself. He was sure to gain a lot of distance on the truck. No matter how he tried, that bastard Keller couldn't manage 80 miles an hour on a hill. But *I* can! cried his mind with fierce elation. He worked up saliva in his mouth and swallowed it. The back of his shirt was drenched. He could feel sweat trickling down his sides. A bath and a drink, first order of the day on reaching San Francisco. A long, hot bath, a long, cold drink. Cutty Sark. He'd splurge, by Christ. He rated it.

The car swept up a shallow rise. Not steep enough, goddamn it! The truck's momentum would prevent its losing speed. Mann felt mindless hatred for the landscape. Already, he had topped the rise and tilted over to a shallow downgrade. He looked at the rearview mirror. *Square*, he thought, everything about the truck was square: the radiator grille, the fender shapes, the bumper ends, the outline of the cab, even the shape of Keller's hands and face. He visualised the truck as some great entity pursuing him, insentient, brutish, chasing him with instinct only.

Mann cried out, horror-stricken, as he saw the ROAD REPAIRS sign up ahead. His frantic gaze leaped down the highway. Both lanes blocked, a huge black arrow pointing towards the alternative route! He groaned in anguish, seeing it was dirt. His foot jumped automatically to the brake pedal and started pumping it. He threw a dazed look at the rearview mirror. The truck was moving as fast as ever! It *couldn't*, though! Mann's expression froze in terror as he started turning to the right.

He stiffened as the front wheels hit the dirt road. For an instant, he was certain that the back part of the car was going to spin; he felt it breaking to the left. 'No, don't!' he cried. Abruptly, he was jarring down the dirt road, elbows braced against his sides, trying to keep from losing control. His tyres battered at the ruts, almost tearing the wheel from his grip. The windows rattled noisily. His neck snapped back and forth with painful jerks. His jolting body surged against the binding of the safety belt and slammed down violently on the seat. He felt the bouncing of the car drive up his spine. His clenching teeth slipped and he cried out hoarsely as his upper teeth gouged deep into his lip.

He gasped as the rear end of the car began surging to the right. He started to jerk the steering wheel to the left, then, hissing, wrenched it in the opposite direction, crying out as the right rear fender cracked into a fence pole, knocking it down. He started pumping at the brakes, struggling to regain control. The car rear yawed sharply to the left, tyres shooting out a spray of dirt. Mann felt a scream tear upward in his throat. He twisted wildly at the steering wheel. The car began careening to the right. He hitched the wheel round until the car was on course again. His head was pounding like his heart now, with gigantic, throbbing spasms. He started coughing as he gagged on dripping blood.

The dirt road ended suddenly, the car regained momentum on the pavement and he dared to look at the rearview mirror. The truck was slowed down but was still behind him, rocking like a freighter on a storm-tossed sea, its huge tyres scouring up a pall of dust. Mann shoved in the accelerator pedal and his car surged forward. A good, steep grade lay just ahead; he'd gain that distance now. He swallowed blood, grimacing at the taste, then fumbled in his trouser pocket and tugged out his handkerchief. He pressed it to his bleeding lip, eyes fixed on the slope ahead. Another 50 yards or so. He writhed his back. His undershirt was soaking wet, adhering to his skin. He glanced at the rearview mirror. The truck had just regained the highway. *Tough!* he thought with venom. Didn't get me, did you, Keller?

His car was on the first yards of the upgrade when steam began to issue from beneath its hood. Mann stiffened suddenly, eyes widening with shock. The steam increased, became a smoking mist. Mann's gaze jumped down. The red light hadn't flashed on yet but had to in a moment. How could this be happening? Just as he was set to get away! The slope ahead was long and gradual, with many curves. He knew he couldn't stop. Could he U-turn unexpectedly and go back down? the sudden thought occurred. He looked ahead. The highway was too narrow, bound by hills on both sides. There wasn't room enough to make an uninterrupted turn and there wasn't time enough to ease around. If he tried that, Keller would shift direction and hit him head on. 'Oh, my God!' Mann murmured suddenly.

He was going to die.

He stared ahead with stricken eyes, his view increasingly obscured by steam. Abruptly, he recalled the afternoon he'd had the engine steam-cleaned at the local car wash. The man who'd done it had suggested he replace the water hoses, because steam-cleaning had a tendency to make them crack. He'd nodded, thinking that he'd do it when he had more time. *More time!* The phrase was like a dagger in his mind. He'd failed to change the hoses and, for that failure, he was now about to die.

He sobbed in terror as the dashboard light flashed on. He glanced at it involuntarily and read the word HOT, black on red. With a breathless gasp, he jerked the transmission into low. Why hadn't he done that right away! He looked ahead. The slope seemed endless. Already, he could hear a boiling throb inside the radiator. How much coolant was there left? Steam was clouding faster, hazing up the windshield. Reaching out, he twisted at a dashboard knob. The wipers started flicking back and forth in fan-shaped sweeps. There had to be enough coolant in the radiator to get him to the top. *Then* what? cried his mind. He couldn't drive without coolant, even downhill. He glanced at the rearview mirror. The truck was falling behind. Mann snarled with maddened fury. *If it weren't for that goddamned hose, he'd be escaping now!*

The sudden lurching of the car snatched him back to terror. If he braked now, he could jump out, run and scrabble up that slope. Later, he might not have the time. He couldn't make himself stop the car, though. As long as it kept on running, he felt bound to it, less vulnerable. God knows what would happen if he left it.

Mann stared up the slope with haunted eyes, trying not to see the red light on the edges of his vision. Yard by yard, his car was slowing down. Make it, make it, pleaded his mind, even though he thought that it was futile. The car was running more and more unevenly. The thumping percolation of its radiator filled his ears. Any moment now, the motor would be choked off and the car would shudder to a stop, leaving him a sitting target. *No*, he thought. He tried to blank his mind.

He was almost to the top, but in the mirror he could see the truck drawing up on him. He jammed down on the pedal and the motor made a grinding noise. He groaned. It had to make the top! Please, God, help me! screamed his mind. The ridge was just ahead. Closer. Closer. Make it. 'Make it.' The car was shuddering and clanking, slowing down—oil, smoke and steam gushing from beneath the hood. The windshield wipers swept from side to side. Mann's head throbbed. Both his hands felt numb. His heartbeat pounded as he stared ahead. Make it, please, God, make it. Make it. *Make* it.'

Over! Mann's lips opened in a cry of triumph as the car began descending. Hand shaking uncontrollably, he shoved the transmission into neutral and let the car go into a glide. The triumph strangled in his throat as he saw that there was nothing in sight but hills and more hills. Never mind! He was on a downgrade now, a long one. He passed a sign that read, TRUCKS USE LOW GEARS NEXT 12 MILES. Twelve miles! Something would come up. It had to.

The car began to pick up speed. Mann glanced at the speed-

ometer. Forty-seven miles an hour. The red light still burned.
He'd save the motor for a long time, too, though; let it cool for
12 miles, if the truck was far enough behind.

His speed increased. Fifty ... 51. Mann watched the needle
turning slowly towards the right. He glanced at the rearview
mirror. The truck had not appeared yet. With a little luck, he
might still get a good lead. Not as good as he might have if the
motor hadn't overheated but enough to work with. There had to
be someplace along the way to stop. The needle edged past 55
and started towards the 60 mark.

Again, he looked at the rearview mirror, jolting as he saw that
the truck had topped the ridge and was on its way down. He
felt his lips begin to shake and crimped them together. His gaze
jumped fitfully between the steam-obscured highway and the
mirror. The truck was accelerating rapidly. Keller doubtless had
the gas pedal floored. It wouldn't be long before the truck caught
up to him. Mann's right hand twitched unconsciously towards the
gearshift. Noticing, he jerked it back, grimacing, glanced at the
speedometer. The car's velocity had just passed 60. Not enough!
He had to use the motor now! He reached out desperately.

His right hand froze in mid-air as the motor stalled; then,
shooting out the hand, he twisted the ignition key. The motor
made a grinding noise but wouldn't start. Mann glanced up, saw
that he was almost on the shoulder, jerked the steering wheel
around. Again, he turned the key, but there was no response.
He looked up at the rearview mirror. The truck was gaining on
him swiftly. He glanced at the speedometer. The car's speed was
fixed at 62. Mann felt himself crushed in a vice of panic. He
stared ahead with haunted eyes.

Then he saw it, several hundred yards ahead; an escape route
for trucks with burned-out brakes. There was no alternative now.
Either he took the turnout or his car would be rammed from
behind. The truck was frighteningly close. He heard the high-
pitched wailing of its motor. Unconsciously, he started easing to
the right, then jerked the wheel back suddenly. He mustn't give
the move away! He had to wait until the last possible moment.
Otherwise, Keller would follow him in.

Just before he reached the escape route. Mann wrenched the
steering wheel round. The car rear started breaking to the left,
tyres shrieking on the pavement. Mann steered with the skid,
braking just enough to keep from losing all control. The rear

tyres grabbed and, at 60 miles an hour, the car shot up the dirt trail, tyres slinging up a cloud of dust. Mann began to hit the brakes. The rear wheels sideslipped and the car slammed hard against the dirt bank to the right. Mann gasped as the car bounced off and started to fishtail with violent whipping motions, angling towards the trail edge. He drove his foot down on the brake pedal with all his might. The car rear skidded to the right and slammed against the bank again. Mann heard a grinding rend of metal and felt himself heaved downward suddenly, his neck snapped, as the car ploughed to a violent halt.

As in a dream, Mann turned to see the truck and trailer swerving off the highway. Paralysed, he watched the massive vehicle hurtle towards him, staring at it with a blank detachment, knowing he was going to die but so stupefied by the sight of the looming truck that he couldn't react. The gargantuan shape roared closer, blotting out the sky. Mann felt a strange sensation in his throat, unaware that he was screaming.

Suddenly, the truck began to tilt. Mann stared at it in choked-off silence as it started tipping over like some ponderous beast toppling in slow motion. Before it reached his car, it vanished from his rear window.

Hands palsied, Mann undid the safety belt and opened the door. Struggling from the car, he stumbled to the trail edge, staring downward. He was just in time to see the truck capsize like a foundering ship. The tanker followed, huge wheels spinning as it overturned.

The storage tank on the truck exploded first, the violence of its detonation causing Mann to stagger back and sit down clumsily on the dirt. A second explosion roared below, its shock wave buffeting across him hotly, making his ears hurt. His glazed eyes saw a fiery column shoot up towards the sky in front of him, then another.

Mann crawled slowly to the trail edge and peered down at the canyon. Enormous gouts of flame were towering upwards, topped by thick, black, oily smoke. He couldn't see the truck or trailer, only flames. He gaped at them in shock, all feeling drained from him.

Then, unexpectedly, emotion came. Not dread, at first, and not regret; not the nausea that followed soon. It was a primeval tumult in his mind: the cry of some ancestral beast above the body of its vanquished foe.

WHO'S BEEN SITTING IN MY CAR?

Antonia Fraser

The contrast between the vehicle in 'Duel' and the car in this next story could not be greater. From a huge, malevolent truck we turn to one of the smallest cars on the road, the evergreen Mini, which celebrated its fortieth anniversary in 1999. Millions of the tiny cars have been sold and cherished by drivers of all ages, and at first glance there would seem to be no more harmless car on the road. But not so in the imagination of Antonia Fraser, the versatile English crime writer and author of the best-selling series of cases about Jemima Shore, the TV investigative journalist, and inspiration of two television series. 'Who's Been Sitting in My Car?' is not one of Jemima's cases, but it is the kind of mystery she would relish solving.

Antonia Fraser (1932–) is as well known as a historian and biographer as she is as a crime writer, and has frequently made use of her research into the past when composing her puzzling and well-crafted mysteries. Her story here, however, is very much of today and begins innocently enough when the owner of a Mini finds her car full of cigarette ends (she doesn't smoke) and out of petrol (when she knows it should have plenty). The girl, Jacobine, begins to think someone is using the vehicle surreptitiously, especially when it disappears one night only to reappear twenty minutes later. What has happened, is happening, to her little car?

*   *   *

'Who's been sitting in my car?' said Jacobine. She said it in a stern gruff voice, like a bear. In fact Jacobine looked more like Goldilocks with her pale fair hair pulled back from her round forehead. The style betokened haste and worry, the worry of a girl late for school. But it was Jacobine's children who were late, and she was supposed to be driving them.

'Someone's been smoking in my car,' Jacobine added, pointing to the ashtray crammed with butts.

'Someone's been driving your car, you mean.' It was Gavin, contradictory as usual. 'People don't just sit in cars. They drive them.' He elaborated. 'Someone's been driving my car, said the little bear —'

'People do sit in cars. We're sitting in a car now.' Tessa, because she was twelve months older, could never let that sort of remark from Gavin pass.

'Be quiet, darlings,' said Jacobine automatically. She continued to sit looking at the ashtray in front of her. It certainly looked quite horrible with all its mess of ash and brown stubs. And there was a sort of violence about the way it had been stuffed: you wondered that the smoker had not bothered to throw at least a few of them out of the window. Instead he had remorselessly gone on pressing them into the little chromium tray, hard, harder, into the stale pyre.

Jacobine did not smoke. Rory, her ex-husband, had been a heavy smoker. And for one moment she supposed that Rory might have used an old key to get into the Mini, and then sat endlessly smoking outside the house . . . It was a mad thought and almost instantly Jacobine recognised it as such. For one thing she had bought the Mini second-hand after the divorce. Since ferrying the children had become her main activity these days, she had spent a little money on making it as convenient as possible. More to the point, Jacobine and Rory were on perfectly good terms.

'Married too young' was the general verdict. Jacobine agreed. She still felt rather too young for marriage, as a matter of fact: in an upside-down sort of way, two children seemed to be all she could cope with. She really quite liked Rory's new wife, Fiona, for her evident competence in dealing with the problem of living with him.

It was only that the mucky filled ashtray had reminded Jacobine of the household details of life with Rory. But if not Rory, who? And why did she feel, on top of disgust, a very strong sensation of physical fear? Jacobine, habitually timid, did not remember feeling fear before in quite such an alarmingly physical manner. Her terrors were generally projections into the future, possible worries concerned with the children. She was suddenly convinced that the smoker had an ugly streak of cruelty in his nature – as well as being of course a potential thief. She had a nasty new image of him sitting there in her car outside her house. Waiting for her. Watching the house. She dismissed it.

'Tessa, Gavin, stay where you are.' Jacobine jumped out of the driver's seat and examined the locks of the car.

'Mummy, we are going to be late,' whined Tessa. That decided Jacobine. Back to the car, key in lock and away. They had reached the corner of Melville Street when the next odd thing happened. The engine died and the little Mini gradually and rather feebly came to a halt.

'No petrol!' shouted Gavin from the back.

'Oh darling, do be quiet,' began Jacobine. Then her eye fell on the gauge. He was right. The Mini was out of petrol. Jacobine felt completely jolted as if she had been hit in the face. It was as uncharacteristic of her carefully ordered existence to run out of petrol as, for example, to run out of milk for the children's break-fast—a thing which had happened once and still gave Jacobine shivers of self-reproach. In any case, another unpleasant dawning realisation, she had only filled up two days ago . . .

'Someone's definitely been driving this car,' she exclaimed before she could stop herself.

'That's what I said!' crowed Gavin. 'Someone's been driving my car, said the little bear.'

'Oh Mummy, we are going to be awfully late,' pleaded Tessa. 'Miss Hamilton doesn't like us to be late. She says Mummies should be more thoughtful.'

The best thing to do was to take them both to school in a taxi and sort out the car's problems later. One way and another, it was lunch-time before Jacobine was able to consider the intruding driver again. And then, sturdily, she dismissed the thought. So that, curiously enough, finding the Mini once more empty of petrol and the ashtray packed with stubs the following morning was even more of a shock. Nor was it possible to escape the sharp eyes of the children, or gloss over the significance of the rapid visit to the petrol station. In any case, Tessa had been agonising on the subject of lateness due to petrol failure since breakfast.

'I shall go to the police,' said Jacobine firmly. She said it as much to reassure herself as to shut up the children. In fact the visit was more irritating than reassuring. Although Jacobine began her complaint with the statement that she had locked her car, and the lock had not been tampered with, she was left with the strong impression that the police did not believe any part of her story. They did not seem to accept either that the doors had been locked or that the petrol was missing, let alone appreciate the significance of the used ashtray. All the same, they viewed her tale quite indulgently, and were positively gallant when Jacobine revealed that she lived, as they put it, 'with no man to look after you'.

'Of course you worry about the car, madam, it's natural. I expect your husband did all that when you were married,' said the man behind the broad desk. 'Tell you what, I know where you live, I'll tell the policeman on the beat to keep a special watch on it, shall I? Set your mind at rest. That's what we're here for. Prevention is better than cure.'

Jacobine trailed doubtfully out of the station. Prevention is better than cure. It was this parting homily which gave her the inspiration to park the Mini for the night directly under the street light, which again lay under the children's window. If the police did not altogether believe her, she did not altogether believe them in their kindly promises. Anyway, the light would make their task easier, if they did choose to patrol the tree-shaded square.

That evening Jacobine paid an unusually large number of visits to the children's room after they went to sleep. Each time she looked cautiously out of the window. The Mini, small and green, looked like a prize car at the motor show, in its new spotlight. You could hardly believe it had an engine inside it. It might have been a newly painted dummy. The shock of seeing the Mini gone on her fifth visit of inspection was therefore enormous. At the same time, Jacobine did feel a tiny pang of satisfaction. Now let the police treat her as a hysterical female she thought, as she dialled 999 with slightly shaking fingers. Her lips trembled too as she dictated the number of the car: 'AST 5690. A bright green Mini. Stolen not more than ten minutes ago. I warned you it might happen.'

'Don't worry, madam, we'll put out a general call for it.' Why did everyone tell her not to worry?

'No, it's my car, not my husband's. I haven't got a husband.'

Jacobine tried to sleep after that, but her mind raced, half in rage at the impudence of the intruder, half in imagined triumph that he would be hauled before her, cigarette hanging from his lips, those tell-tale polluting cigarettes . . . It was the door bell weaving in and out of these hazy dreams which finally ended them. At first she assumed they were bringing round the thief, even at this time of night.

It was a policeman, a new one from the morning's encounter. But he was alone.

'Mrs Esk?' Sorry to call so late. About your stolen Mini—'

'Have you found it? Who took it?'

'Well that's the point, madam. A green Mini, number AST 5690, reported stolen twenty minutes ago at Ferry Road police station, is now outside your door.'

Jacobine stared. It was true. The Mini was back.

'He must have known you were looking for him.' She blurted out the remark and then regretted it. Silently, Jacobine in her quilted dressing-gown and slippers, and the policeman in thick night-black uniform, examined the Mini from every angle. The locks were pristine, and the car itself was locked. They examined the dashboard. It was untouched.

'Perhaps there was some mistake?' suggested the policeman in the gentle tone Jacobine had come to associate with his colleagues. 'You only looked out of the window, you said. In the lamplight, you know . . . Well, I'd better be getting back to the station and report that all is well. You don't want to be arrested for driving your own Mini tomorrow, do you?' He sounded quite paternal.

'Look, he only had time for two cigarettes,' said Jacobine suddenly. At least she had curtailed the nocturnal pleasures of her adversary. On the other hand there was a new and rather horrible development. The car positively *smelt*. It did. She did not like to point that out to the policeman, since he had not mentioned it. Perhaps he was embarrassed. It was a strong, pungent, human smell which had nothing to do with Jacobine or the children or even cigarettes. As Jacobine had envisaged someone cruel and even violent when she first saw the ashtray, she now conjured up involuntarily someone coarse and even brutal.

Jacobine had not thought much about sex since the end of her marriage. Now she found herself thinking of it, in spite of herself. It was the unmistakable animal smell of sex which overpoweringly filled her nostrils.

The next night she put the children to bed early. Still fully dressed, with a new large torch beside her, she took up her vigil

in the lobby next to the front door. A little after eleven o'clock,
with apprehension but also with excitement, she heard the noise
of an engine running. It was close to the house. It was the peculiar
coughing start of her own car.

Without considering what she was doing, Jacobine flung open
the front door, ran towards the kerb and shouted: 'Stop it, stop
it, stop, thief!' The engine stopped running instantly. It was as
though it had been cut short in mid-sentence. She wrenched upon
the handle of the passenger seat, her fingers trembling so much
that she fumbled with the familiar door. It did not open. Even
locked against her: her own car! In her passion, Jacobine rapped
hard on the window.

Nothing happened. Very slowly, she realised that the driver's
seat, and indeed the whole of the tiny car, was empty. In the
ashtray, illuminated by the street lamp like a detail in a moonlight
picture, lay one cigarette, still alight. Jacobine was now suddenly
aware of her thumping heart as the anger which had driven her
on drained away. For the first time she had no idea what to do.
After a pause, during which she stood gazing at the locked Mini
and the gradually disintegrating cigarette, she walked back into
the house. She picked up the car keys. Even more slowly, she
returned to the car and unlocked it. Deliberately, but very
gingerly she climbed into the front seat and touched the cigarette.
Yes, warm. The car smelt fearfully.

'Sweetheart,' said a voice very close to her ear. 'You shouldn't
have told the police, you know. You shouldn't have done that.
You have to be punished for that, don't you?'

Jacobine felt herself grasped roughly and horribly. What happened next was so unexpected in its outrageous nature that she
tried to scream out her revulsion. But at the same time a pair of
lips, thick hard rubbery lips, were pressed on to her own. The
car was still, to her staring frantic eyes above her muted mouth,
palpably empty.

'Oh God, I've been taken,' she thought, as she choked and
struggled.

'But you like it, don't you, Sweetheart?' as though she had
managed to speak it out loud. It was not true.

'I'm going to be sick, I think,' said Jacobine. This time she did
manage to say it out loud.

'But you'll come back for more tomorrow night, won't you,
Sweetheart,' said the voice. 'And we'll go for a drive together.'

She was released. Jacobine fumbled with the door once more and, half-retching, fled towards the house.

She did not dare leave it again that night but lay in her bed, trembling and shaking. Even a bath did not help to wash away her body's memories of the assault. The next morning, as soon as the children were at school, Jacobine went to the police station. From the start, the man behind the desk was altogether more wary of her, she thought. He listened to her new story with rather a different expression, no less kind, but somewhat more speculative. At the end, without commenting on Jacobine's nocturnal experience, he asked her abruptly if she had ever seen a doctor since the break-up of her marriage.

'I need the police, not a doctor, for something like this,' said Jacobine desperately. 'I need protection.'

'I'm not quite so sure, Mrs Esk,' said the policeman. 'Now look here, why don't you have a word first of all with your GP? It's not very pleasant being a woman on your own, is it, and maybe a few pills, a few tranquillisers . . .'

When Jacobine left the station, it was with a sinking feeling that he had not believe her at all. The rest of the day she agonised over what to do. Ring Rory? That was ridiculous. But Jacobine had no other figure of authority in her life. A lawyer might help, she thought vaguely, remembering the sweet young man who had helped her over the divorce. Yet even a lawyer would ask for more proof, if the police had proved so sceptical. With dread, Jacobine realised that it was up to her to provide it.

About eleven o'clock that night, therefore, she took up her position in the driver's seat. She was not quite sure what to expect, except that there would be a moment's wait while she settled herself.

'I'm glad you're early, Sweetheart,' said the voice conversationally. 'Because we'll be able to go for a really long drive. We've got so much to talk about, haven't we? The children, for example. I don't really like your children. You'll have to get rid of them, you know.'

'Don't you dare touch my children,' gasped Jacobine.

'Oh, rather you than me,' said the voice. 'My methods aren't as pretty as yours. A car crash on the way to school, for example, which would leave you uninjured . . .'

Jacobine gave a little sick cry. She envisaged those precious tender bodies . . . the recurring nightmare of motherhood.

'I know all about crashes and children, their precious bodies,' went on the voice. He seemed to read her thoughts, her ghastly images. 'Poor little mangled things.'

Jacobine could no longer bear it. The smell combined with terror overwhelmed her. And the police station was so near. Jumping out of the car, abandoning her persecutor, she ran along the road in the general direction of the station. A few minutes later she heard the engine start up. The car was following her. Her heart banged in her chest. She had time to think that it was more frightening being pursued by a car, an empty car, than by anything in the world human and alive, when she gained the safety of the steps. The car stopped, neatly, and remained still.

'He's threatening the children now. He say's he's going to kill them,' Jacobine began her story. It seemed that she had hardly gulped it out before a policewoman was taking her back — on foot — to her house. The policewoman concentrated on the fact that Jacobine had left her children alone in the house while she went out to the car. Indeed, although it had not occurred to Jacobine at the time, it was very much outside her usual character. The car was driven back by a policeman. It looked very chic and small and harmless when it came to rest once more outside her front door.

It was two days later that Rory rang up. In between Jacobine had not dared to leave the intruder alone in the car at night in case he carried out his threat against the children during the day. On Saturday he performed the same act of possession which had initiated their relationship. On Sunday he brought up the subject of the children again. First he made Jacobine drive as far as Arthur's Seat, then round through silent Edinburgh. Jacobine was tired when she got back, and the Mini was allowed to park beside her house once more. A policeman noted her sitting there, a smouldering cigarette propped above the dashboard, and he heard her cry out. In answer to his questions, she would only point to the cigarette. She was wearing, he saw, a nightdress under her coat. At the time, the policeman was not quite sure whether Jacobine was crying out in terror or delight.

Actually what had forced that strange hoarse sound out of Jacobine was neither fear nor pleasure. It was, in its weird way, a sort of cry of discovery, a confirmation of a dread, but also bringing relief from the unknown.

She had got to know, perforce, the voice a little better during their long night drive. It was some chance remark of his about the car, some piece of mechanical knowledge, which gave her the clue. Proceeding warily—because the voice could often, but not always, read her thoughts—Jacobine followed up her suspicions. In any case, she preferred talking about the car to listening to the voice on the subject of her children. She tried to shut her mind to his gibes and sometimes quite surprisingly petty digs against Tessa and Gavin. He seemed to be out to belittle the children as well as eliminate them from Jacobine's life.

'Fancy Gavin not being able to read – at seven,' he would say. 'I heard him stumbling over the smallest words the other day. What a baby!' And again: 'Tessa makes an awful fuss about being punctual for one so young, doesn't she? I can just see her when she grows up. A proper little spinster. If she grows up, that is . . .'

Jacobine interrupted this by wondering aloud how she had got such a bargain in the shape of a second-hand Mini which had hardly done a thousand miles.

'Oh yes, Sweetheart,' exclaimed the voice, 'you certainly did get a bargain when you bought this car. All things considered. It had always been very well looked after, I can tell you—'

'Then it was your car,' Jacobine tried to stop her own voice shaking as she burst out with her discovery. 'This was your car once, wasn't it?'

'There was an accident,' replied the voice. He spoke in quite a different tone, she noticed, dully, flatly, nothing like his usual accents which varied from a horrid predatory kind of lustfulness to the near frenzy of his dislike for the children.

'Tell me.'

'It was her children. On the way to school. There was an accident.' It was still quite a different tone, so much so that Jacobine almost thought—it was a ridiculous word to use under the circumstances—that he sounded quite human. The smell in the car lessened and even the grip which he habitually kept on her knee, that odious grip, seemed to become softer, more beseeching than possessing.

'She worked so hard. She always had so many things to do for them. I was just trying to help her, taking them to school for her. It was an accident. A mistake. Otherwise why didn't I save myself? An accident, I tell you. And she won't forgive me. Oh, why won't she forgive me? I can't rest till she forgives me.' It was piteous now and Jacobine heard a harsh, racking sobbing, a man's sobbing which hurts the listener. She yielded to some strange new impulse and tentatively put out her hand towards the passenger seat. The next moment she was grasped again, more firmly than before; the assault began again, the smell intensified.

'I've got you now, Sweetheart, haven't I?' said the voice. 'It doesn't matter about her any more. Let her curse me all she likes. We've got each other. Once we get rid of your children, that is. And I'm awfully good at getting rid of children.'

When Rory rang on Monday he was uneasy and embarrassed.

'It's all so unlike Jacobine,' he complained later to Fiona. 'She's really not the type. And you should have heard some of the things she told the policeman this fellow in the car had done to her.'

'Oh those quiet types,' exclaimed Fiona. Without knowing Jacobine intimately, she had always thought it odd that she should have surrendered such an attractive man as Rory, virtually without a struggle. 'Still waters,' Fiona added brightly.

Rory suggested a visit to the doctor. He also wondered whether the strain of running a car . . . Jacobine felt the tears coming into her eyes. Why hadn't she thought of that? Get rid of him. Get rid of the car. Free herself.

'Oh, Rory,' she begged. 'Would you take Tessa and Gavin for a few days? I know it's not your time, and I appreciate that Fiona's job — '

'I'll have them at the weekend,' suggested Rory, always as placating as possible, out of guilt that Jacobine, unlike him, had not married again. 'Fiona's got a marketing conference this week and I'll be in Aberdeen.'

'No, please, Rory, today, I implore you. I tell you what, I'll send them round in a taxi. I won't come too. I'll just put them in a taxi this afternoon.'

But Rory was adamant. It would have to be the weekend.

That afternoon, picking up Tessa and Gavin from school, Jacobine very nearly hit an old woman on a zebra crossing. She had simply not seen her. She could not understand it. She always slowed down before zebra crossings and yet she had been almost speeding across this one. Both children bumped themselves badly and Gavin in the front seat who was not wearing his safety belt (another odd factor, since Jacobine could have sworn she fastened it herself), cut himself on the driving mirror.

'That's your warning,' he said that night. 'The children must go. You spend too much time thinking about them and bothering about them. Tiresome little creatures. I'm glad they hurt themselves this afternoon. Cry babies, both of them. Besides, I don't want you having any other calls on your time.'

And Jacobine was wrenched very violently to and fro, shaken like a bag of shopping. The next moment was worse. A cigarette was stubbed, hard, on her wrist, just where the veins ran.

Even at the instant of torture, Jacobine thought:

'Now they'll have to believe me.'

But it seemed that they didn't. In spite of the mark and in spite of the fact that surely everyone knew Jacobine did not smoke. A doctor came. And Rory came. Jacobine got her wish in the sense that Tessa and Gavin were taken away by Rory. Fiona had to break off halfway through her marketing conference, although you would never have guessed it from the cheery way she saluted the children.

'Just because their mother's gone nuts,' Fiona said sensibly to Rory afterwards, 'it doesn't mean that I can't give them a jolly good tea. And supper too. I have no idea what happened about their meals with all that jazzing about at night, and running around in her nightie, and screaming.'

Then Rory took Jacobine down to a really pleasant countrified place not far from Edinburgh, recommended by the doctor. It had to be Rory: there was no one else to do it. Jacobine was very quiet all the way. Rory wondered whether it was because he was driving her car — the car. But Fiona needed the Cortina to fetch the children from school. Once or twice he almost thought Jacobine was listening to something in her own head. It gave him a creepy feeling. Rory put on the radio.

'Don't do that,' said Jacobine, quite sharply for her. 'He doesn't like it.' Rory thought it prudent to say nothing. But he made a mental note to report back to Fiona when he got home. For it was Fiona who felt some concern about despatching Jacobine in this way.

'It's really rather awful, darling,' she argued, 'taking her children away from her. They're all she had in her life. Poor dotty girl.'

'They are my children too,' said Rory humbly. But he knew just what Fiona meant. He admired her more than ever for being so resolutely kind-hearted: it was wonderful how well she got on with both Tessa and Gavin as a result. Fiona also took her turn visiting Jacobine when Rory was too busy. There were really no limits to her practical good nature. And so it was Fiona who brought back the news.

'She wants the car.'

'The car!' cried Rory. 'I should have thought that was the very last thing she should have under the circumstances.'

'Not to drive. She doesn't even want the keys. Just the car. She says she likes the idea of sitting in it. It makes her feel safe to know the car's there and not free to go about wherever it likes. I promise you, those were her very words.'

'What did Dr Mackie say? It seems very rum to me.'

'Oh, he seemed quite airy about it. Talked about womb trans-ference — can that be right? — anyway that sort of thing. He said it could stay in the grounds. Like a sort of Wendy house, I sup-pose. She hasn't been making very good progress. She cries so much, you see. It's pathetic. Poor thing, let her have the car. She has so little,' ended Fiona generously.

So Jacobine got her car back. Dr Mackie had it parked as promised in a secluded corner of the gardens. He was encouraged to find that Jacobine cried much less now. She spent a great deal of time sitting alone in the driver's seat, talking to herself. She was clearly happier.

'It's much better like this,' said the voice. 'I'm glad we got rid of your children the *nice* way. You won't ever see them again, you know.' Jacobine did not answer. She was getting quite prac-tised at pleasing him. He was generally waiting for her when she arrived at the Mini in its shady corner.

'Who's been sitting in my car?' she would say in a mock gruff voice, pointing to the heap of butts in the ashtray. But in spite of everything Jacobine still looked more like Goldilocks than a bear. Indeed, her face had come to look even younger since she lost the responsibility of the children – or so Fiona told Rory.

Jacobine had to be specially charming on the days when Fiona came down to see her, in case He got into her car and went back to find the children after all. She thought about them all the time. But she no longer cried in front of Him. Because that made Him angry and then He would leave her. She had to keep Him sitting beside her. That way the children would be safe. From Him.

NOT FROM DETROIT

Joe R. Lansdale

It is one of the oldest traditions in folklore that Death sometimes comes to collect his own in a coach or buggy. In this story, Joe R. Lansdale suggests that the Grim Reaper has been keeping up with progress and now uses an automobile on his missions. But when Death meets Alex Brooks, a grizzled old mechanic who runs a repair and wrecking service on Highway 59, he finds himself confronted by an adversary who proves to be smart at more than just fixing cars.

Joe R. Lansdale (1951–) is an award-winning mystery writer from Texas who was recently hailed as 'the hottest writer of Gothic goings-on', by the London Evening Standard. *Lansdale's tough, impoverished upbringing in East Texas, followed by a string of blue collar jobs, provided him with much of the material for his violent and sexually-charged stories of racism and sex crimes 'At 16 I worked on garbage trucks scraping dead dogs off the road,' he has recalled, 'and did a mess of other things until I got a janitor's job which allowed me to spend all day writing.' The success of his work has subsequently won him three Bram Stoker awards, the American Mystery Award and the British Fantasy Award, while* Time Out *referred to his most recent best-sellers,* Two Bear Mambo (1996) *and* Mucho Mojo (1998) *as 'red-hot gonzo stuff with all barrels firing point blank'. Cars have featured in a number of Lansdale's short stories, including 'Incident on and off a Mountain Road', 'The Job', 'Drive-in Date' and 'Hell Through a Windshield'. In the last of these he wrote, 'Texas is the champion state for automobile registration, and Texans have this thing about their cars. The automobile has replaced the horse, not only as a mode of transportation, but as a source of mythology.' Joe takes this idea further in 'Not From Detroit', a story which mixes the darkest ideas with humour and was first published in* Midnight Graffiti *in Autumn 1988.*

Outside it was cold and wet and windy. The storm rattled the shack, slid like razor blades through the window, door and wall cracks, but it wasn't enough to make any difference to the couple. Sitting before the crumbling fireplace in their creaking rocking-chairs, shawls across their knees, fingers entwined, they were warm.

A bucket behind them near the kitchen sink collected water dripping from a hole in the roof. The drops had long since passed the noisy stage of sounding like steel bolts falling on tin, and were now gentle plops.

The old couple were husband and wife; had been for over fifty years. They were comfortable with one another and seldom spoke. Mostly they rocked and looked at the fire as it flickered shadows across the room.

Finally Margie spoke. 'Alex,' she said. 'I hope I die before you.'

Alex stopped rocking. 'Did you say what I thought you did?'

'I said, I hope I die before you.' She wouldn't look at him, just the fire. 'It's selfish, I know, but I hope I do. I don't want to live on with you gone. It would be like cutting out my heart and making me walk around. Like one of them zombies.'

'There are the children,' he said. 'If I died, they'd take you in.'

'I'd just be in the way. I love them, but I don't want to do that. They got their own lives. I'd just as soon die before you. That would make things simple.'

'Not simple for me,' Alex said. 'I don't want you to die before me. So how about that? We're both selfish, aren't we?'

She smiled thinly. 'Well, it ain't a thing to talk about before bed-time, but it's been on my mind, and I had to get it out.'

'Been thinking on it too, honey. Only natural we would. We ain't spring chickens any more.'

'You're healthy as a horse, Alex Brooks. Mechanic work you did all your life kept you strong. Me, I got the bursitis and the miseries and I'm tired all the time. Got the old age bad.'

Alex started rocking again. They stared into the fire. 'We're going to go together, hon,' he said. 'I feel it. That's the way it ought to be for folks like us.'

'I wonder if I'll see him coming. Death, I mean.'

'What?'

'My grandma used to tell me she seen him the night her daddy died.'

'You've never told me this.'

'Ain't a subject I like. But grandma said this man in a black buggy slowed down out front of their house, cracked his whip three times, and her daddy was gone in instants. And she said she'd heard her grandfather tell how he had seen Death when he was a boy. Told her it was early morning and he was up, about to start his chores, and when he went outside he seen this man dressed in black walk by the house and stop out front. He was carrying a stick over his shoulder with a chequered bundle tied to it, and he looked at the house and snapped his fingers three times. A moment later they found my great-grandfather's brother, who had been sick with the smallpox, dead in bed.'

'Stories, hon. Stories. Don't get yourself worked up over a bunch of old tall tales. Here, I'll heat us some milk.'

Alex stood, laid the shawl in the chair, went over to put milk in a pan and heat it. As he did, he turned to watch Margie's back. She was still staring into the fire, only she wasn't rocking. She was just watching the blaze, and Alex knew, thinking about dying.

After the milk they went to bed, and soon Margie was asleep, snoring like a busted chainsaw. Alex found he could not rest. It was partly due to the storm, it had picked up in intensity. But it was mostly because of what Margie had said about dying. It made him feel lonesome.

Like her, he wasn't so much afraid of dying, as he was of being left alone. She had been his heartbeat for fifty years, and without her, he would only be going through motions of life, not living.

God, he prayed silently. When we go, let us go together.

He turned to look at Margie. Her face looked unlined and strangely young. He was glad she could turn off most anything with sleep. He, on the other hand, could not.

Maybe I'm just hungry.

He slid out of bed, pulled on his pants, shirt and houseshoes; those silly things with the rabbit face and ears his granddaughter had bought him. He padded silently to the kitchen. It was not only the kitchen, it served as a den, living-room and dining-room. The house was only three rooms and a closet, and one of the rooms was a small bathroom. It was times like this that Alex thought he could have done better by Margie. Got her a bigger house, for one thing. It was the same house where they had raised their kids, the babies sleeping in a crib here in the kitchen.

He sighed. No matter how hard he had worked, he seemed to stay in the same place. A poor place.

He went to the refrigerator and took out a half-gallon of milk, drank directly from the carton.

He put the carton back and watched the water drip into the bucket. It made him mad to see it. He had let the little house turn into a shack since he retired, and there was no real excuse for it. Surely, he wasn't that tired. It was a wonder Margie didn't complain more.

Well, there was nothing to do about it tonight. But he vowed that when dry weather came, he wouldn't forget about it this time. He'd get up there and fix that damn leak.

Quietly, he rummaged a pan from under the cabinet. He'd have to empty the bucket now if he didn't want it to run over before morning. He ran a little water into the pan before substituting it for the bucket so the drops wouldn't sound so loud.

He opened the front door, went out on the porch, carrying the bucket. He looked out at his mud-pie yard and his old, red wrecker, his white logo on the side of the door faded with time: ALEX BROOKS WRECKING AND MECHANIC SERVICE.

Tonight, looking at the old warhorse, he felt sadder than ever. He missed using it the way it was meant to be used. For work. Now it was nothing more than transportation. Before he retired, his tools and hands made a living. Now nothing. Picking up a Social Security Cheque was all that was left.

Leaning over the edge of the porch, he poured the water into the bare and empty flowerbed. When he lifted his head and looked at his yard again, and beyond Highway 59, he saw a light. Headlights, actually, looking fuzzy in the rain, like filmed-over amber eyes. They were way out there on the highway, coming from the South, winding their way towards him, moving fast.

Alex thought that whoever was driving that crate was crazy. Cruising like that on bone-dry highways with plenty of sunshine would have been dangerous, but in this weather, they were asking for a crackup.

As the car neared, he could see it was long, black and strangely-shaped. He'd never seen anything like it, and he knew cars fairly well. This didn't look like something off the assembly line from Detroit. It had to be foreign.

Miraculously, the car slowed without so much as a quiver or

a screech of brakes and tyres. In fact, Alex could not even hear its motor, just the faint whispering of rubber on wet cement.

The car came even of the house just as lightning flashed, and in that instant, Alex got a good look at the driver, or at least the shape of the driver outlined in the flash, and he saw that it was a man with a cigar in his mouth and a bowler hat on his head. And the head was turning towards the house.

The lightning flash died, and now there was only the dark shape of the car and the red tip of the cigar jutting at the house. Alex felt stalactites of ice dripping down from the roof of his skull, extended through his body and out the soles of his feet.

The driver hit down on his horn; three sharp blasts that pricked at Alex's mind.

Honk. (visions of blooming roses, withering going black)

Honk. (funerals remembered, loved ones in boxes, going down)

Honk. (worms crawling through rotten flesh)

Then came a silence louder than the horn blasts. The car picked up speed again. Alex watched as its tail-lights winked away in the blackness. The chill became less chill. The stalactites in his brain and mind melted away.

But as he stood there, Margie's words of earlier that evening came at him in a rush: 'Seen Death once . . . buggy slowed down out front . . . cracked his whip *three times* . . . man looked at the house, snapped his fingers *three times* . . . found dead a moment later . . .'

Alex's throat felt as if a pine knot had lodged there. The bucket slipped from his fingers, clattered on the porch and rolled into the flowerbed. He turned into the house and walked briskly towards the bedroom.

(*Can't be, just a wive's tale*)

his hands vibrating with fear.

(*Just a crazy coincidence*)

Margie wasn't snoring.

Alex grabbed her shoulder, shook her.

Nothing.

He rolled her on her back and screamed her name.

Nothing.

'Oh, baby. No.'

He felt for her pulse.

None.

He put an ear to her chest, listening for a heartbeat (the other half of his life bongos), and there was none.

Quiet. Perfectly quiet.

'You can't . . .' Alex said. 'You can't . . . We're supposed to go together . . . Got to be that way.'

And then it came to him. He had *seen* Death drive by, had *seen* him heading on down the highway.

He came to his feet, snatched his coat from the back of the chair, raced towards the door. 'You won't have her,' he said aloud. 'You won't.'

Grabbing the wrecker keys from the nail beside the door, he leaped to the porch and dashed out into the cold and the rain.

A moment later he was heading down the highway, driving fast and crazy in pursuit of the strange car.

The wrecker was old and not built for speed, but since he kept it well tuned and it had new tyres, it ran well over the wet highway. Alex kept pushing the pedal gradually until it met the floor. Faster and faster and faster.

After an hour, he saw Death.

Not the man himself but the licence plate. Personalised and clear in his headlights. It read: DEATH / EXEMPT.

The wrecker and the strange black car were the only ones on the road. Alex closed in on him, honked his horn. Death tootled back (not the same horn sound he had given in front of Alex's house), stuck his arm out the window and waved the wrecker around.

Alex went, and when he was alongside the car, he turned his head to look at Death. He could still not see him clearly, but he could make out the shape of his bowler, and when Death turned to look at him, he could see the glowing tip of the cigar, like a bloody bullet wound.

Alex whipped hard right into the car, and Death swerved to the right, then back onto the road. Alex rammed again. The black car's tyres hit roadside gravel and Alex swung closer, preventing it from returning to the highway. He rammed yet another time, and the car went into the grass alongside the road, skidded and went sailing down an embankment and into a tree.

Alex braked carefully, backed off the road and got out of the wrecker. He reached a small pipe wrench and a big crescent wrench out from under the seat, slipped the pipe wrench into his coat pocket for insurance, then went charging down the embankment waving the crescent.

Death opened his door and stepped out. The rain had subsided and the moon was peeking through the clouds like a shy child through gossamer curtains. Its light hit Death's round, pink face and made it look like a waxed pomegranate. His cigar hung from his mouth by a tobacco strand.

Glancing up the embankment, he saw an old, but strong-looking black man brandishing a wrench and wearing bunny slippers, charging down at him.

Spitting out the ruined cigar, Death stepped forward, grabbed Alex's wrist and forearm, twisted. The old man went up and over, the wrench went flying from his hand. Alex came down hard on his back, the breath bursting out of him in spurts.

Death leaned over Alex. Up close, Alex could see that the pink face was slightly pocked and that some of the pinkness was due to makeup. That was rich. Death was vain about his appearance. He was wearing a black tee-shirt, pants and sneakers, and of course his derby, which had neither been stirred by the wreck nor by the ju-jitsu manoeuvre.

'What's with you, man?' Death asked.

Alex wheezed, tried to catch his breath. 'You . . . can't . . . have . . . her.'

'Who? Who are you talking about?'

'Don't play . . . dumb with me.' Alex raised up on one elbow, his wind returning. 'You're Death and you took my Margie's soul.'

Death straightened. 'So you know who I am. All right. But what of it? I'm only doing my job.'

'It ain't her time.'

'My list says it is, and my list is never wrong.'

Alex felt something hard pressing against his hip, realised what it was. The pipe wrench. Even the throw Death had put on him had not hurled it from his coat pocket. It had lodged there and the pocket had shifted beneath his hip, making his old bones hurt all the worse.

Alex made as to roll over, freed the pocket beneath him, shot his hand inside and produced the pipe wrench. He hurled it at Death, struck him just below the brim of the bowler and sent him stumbling back. This time the bowler fell off. Death's forehead was bleeding.

Before Death could collect himself, Alex was up and rushing.

He used his head as a battering ram and struck Death in the stomach, knocking him to the ground. He put both knees on Death's arms, pinning them, clenched his throat with his strong, old hands.

'I ain't never hurt nobody before,' Alex said. 'Don't want to now. I didn't want to hit you with that wrench, but you give Margie back.'

Death's eyes showed no expression at first, but slowly a light seemed to go on behind them. He easily pulled his arms out from under Alex's knees, reached up, took hold of the old man's wrist and pulled the hands away from his throat.

'You old rascal,' Death said. 'You outsmarted me.'

Death flopped Alex over on his side, then stood up to once more lord over the man. Grinning, he turned, stooped to recover his bowler, but he never laid a hand on it.

Alex moved like a crab, scissored his legs and caught Death above and behind the knees, twisted, brought him down on his face.

Death raised up on his palms and crawled from behind Alex's legs like a snake, effortlessly. This time he grabbed the hat and put it on his head and stood up. He watched Alex carefully.

'I don't frighten you much, do I?' Death asked.

Alex noted that the wound on Death's forehead had vanished. There wasn't even a drop of blood. 'No,' Alex said. 'You don't frighten me much. I just want my Margie back.'

'All right,' Death said.

Alex sat bolt upright.

'What?'

'I said, all right. For a time. Not many have outsmarted me, pinned me to the ground. I give you credit, and you've got courage. I like that. I'll give her back. For a time. Come here.'

Death walked over to the car that was not from Detroit. Alex got to his feet and followed. Death took the keys out of the ignition, moved to the trunk, worked the key in the lock. It popped up with a hiss.

Inside were stacks and stacks of matchboxes. Death moved his hand over them, like a careful man selecting a special vegetable at the supermarket. His fingers came to rest on a matchbox that looked to Alex no different than the others.

Death handed Alex the matchbox. 'Her soul's in here, old man. You stand over her bed, open the box. Okay?'

'That's it?'

'That's it. Now get out of here before I change my mind. And remember, I'm giving her back to you. But just for a while.'

Alex started away, holding the matchbox carefully. As he walked past Death's car, he saw the dents he had knocked in the side with his wrecker were popping out. He turned to look at Death, who was closing the trunk.

'Don't suppose you'll need a tow out of here?'

Death smiled thinly. 'Not hardly.'

Alex stood over their bed; the bed where they had loved, slept, talked and dreamed. He stood there with the matchbox in his hand, his eyes on Margie's cold face. He ever so gently eased the box open. A small flash of blue light, like Peter Pan's friend Tinkerbelle, rushed out of it and hit Margie's lips. She made a sharp inhaling sound and her chest rose. Her eyes came open. She turned and looked at Alex and smiled.

'My lands, Alex. What are you doing there, and half-dressed? What you been up to . . . is that a matchbox?'

Alex tried to speak, but he found he could not. All he could do was grin.

'Have you gone nuts?' she asked.

'Maybe a little.' He sat down on the bed and took her hand. 'I love you Margie.'

'And I love you . . . You been drinking?'

'No.'

Then came the overwhelming sound of Death's horn. One harsh blast that shook the house, and the headbeams shone brightly through the window and the cracks and lit up the shack like a cheap nightclub act.

'Who in the world?' Margie asked.

'Him. But he said . . . Stay here.'

Alex got his shotgun out of the closet. He went out on the porch. Death's car was pointed towards the house, and the head-beams seemed to hold Alex, like a fly in butter.

Death was standing on the bottom porch step, waiting.

Alex pointed the shotgun at him. 'You git. You gave her back. You gave your word.'

'And I kept it. But I said for a while.'

'That wasn't any time at all.'

'It was all I could give. My present.'

'Short time like that's worse than no time at all.'

'Be good about it, Alex. Let her go. I got records and they have to be kept. I'm going to take her anyway, you understand that?'

'Not tonight, you ain't.' Alex pulled back the hammers on the shotgun. 'Not tomorrow night either. Not anytime soon.'

'That gun won't do you any good, Alex. You know that. You can't stop Death. I can stand here and snap my fingers three times, or click my tongue, or go back to the car and honk my horn, and she's as good as mine. But I'm trying to reason with you, Alex. You're a brave man. I did you a favour because you bested me. I didn't want to just take her back without telling you. That's why I came here to talk. But she's got to go. Now.'

Alex lowered the shotgun. 'Can't . . . can't you take me in her place? You can do that can't you?'

'I . . . I don't know. It's highly irregular.'

'Yeah, you can do that. Take me. Leave Margie.'

'Well, I suppose.'

The screen door creaked open and Margie stood there in her housecoat. 'You're forgetting, Alex, I don't want to be left alone.'

'Go in the house, Margie,' Alex said.

'I know who this is. I heard you talking, Mr Death, I don't want you taking my Alex. I'm the one you came for. I ought to have the right to go.'

There was a pause, no one speaking. Then Alex said, 'Take both of us. You can do that, can't you? I know I'm on that list of yours, and pretty high up. Man my age couldn't have too many years left. You can take me a little before my time, can't you? Well, can't you?'

Margie and Alex sat in their rocking chairs, their shawls over their knees. There was no fire in the fireplace. Behind them the bucket collected water and outside the wind whistled. They held hands. Death stood in front of them. He was holding a King Edward cigar box.

'You're sure of this?' Death asked. 'You don't both have to go.'

Alex looked at Margie, then back at Death.

'We're sure,' he said. 'Do it.'

Death nodded. He opened the cigar box and held it out on one palm. He used his free hand to snap his fingers.

Once. (*the wind picked up, howled*)

Twice. (*the rain beat like drumsticks on the roof*)

Three times. *(lightning ripped and thunder roared)*

'And in you go,' Death said.

A little blue light came out of the couple's mouths and jetted into the cigar box with a thump, and Death closed the lid.

The bodies of Alex and Margie slumped and their heads fell together between the rocking chairs. Their fingers were still entwined.

Death put the box under his arm and went out to the car. The rain beat on his derby hat and the wind sawed at his bare arms and tee-shirt. He didn't seem to mind.

Opening the trunk, he started to put the box inside, then hesitated.

He closed the trunk.

'Damn,' he said, 'if I'm not getting to be a sentimental old fool.'

He opened the box. Two blue lights rose out of it, elongated, touched ground. They took on the shape of Alex and Margie. They glowed against the night.

'Want to ride up front?' Death asked.

'That would be nice,' Margie said.

'Yes, nice,' Alex said.

Death opened the door and Alex and Margie slid inside. Death climbed in behind the wheel. He checked the clipboard dangling from the dash. There was a woman in a Tyler hospital, dying of brain damage. That would be his next stop.

He put the clipboard down and started the car that was not from Detroit.

'Sounds well tuned,' Alex said.

'I try to keep it that way,' Death said.

They drove out of there then, and as they went, Death broke into song. 'Row, row row your boat, gently down the stream,' and Margie and Alex chimed in with, 'Merrily, merrily, merrily, life is but a dream.'

Off they went down the highway, the tail-lights fading, the song dying, the black metal of the car melting into the fabric of night, and then there was only the whispery sound of good tyres on wet cement and finally not even that. Just the blowing sound of the wind and the rain.

(With thanks to Richard Matheson and Richard Christian Matheson)

TWO

MOTORWAY MADNESS

Murder in the Fast Lane

NEVER STOP ON THE MOTORWAY

Jeffrey Archer

'Road rage' — aggression between drivers on busy roads — has become almost a worldwide epidemic. The term originated in America where as many as a hundred people are killed every year over traffic arguments, and it has been in use in Britain since the long, hot summer of 1992 when motorists' tempers everywhere ran high. In one instance in May of that year, a 79-year-old man was killed by another after an overtaking incident in Yorkshire, while a second was stabbed with a screwdriver by a motorist who claimed he had been cut up on the M27. The most horrific incidents have almost all been on motorways, and although men are said to be the worst offenders, a large number of women have also been involved. One suggested explanation for 'road rage' has been offered by a spokesman of the Transport Studies Unit in the UK, who put it down to 'a driver's sense of isolation from real life when enclosed in a vehicle, which results in a tendency to treat other motorists in highly anti-social ways.' This next story draws on the phenomenon with quite shattering results for those involved.

Jeffrey Archer (1940–) has been described as 'Britain's top-selling novelist' as well as one of the leading high-profile figures on the political scene. He came to public attention during his time as MP for Louth, when he resigned from the Houses of Parliament after a financial disaster. In order to pay his debts, he turned to writing fiction and his first book, Not a Penny More, Not a Penny Less (1975), based on his own experiences, became an immediate best-seller. His subsequent works, including Kane and Abel (1979) which was made into a television series, Honour Among Thieves (1993) and The Proprietors (1996), have all been hugely popular. He has also written plays and in 1992 was made a life peer. Archer's short stories have also earned him praise from the Daily Express as 'a suspense-filled rival to Roald Dahl', and like those of Dahl his stories are notable for their 'sting in the tail'.

'Never Stop on the Motorway' is just such a tale, in which a young woman finds herself being relentlessly pursued along a motorway by a youth in a black van. What awaits Diana as she tries vainly to shake off the man will surprise the reader as much as it does her. Jeffrey Archer has admitted, enigmatically, that the story is 'actually based on a known incident'.

*   *   *

Diana had been hoping to get away by five, so she could be at the farm in time for dinner. She tried not to show her true feelings when at 4.37 her deputy, Phil Haskins, presented her with a complex twelve-page document that required the signature of a director before it could be sent out to the client. Haskins didn't hesitate to remind her that they had lost two similar contracts that week.

It was always the same on Friday. The phones would go quiet in the middle of the afternoon and then, just as she thought she could slip away, an authorisation would land on her desk. One glance at this particular document and Diana knew there would be no chance of escaping before six.

The demands of being a single parent as well as a director of a small but thriving City company meant there were few moments left in any day to relax, so when it came to the one weekend in four that James and Caroline spent with her ex-husband, Diana would try to leave the office a little earlier than usual to avoid getting snarled up in the weekend traffic.

She read through the first page slowly and made a couple of emendations, aware that any mistake made hastily on a Friday night could be regretted in the weeks to come. She glanced at the clock on her desk as she signed the final page of the document. It was just flicking over to 5.51.

Diana gathered up her bag and walked purposefully towards the door, dropping the contract on Phil's desk without bothering to suggest that he have a good weekend. She suspected that the paperwork had been on his desk since nine o'clock that morning, but that holding it until 4.37 was his only means of revenge now that she had been made head of department. Once she was safely in the lift, she pressed the button for the basement carpark, calculating that the delay would probably add an extra hour to her journey.

She stepped out of the lift, walked over to her Audi estate, unlocked the door and threw her bag onto the back seat. When she drove up onto the street the stream of twilight traffic was just about keeping pace with the pinstriped pedestrians who, like worker ants, were hurrying towards the nearest hole in the ground.

She flicked on the six o'clock news. The chimes of Big Ben rang out, before spokesmen from each of the three main political parties gave their views on the European election results. John Major was refusing to comment on his future. The Conservative Party's explanation for its poor showing was that only forty-two per cent of the country had bothered to go to the polls. Diana felt guilty — she was among the fifty-eight per cent who had failed to register their vote.

The newscaster moved on to say that the situation in Bosnia remained desperate, and that the UN was threatening dire consequences if Radovan Karadzik and the Serbs didn't come to an agreement with the other warring parties. Diana's mind began to drift — such a threat was hardly news any longer. She suspected that if she turned on the radio in a year's time they would probably be repeating it word for word.

As her car crawled round Russell Square, she began to think about the weekend ahead. It had been over a year since John had told her that he had met another woman and wanted a divorce. She still wondered why, after seven years of marriage, she hadn't been more shocked — or at least angry — at his betrayal. Since her appointment as a director, she had to admit they had spent less and less time together. And perhaps she had become anaesthetised by the fact that a third of the married couples in Britain were now divorced or separated. Her parents had been unable to hide their disappointment, but then they had been married for forty-two years.

The divorce had been amicable enough, as John, who earned less than she did — one of their problems, perhaps — had given in to most of her demands. She had kept the flat in Putney, the Audi estate and the children, to whom John was allowed access one weekend in four. He would have picked them up from school earlier that afternoon, and, as usual, he'd return them to the flat in Putney around seven on Sunday evening.

Diana would go to almost any lengths to avoid being left on her own in Putney when they weren't around, and although she regularly grumbled about being landed with the responsibility of bringing up two children without a father, she missed them desperately the moment they were out of sight.

She hadn't taken a lover and she didn't sleep around. None of the senior staff at the office had ever gone further than asking her out to lunch. Perhaps because only three of them were unmarried—and not without reason. The one person she might have considered having a relationship with had made it abundantly clear that he only wanted to spend the night with her, not the days.

In any case, Diana had decided long ago that if she was to be taken seriously as the company's first woman director, an office affair, however casual or short-lived, could only end in tears. Men are so vain, she thought. A woman only had to make one mistake and she was immediately labelled as promiscuous. Then every other man on the premises either smirks behind your back, or treats your thigh as an extension of the arm on his chair.

Diana groaned as she came to a halt at yet another red light. In twenty minutes she hadn't covered more than a couple of miles. She opened the glove box on the passenger side and fumbled in the dark for a cassette. She found one and pressed it into the slot, hoping it would be Pavarotti, only to be greeted by the strident tones of Gloria Gaynor assuring her 'I will survive'. She smiled and thought about Daniel, as the light changed to green.

She and Daniel had read Economics at Bristol University in the early 1980s, friends but never lovers. Then Daniel met Rachael, who had come up a year after them, and from that moment he had never looked at another woman. They married the day he graduated, and after they returned from their honeymoon Daniel took over the management of his father's farm in Bedfordshire. Three children had followed in quick succession, and Diana had been proud when she was asked to be godmother to Sophie, the eldest. Daniel and Rachael had now been married for twelve years, and Diana felt confident that they wouldn't be disappointing *their* parents with any suggestion of a divorce. Although they were convinced she led an exciting and fulfilling life, Diana often envied their gentle and uncomplicated existence.

She was regularly asked to spend the weekend with them in the country, but for every two or three invitations Daniel issued, she only accepted one—not because she wouldn't have liked to join them more often, but because since her divorce she had no desire to take advantage of their hospitality.

Although she enjoyed her work, it had been a bloody week. Two contracts had fallen through, James had been dropped from the school football team, and Caroline had never stopped telling her that her father didn't mind her watching television when she ought to be doing her prep.

Another traffic light changed to red.

It took Diana nearly an hour to travel the seven miles out of the city, and when she reached the first dual carriageway, she glanced up at the A1 sign, more out of habit than to seek guidance, because she knew every yard of the road from her office to the farm. She tried to increase her speed, but it was quite impossible, as both lanes remained obstinately crowded.

Damn.' She had forgotten to get them a present, even a decent bottle of claret. 'Damn,' she repeated: Daniel and Rachael always did the giving. She began to wonder if she could pick something up on the way, then remembered there was nothing but service stations between here and the farm. She couldn't turn up with yet another box of chocolates they'd never eat. When she reached the roundabout that led onto the A1, she managed to push the car over fifty for the first time. She began to relax, allowing her mind to drift with the music.

There was no warning. Although she immediately slammed her foot on the brakes, it was already too late. There was a dull thump from the front bumper, and a slight shudder rocked the car.

A small black creature had shot across her path, and despite her quick reactions, she hadn't been able to avoid hitting it. Diana swung onto the hard shoulder and screeched to a halt, wondering if the animal could possibly have survived. She reversed slowly back to the spot where she thought she had hit it as the traffic roared past her.

And then she saw it, lying on the grass verge—a cat that had crossed the road for the tenth time. She stepped out of the car, her headlights shining on the lifeless body. Suddenly Diana felt sick. She had two cats of her own, and she knew she would never be able to tell the children what she had done. She picked up the dead animal and laid it gently in the ditch by the roadside.

'I'm so sorry,' she said, feeling a little silly. She gave it one last look before walking back to her car. Ironically, she had chosen the Audi for its safety features.

She climbed back into the car and switched on the ignition to find Gloria Gaynor was still belting out her opinion of men. She turned her off, and tried to stop thinking about the cat as she waited for a gap in the traffic large enough to allow her to ease her way back into the slow lane. She eventually succeeded, but was still unable to erase the dead cat from her mind.

Diana had accelerated up to fifty again when she suddenly became aware of a pair of headlamps shining through her rear windscreen. She put up her arm and waved in her rear-view mirror, but the lights continued to dazzle her. She slowed down to allow the vehicle to pass, but the driver showed no interest in doing so. Diana began to wonder if there was something wrong with her car. Was one of her lights not working? Was the exhaust billowing smoke? Was . . .

She decided to speed up and put some distance between herself and the vehicle behind, but it remained within a few yards of her bumper. She tried to snatch a look at the driver in her rear-view mirror, but it was hard to see much in the harshness of the lights. As her eyes became more accustomed to the glare, she could make out the silhouette of a large black van bearing down on her, and what looked like a young man behind the wheel. He seemed to be waving at her.

Diana slowed down again as she approached the next round-about, giving him every chance to overtake her on the outside lane, but once again he didn't take the opportunity, and just sat on her bumper, his headlights still undimmed. She waited for a small gap in the traffic coming from her right. When one appeared she slammed her foot on the accelerator, shot across the roundabout and sped on up the A1.

She was rid of him at last. She was just beginning to relax and to think about Sophie, who always waited up so that she could read to her, when suddenly those high-beam headlights were glaring through her rear windscreen and blinding her once again. If anything, they were even closer to her than before.

She slowed down, he slowed down. She accelerated, he accelerated. She tried to think what she could do next, and began waving frantically at passing motorists as they sped by, but they remained oblivious to her predicament. She tried to think of other ways she might alert someone, and suddenly recalled that when she had joined the board of the company they had suggested she have a car phone fitted. Diana had decided it could wait until the car went in for its next service, which should have been a fortnight ago.

She brushed her hand across her forehead and removed a film of perspiration, thought for a moment, then manoeuvred her car into the fast lane. The van swung across after her, and hovered so close to her bumper that she became fearful that if she so much as touched her brakes she might unwittingly cause an enormous pile-up.

Diana took the car up to ninety, but the van wouldn't be shaken off. She pushed her foot further down on the accelerator and touched a hundred, but it still remained less than a car's length behind.

She flicked her headlights onto high-beam, turned on her hazard lights and blasted her horn at anyone who dared to remain in her path. She could only hope that the police might see her, wave her onto the hard shoulder and book her for speeding. A fine would be infinitely preferable to a crash with a young tearaway, she thought, as the Audi estate passed a hundred and ten for the first time in its life. But the black van couldn't be shaken off.

Without warning, she swerved back into the middle lane, and took her foot off the accelerator, causing the van to draw level with her, which gave her a chance to look at the driver for the first time. He was wearing a black leather jacket and pointing menacingly at her. She shook her fist at him and accelerated away, but he simply swung across behind her like an Olympic runner determined not to allow his rival to break clear.

And then she remembered, and felt sick for a second time that night. 'Oh my God,' she shouted aloud in terror. In a flood, the details of the murder that had taken place on the same road a few months before came rushing back to her. A woman had been raped before having her throat cut with a knife with a serrated edge and dumped in a ditch. For weeks there had been signs posted on the A1 appealing to passing motorists to phone a certain number if they had any information that might assist the police with their enquiries. The signs had now disappeared, but the police were still searching for the killer. Diana began to tremble as she remembered their warning to all women drivers: 'Never stop on the motorway'.

A few seconds later she saw a road sign she knew well. She had reached it far sooner than she had anticipated. In three miles she would have to leave the motorway for the sliproad that led to the farm. She began to pray that if she took her usual turning, the black-jacketed man would continue on up the A1 and she would finally be rid of him.

Diana decided that the time had come for her to speed him on his way. She swung back into the fast lane and once again put her foot down on the accelerator. She reached a hundred miles per hour for the second time as she sped past the two-mile sign. Her body was now covered in sweat, and the speedometer touched a hundred and ten. She checked her rear-view mirror, but he was still right behind her. She would have to pick the exact moment if she was to execute her plan successfully. With a mile to go, she began to look to her left, so as to be sure her timing would be perfect. She no longer needed to check in her mirror to know that he would still be there.

The next signpost showed three diagonal white lines, warning her that she ought to be on the inside lane if she intended to leave the motorway at the next junction. She kept the car in the outside lane at a hundred miles per hour until she spotted a large enough gap. Two white lines appeared by the roadside: Diana knew she would have only one chance to make her escape. As she passed the sign with a single white line on it she suddenly swung across the road at ninety miles per hour, causing cars in the middle and inside lanes to throw on their brakes and blast out their angry opinions. But Diana didn't care what they thought of her, because she was now travelling down the sliproad to safety, and the black van was speeding on up the A1.

She laughed out loud with relief. To her right, she could see the steady flow of traffic on the motorway. But then her laugh turned to a scream as she saw the black van cut sharply across the motorway in front of a lorry, mount the grass verge and career onto the sliproad, swinging from side to side. It nearly drove over the edge and into a ditch, but somehow managed to steady itself, ending up a few yards behind her, its lights once again glaring through her rear windscreen.

When she reached the top of the sliproad, Diana turned left in the direction of the farm, frantically trying to work out what she should do next. The nearest town was about twelve miles away on the main road, and the farm was only seven, but five of those miles were down a winding, unlit country lane. She checked her petrol gauge. It was nearing empty, but there should still be enough in the tank for her to consider either option. There was less than a mile to go before she reached the turning, so she had only a minute in which to make up her mind.

With a hundred yards to go, she settled on the farm. Despite the unlit lane, she knew every twist and turn, and she felt confident that her pursuer wouldn't. Once she reached the farm she could be out of the car and inside the house long before he could catch her. In any case, once he saw the farmhouse, surely he would flee.

The minute was up. Diana touched the brakes and skidded into a country road illuminated only by the moon.

Diana banged the palms of her hands on the steering wheel. Had she made the wrong decision? She glanced up at her rear-view mirror. Had he given up? Of course he hadn't. The back of a Land Rover loomed up in front of her. Diana slowed down, waiting for a corner she knew well, where the road widened slightly. She held her breath, crashed into third gear, and overtook. Would a head-on collision be preferable to a cut throat? She rounded the bend and saw an empty road ahead of her. Once again she pressed her foot down, this time managing to put a clear seventy, perhaps even a hundred, yards between her and her pursuer, but this only offered her a few minutes' respite. Before long the familiar headlights came bearing down on her once again.

With each bend Diana was able to gain a little time as the van continued to lurch from side to side, unfamiliar with the road, but she never managed a clear break of more than a few seconds. She checked the milometer. From the turn-off on the main road to the farm it was just over five miles, and she must have covered about two by now. She began to watch each tenth of a mile clicking up, terrified at the thought of the van overtaking her and forcing her into the ditch. She stuck determinedly to the centre of the road.

Another mile passed, and still he clung on to her. Suddenly she saw a car coming towards her. She switched on her headlights to full beam and pressed on the horn. The other car retaliated by mimicking her actions, which caused her to slow down and brush against the hedgerow as they shot past each other. She checked the milometer once again. Only two miles to go.

Diana would slow down and then speed up at each familiar bend in the road, making sure the van was never given enough room to pull level with her. She tried to concentrate on what she should do once the farmhouse came into sight. She reckoned that the drive leading up to the house must be about half a mile long. It was full of potholes and bumps which Daniel had often explained he couldn't afford to have repaired. But at least it was only wide enough for one car.

The gate to the driveway was usually left open for her, though on the odd rare occasion Daniel had forgotten, and she'd had to get out of the car and open it for herself. She couldn't risk that tonight. If the gate was closed, she would have to travel on to the next town and stop outside the Crimson Kipper, which was always crowded at this time on a Friday night, or, if she could find it, on the steps of the local police station. She checked her petrol gauge again. It was now touching red. 'Oh my God,' she said, realising she might not have enough petrol to reach the town.

She could only pray that Daniel had remembered to leave the gate open.

She swerved out of the next bend and speeded up, but once again she managed to gain only a few yards, and she knew that within seconds he would be back in place. He was. For the next few hundred yards they remained within feet of each other, and she felt certain he must run into the back of her. She didn't once dare to touch her brakes – if they crashed in that lane, far from any help, she would have no hope of getting away from him.

She checked her milometer. A mile to go.

'The gate must be open. It must be open,' she prayed. As she swung round the next bend, she could make out the outline of the farmhouse in the distance. She almost screamed with relief when she saw that the lights were on in the downstairs rooms.

She shouted 'Thank God!' then remembered the gate again, and changed her plea to 'Dear God, let it be open.' She would know what needed to be done as soon as she came round the last bend. 'Let it be open, just this once,' she pleaded. 'I'll never ask for anything again, ever.' She swung round the final bend only inches ahead of the black van. 'Please, please, please.' And then she saw the gate.

It was open.

Her clothes were now drenched in sweat. She slowed down,

wrenched the gearbox into second, and threw the car between the gap and into the bumpy driveway, hitting the gatepost on her right-hand side as she careered on up towards the house. The van didn't hesitate to follow her, and was still only inches behind as she straightened up. Diana kept her hand pressed down on the horn as the car bounced and lurched over the mounds and potholes.

Flocks of startled crows flapped out of overhanging branches, screeching as they shot into the air. Diana began screaming, 'Daniel! Daniel!' Two hundred yards ahead of her, the porch light went on.

Her headlights were now shining onto the front of the house, and her hand was still pressed on the horn. With a hundred yards to go, she spotted Daniel coming out of the front door, but she didn't slow down, and neither did the van behind her. With fifty yards to go she began flashing her lights at Daniel. She could now make out the puzzled, anxious expression on his face.

With thirty yards to go she threw on her brakes. The heavy estate car skidded across the gravel in front of the house, coming to a halt in the flowerbed just below the kitchen window. She heard the screech of brakes behind her. The leather-jacketed man, unfamiliar with the terrain, had been unable to react quickly enough, and as soon as his wheels touched the gravelled forecourt he began to skid out of control. A second later the van came crashing into the back of her car, slamming it against the wall of the house and shattering the glass in the kitchen window.

Diana leapt out of the car, screaming, 'Daniel! Get a gun, get a gun!' She pointed back at the van. 'That bastard's been chasing me for the last twenty miles!'

The man jumped out of the van and began limping towards them.

Diana ran into the house. Daniel followed and grabbed a shotgun, normally reserved for rabbits, that was leaning against the wall. He ran back outside to face the unwelcome visitor, who had come to a halt by the back of Diana's Audi.

Daniel raised the shotgun to his shoulder and stared straight at him. 'Don't move or I'll shoot,' he said calmly. And then he remembered the gun wasn't loaded. Diana ducked back out of the house, but remained several yards behind him.

'Not me! Not me!' shouted the leather-jacketed youth, as Rachael appeared in the doorway.

'What's going on?' she asked nervously.

'Ring for the police,' was all Daniel said, and his wife quickly disappeared back into the house.

Daniel advanced towards the terrified-looking young man, the gun aimed squarely at his chest.

'Not me! Not me!' he shouted again, pointing at the Audi. 'He's in the car!' He quickly turned to face Diana. 'I saw him get in when you were parked on the hard shoulder. What else could I have done? You just wouldn't pull over.'

Daniel advanced cautiously towards the rear door of the car and ordered the young man to open it slowly, while he kept the gun aimed at his chest.

The youth opened the door, and quickly took a pace backwards. The three of them stared down at a man crouched on the floor of the car. In his right hand he held a long-bladed knife with a serrated edge. Daniel swung the barrel of the gun down to point at him, but said nothing.

The sound of a police siren could just be heard in the distance.

THE DEATH CAR

Peter Haining

*The Interstate Highway 15, which passes through Las Vegas on its way
to California and the coast, is one of the most notorious motorways in
America in terms of 'road rage' and murder. It has a history of killings
associated with automobiles going back to the Roaring Twenties.
Nowhere is this tradition more gruesomely acknowledged than in the
town of Rhyolite, close to the Nevada/California border, where a huge
neon sign invites passing motorists to stop and see 'The Death Car'.
Beneath it is a painting of a 1934 Ford V8 saloon which, at a distance,
seems just like any other of the millions that were mass-produced for
almost a generation. But leave Highway 15 for a look at this particular
V8, battered and riddled with bullet holes, and an extraordinary story
of crime and murder unravels, linking America's greatest motor mag-
nate with one of her most infamous gangsters.*

*Peter Haining (1940–) is a former journalist and publisher whose
anthologies, novels and works of non-fiction have been published all
over the world. He has reprinted short stories about automobiles in a
number of earlier collections, and is the author of a best-selling 'biogra-
phy' of the world's favourite sports car,* The MG Log *(1993). He was
inspired to write 'The Death Car' after seeing the actual vehicle some
years ago. Neither the names nor the events have been changed.*

*   *   *

Jesse Warren stood on the driveway and admired his handiwork.
He had washed and polished the Ford V8-40 until it gleamed in
the April sunshine. Through the kitchen window, a woman
looked up from her chores and saw the grin of satisfaction spread
across her husband's face. *He loves that damn car more'n me,*
she thought.

The car certainly wasn't the only new V8 in Topeka that spring of 1934, but Jesse reckoned you'd have to go a long way across Kansas to find an automobile that was better looked after. He sure *did* love the saloon, not only because it looked good, but because it was also pretty nifty to drive. OK, so Ruth didn't like him driving fast when she was along for the ride, but on his own he knew he could show most of those sporty models a clean pair of wheels.

For a while Jesse continued cleaning up the inside of the car. He brushed the seats, shook out the mats, and polished the dashboard until he could see his face in it. He gave the windows a final shine with his leather and, satisfied, decided he was all through.

Jesse looked up at the sky. It was clear blue to the horizon. No sign of any clouds. The forecast was good, he had heard that on the radio, so he could reckon without any rain to spoil his hard work. He'd leave the car on the drive just so his neighbours could see. Maybe make them a mite jealous. That was to be his big mistake.

Several times that evening he glanced out of his front window at the V8. The bodywork still shone even after darkness had fallen. Tomorrow, he decided, he would take Ruth for a ride. To hell with speeding for once.

But when Jesse Warren got up the next day and looked at the driveway, he suddenly got sick to his stomach. The V8 was gone.

In his office overlooking the huge plant at River Rouge that bore his name, Henry Ford was reading through the morning mail. Below him, the assembly line was busy as ever. Although the old man couldn't see the faces of his employees, he knew they were a pretty happy bunch. After all, didn't he pay them more than the normal rate for the auto industry? And hadn't that got up the noses of those guys in Washington running Roosevelt's recovery programme? Ford smiled at the thought.

But, no matter, Detroit was a long way from Washington and this was *his* kingdom. Folks hereabouts liked working for Henry Ford, and all across America people sure loved to drive his motor cars. You only had to read the letters he got to see that. Just like the one he was holding now, with its scrawly handwriting that made it hard to read. The poor spelling didn't help much, either.

Ford could make out that the writer thought the V8 was a

'right dandy car'. In another paragraph the man had written, 'For sustained speed and freedom from trouble, the Ford has got every other car skinned.'

The motor manufacturer paused and allowed himself another smile. Nice phrase. Perhaps his ad men could use it in a campaign. What he deciphered next, however, surprised him more than a little.

'Even if my business hasn't been strickly legal,' the writer confided, 'it don't hurt enything to tell you what a fine car you got in the V8.'

For several moments Henry Ford tried to make out the signature, then with a puzzled shrug of his shoulders he dropped the letter with all the others.

It didn't take the young couple who were moving stealthily in the shadows along the street more than a glance to know that the V8 on the driveway was just the kind of top notch car they needed.

Without hesitation the man, a fedora pulled down over his handsome features, opened the back door of the car and laid the bulky sack he was carrying on the seat. Just as carefully he opened the driver's door and leaned across to free the opposite door. The other figure, a pretty young girl, her blonde hair stuffed into a beret, slid into the passenger's seat. Even as she silently closed the door, her companion released the car's handbrake and allowed it to roll slowly down the drive and into the street. A moment later, with the house almost out of view, he switched on the ignition, eased the car into gear, and drove off into the night.

In the hours and days that followed, the couple took turns at the wheel as they put distance between themselves and Topeka—as well as the law officers they knew were hard on their trail. All the while the engine purred smoothly beneath the hood. Jesse Warren's pride and joy would suit them mighty well, the couple agreed. After all, not for nothing was the V8 known as the gangster's ideal getaway car.

Henry Ford had not even begun to read his mail at River Rouge on the morning, six weeks later, when a front page story in his newspaper caught his eye. The article was datelined 24 May and described how two fugitives had been stopped by a hail of bullets when they drove into a police ambush between Sailes and Gibs-land in Louisiana. Beneath a photograph of the vehicle the paper reported, 'The car, running wild, crashed into an embankment. As the wheels spun the posse continued to fire until the car was almost shot to pieces.'

A frown creased Ford's brow. Goddammit, if that wasn't one of *his* cars. There was no mistaking the V8-40 sedan. The report also said that on the back seat behind the bloodstained bodies of the two occupants a whole heap of weapons had been found: three Colt automatics and a Colt revolver, two sawn-off shotguns, a pair of Browning automatics and over 3,000 rounds of ammu-nition.

Henry Ford let a slow whistle escape between his teeth. Damn, he knew a lot of crooks had taken a fancy to his new V8. Hadn't John Dillinger, the man they called 'Public Enemy Number One', boasted he would never do a job without one? But Ford's name had never before been associated with this kind of carnage. It was the sort of publicity he could well do without.

He was just about to put a call through to his assistant when he saw the name of the driver of the car. Clyde Barrow. The girl who had died alongside him was named as Bonnie Parker. Like a shiver up the spine, memories of an almost indecipherable letter stirred in his head.

Henry Ford let out another sigh. Sure as hell, he thought, there was one driver of his cars who would never be hurt by anything again.

NIGHT COURT

Mary Elizabeth Counselman

Bob Trask is a typical aggressive motorist, impatient and reckless, who has already twice been involved in major accidents. When he is cleared of knocking down and killing an old man, thanks to the leniency of a judge with family connections, his smugness is such that it even angers his wife. But when Trask fails to learn even from this tragedy and drives into a little girl on Highway 31, judgement is visited upon him in the most dramatic manner. 'Night Court' is a story of horror and retribution written in the tradition of Charles Dickens' 'A Christmas Carol'.

Mary Elizabeth Counselman (1911–95) began writing poetry at six, was contributing short stories to magazines as a teenager, and in her adult years was acknowledged as a fine novelist and brilliant creative writing teacher in her native Alabama. Born in Birmingham, she claimed to have had several psychic experiences which inspired her to write supernatural stories. A number of these, including 'Night Court' written in 1953, she contributed to the legendary Weird Tales, *and they earned her the reputation of being 'one of the most original writers for the magazine', as well as drawing comparison with the 'Gothic tales' of Faulkner, McCullers and O'Connor. The American South is also the setting of this story, in which one of the characters remarks with grim conviction, 'There is no such thing as an accidental death! Accidents are murders — because someone could have prevented them . . .'*

*   *   *

Bob waited, humming to himself in the stifling telephone booth, his collar and tie loosened for comfort in the late August heat, his Panama tilted rakishly over one ear to make room for the instrument. Through it he could hear a succession of female

voices: 'Gareyville calling Oak Grove thuh-ree, tew, niyun, six ...
collect ...' 'Oak Grove. What was that number ...?' 'Thuh-ree,
tew ...'

He stiffened as a low, sweetly familiar voice joined the chorus:
'Yes, yes! I—I accept the charges ... Hello? Bob ...?'

Instinctively he pressed the phone closer to his mouth, the
touch of it conjuring up the feel of cool lips, soft blonde hair,
and eyes that could melt a steel girder.

'Marian? Sure it's me! ... Jail? No! No, honey, that's all over.
I'm free! Free as a bird, yeah! The judge said it was unavoidable.
Told you, didn't I?' He mugged into the phone as though somehow, in this age of speed, she could see as well as hear him
across the twenty-odd miles that separated them. 'It was the
postponement that did it. Then they got this new judge—and
guess what? He used to go to school with Dad and Uncle Harry!
It was a cinch after that ... Huh?'

He frowned slightly, listening to the soft voice coming over
the wire; the voice he could not wait to hear congratulating him.
Only, she wasn't. She was talking to him—he grinned sheepishly—the way Mom talked to Dad sometimes, when he came
swooping into the driveway. One drink too many at the country
club after his Saturday golf ...

'Say!' he snorted. 'Aren't you *glad* I don't have to serve ten to
twenty years for manslaughter ...?'

'Oh, Bob.' There was a sadness in his fiancée's voice, a troubled
note. 'I ... I'm glad. Of course I'm glad about it. But ... it's just
that you sound so smug, so ... That poor old Negro ...'

'Smug!' He stiffened, holding the phone away slightly as if it
had stung him. 'Honey ... how can you say a thing like that!
Why, I've done everything I could for his family. Paid his mort-
gage on that little farm! Carted one of his kids to the hospital
every week for two months, like ...' His voice wavered, laden
with a genuine regret. 'Like the old guy would do himself, I
guess, if he was still ... *Marian*! You think I'm not *sorry* enough;
is that it?' he demanded.

There was a little silence over the wire. He could picture her,
sitting there quietly in the Marshalls' cheery-chintz living-room.
Maybe she had her hair pinned back in one of those ridiculous,
but oddly attractive, 'pony-tails' the teenagers were wearing this
year. Her little cat-face would be tilted up to the lamp, eyes
closed, the long fringe of lashes curling up over shadowy lids.

Bob fidgeted, wanting miserably to see her expression at that moment.

'Well? Say something!'

The silence was broken by a faint sigh.

'Darling . . . what is there to say? You're so thoughtless! Not callous; I don't mean that. Just . . . *careless*! Bob, you've got to unlearn what they taught you in Korea. You're . . . you're home again, and this is what you've been fighting for, isn't it? For . . . for the people around us to be safe? For life not to be cheap, something to be thrown away just to save a little *time* . . .'

'Say, listen!' He was scowling now, anger hardening his mouth into ugly lines. 'I've had enough lectures these past two months — from Dad, from the sheriff, from Uncle Harry. You'd think a guy twenty-two years old, in combat three years and got his feet almost frozen off, didn't know the score! What's the matter with everybody?' Bob's anger was mounting. 'Listen! I got a medal last year for killing fourteen North Koreans. For gunning 'em down! Deliberately! But now, just because I'm driving a little too fast and some old creep can't get his wagon across the highway . . .'

'Bob!'

'. . . now, all at once, I'm not a hero, I'm a murderer! I don't know the value of human life! I don't give a hoot how many people I . . .'

'*Darling!*'

A strangled sob came over the long miles. That stopped him. He gripped the phone, uncertainty in his oddly tip-tilted eyes that had earned him, in service, the nickname of 'Gook'.

'Darling, you're all mixed up, Bob . . . ? Bob dear, are you listening? If I could just *talk* to you tonight . . . ! What time is it? Oh, it's after *six*! I . . . I don't suppose you could drive over here tonight . . .'

The hard line of his mouth wavered, broke. He grinned.

'No? Who says I can't?' His laughter, young, winged and exultant, floated up. 'Baby, I'll burn the road . . . Oops! I mean . . .' He broke off sheepishly. 'No, no; I'll keep 'er under fifty. Honest!' Laughing, he crossed his heart — knowing Marian so well that he knew she would sense the gesture left over from their school days. 'There's so much to talk over now,' he added eagerly. 'Uncle Harry's taking me into the firm. I start peddling real estate for him next week. No kiddin'! And . . . and that little house we looked at . . . It's for sale, all right! Nine hundred down, and . . .'

'Bob . . . Hurry! Please!' The voice over the wire held, again, the tone he loved, laughing and tender. 'But drive carefully. Promise!'

'Sure, sure! Twenty miles, twenty minutes!'

He hung up, chuckling, and strode out into the street. Dusk was falling, the slow Southern dusk that takes its time about folding its dark quilt over the Blue Ridge foothills. With a light, springy step Bob walked to where his blue convertible was parked outside the drugstore, sandwiched between a pickup truck and a sedan full of people. As he climbed under the steering wheel, he heard a boy's piping voice, followed by the shushing monotone of an elder:

'Look! That's Bob Trask! He killed that old Negro last Fourth-o-July . . .'

'Danny, hush! Don't talk so loud! He can hear . . .'

'Benny Olsen told me it's his second bad wreck . . .'

'Danny!'

'. . . and that's the third car he's tore up in two years. Boy, you oughta seen that roadster he had! Sideswiped a truck and tore off the whole . . .'

'Hmph! Licence was never revoked, either! Politics! If his uncle wasn't city commissioner . . .'

Bob's scowl returned, cloudy with anger. People! They made up their own version of how an accident happened. That business with the truck, for instance. Swinging out into the highway just as he had tried to pass! Who could blame him for *that*? Or the fact that, weeks later, the burly driver had happened to die? From a ruptured appendix! The damage suit had been thrown out of court, because nobody could prove the collision had been what caused it to burst.

Backing out of the parking space in a bitter rush, Bob drove the convertible south, out of Gareyville on 31, headed for Oak Grove. Accidents! Anybody could be involved in an accident! Was a guy supposed to be lucky all the time? Or a mind-reader, always clairvoyant about the other driver?

As the white ribbon of highway unreeled before him, Bob's anger cooled. He smiled a little, settling behind the steering wheel and switching on the radio. Music poured out softly. He leaned back, soothed by its sound and and the rush of wind tousling his dark hair.

The law had cleared him of reckless driving; and that was all that counted. The landscape blurred as the sun sank. Bob switched on his headlights, dimmed. There was, at this hour, not much traffic on Chattanooga Road.

Glancing at his watch, Bob pressed his foot more heavily on the accelerator. Six-fifteen already? Better get to Marian's before that parent of hers insisted on dragging her off to a movie. He chuckled. His only real problem now was to win over Marian's mother, who made no bones of her disapproval of him, ever since his second wreck. '*Show me the way a man drives a car, and I'll tell you what he's like inside* . . .' Bob had laughed when Marian had repeated those words. A man could drive, he had pointed out, like an old-maid schoolteacher and still be involved in an accident that was not legally his fault. All right, *two* accidents! A guy could have lousy luck twice, couldn't he? Look at the statistics! Fatal accidents happened every day . . .

Yawning, at peace with himself and the lazy countryside sliding past his car window, Bob let the speedometer climb another ten miles an hour. Sixty-five? He smiled, amused. Marian was such an old grandma about driving fast! After they were married, he would have to teach her, show her. Why, he had had this old boat up to ninety on this same tree-shaded stretch of highway! A driver like himself, a good driver with a good car, had perfect control over his vehicle at any . . .

The child seemed to appear out of nowhere, standing in the centre of the road. A little girl in a frilly pink dress, her white face turned up in sudden horror, picked out by the headlights' glare.

Bob's cry was instinctive as he stamped on the brakes, and wrenched at the steering wheel. The car careened wildly, skidding sideways and striking the child broadside. Then, in a tangle of wheels and canvas top, it rolled into a shallow ditch, miraculously right side up. Bob felt his head strike something hard – the windshield. It starred out with tiny shimmering cracks, but did not shatter. Darkness rushed over him; the sick black darkness of the unconscious; but through it, sharp as a knife thrust, bringing him back to hazy awareness, was the sound of a child screaming.

'*Oh, no ohmygodohgod* . . .' Someone was sobbing, whimpering the words aloud. Himself.

Shaking his head blurrily. Bob stumbled from the tilted vehicle and looked about. Blood was running from a cut on his forehead, and his head throbbed with a surging nausea. But, ignoring the pain, he sank to his knee and peered under the car.

She was there. A little girl perhaps five years old. Ditch water matted the soft blonde hair and trickled into the half-closed eyes, tip-tilted at a pixie-like angle and fringed with long silky lashes. Bob groaned aloud, cramming his knuckles into his squared mouth to check the sob that burst out of him like a gust of desperate wind. She was pinned under a front wheel. Such a lovely little girl, appearing out here, miles from town, dressed as for a party. A sudden thought struck him that he knew this child, that he had seen her somewhere, sometime. On a bus? In a movie lobby . . . ? Where?

He crawled under the car afraid to touch her, afraid not to. She did not stir. Was she dead? Weren't those frilly little organdy ruffles on her small chest moving, ever so faintly . . . ? If he could only get her out from under that wheel! Get the car moving, rush her to a hospital . . . ! Surely, surely there was some spark of life left in that small body . . . !

Bob stood up, reeling, rubbing his eyes furiously as unconsciousness threatened to engulf him again. It was at that moment that he heard the muffled roar of a motorcycle. He whirled. Half in eagerness, half in dread, he saw a shadowy figure approaching him down the twilight-misted highway.

The figure on the motorcycle, goggled and uniformed as a state highway patrolman, braked slowly a few feet away. With maddening deliberateness of movement, he dismounted, flipped out a small report-pad, and peered at the convertible, jotting down its licence number. Bob beckoned frantically, pointing at the child pinned under the car. But the officer made no move to help him free her; took no notice of her beyond a cursory glance and a curt nod.

Instead, tipping back his cap from an oddly pale face, he rested one booted foot on the rear bumper and beckoned Bob to his side.

'All right, buddy . . .' His voice, Bob noted crazily, was so low that he could scarcely hear it; a whisper, a lip-movement pronouncing sounds that might have been part of the wind soughing in the roadside trees. 'Name: Robert Trask? I had orders to be on the lookout for you . . .'

'Orders?' Bob bristled abruptly, caught between anxiety for the child under his car and an instinct for self-preservation. 'Now, wait! I've got no record of reckless driving. I . . . I was involved in a couple of accidents; but the charges were dropped . . . Look!' he burst out. 'While you're standing here yapping, this child may be . . . Get on that scooter of yours and go phone an ambulance, you! I'll report you for dereliction of duty! . . . Say!' he yelled, as the officer did not move, but went on scribbling in his book. 'What kind of a man *are* you, anyway? Wasting time booking me, when there still may be time to save this . . . this poor little . . . !'

The white, goggle-obscured face lifted briefly, expressionless as a mask. Bob squirmed under the scrutiny of eyes hidden behind the green glass; saw the lips move . . . and noticed, for the first time, how queerly the traffic officer held his head. His pointed chin was twisted sideways, almost meeting the left shoulder. When he looked up, his whole body turned, like a man with a crick in his neck . . .

'What kind of man are *you*?' said the whispering lips. 'That's what we have to find out . . . And that's why I got orders to bring you in. *Now!*'

'Bring me in . . . ?' Bob nodded dully. 'Oh, you mean I'm under arrest? Sure, sure . . . but the little girl!' He glared, suddenly enraged by the officer's stolid indifference to the crushed form under the car. 'Listen, if you don't get on that motorbike and go for help, I . . . I'll knock you out and go myself! Resisting arrest; leaving the scene of an accident . . . Charge me with anything you like! But if there's still time to save her . . .'

The goggled eyes regarded him steadily for a moment. Then, nodding, the officer scribbled something else in his book.

'Time?' the windy whisper said, edged with irony. 'Don't waste time, eh? . . . Why don't you speed-demons think about other people's time before you cut it off? Why? *Why?* That's what we want to find out, what we *have* to find out . . . *Come on!*' The whisper lashed out, sibilant as a striking snake. 'Let's go, buddy! *Walk!*'

Bob blinked, swayed. The highway patrolman, completely ignoring the small body pinned under the convertible, had strode across the paved road with a peremptory beckoning gesture. He seemed headed for a little byroad that branched off the highway, losing itself among a thick grove of pine trees. It must, Bob decided eagerly, lead to some farmhouse where the officer meant to phone for an ambulance. Staggering, he followed, with a last anxious glance at the tiny form spreadeagled under his car wheel.

Where had he seen that little face? *Where* ... ? Some neighbour's child, visiting out here in the country ... ?

'You ... you think she's ... dead?' he blurted, stumbling after the shadowy figure ahead of him. 'Is it too late ... ?'

The officer with the twisted neck half turned, swivelling his whole body to look back at him.

'That,' the whispering voice said, 'all depends. Come on, you—snap it up! We got all night, but there's no sense wastin' time! Eh, buddy?' The thin lips curled ironically. 'Time! That's the most important thing in the world ... to them as still have it!'

Swaying dizzily, Bob hurried after him up the winding little byroad. It led, he saw with a growing sense of unease, through a country cemetery ... Abruptly, he brought up short, peering ahead at a grey gleam through the pines. Why, there was no farmhouse ahead! A fieldstone chapel with a high peaked roof loomed against the dusk, its arched windows gleaming redly in the last glow of sunset.

'Hey!' he snapped. 'What *is* this? Where the hell are you taking me?'

The highway patrolman turned again, swivelling his body instead of his stiff, twisted neck.

'Night court,' his whisper trailed back on a thread of wind.

'*Night* court!' Bob halted completely, anger stiffening his resolve not to be railroaded into anything, no matter what he had done to that lovely little girl back there in the ditch. 'Say! Is this some kind of a gag? A kangaroo court, is it? You figure on lynching me after you've ... ?'

He glanced about the lonely graveyard in swift panic, wondering if he could make a dash for it. This was no orderly minion of the law, this crazy deformed figure stalking ahead of him! A crank, maybe? Some joker dressed up as a highway patrolman ... ? Bob backed away a few steps, glancing left and right. A mental case, a crackpot ... ?

He froze. The officer held a gun levelled at his heart.

'Don't try it!' The whisper cracked like a whiplash. 'Come on, bud. You'll get a fair trial in this court—fairer than the likes of you deserve!'

Bob moved forward, helpless to resist. The officer turned his back, almost insolently, and stalked on up the narrow road. At the steps of the chapel he stood aside, however, waving his gun for Bob to open the heavy doors. Swallowing on a dry throat, he obeyed — and started violently as the rusty hinges made a sound like a hollow groan.

Then, hesitantly, his heart beginning to hammer with apprehension, Bob stepped inside. Groping his way into the darker interior of the chapel, he paused for a moment to let his eyes become accustomed to the gloom. Row on row of hardwood benches faced a raised dais, on which was a pulpit. Here, Bob realised with a chill coursing down his spine, local funeral services were held for those to be buried in the churchyard outside. As he moved forward, his footsteps echoed eerily among the beamed rafters overhead . . .

Then he saw them. People in those long rows of benches! There seemed to be over a hundred of them, seated in silent groups of twos and threes, facing the pulpit. In a little alcove, set aside for the choir, Bob saw another, smaller group — and found himself suddenly counting them with a surge of panic. There were twelve in the choir box. Twelve, the number of a jury! Dimly he could see their white faces, with dark hollows for eyes, turning to follow his halting progress down the aisle.

Then, like an echo of a voice, deep and reverberating, someone called his name.

'The defendant will please take the stand. . . !'

Bob stumbled forward, his scalp prickling at the ghostly resemblance of this mock-trial to the one in which he had been acquitted only that morning. As though propelled by unseen hands, he found himself hurrying to a seat beside the pulpit, obviously reserved for one of the elders, but now serving as a witness-stand. He sank into the big chair, peering through the half-darkness in an effort to make out some of the faces around him . . .

Then, abruptly, as the 'bailiff' stepped forward to 'swear him in', he stifled a cry of horror.

The man had no face. Where his features had been there was a raw, reddish mass. From this horror, somehow, a nightmare slit of mouth formed the words: '. . . to tell the truth, the whole truth, and nothing but the truth, so help you God?'

'I . . . I do,' Bob murmured; and compared to the whispered tones of the bailiff, his own voice shocked him with its loudness.

'State your name.'

'R-robert Trask . . .'

'Your third offence, isn't it, Mr Trask?' the judge whispered drily. 'A habitual reckless driver . . .'

Bob was shaking now, caught in the grip of a nameless terror. What was this? Who were all these people, and why had they had him brought here by a motorcycle cop with a twisted . . . ?

He caught his breath again sharply, stifling another cry as the figure of a dignified elderly man became visible behind the pulpit, where he had been half-shrouded in shadow. Bob blinked at him, sure that his stern white face was familiar — very familiar, not in the haunting way in which that child had seemed known to him, lying there crushed under his car. This man . . .

His head reeled all at once. Of course! Judge Abernathy! Humorous, lenient old Judge Ab, his father's friend, who had served in the Gareyville circuit court . . . Bob gulped. In 1932! Why, he had been only a youngster then! Twenty years would make this man all of ninety-eight years old, if . . . And it was suddenly that 'if' which made Bob's scalp prickle with uneasiness. *If he were alive.* Judge Ab was *dead*! Wasn't he? Hadn't he heard his mother and dad talking about the old man, years ago; talking in hushed, sorrowful tones about the way he had been killed by a hit-and-run driver who had never been caught?

Bob shook his head, fighting off the wave of dizziness and nausea that was creeping over him again. It was crazy, the way his imagination was running away with him! Either this was not Judge Ab, but some old fellow who vaguely resembled him in this half-light . . . Or it *was* Judge Ab, alive, looking no older than he had twenty-odd years ago, at which time he was supposed to have been killed.

Squinting out across the rows of onlookers, Bob felt a growing sense of unreality. He could just make out, dimly, the features of the people seated in the first two rows of benches. Other faces, pale blurs against the blackness, moved restlessly as he peered at them . . . Bob gasped. His eyes made out things in the semi-gloom that he wished he had not seen. Faces mashed and cut beyond the semblance of a face! Bodies without arms! One girl . . . He swayed in his chair sickly; her shapely form was without a head!

He got a grip on his nerves with a tremendous effort. Of course! It wasn't real; it was all a horrible, perverted sort of practical joke! All these people were tricked up like corpses in a Chamber-of-Commerce 'horror' parade. He tried to laugh, but his lips jerked with the effort . . . Then they quivered, sucking in breath.

The 'prosecuting attorney' had stepped forward to question him – as, hours ago, he had been questioned by the attorney for Limestone County. Only . . . Bob shut his eyes quickly. It couldn't be! They wouldn't, whoever these people in this lonely chapel might be, they *wouldn't* make up some old Negro to look like the one whose wagon he had . . . had . . .

The figure moved forward, soundlessly. Only someone who had seen him on the morgue slab, where they had taken him after the accident, could have dreamed up that woolly white wig, that wrinkled old black face, and . . . and that gash at his temple, on which now the blood seemed to have dried forever . . .

'Hidey, Cap'm,' the figure said in a diffident whisper. 'I got to ast you a few questions. Don't lie, now! Dat's de *wust* thing you could do — tell a lie in dis-*yeah* court! . . .'Bout how fast you figger you was goin' when you run over de girl-baby?'

'I . . . Pretty fast,' he blurted. 'Sixty-five, maybe seventy an hour.'

The man he had killed nodded, frowning. 'Yassuh. Dat's about right, sixty-five accordin' to de officer here.' He glanced at the patrolman with the twisted neck, who gave a brief, grotesque nod of agreement.

Bob waited sickly. The old Negro — or whoever was dressed up as a dead man — moved towards him, resting his hand on the ornate rail of the chapel pulpit.

'Cap'm . . .' His soft whisper seemed to come from everywhere, rather than from the moving lips in that black face. 'Cap'm . . . *why?* How come you was drivin' fifteen miles over the speed-limit on this-yeah road? Same road where you run into my wagon . . .'

The listeners in the tiers of pews began to sway all at once, like reeds in the wind. '*Why?*' someone in the rear took up the word, and then another echoed it, until a faint rhythmic chant rose and fell all over the crowded chapel:

'*Why? Why? Why? . . . Why? Why? Why?*'

'*Order!*' The 'judge', the man who looked like the judge long dead, banged softly with his gavel; or it could have been a shutter banging at one of those arched chapel windows, Bob thought strangely.

The chanting died away. Bob swallowed nervously. For the old Negro was looking up at him expectantly, waiting for an answer to his simple question — the question echoed by those looking and listening from that eerie 'courtroom'. *Why?* Why was he driving so fast? If he could only make up something, some good reason . . .

'I . . . I had a date with my girl,' Bob heard his own voice, startling in its volume compared to the whispers around him.

'Yassuh?' The black prosecutor nodded gently. 'She was gwine off someplace, so's you had to hurry to catch up wid her? Or else, was she bad-off sick and callin' for you . . . ?'

'I . . . No,' Bob said, miserably honest. 'No. There wasn't any hurry. I just . . . didn't want to . . .' He gestured futilely. 'I wanted to be with her as quick as I could! Be-because I love her . . .' He paused, waiting to hear a titter of mirth ripple over the listeners.

There was no laughter. Only silence, sombre and accusing.

'Yassuh.' Again the old Negro nodded his greying head, the head with the gashed temple. 'All of us wants to be wid the ones we love. We don't want to waste no time doin' it . . . Only, you got to remember de Lawd give each of us a certain po'tion of time to use. And he don't aim for us to cut off de supply dat belong to somebody else. They got a right to live and love and be happy, too!'

The grave words hit Bob like a hammer blow – or like, he thought oddly, words he had been forming in his own mind, but holding off, not letting himself think because they might hurt. He fidgeted in the massive chair, twisting his hands together in sudden grim realisation. Remorse had not, up to this moment, touched him deeply. But it now brought tears welling up, acid-like, to burn his eyes.

'Oh . . . please!' he burst out. 'Can't we get this over with, this . . . this crazy mock-trial? I don't know who you are, all you people here. But I know you've . . . you've been incensed because my . . . my folks pulled some wires and got me out of two traffic accidents that I . . . I should have been punished for! Now I've . . . I've run over a little girl, and you're afraid if I go to regular court-trial, my uncle will get me free again; is that it? That's it, isn't it . . . ?' he lashed out, half rising. 'All this . . . this masquer-ade! Getting yourselves up like . . . like people who are dead . . . ! You're doing it to scare me!' He laughed harshly. 'But it doesn't scare me, kid tricks like . . . like . . .'

He broke off, aware of another figure that had moved forward, rising from one of the forward benches. A burly man in overalls, wearing a trucker's cap ... One big square hand was pressed to his side, and he walked as though in pain. Bob recognised those rugged features with a new shock.

'Kid ... listen!' His rasping whisper sounded patient, tired. 'We ain't here to scare nobody ... Hell, that's for Hallowe'en parties! The reason we hold court here, night after night, tryin' some thick-skinned jerk who thinks he owns the road ... Look, we just want t' know *why*; see? Why we had to be killed. Why some nice joe like you, with a girl and a happy future ahead of 'im, can't understand that ... that *we* had a right to live, too! Me! Just a dumb-lug of a truck jockey, maybe ... But I was doin' all right. I was gettin' by, raisin' my kids right ...' The square hand moved from the man's side, gestured briefly, and pressed back again.

'I figured to have my fool appendix out, soon as I made my run and got back home that Sunday. Only, you ... Couldn't you have spared me ten seconds, mac?' the hoarse whisper accused. 'Wouldn't you loan me that much of your ... your precious time, instead of takin' away all of mine? Mine, and this ole darkey's? And tonight ...'

An angry murmur swept over the onlookers, like a rising wind.

'*Order!*' The gavel banged again, like a muffled heartbeat. 'The accused is not on trial for previous offences. Remarks of the defence attorney—who is distinctly out of order—will be stricken from the record. Does the prosecution wish to ask the defendant any more questions to determine the *reason* for the accident?'

The old Negro shook his head, shrugging. 'Nawsuh, Jedge. Reckon not.'

Bob glanced sideways at the old man who looked so like Judge Ab. He sucked in a quick breath as the white head turned, revealing a hideously crushed skull matted with some dark brown substance. Hadn't his father said something, years ago, about that hit-and-run driver running a wheel over his old friend's head? Were those ... where those tyre-tread marks on this man's white collar ... ? Bob ground his teeth. How far would these Hallowe'en mummers go to make their macabre little show realistic ... ?

But now, to his amazement, the burly man in truck's garb moved forward, shrugging.

'Okay, your Honour,' his hoarse whisper apologised. 'I ... I know it's too late for justice, not for us here. And if the court appoints me to defend this guy, I'll try ... Look buddy,' his whisper softened. 'You have reason to believe your girl was steppin' out on you? That why you was hurryin', jumpin' the speed-limit, to get there before she ...? You were out of your head, crazy-jealous?'

Bob glared. 'Say!' he snapped. 'This is going too far, dragging my fiancée's name into this ... this fake trial ... Go ahead! I'm guilty of reckless driving—three times! I admit it! There was no reason on this earth for me to be speeding, no excuse for running over that ... that poor little kid! It's ... it's just that I ...' His voice broke, 'I didn't *see* her! Out here in the middle of nowhere—a child! How was I to know? The highway was clear, and then all at once, there she was right in front of my car ... But ... but I *was* going too fast. I deserve to be lynched! Nothing you do to me would be enough ...'

He crumpled in the chair, stricken with dry sobs of remorse. But fear, terror of this weirdly made-up congregation, left him slowly, as, looking from the judge to the highway patrolman, from the old Negro to the trucker, he saw only pity in their faces, and a kind of sad bewilderment.

'But—why? Why need it happen?' the elderly judge asked softly, in a stern voice Bob thought he could remember from childhood. 'Why does it go on and on? This senseless slaughter! If we could only *understand* ...! If we could only make the living understand, and stop and think, before it's too late for ... another such as we. There is no such thing as an accidental death! Accidents are murders – because someone could have prevented them!'

The white-haired man sighed, like a soft wind blowing through the chapel. The sigh was caught up by others, until it rose and fell like a wailing gust echoing among the rafters.

Bob shivered, hunched in his chair. The hollow eyes of the judge fixed themselves on him, stern but pitying. He hung his head, and buried his face in his hands, smearing blood from the cut on his forehead.

'I ... I ... Please! Please don't say any more!' he sobbed. 'I guess I just didn't realise, I was too wrapped up in my own selfish ...' His voice broke. 'And now it's too late ...'

Silently, the shadowy figures of the old Negro and the burly truck driver moved together in a kind of grim comradeship. They looked at the judge mutely as though awaiting his decision. The gaunt figure with the crushed skull cleared his throat in a way Bob thought he remembered . . .

'Too late? Yes . . . for these two standing before you. But the dead,' his sombre whisper rose like a gust of wind in the dark chapel, 'the dead cannot punish the living. They are part of the past, and have no control over the present . . . or the future.'

'Yet, sometimes,' the dark holes of eyes bored into Bob's head sternly, 'the dead can guide the living, by giving them a glimpse into the future. The future as it will be . . . unless the living use their power to change it! Do you understand, Robert Trask? Do you understand that you are on trial in this night court, not for the past but for the future . . . ?'

Bob shook his head, bewildered. 'The . . . future? I don't understand. I . . .' He glanced up eagerly. 'The little girl! You . . . you mean, she's all right? She isn't dead . . . ?' he pressed, hardly daring to hope.

'She is not yet born,' the old man whispered quietly. 'But one day you will see her, just as you saw her tonight, lying crushed under your careless wheels . . . unless . . .' The whisper changed abruptly; became the dry official voice of a magistrate addressing his prisoner. 'It is therefore the judgement of this court that, in view of the defendant's plea of guilty and in view of his extreme youth and of his war-record, sentence will be suspended pending new evidence of criminal behaviour in the driver's seat of a motor vehicle. If such new evidence should be brought to the attention of this court, sentence shall be pronounced and the extreme penalty carried out . . . Do you understand, Mr Trask?' the grave voice repeated. '*The extreme penalty!* . . . Case dismissed.'

The gavel banged. Bob nodded dazedly, again burying his face in his hands and shaking with dry sobs. A wave of dizziness swept over him. He felt the big chair tilt, it seemed, and suddenly he was falling, falling forward into a great black vortex that swirled and eddied . . .

Light snatched him back to consciousness, a bright dazzling light that pierced his eyeballs and made him gag with nausea. Hands were pulling at him, lifting him. Then, slowly, he became aware of two figures bending over him: a gnome-like little man with a lantern, and a tall, sunburned young man in the uniform of a highway patrolman. It was not, Bob noted blurrily, the same one, the one with the twisted neck ... He sat up, blinking.

'My, my, young feller!' The gnome with the lantern was trying to help him up from where he lay on the chapel floor in front of the pulpit. 'Nasty lump on your head there! I'm the sexton: live up the road a piece. I heard your car hit the ditch a while ago, and called the Highway Patrol. Figgered you was drunk...' He sniffed suspiciously, then shrugged. 'Don't smell drunk. What happened? You fall asleep at the wheel?'

Bob shut his eyes, groaning. He let himself be helped to one of the front pews and leaned back against it heavily before answering. Better tell the truth now. Get it over with...

'The ... little girl. Pinned under my car—you found her?' He forced out the words sickly. 'I ... didn't see her, but ... It was my fault. I was ... driving too fast. Too fast to stop when she stepped out right in front of my ...'

He broke off, aware that the tall tanned officer was regarding him with marked suspicion.

'What little girl?' he snapped. 'There's nobody pinned under your car, buddy! I looked. Your footprints were the only ones leading away from the accident ... and I traced them here! Besides, you were dripping blood from that cut on you ... Say! You trying to kid somebody?'

'No, no!' Bob gestured wildly. 'Who'd kid about a thing like ... ? Maybe the other highway patrolman took her away on his motorcycle! He ... All of them ... There didn't seem any doubt that she'd been killed instantly. But then, the judge said she ... she wasn't even born yet! They made me come here, to ... to try me! In ... night court, they called it! All of them pretending to be ... dead people, accident victims. Blood all over them! Mangled ...' He checked himself, realising how irrational he sounded. 'I fainted,' his voice trailed uncertainly. 'I guess when they ... they heard you coming, they all ran away ...'

'Night court?' The officer arched one eyebrow, tipped back his cap, and eyed Bob dubiously. 'Say, you sure you're sober, buddy? Or maybe you got a concussion ... There's been nobody here. Not a soul; has there, Pop?'

'Nope.' The sexton lifted his lamp positively, causing shadows to dance weirdly over the otherwise empty chapel. A film of dust covered the pews, undisturbed save where Bob himself now sat. 'Ain't been nary a soul here since the Wilkins funeral; that

was Monday three weeks ago. My, you never saw the like o'
flowers . . .'

The highway patrolman gestured him to silence, peering at
Bob once more. 'What was that you said about another speed
cop? There was no report tonight. What was his badge number?
You happen to notice?'

Bob shook his head vaguely; then dimly recalled numbers he
had seen on a tarnished shield pinned to that shadowy uniform.

'Eight something . . . 84! That was it! And . . . and he had a
kind of twisted set to his head . . .'

The officer scowled suddenly, hands on hips. 'Sa-ay!' he said
in a cold voice. 'What're you tryin' to pull? Nobody's worn Badge
No. 84 since Sam Lacy got killed two years ago. Chasin' a speed-
crazy high school kid, who swerved and made him fall off his
motor. Broke his neck!' He compressed his lips grimly. 'You're
tryin' to pull some kind of gag about *that*?'

'No! N-no . . . !' Bob rose shakily to his feet. 'I . . . I . . . Maybe
I just dreamed it all! That clonk on the head . . .' He laughed all
at once, a wild sound, full of hysterical relief. 'You're positive
there was no little girl pinned under my wheel? No . . . no signs
of . . . ?'

He started towards the wide-flung doors of the chapel, reeling
with laughter. But it had all seemed so real! Those nightmare
faces, the whispering voices: that macabre trial for a traffic fatality
that had never happened anywhere but in his own overwrought
imagination . . . !

Still laughing, he climbed into his convertible; found it undam-
aged by its dive into the ditch, and backed out onto the road
again. He waved. Shrugging, grinning, the highway officer and
the old sexton waved back, visible in a yellow circle of lantern
light.

Bob gunned his motor and roared away. A lone tourist, round-
ing a curve, swung sharply off the pavement to give him room
as he swooped over on the wrong side of the yellow line. Bob
blew his horn mockingly, and trod impatiently on the accelerator.
Marian must be tired of waiting! And the thought of holding
her in his arms, laughing with her, telling her about the crazy,
dream-trial . . . Dead men! Trying him, the living, for the traffic
death of a child yet to be born! 'The extreme penalty!' If not
lynching, what would that be? He smiled, amused. Was anything

that could happen to a man really 'a fate worse than death . . .'?
Bob's smile froze.

Quite suddenly his foot eased up on the accelerator. His eyes
widened, staring ahead at the dark highway illuminated by the
twin glare of his headlights. Sweat popped out on his cool forehead all at once. Jerkily his hands yanked at the smooth plastic
of the steering wheel, pulling the convertible well over to the
right side of the highway . . .

In that instant, Bob thought he knew where he had seen the
hauntingly familiar features of that lovely girl lying dead,
crushed, under the wheel of his car. 'The extreme penalty?' He
shuddered, and slowed down, driving more carefully into the
darkness ahead. The darkness of the future . . .

For, the child's blonde hair and long lashes, he knew with a
swift chill of dread, had been a tiny replica of Marian's . . . and
the tip-tilted pixie eyes, closed in violent death, had borne a
startling resemblance to his own.

ACCIDENT ZONE

Ramsey Campbell

There are certain stretches of road that earn themselves the reputation of being particularly deadly. Some are open lanes of motorway; others meandering roads in rural or mountainous districts. On all of them, drivers have spoken of suddenly being overcome by fear for no apparent reason, of the car inexplicably breaking down, or, most unnerving of all, of being conscious of supernatural forces at work. In Wyoming in the USA, for example, there is a stretch of road where dozens of drivers have braked and skidded to avoid a car with blazing headlights when there proved to be nothing there, and in the UK at a point on the A40, the ghost of a 'man' has been regularly reported walking directly into the paths of vehicles . . . although no body is ever found. Ramsey Campbell takes just such a locality as his theme in 'Accident Zone'.

Ramsey Campbell (1946–) is the British writer whose discovery of the horror stories of H. P. Lovecraft — another of the famous contributors to Weird Tales *—inspired him to become a writer of macabre fiction, now regarded as one of the finest contemporary practitioners in the genre. From early successes like the Lovecraft-influenced* Demons by Daylight *(1973), he became more focused on the evil in mankind with* The Doll who Ate his Mother *(1976) and, more recently still, he has dealt with alienation and possession in novels such as* The Nameless *(1981),* The One Safe Place *(1995) and* The Last Voice They Hear *(1998). His collection of 30 years of short stories,* Alone With the Horrors *(1993), won a World Fantasy Award and the Bram Stoker Award. Of Campbell's various stories that take driving as their theme — including 'The Sneering' and 'Root Cause', both of which are highly recommended — 'Accident Zone' is my particular favourite and is here reprinted after being unavailable for more than a decade.*

Blake had walked some miles from his hotel when he saw the mirror. He'd exhausted Keswick and its environs within three days, or the weather had exhausted him; he disliked having to wait outside his hotel for the hourly bus while rain teemed on his head, and disliked being blinded by the grey steamed windows as he rode the bus to the Lakeland coach-tour station. Today had been the first fine day of his holiday in the Lakes. He'd had them make him a box lunch and had set out from his hotel, away from Keswick. He was tired of towns.

At noon clouds still overlapped the hills and streamed like smoke between the trees. The sun glinted dully, then as the afternoon progressed began to blaze. Blake followed the road for a while, crossing from one meagre verge to the other to protect himself from blind corners. Eventually, offended by the belches of cars and the glare of litter, he left the road and climbed a hill. The wet earth smacked its lips at his feet. He reached the top, where pale rock protruded like teeth from the grass, and gazed down.

Four hundred feet below, cars scurried like spiders on threads. Blake took deep breaths and felt victorious. For the first time this year he could ignore cars. In Keswick they challenged each other in the narrow streets, snarling; in Liverpool they demanded that he help design housing projects to accommodate them as well as the tenants. He stood up and urinated towards them. Then he sat down on the rocks and ate his lunch.

It was as he threw his head back to catch the dregs of coffee that he saw the mirror. Near the foot of the hill, on the side opposite that he'd climbed, was a hairpin bend. The pin was hardly open. At the hinge of the bend, stuck into a rough green mat of bushes, was a large mirror on a pole. Equidistant from it two cars were parked, at the verge of each approach to the bend.

Blake frowned. He had planned to descend that side of the hill, but the mirror troubled him. It seemed trivial and in bad taste, like a glass-headed pin thrust into a tapestry. Still, he thought, it was absurd enough to be enjoyable. If he responded to it with the shocked laugh it deserved, it wouldn't spoil his landscape. In Liverpool, to the dismay of passers-by, he sometimes laughed at the sight of the white boxes of highrise flats against blue sky and clouds; Magritte in three dimensions.

We need surrealism more than ever, he thought. For sanity.

The mirror's there to prevent accidents, he responded.

Oh shut up, he thought. This is my landscape today. The drivers can have it tomorrow.

He descended the hill. The ground was beginning to steam; each hundred feet further down he felt as if he'd pulled on another set of clothes. From the top he'd seen a lake, some miles across the fields. He intended to make for it, avoiding the mirror, but the hill seemed patched with sponge, and his zig-zag descent across firmer ground brought him slithering to the slope just above the mirror. There he stopped, gasping, for he felt as if he'd stepped from a hot bath and plunged into ice.

It must be an effect of shade, he thought. But he couldn't see how; the sunlight was pouring over him. Perhaps, there was a pond near, steeping the area in clamminess. Shivering, he stepped into the road.

The brandished mirror loomed above him. As he crossed the road his head bulged in the mirror and his body dwindled. He recoiled, reminded of humanoid balloons he'd tried to inflate when a child, squeezing air up into the head and blowing again until the head burst. He surveyed both stretches of road, looking for a route to the lake, but both were edged by tangles of bushes beyond which lay muddy fields. He sensed the mirror staring over his head and turned again, angry with himself. God, the quiet ached. Too much so, he thought suddenly, given the nearby cars. Well, there was no point in standing about. He would follow the road away from Keswick. Sooner or later there must be a path towards the lake.

He strode away from the mirror. There was a sign just beyond the parked car; that might help him. Though it seemed odd to park the car with its bonnet between the uprights of the sign. In fact, now Blake came closer, he began to suspect that the car had been dumped. Yes, it had: the front of the car looked like a trampled can. Cursing whoever had abandoned it, Blake came abreast of the car and read the sign. ACCIDENT ZONE, it said. DON'T LET THIS HAPPEN TO YOU.

From the edge of his eye Blake glimpsed movement. He glanced towards the mirror. For a moment he was sure he'd seen an object appear in the mirror and dodge out of sight again. An animal, no doubt, which had brushed the edge of the reflection. From his position by the sign he could see the door and a smashed windscreen. The second car was also displayed beneath a sign. Blake stared at the empty rusting cars, the attentive mirror, the emphatic almost suburban silence. Then he began to hurry away down the road.

He had taken only a few paces when he heard a car rattling towards him. It swerved around a bend ahead and rushed closer. He retreated onto the verge and the car sped by, deafening him and spouting fumes. Blake stared after it furiously. The students piled inside it ignored the wrecked car. As they reached the mirror Blake was attacked by nausea: hot with rage, he'd suddenly felt as if all his heat had been drained from him. The car skidded across the bend, its reflection squeezed like rubber into a curve, regained control at the last moment and sped on.

Blake took a step towards the mirror. Then he turned and made off down the road. He was still shivering from the gulp of heat that had seemed to be drawn from him. An odd image persisted in his mind: as the car had been caught in the mirror, the glass had trembled like a bubble and small pale globules, or so his memory interpreted them, had appeared around the rim. Distortion caused by the heat and the exhaust of the car, no doubt. But he was sure there must be a flaw in the glass.

He was still shivering as he walked. A wind had started to hiss in the trees bordering the road. The clouds were gathering again, and trickled down the hills. Beyond the trees he encountered a path leading from the road in the direction of the lake; it was composed of brown mud and stones. He would have attempted it, but felt weak. He blamed the chill that had crept into him near the mirror, and an insidious depression that he had taken away with him. Should have known cars wouldn't let me alone, he thought.

He continued walking, but mechanically; the depression had robbed him of motive. Above him chiselled rock caught tatters of cloud. After half an hour's walk the landscape softened; trees swayed, asleep on their roots, and butterflies bloomed on the trunks. He rounded a bend and saw a small white cottage before which stood several white wicker tables and chairs. A pole held up a rotating double-headed string: TEAS.

This time he didn't question its taste. He sat down at a table in the artificial glade. He was still weak, and felt exhausted and hungry. He glanced about for a waitress and saw a hoarding which had been screened from him by the trees, on the edge of the glade. Protected by glass, a huge enlargement of a newspaper

report gleamed between the trunks. I WAS HOSTILE AND
AFRAID, SAYS DRIVER.

A car engine whined like a dentist's drill across the hills. Blake
read the hoarding; patches of light surrounded by leaf-shadow
fluttered and slipped across the words. 'In the two-year period
since the erection of the mirror more fatal accidents have occurred
at the bend, five less than in the previous two years. Is there a
case for stronger action? Mr Eric Mayne, 42, of Blubberfosters,
survived an accident at the bend. "I saw a car coming in the
other direction," he told us. "I slowed down but I still thought
we were both going too fast. I was afraid there would be an
accident. Then I got angry and turned my headlights on full. I
was being very aggressive, I felt it was his turn to slow down. I
think the lights blinded him." Mr Mayne was lucky; the other
driver died. It is up to the drivers not to turn our country into
a jungle, and up to us to make sure they do.'

Forthright but ungrammatical, Blake thought. He turned his
back on the hoarding and gazed across the landscape. Clouds
were now pouring down the higher hills. An old lady in an
ankle-length kaftan, with white hair like a poodle's fur, emerged
from the cottage and took his order for tea and scones. 'You're
not in a car, are you?' she said. 'I saw you looking at my board.
Well, I'm glad to see someone's still walking.'

Five minutes later she returned with the tea. Shadows were
rushing across the landscape. 'Yes, I do like the Lakes very much,'
Blake said.

'Any life would be bearable if it ended here. That was always
my scheme of things,' she said. 'It's the atmosphere I love. In ten
years it's made me its own.'

'I'm fond of atmospheres,' Blake said.

'One thing spoils it. That.' She pointed to the hoarding. 'Oh,
not the report. I put that up myself. I meant the place they're
talking about. I wish it weren't so near. The bus to Keswick goes
through it, and I dread going.'

'I don't think I would dread it, just dislike it,' Blake said.

'Ah, but have you been there? Well, tell me your opinion.'

'I thought it was grotesque,' Blake said. 'Entirely out of place.
But necessary, perhaps.'

'You'll have to take the bus to Keswick to get back to your
hotel, unless you intend to walk. You'll probably be soaked if
you walk. Now, you remember what I'm going to tell you. Notice

what happens when the bus comes near the bend. Everyone will stop talking. They always do, and they couldn't tell you why. They'd probably say they're afraid to distract the driver. But why should they be? Driving's his job, and he knows the road. Why should he crash there, particularly? You tell me that.'

'I'm not sure what you're saying,' Blake said.

'I'm talking about fear and hostility,' she said, gesturing towards the hoarding. 'So much of that in a place must leave its mark. It's even there when you're walking, let alone driving. You must have felt it.'

'What, fear and hostility?' Blake said. 'Not at all.'

He stood up and paid. 'You're welcome to wait here for the bus,' she said. 'Look at the sky.'

'I'll survive. I think I'll walk until the bus comes,' Blake said. 'Good for me.'

Twenty minutes later he heard the bus behind him. He hesitated, then strode on. The bus swept by, and he hurried up a slope at the edge of the road. From there he could watch the lights of the bus dwindling towards the mirror. Clouds had seeped into the sun, dousing it. He strained his eyes. The lighted windows slipped through the mirror, and as they did so they shuddered. The bus itself negotiated the bend with ease. Blake ran down the slope, frowning. Rage was beginning to sputter inside him. He hurried towards the mirror. He was determined to discover exactly what had spoilt his day.

Near the mirror he left the road. He picked his way in the draining light across the side of the hill. Cars were already casting paths of light before them and rolling them up. He sat on a rock shelving from the hill, and gazed down. The landscape glimmered with the threat of a storm, and the glow coated the wrecked cars. Between them the mirror reared up, an empty eye.

Soon the landscape had lost all its colour. Sky and earth merged. Blake yawned and shivered, for his body heat was dissipating. He'd thought the ground would give out heat at twilight; on the contrary, it seemed to be drinking his own heat. The mirror was only faintly visible now, a thick blob of grey. He drummed his heels on the rock, wishing for the first time in months that he had a cigarette. What the hell he was doing here he didn't know. So much for gestures. No doubt there wouldn't be another bus for almost an hour.

A car crept towards the bend, its headlights awakening almost at the mirror. Blake shook himself alert. The headlights peered out of the mirror, and silhouetted on their reflection a small round shape bobbed up, like a teasing target in a shooting gallery. Blake stood up, squinting, and the headlights swung at him before sweeping away. No, there was nothing except the smouldering impression of the headlights on his eyes. Not so odd, he thought; it had probably been a moth, made to look nearly spherical by the blaze of the lights. The mirror would attract night flyers.

He sat down again. His weakness had returned. Not surprisingly, when it was so cold. If it hadn't been for that bloody woman he would be halfway to Keswick by now. Talking about fear and hostility – well, he wasn't hostile except to the situation he'd allowed to take him over, he wished he could go back and stuff that down her throat. And I'm certainly not afraid, he shouted to himself. Just because he jumped when something appeared in the mirror it didn't mean he was afraid. He would sit for a few minutes to see whether he regained his strength. If not he would walk away.

He watched two cars approaching. Their headlights trickled thinly down the distant roads, then began to widen as they poured closer. As the headlights of one touched the mirror the glass began to shift like a bubble about to burst.

No, it wasn't his eyes. The surface of the mirror was perceptibly trembling. It must be a vibration set up by the approach of the car. When the second car drew near and the mirror's shivering increased Blake was sure he was right. The beam was swinging out of the mirror like an uncontrolled searchlight; it roamed across the side of the hill as if searching for him. The second car drew into the verge and allowed the first to pass. Don't blame him, Blake thought. I'd be afraid too.

The second car moved off slowly. As its lights returned to the mirror the reflection was surrounded. Blake leaned forward. An iris of small pale shapes had appeared around the light, jostling like bubbles on the rim of a pan coming to the boil.

Blake ran down the hill, fixing his gaze on the mirror. It couldn't be a flaw in the glass, not one that moved around the edge of the mirror and sank back out of sight and reappeared. He ran faster to reach the mirror before the light withdrew, and tripped on a loose rock. He hit the ground with a sucking thud.

A prickling touched the back of his neck. The grass before him hissed. It was raining.

Raindrops on a mirror and I almost break my leg, he thought. My God, I'm overwrought. The rain was springing back from the ground. He ran towards the shelter of the bushes behind the mirror. As he passed the mirror he peered up. As far as he could see the glass was beaded by drops, but few of them were around the edge. He shrugged angrily and made for the bushes.

The leaves sizzled around him. After perhaps ten minutes the rain ceased. He emerged, shaking himself like a dog. His hair dripped about his face; his clothes clung to him like seaweed. He stood beneath the mirror and laughed. No, I'm not going to blame you, he thought. This entire absurd business is my own doing.

He heard a car approaching. Perhaps he could thumb a lift. He waited beneath the mirror, leaning forward to avoid its tassels of rain. Points of light flashed from bush to bush as the car neared the bend. No use; it was coming from Keswick. Might have known, Blake thought. Ah well, I'm saved from importuning. He turned to begin walking, then halted. No point in giving the driver more to avoid. The headlights felt their way towards him, and the mirror sprang up at his feet.

It was reflected in a puddle which had gathered in a dip in the road. For a moment it shone like the moon. Then it shrank. The iris had reappeared; the bubbles crowded and fought for place. Leaning closer, Blake saw that the lowest bubble was nothing of the kind. It contained a vicious grin and glaring eyes.

All his heat rushed out of him. His skin shuddered. He twisted to stare at the mirror. Apart from the probing headlights it was empty. But he had the impression that as he had turned, a darker iris had retreated into the frame of the mirror. He was still staring upward when the car whipped past, lifting a wave from the puddle and drenching him.

Blake shouted in rage, glaring up at the mirror. How many deaths had been focused in the glass? Ten that he'd read of, and there had been more than a dozen small round shapes in the mirror. The puddle might have given them faces, earth for eyes and ripples for grins, he argued with himself. They hadn't been clear. But he was already struggling up the hillside, searching in the sodden grass for the loose rock.

When he found it he slithered down to the mirror. He imagined the faces peering down at him through the dark. You won't take any more with you, he shouted. Shaking with anger and revulsion and renewed cold, he threw the rock.

The mirror was stouter than he had anticipated. The rock thudded at his feet. He thought he could hear a dry sound like that of disturbed mice. Oh no you don't, he thought. He hurled the rock again. Three more throws and shattered glass plunged into the earth in front of him.

He smiled grimly and let his shoulders slump. Then he heard two cars converging towards him.

My God, what have I done? he shouted. I must be mad. It's the mirror's fault, no, this whole morbid area. Headlights slashed around bends on both sides of him. He threw the rock into the bushes and ran into the road. Perhaps he could stop them. Perhaps one would drive him into Keswick, where he could report someone's act of vandalism on the mirror.

The car coming from Keswick was nearer. He raised his arms and urged it to slow down. He pushed it back with his hands. It slowed for a moment as the driver surveyed him. Then it gathered speed and swerved past him, missing him by inches.

The second car did not.

He heard a metallic squeal and felt a dull agonising thud across the back of his thighs. He was scooped up and slid clawing wildly over metal. His head struck glass. Then the metal whipped from beneath him and he thumped into the mud of the road.

Pain burned through his legs. Above him he heard the chop of car doors, men saying 'Oh Christ', 'Now for heaven's sake keep calm,' and a woman screaming. He turned his head and laid his cheek in bright spotlighted mud. He saw boots walking past his face, squeezing up walls of mud around their footprints. He saw a trailing bootlace drag by, coated with mud like a worm. He heard voices saying 'I think it looks worse than it is, don't worry.' Everything, even the pulse of agony in his legs, felt distant as delirium.

Even the mirror at the top of the pole. Even the jagged black hole in it. 'I know first aid,' someone said. 'Give me a few minutes and I think we can move him. We can't leave him here.' Even the pale struggling blobs which had appeared at the hole in the mirror, like the contents of a spider's torn cocoon. Someone was tying something around his legs. 'We'll have to make a stretcher,' a voice said. 'Can you hear me? We're leaving you for a minute but we'll still be here. You'll be all right.'

No I won't, Blake thought, but he felt detached. He watched the faces stream out of the crack in the mirror, falling through the light like slow leaden bubbles. He watched the string of faces balance on the air and float towards him in disorder, some on their backs, some hanging towards the ground. He closed his eyes. It was worse than delirium. Not until he felt them settle on him like a swarm of insects did he begin to mutter and scream.

'We're coming, just give us a minute, lie still, we're coming,' a voice called. But Blake was writhing as his skin crawled, as light soft objects roved over his body, pulling feebly at him, seeking him beneath the skin. They were trying to prise him out. His skin, or his sense of it, was attenuating.

'My God, what's that?' 'Moths, I think. Look, there they go. Like bloody scavengers,' and he felt himself rolled onto a hard support and lifted. He jolted and sank onto metal. Doors slammed behind him. An engine whirred and he felt the gears engage. He opened his eyes. The mirror and the other car shrank. The displayed wreck swung by, and a chain of pale blobs rose from it and rushed towards the back windows of the car before drifting scattered across the field. Blake moaned. 'Hold on. We'll be in Keswick before you know it,' the driver said, driving Blake towards a wheelchair in Liverpool, a fear of mirrors, and a crawling of the skin which he would scratch until blood flowed.

THE LAST RUN

Alan Dean Foster

Illegal high-speed road races on the motorways of Britain, Europe, America and much of the rest of the world have become increasingly popular in recent years. In England, for instance, such 'road raves' often attract more than a hundred drivers and ten times as many spectators to the motorways of the South and Midlands, while in Germany thousands line the autobahn network whenever they learn from the Internet of a forthcoming road race. Horrendous crashes, serious injuries and deaths are not infrequent occurrences in all these places, and especially in America where the multi-lane highways and long stretches of desert roads in California gave birth to the craze for renegade racing. 'The Last Run' puts the reader right at the heart of this world of raw, howling horsepower.

Alan Dean Foster (1946–), who grew up in one of the road-racing centres of the world, Los Angeles, was inspired to become a writer by the cartoonist Carl Banks and has brought a similar visual brilliance to his storytelling. Foster became well known to readers through his novelisations of several famous movies — among them The Star Trek Log *(1974),* Star Wars *(1976) and* Alien *(1979) — but it was his fantasy trilogy,* Icerigger *(1974),* Mission to the Moulokin *(1979) and* The Deluge Drivers *(1987), that won critical acclaim and big sales on both sides of the Atlantic. 'The Last Run', which Foster wrote for* Fantasy & Science Fiction *magazine in 1982, introduces the Banzai Runners of Interstate 10 and, in particular, a street-racing wizard named Bill Switch who has always been able to outdrive any rival . . . until the day he is suddenly in the race of his life and for his life . . .*

*   *   *

Banzai Runner ain't got no home
Empty highway is where he roam
Gas in his bloodstream
Oil on the brain
Make for a man who drives insane

Everyone knew Bill Switch didn't give a damn about death. People who indulged in the special type of street racing Bill enjoyed couldn't afford to think about it. Not that he and his competitors were *really* crazy. Just indifferent.

When he was fifteen, Switch took an old Willys Jeep belonging to his father and turned it into a passable street racer. Now, to fully appreciate what that means, you have to know something about the structure of a Willys Jeep. Bill's accomplishment was comparable to transforming a Mexican plaster pot into something out of Benvenuto Cellini.

When they sent him to Nam they had the rare good sense to assign him to a motor pool. Bill spent a perfectly happy war toying with armoured personnel carriers and trucks. He turbo-charged a tank long before pentagon researchers and the Chrysler Corporation decided that would be a good idea.

When he came back he opened his own little garage. Speciality work. It could have made him rich. God knows how many professional racing teams wanted the wizard of San Bernardino prepping their formula ones.

Bill always turned them down. That wasn't his style. He got his satisfaction from tricking up street cars and then beating their owners with his own machines. The streets of Southern California became his racetrack, the freeway system his Indianapolis 500.

There were a few others who felt the way Bill did about street racing. Most of them knew Bill, or of him. If they didn't know him they found out fast enough when the quiet big man beat the crap out of them some night on the freeway.

See, Bill Switch and these few others, they weren't your usual street racer. They didn't match hopped-up Fords on Kester in the Valley or low-riding Chevys on the East Side. To this little group, getting a street car up to a hundred and fifty wasn't worth the gas it burnt.

They did their racing on the freeways that encircle greater Los Angeles, in the early morning dark when few other cars were on the road and when the Highway Patrol could look the other way in search of stranded campers and groping adolescents.

A race could cover twenty miles to a hundred or more. The men and women who matched up this way were usually very rich. They had to be, to afford the cars they used. You couldn't call them hot rodders, or street racers.

Even the police called them banzai runners.

> *Banzai Runner, you better watch out*
> *Check your real-view mirror*
> *Got Smokey in a dither*
> *Gonna try and getcha whether*
> *You're ready or not*

I knew Bill because once in a while he deigned to work on my Corvette, a pretty but unmuscular '69 with side pipes but little else. Nice little commuter car, suitable for old ladies and men with delusions of grandeur. Bill's shop was in San Berdoo, and I'd unknowingly dropped by there one day in hopes of getting one of the custom mufflers replaced.

Well, Bill took pity on me and repaired the muffler. He also did something unseen under the hood which took five years and fifty thousand miles off that 'vette's life. In the unpredictable manner of events, we became friends. Not real close. Just Hi, howareya, smile and wave. That sort of thing. Bill liked to pick my brain, which I willingly gave him access to. In turn, he'd usually let me know on what night he'd have a little match race set up.

I'll never forget that particular night. Sultry Southern Californian September midnight, all grey outlines clad in tropical overtones. There were two challenging Bill. It's unusual for more than one at a time to take on a competitor. Bill relished the opportunity.

One of them was a prominent actor. You'd recognise the name, so I better keep my mouth shut, just in case. I'm not the litigious type.

He drove a Ferrari Boxer. Decent car, smooth of line and painted fire-engine red as a whore's nail polish. The actor shammied it lovingly, boasting to anyone who'd listen how he was going to cream the Wisp's ass. That was Bill's nickname. The Wisp, as in Will-o'-the.

In his enthusiasm he forgot about the other driver. He shut up a little when the rest of the competition drove up.

The man who climbed out of the driver's seat wasn't much over five feet in height. He was a plastic surgeon who'd driven all the way out from Beverly Hills just for the race. What you could interpret through the single-piece beige driving suit had about as much fat on it as a culotte steak, despite the body's sixty years.

His car was a Lambourghini Countach, silver, tricked up with special front and rear spoilers, special flare work, and a suspension low enough to decapitate any caterpillar that didn't duck. When he revved that engine it sounded like one of the turbines at Hoover Dam, where I once spent an awed summer day.

The actor paled a little, but then his resolve stiffened and he climbed back into his own car. The Ferrari was tuned perfectly. Its driver might be intimidated but the Boxer was not.

Then Bill arrived. The starting point was just past the Kaiser Steel plant in Fontana. The race would be a short one, just a few miles to the Highland off-ramp. The surgeon and the actor had their first look at Bill's famous Wisp car. they started to laugh, thought better of it, and ended up by looking plain confused.

Bill drove what appeared to be a stock Plymouth station wagon, painted powder blue, with blue curtains on the windows. Except for the low front shocks and oversized tyres it would not have looked out of place carrying groceries from a supermarket.

The actor and the surgeon put their confusion aside and turned serious. Each of them, Bill included, had put up ten thousand, winner take all. The three cars eased out onto the freeway. This early in the morning the little-used stretch of concrete was empty.

The starter fired his pistol. The Lambourghini bellowed and the Ferrari rumbled. You could hardly hear Bill's engine among them.

There was a soft, rising growl from the three cars as they accelerated. I waited with a couple of others at the halfway point, our own cars parked inconspicuously on the shoulder.

As they neared we could see that the Countach was slightly in the lead, the Boxer close but seemingly losing ground, with Bill bringing up the rear. I was trying to watch the surgeon's face through my night binoculars. At the moment he didn't wear the expression of a man I'd want slicing into my guts.

Suddenly above the steady roar a new tone sounded, a deep-throated barrooommm like a five-hundred-pound bomb going off. The Wisp materialised from the darkness. I clocked the Countach at two hundred and thirty miles per as they passed us. The Wisp went by it like a Harley passing a training bike. I wish I could've seen what the surgeon was thinking.

There was a real explosion soon after, as the Countach's straining engine blew. We rushed out and helped the doctor from his car. Somebody put a fire extinguisher on it. Fifty thousand bucks, up in pouf.

The actor lasted a minute or so longer, but slow and steady wasn't going to win this race. He pulled off the freeway too fast to slow down in time, lost control. The Boxer ended up among the heavily taxed grape vines. He came out shaken, more concerned for his face than the car.

> *Ready or not don't worry Wisp none*
> *Over two hundred he's just havin' fun*
> *Lambourghini blown its engine*
> *Ferrari in the ditch*
> *Ain't a one can catch that Wisp,*
>   *Bill Switch*

I was the only one to drive out to meet Bill. He'd pulled off onto Highland, the street as deserted as the freeway. He was lying on a crawly under the car, using a light. He barely fit. Bill Switch was six five, weighed two forty, and couldn't look nasty-mean if he had to.

'Hi,' he called out to my feet. 'How're the others?'

'Okay. The surgeon had guts. He gave it everything he had.'

'Yeah,' echoed Bill's voice from beneath the station wagon. 'You put some of these respectable citizen types in a real vehicle, they go from Jekyll to Hyde in seconds.'

Bill had a 454 Chevy under the hood of the wagon. But that was for casual racing, for going to the market. It only powered the front wheels. Taking up most of the back of the wagon and connected to the rear drive train was a 900-hp Pratt and Whitney aircraft engine, built to go into small racing planes, the kind that zip and snort around chequered pylons. Bill would use the 454 to toy his opponents and then he'd kick in that hibernating airplane plant. With turbocharging, that boosted his total horsepower *way* up over a thousand. That station wagon looked stock, but it had more bracing inside than the Brooklyn Bridge.

But Bill wasn't satisfied. He told me that someday he wanted to put a jet engine into a van, if he could figure out a way to stabilise the damn thing.

We were all alone, with the grape vines and crickets. The others were still helping to tow the doctor's Countach off the freeway and pull the Boxer from the vineyard, when the stranger drove up.

It eased out from the dark hole beneath the overpass and pulled up behind the Wisp wagon. It was painted the blackest black I'd ever seen, so black it was almost purple. Must've been thirty coats of lacquer on it. The headlights burned red because of the special rock shields over them.

I didn't recognise the car, but, then, I was hardly an expert. It wasn't an Indy type, not formula. It didn't look like a Lotus or the custom Mazda. It hardly had any lines at all. The windshield was barely six inches high.

The driver who stepped out was dressed in matching black, a fashion affected by many runners (Bill preferred Jeans and a sweatshirt). He was as tall as Bill but much thinner. I guessed him to be in his forties and wondered what he did for a living. The occupations of banzai runners were often as interesting as their cars.

He leaned against the wagon and waited patiently, smiling unpleasantly at me while he waited for Bill to emerge. The crawly squeaked. Bill saw the newcomer, rose, wiped his hands. His gaze flicked past him to the ebony car behind.

'I hear you like racing,' said the stranger. He nodded towards the freeway. 'You just proved that you could. How'd you like to race me?'

> *Banzai Runner got a challenge now*
> *Funny sort o' guy*
> *Has fire in his eye*
> *Talks funny, kinda wry*
> *And his car . . . oh, wow!*

Bill rubbed his nose. 'I don't know. Don't know your car. That's something of a first for me.'

The stranger's grin widened. 'It's an import. Not Italian, not French.'

'Israeli? I hear they're doing some interesting things over there.'

The man shook his head. 'Not Japanese, either. It's kind of a hybrid of my own design. Does that matter?'

'Nope. Not to me. Just curious.'

'They say you're the best.'

Now it was Bill's turn to smile. 'They're right.'

'I've got five hundred thousand here. In unmarked hundred dollar bills. That'd buy you the engine you want and plenty of time to play with it. You'd never have to work on another old lady's car.'

Bill eyed the money. 'I can't match that, not even if I threw in my shop in the bargain.'

'I wouldn't have any use for your shop,' said the stranger.

'Then what'll I bet?'

The stranger put his arm around Bill's shoulders and the two of them walked out into the grape vines. My skin was beginning to crawl and I was having cold chills despite the heat of the night. I didn't like this guy. I didn't like his smile, his attitude, the funny moan his idling black stiletto of a car made.

None of it seemed to trouble Bill. They strolled back towards the road and I could see them shaking hands. I felt bad about it, but it wasn't my decision to make.

'To be fair we should test endurance as well as speed,' the stranger was saying. 'Of the drivers as well as the cars.'

'I'm agreeable,' said Bill thoughtfully. 'How about from Indio to the border? First one across the bridge is the winner.'

> The Wisp never turned a challenge down
> No black-clad stranger's about to make him frown
> San Berdoo to the River
> Only two hundred mile
> 'It's a race,' said the stranger, with a terrible smile

'Sounds exciting,' said the other driver.

Bill nodded towards the black car. 'You run on alcohol?'

The stranger shook his head. 'Something not nearly so exotic. I propose next Monday night, at two a.m.'

'Good enough.'

Bill never worked as hard as he did that following week. I saw him in his shop on Thursday and he barely glanced up long enough to acknowledge my presence. I knew he was seeing that half million and the jet engine van he'd dreamed of.

I asked Mario, one of his mechanics, what Bill was up to in the stern of the powder-blue wagon.

'Beats the hell out of me, man. He's puttin' in some kind of overdrive or somethin'. Tryin' to drag another five hundred horse out of it.'

I shook my head. 'He's crazy. He'll blow himself up over that distance.'

'It's not for the whole race, I think.' The mechanic spat on the oil-stained concrete. 'If anybody can do it, the Wisp can.'

I was waiting across the bridge Monday night morning. Not too many people knew about the race. Those who did were spread out along the length of the chosen route. A big crowd would tip off the Highway Patrol that something unusual was up. We all had CBs and hf monitors, both to keep track of the man and warn over the truckers.

I didn't see the start, of course, but we could follow the progress over the CBs.

They started out near even. By the time they passed Desert Center, Bill had pulled slightly ahead. The four fifty-four and the Pratt and Whitney were doing their job, meshing efficiently, burning up fuel and distance with incredible precision. Later we learned that the noise was so loud the people in Desert Center woke up and badgered Civil Defence, wanting to know if the munitions depot outside Barstow had gone up.

> *Banzai Runner on Interstate Ten*
> *Doin' two hundred twenty-five*
> *Hardly a man alive*
> *Could match that drive*
> *Only somethin' far past human ken*

Outside Blythe, coming up on the last leg of the race, the stranger made his move. The spectators assembled there said the black car didn't roar or rumble, just gave out a kind of rising shriek that steadily intensified, until it finally drowned out even the Pratt and Whitney.

Someone with binocs said she got a look at Bill's face as he went by and that it was taut and sweaty. No fear, though. Not in Bill Switch.

We had our first glimpse of them as they roared through town. Sirens began to sound all over the place as the Highway Patrol's patience finally ran out. But there wasn't much they could do except watch until the runners burned themselves out. No patrol car could catch a banzai runner.

The black car was in the lead. We could make out those flaming headlights clearly from our position on the bluff across the Colorado.

Then there sounded a distant explosion, like a plummeting jumbo jet. Lights were winking on all over the sleeping town as the citizens awoke to something unnatural in their midst.

> That black demon car was pulling ahead
> Watchers 'cross the River thought the Wisp was dead
> The Wisp looked down
> Kicked the overdrive in
> Came up on that demon near enough to win

The explosion was the sound of Bill kicking in his special trick overdrive. Through our scopes and binoculars we could clearly see the pale station wagon pulling up, making ground on the black racer. They were barely a mile from the California side of the bridge. First one across would win. Then they were even, and then, unbelievably, Bill was ahead!

Those monster engines were making too much noise for us to hear the tyre blow. At nearly three hundred miles an hour Bill's car swerved left. He fought to straighten out, brought it momentarily back on line before it squealed rightward. It went through the flimsy guard rail, hit a bump, and soared gracefully into the air, describing an arc like a dying pelican as it fell. Even this far south the breadth of the Colorado was substantial. The Wisp didn't make much of a splash. There was no explosion. It must've gone straight to the bottom.

> Banzai Runner you've gone too fast
> At two ninety-six
> The accelerator sticks
> Flesh and rock don't mix
> Road and bridge you've passed

I never saw a car going that fast brake as rapidly as that black
bullet. The driver went only a mile or two into Arizona before
slowing enough to turn round and rush back towards us. He
parked and climbed out, and you could see that he'd been in a
race. His formerly icy demeanour was shattered, and that
unshakeable self-confidence I'd seen in him that night in San
Bernardino was missing. He'd won, but barely. If Bill hadn't lost
that tyre it might've been a different story, and the stranger knew
it.

He gazed respectfully down at the limpid sheet of grey that
was the Colorado. I was nearest to him. Most of the others had
scrambled down the bluff, and a few were already swimming
out to where Bill's wagon had sunk. I knew they wouldn't find
a thing. So did the stranger standing next to me. I moved a couple
of steps away from him.

> *The Devil slowed down and got outta his car*
> *That was powered by souls who'd fallen too far*
> *Eyed the wreck in the River*
> *That held Bill Switch*
> *Said, 'You nearly beat me boy,*
>   *I'm sorry 'bout the hitch'*

'Tell me,' I asked hesitantly, 'if the tyre had held, *could* he have
beaten you?'

The stranger considered. 'I don't honestly know.' He smiled
down at me. 'Of course, you can't believe anything I say, can
you?' I noticed now that his eyes were yellow, and it wasn't due
to contact lenses. Funny that I hadn't picked up on that before.
Or maybe I hadn't wanted to.

I'm not an especially brave man, but I have an unreasonable
disregard for death. So I said, 'I think he had you beat cleanly.'

Those awful pupils brightened ever so slightly, just enough to
make me tremble a little. But I had made no bet with this banzai
runner, and he knew it.

> *Banzai Runner, you've lost your soul*
> *Now the Devil take you home*
> *On his hot roads to roam*
> *Cars of fire, not of chrome*
> *No more chance to rock 'n' roll.*

'Could be he had. He was the best I've ever raced against. He was better than his machine, which is unusual in a man. Very unusual. But he lost.' He turned and started back towards his car. I heard him mumbling to himself.

'Maybe some of the forfeit is salvageable. We'll see.'

I never saw that black car or its driver again, and I never hope to. I no longer go out in the dark hours of early morning to watch the banzai runners race. I just stick to my papers and pen advertising jingles.

Oh, and I never exceed the speed limit. Someone might think to challenge me to a race.

> *Now the Devil knows a good thing whenever he sees it*
> *Gave the Wisp a uniform and driver's work kit*
> *So the next bus you board*
> *Better listen to the bell*
> *Might be the Devil's chauffeur*
>   *Wisp drivin' you down to*
>   *Hell . . .*

THE HITCH-HIKER

Roald Dahl

Among the most curious phenomena associated with motoring are the
'phantom hitch-hikers'. These ghosts of the road have apparently been
reported for centuries, since roads were little more than beaten tracks
and in Japan as far back as medieval times. Many people have dismissed
the stories as myths or hallucinations, although author Michael Goss
managed to collect enough instances to fill a book, The Evidence for
Phantom Hitch-Hikers (1984), which contained what many drivers
insisted were genuine experiences. Whether Roald Dahl, that master of
the macabre twist-in-the-tail story, ever had such an encounter is
unknown, but the flesh and blood hitch-hiker who features in this tale
certainly provides more than enough surprises for the motorist who
picks him up on the road to London.

   Roald Dahl (1916–90) was not only a hugely successful children's
writer, but a master of the gruesome adult horror story. His collections of macabre tales, including Someone Like You (1953), Kiss
Kiss (1960) and Switch Bitch (1974), have remained constantly in
print and have provided material for numerous television series,
among them Alfred Hitchcock Presents (1955–64), Way Out
(1961–62) and Tales of the Unexpected (1979–84). Initially the
latter consisted solely of his work, but it proved so successful that
more stories in the same style had to be found and adapted for the
screen.

   Dahl was a motoring enthusiast and enjoyed writing the screenplay
for the fantasy movie about a flying automobile, Chitty, Chitty, Bang,
Bang (1968) which starred Dick Van Dyke. He was also well aware of
the darker side of driving, as he showed in 'The Man From the South' —
about a boy who bets his car for fingers — and 'The Hitch-Hiker'. There
is no evidence that this 1977 story, about a pick-up who goads a driver
into excessive speeding with alarming results, contributed to the

increasing reluctance of drivers to pick up people from the side of the road — but it certainly must have helped!

*   *   *

I had a new car. It was an exciting toy, a big BMW 3.3 Li, which means 3.3 litre, long wheelbase, fuel injection. It had a top speed of 129 mph and terrific acceleration. The body was pale blue. The seats inside were darker blue and they were made of leather, genuine soft leather of the finest quality. The windows were electrically operated and so was the sun-roof. The radio aerial popped up when I switched on the radio, and disappeared when I switched it off. The powerful engine growled and grunted impatiently at slow speeds, but at sixty miles an hour the growling stopped and the motor began to purr with pleasure.

I was driving up to London by myself. It was a lovely June day. They were haymaking in the fields and there were buttercups along both sides of the road. I was whispering along at seventy miles an hour, leaning back comfortably in my seat, with no more than a couple of fingers resting lightly on the wheel to keep her steady. Ahead of me I saw a man thumbing a lift. I touched the footbrake and brought the car to a stop beside him. I always stopped for hitch-hikers. I knew just how it used to feel to be standing on the side of a country road watching the cars go by. I hated the drivers for pretending they didn't see me, especially the ones in big cars with three empty seats. The large expensive cars seldom stopped. It was always the smaller ones that offered you a lift, or the old rusty ones, or the ones that were already crammed full of children and the driver would say, 'I think we can squeeze in one more.'

The hitch-hiker poked his head through the open window and said, 'Going to London, guv'nor?'

'Yes,' I said. 'Jump in.'

He got in and I drove on.

He was a small ratty-faced man with grey teeth. His eyes were dark and quick and clever, like a rat's eyes, and his ears were slightly pointed at the top. He had a cloth cap on his head and he was wearing a greyish-coloured jacket with enormous pockets. The grey jacket, together with the quick eyes and the pointed ears, made him look more than anything like some sort of a huge human rat.

'What part of London are you headed for?' I asked him.

'I'm goin' right through London and out the other side,' he said. 'I'm goin' to Epsom for the races. It's Derby Day today.'

'So it is,' I said. 'I wish I were going with you. I love betting on horses.'

'I never bet on horses,' he said. 'I don't even watch 'em run. That's a stupid silly business.'

'Then why do you go?' I asked.

He didn't seem to like that question. His little ratty face went absolutely blank and he sat there staring straight ahead at the road, saying nothing.

'I expect you help to work the betting machines or something like that,' I said.

'That's even sillier,' he answered. 'There's no fun working them lousy machines and selling tickets to mugs. Any fool could do that.'

There was a long silence. I decided not to question him any more. I remembered how irritated I used to get in my hitch-hiking days when drivers kept asking *me* questions. Where are you going? Why are you going there? What's your job? Are you married? Do you have a girl-friend? What's her name? How old are you? And so on and so forth. I used to hate it.

'I'm sorry,' I said. 'It's none of my business what you do. The trouble is, I'm a writer, and most writers are terrible nosey parkers.'

'You write books?' he asked.

'Yes.'

'Writin' books is okay,' he said. 'It's what I call a skilled trade. I'm in a skilled trade too. The folks I despise is them that spend all their lives doin' crummy old routine jobs with no skill in 'em at all. You see what I mean?'

'Yes.'

'The secret of life,' he said, 'is to become very very good at somethin' that's very very 'ard to do.'

'Like you,' I said.

'Exactly. You and me both.'

'What makes you think that *I'm* any good at my job?' I asked. 'There's an awful lot of bad writers around.'

'You wouldn't be drivin' about in a car like this if you weren't no good at it,' he answered. 'It must've cost a tidy packet, this little job.'

'It wasn't cheap.'

'What can she do flat out?' he asked.

'One hundred and twenty-nine miles an hour,' I told him.

'I'll bet she won't do it.'

'I'll bet she will.'

'All car makers is liars,' he said. 'You can buy any car you like and it'll never do what the makers say it will in the ads.'

'This one will.'

'Open 'er up then and prove it,' he said. 'Go on, guv'nor, open 'er right up and let's see what she'll do.'

There is a roundabout at Chalfont St Peter and immediately beyond it there's a long straight section of dual carriageway. We came out of the roundabout on to the carriageway and I pressed my foot down on the accelerator. The big car leaped forward as though she'd been stung. In ten seconds or so, we were doing ninety.

'Lovely!' he cried. 'Beautiful! Keep goin'!'

I had the accelerator jammed right down against the floor and I held it there.

'One hundred!' he shouted ... 'A hundred and five ...! A hundred and ten ...! A hundred and fifteen! Go on! Don't slack off!'

I was in the outside lane and we flashed past several cars as though they were standing still—a green Mini, a big cream-coloured Citroën, a white Land-Rover, a huge truck with a container on the back, an orange-coloured Volkswagen Minibus ...

'A hundred and twenty!' my passenger shouted, jumping up and down. 'Go on! Go on! Get 'er up to one-two-nine!'

At that moment, I heard the scream of a police siren. It was so loud it seemed to be right inside the car, and then a policeman on a motor-cycle loomed up alongside us on the inside lane and went past us and raised a hand for us to stop.

'Oh, my sainted aunt!' I said. 'That's torn it!'

The policeman must have been doing about a hundred and thirty when he passed us, and he took plenty of time slowing down. Finally, he pulled into the side of the road and I pulled in behind him. 'I didn't know police motor-cycles could go as fast as that,' I said rather lamely.

'That one can,' my passenger said. 'It's the same make as yours. It's a BMW R90S. Fastest bike on the road. That's what they're usin' nowadays.'

The policeman got off his motor-cycle and leaned the machine sideways on to its prop stand. Then he took off his gloves and placed them carefully on the seat. He was in no hurry now. He had us where he wanted us and he knew it.

'This is real trouble,' I said. 'I don't like it one bit.'

'Don't talk to 'im any more than is necessary, you understand,' my companion said. 'Just sit tight and keep mum.'

Like an executioner approaching his victim, the policeman came strolling slowly towards us. He was a big meaty man with a belly, and his blue breeches were skintight around his enormous thighs. His goggles were pulled up on to the helmet, showing a smouldering red face with wide cheeks.

We sat there like guilty schoolboys, waiting for him to arrive.

'Watch out for this man,' my passenger whispered. ''Ee looks mean as the devil.'

The policeman came round to my open window and placed one meaty hand on the sill. 'What's the hurry?' he said.

'No hurry, officer,' I answered.

'Perhaps there's a woman in the back having a baby and you're rushing her to hospital? Is that it?'

'No, officer.'

'Or perhaps your house is on fire and you're dashing home to rescue the family from upstairs?' His voice was dangerously soft and mocking.

'My house isn't on fire, officer.'

'In that case,' he said, 'you've got yourself into a nasty mess, haven't you? Do you know what the speed limit is in this country?'

'Seventy,' I said.

'And do you mind telling me exactly what speed you were doing just now?'

I shrugged and didn't say anything.

When he spoke next, he raised his voice so loud that I jumped. '*One hundred and twenty miles per hour!*' he barked. 'That's *fifty* miles an hour over the limit!'

He turned his head and spat out a big gob of spit. It landed on the wing of my car and started sliding down over my beautiful blue paint. Then he turned back again and stared hard at my passenger. 'And who are you?' he asked sharply.

'He's a hitch-hiker,' I said. 'I'm giving him a lift.'

'I didn't ask you,' he said. 'I asked him.'

''Ave I done somethin' wrong?' my passenger asked. His voice was as soft and oily as haircream.

'That's more than likely,' the policeman answered. 'Anyway, you're a witness. I'll deal with you in a minute. Driving-licence,' he snapped, holding out his hand.

I gave him my driving-licence.

He unbuttoned the left-hand breast-pocket of his tunic and brought out the dreaded books of tickets. Carefully, he copied the name and address from my licence. Then he gave it back to me. He strolled round to the front of the car and read the number from the number-plate and wrote that down as well. He filled in the date, the time and the details of my offence. Then he tore out the top copy of the ticket. But before handing it to me, he checked that all the information had come through clearly on his own carbon copy. Finally, he replaced the book in his tunic pocket and fastened the button.

'Now you,' he said to my passenger, and he walked around to the other side of the car. From the other breast-pocket he produced a small black notebook. 'Name?' he snapped.

'Michael Fish,' my passenger said.

'Address?'

'Fourteen, Windsor Lane, Luton.'

'Show me something to prove this is your real name and address,' the policeman said.

My passenger fished in his pockets and came out with a driving-licence of his own. The policeman checked the name and address and handed it back to him. 'What's your job?' he asked sharply.

'I'm an 'od carrier.'

'A *what*?'

'An 'od carrier.'

'Spell it.'

'H-O-D C-A- . . .'

'That'll do. And what's a hod carrier, may I ask?'

'An 'od carrier, officer, is a person 'oo carries the cement up the ladder to the bricklayer. And the 'od is what 'ee carries it in. It's got a long 'andle, and on the top you've got two bits of wood set at an angle . . .'

'All right, all right. Who's your employer?'

'Don't 'ave one. I'm unemployed.'

The policeman wrote all this down in the black notebook. Then he returned the book to its pocket and did up the button.

'When I get back to the station I'm going to do a little checking up on you,' he said to my passenger.

'Me? What've I done wrong?' the rat-faced man asked.

'I don't like your face, that's all,' the policeman said. 'And we just might have a picture of it somewhere in our files.' He strolled round the car and returned to my window.

'I suppose you know you're in serious trouble,' he said to me.

'Yes, officer.'

'You won't be driving this fancy car of yours again for a very long time, not after *we've* finished with you. You won't be driving *any* car again come to that for several years. And a good thing, too. I hope they lock you up for a spell into the bargain.'

'You mean prison?' I asked, alarmed.

'Absolutely,' he said, smacking his lips. 'In the clink. Behind the bars. Along with all the other criminals who break the law. *And* a hefty fine into the bargain. Nobody will be more pleased about that than me. I'll see you in court, both of you. You'll be getting a summons to appear.'

He turned away and walked over to his motor-cycle. He flipped the prop stand back into position with his foot and swung his leg over the saddle. Then he kicked the starter and roared off up the road out of sight.

'Phew!' I gasped. 'That's done it.'

'We was caught,' my passenger said. 'We was caught good and proper.'

'I was caught, you mean.'

'That's right,' he said. 'What you goin' to do now, guv'nor?'

'I'm going straight up to London to talk to my solicitor,' I said. I started the car and drove on.

'You mustn't believe what 'ee said to you about goin' to prison,' my passenger said. 'They don't put nobody in the clink just for speedin'.'

'Are you sure of that?' I asked.

'I'm positive,' he answered. 'They can take your licence away and they can give you a whoppin' big fine, but that'll be the end of it.'

I felt tremendously relieved.

'By the way,' I said, 'why did you lie to him?'

'Who, me?' he said. 'What makes you think I lied?'

'You told him you were an unemployed hod carrier. But you told *me* you were in a highly skilled trade.'

'So I am,' he said. 'But it don't pay to tell everythin' to a copper.'

'So what *do* you do?' I asked him.

'Ah,' he said slyly. 'That'd be tellin', wouldn't it?'

'Is it something you're ashamed of?'

'Ashamed?' he cried. 'Me, ashamed of my job? I'm about as proud of it as anybody could be in the entire world!'

'Then why won't you tell me?'

'You writers really is nosey parkers, aren't you?' he said. 'And you ain't goin' to be 'appy, I don't think, until you've found out exactly what the answer is?'

'I don't really care one way or the other,' I told him, lying.

He gave me a crafty little ratty look out of the sides of his eyes. 'I think you do care,' he said. 'I can see it on your face that you think I'm in some kind of a very peculiar trade and you're just achin' to know what it is.'

I didn't like the way he read my thoughts. I kept quiet and stared at the road ahead.

'You'd be right, too,' he went on. 'I *am* in a very peculiar trade. I'm in the queerest peculiar trade of 'em all.'

I waited for him to go on.

'That's why I 'as to be extra careful 'oo I'm talkin' to, you see. 'Ow am I to know, for instance, you're not another copper in plain clothes?'

'Do I look like a copper?'

'No,' he said. 'You don't. And you ain't. Any fool could tell that.'

He took from his pocket a tin of tobacco and a packet of cigarette papers and started to roll a cigarette. I was watching him out of the corner of one eye, and the speed with which he performed this rather difficult operation was incredible. The cigarette was rolled and ready in about five seconds. He ran his tongue along the edge of the paper, stuck it down and popped the cigarette between his lips. Then, as if from nowhere, a lighter appeared in his hand. The lighter flamed. The cigarette was lit. The lighter disappeared. It was altogether a remarkable performance.

'I've never seen anyone roll a cigarette as fast as that,' I said.

'Ah,' he said, taking a deep suck of smoke. 'So you noticed.'

'Of course I noticed. It was quite fantastic.'

He sat back and smiled. It pleased him very much that I had noticed how quickly he could roll a cigarette. 'You want to know what makes me able to do it?' he asked.

'Go on then.'

'It's because I've got fantastic fingers. These fingers of mine,' he said, holding up both hands high in front of him, 'are quicker and cleverer than the fingers of the best piano player in the world!'

'Are you a piano player?'

'Don't be daft,' he said. 'Do I look like a piano player?'

I glanced at his fingers. They were so beautifully shaped, so slim and long and elegant, they didn't seem to belong to the rest of him at all. They looked more like the fingers of a brain surgeon or a watchmaker.

'My job,' he went on, 'is a hundred times more difficult than playin' the piano. Any twerp can learn to do that. There's titchy little kids learnin' to play the piano in almost any 'ouse you go into these days. That's right, ain't it?'

'More or less,' I said.

'Of course it's right. But there's not one person in ten million can learn to do what I do. Not one in ten million! 'Ow about that?'

'Amazing,' I said.

'You're darn right it's amazin',' he said.

'I think I know what you do,' I said. 'You do conjuring tricks. You're a conjuror.'

'Me?' he snorted. 'A conjuror? Can you picture me goin' round crummy kids' parties makin' rabbits come out of top 'ats?'

'Then you're a card player. You get people into card games and deal yourself marvellous hands.'

'Me! A rotten card-sharper!' he cried. 'That's a miserable racket if ever there was one.'

'All right. I give up.'

I was taking the car along slowly now, at no more than forty miles an hour, to make quite sure I wasn't stopped again. We had come on to the main London–Oxford road and were running down the hill towards Denham.

Suddenly, my passenger was holding up a black leather belt in his hand. 'Ever seen this before?' he asked. The belt had a brass buckle of unusual design.

'Hey!' I said. 'That's mine, isn't it? It *is* mine! Where did you get it?'

He grinned and waved the belt gently from side to side. 'Where d'you think I got it?' he said. 'Off the top of your trousers, of course.'

I reached down and felt for my belt. It was gone.

'You mean you took it off me while we've been driving along?' I asked, flabbergasted.

He nodded, watching me all the time with those little black ratty eyes.

'That's impossible,' I said. 'You'd have had to undo the buckle and slide the whole thing out through the loops all the way round. I'd have seen you doing it. And even if I hadn't seen you, I'd have felt it.'

'Ah, but you didn't, did you?' he said, triumphant. He dropped the belt on his lap, and now all at once there was a brown shoelace dangling from his fingers. 'And what about this, then?' he exclaimed, waving the shoelace.

'What about it?' I said.

'Anyone around 'ere missin' a shoelace?' he asked, grinning.

I glanced down at my shoes. The lace of one of them was missing. 'Good grief!' I said. 'How did you do that? I never saw you bending down.'

'You never saw nothin',' he said proudly. 'You never even saw me move an inch. And you know why?'

'Yes,' I said. 'Because you've got fantastic fingers.'

'Exactly right!' he cried. 'You catch on pretty quick, don't you?' He sat back and sucked away at his home-made cigarette, blowing the smoke out in a thin stream against the windshield. He knew he had impressed me greatly with those two tricks, and this made him very happy. 'I don't want to be late,' he said. 'What time is it?'

'There's a clock in front of you,' I told him.

'I don't trust car clocks,' he said. 'What does your watch say?'

I hitched up my sleeve to look at the watch on my wrist. It wasn't there. I looked at the man. He looked back at me, grinning.

'You've taken that, too,' I said.

He held out his hand and there was my watch lying in his palm. 'Nice bit of stuff, this,' he said. 'Superior quality. Eighteen-carat gold. Easy to flog, too. It's never any trouble gettin' rid of quality goods.'

'I'd like it back, if you don't mind,' I said rather huffily.

He placed the watch carefully on the leather tray in front of him. 'I wouldn't nick anything from you, guv'nor,' he said. 'You're my pal. You're giving me a lift.'

'I'm glad to hear it,' I said.

'All I'm doin' is answerin' your questions,' he went on. 'You asked me what I did for a livin' and I'm showin' you.'

'What else have you got of mine?'

He smiled again, and now he started to take from the pocket of his jacket one thing after another that belonged to me—my driving-licence, a key-ring with four keys on it, some pound notes, a few coins, a letter from my publishers, my diary, a stubby old pencil, a cigarette-lighter, and last of all, a beautiful old sapphire ring with pearls around it belonging to my wife. I was taking the ring up to the jeweller in London because one of the pearls was missing.

'Now *there's* another lovely piece of goods,' he said, turning the ring over in his fingers. 'That's eighteenth century, if I'm not mistaken, from the reign of King George the Third.'

'You're right,' I said, impressed. 'You're absolutely right.'

He put the ring on the leather tray with the other items.

'So you're a pickpocket,' I said.

'I don't like that word,' he answered. 'It's a coarse and vulgar word. Pickpockets is coarse and vulgar people who only do easy little amateur jobs. They lift money from blind old ladies.'

'What do you call yourself, then?'

'Me? I'm a fingersmith. I'm a professional fingersmith.' He spoke the words solemnly and proudly, as though he were telling me he was the President of the Royal College of Surgeons or the Archbishop of Canterbury.

'I've never heard that word before,' I said. 'Did you invent it?'

'Of course I didn't invent it,' he replied. 'It's the name given to them who's risen to the very top of the profession. You've 'eard of a goldsmith and a silversmith, for instance. They're experts with gold and silver. I'm an expert with my fingers, so I'm a fingersmith.'

'It must be an interesting job.'

'It's a marvellous job,' he answered. 'It's lovely.'

'And that's why you go to the races?'

'Race meetings is easy meat,' he said. 'You just stand around after the race, watchin' for the lucky ones to queue up and draw their money. And when you see someone collectin' a big bundle of notes, you simply follows after 'im and 'elps yourself. But don't get me wrong, guv'nor. I never takes nothin' from a loser. Nor from poor people neither. I only go after them as can afford it, the winners and the rich.'

'That's very thoughtful of you,' I said. 'How often do you get caught?'

'Caught?' he cried, disgusted. '*Me* get caught! It's only pick-pockets get caught. Fingersmiths never. Listen, I could take the false teeth out of your mouth if I wanted to and you wouldn't even catch me!'

'I don't have false teeth,' I said.

'I know you don't,' he answered. 'Otherwise I'd 'ave 'ad 'em out long ago!'

I believed him. Those long slim fingers of his seemed able to do anything.

We drove on for a while without talking.

'That policeman's going to check up on you pretty thoroughly,' I said. 'Doesn't that worry you a bit?'

'Nobody's checkin' up on me,' he said.

'Of course they are. He's got your name and address written down most carefully in his black book.'

The man gave me another of his sly, ratty little smiles. 'Ah,' he said. 'So 'ee 'as. But I'll bet 'ee ain't got it all written down in 'is memory as well. I've never known a copper yet with a decent memory. Some of 'em can't even remember their own names.'

'What's memory got to do with it?' I asked. 'It's written down in his book, isn't it?'

'Yes, guv'nor, it is. But the trouble is, 'ee's lost the book. 'Ee's lost both books, the one with my name in it *and* the one with yours.'

In the long delicate fingers of his right hand, the man was holding up in triumph the two books he had taken from the policeman's pockets. 'Easiest job I ever done,' he announced proudly.

I nearly swerved the car into a milk-truck, I was so excited.

'That copper's got nothin' on either of us now,' he said.

'You're a genius!' I cried.

' 'Ee's got no names, no addresses, no car number, no nothin',' he said.

'You're brilliant!'

'I think you'd better pull in off this main road as soon as possible,' he said. 'Then we'd better build a little bonfire and burn these books.'

'You're a fantastic fellow,' I exclaimed.

'Thank you, guv'nor,' he said. 'It's always nice to be appreciated.'

CRASH

J. G. Ballard

At the time of writing, the most controversial film about the motor car has undoubtedly been Crash *(1996), which was the subject of a fierce campaign (ultimately unsuccessful) to have it banned for fear it would 'deprave and corrupt' viewers. Directed by David Cronenberg, himself a racer and vintage car collector, the story concerns a group of people who find car crashes and the resulting injuries erotic. It was described by* The Times *critic as 'the worst film even duty has ever made me watch: the* Oh Calcutta! *of the used car lot.' Ferocious arguments raged throughout the media about the film which starred James Spader and Holly Hunter as two car crash victims seeking to re-ignite their traumatised passions by exploring the sexual corollaries of cars. For author J. G. Ballard, however, it was a 'brilliant picture, provocative, unsettling and a very faithful adaptation'. The views of cinema audiences also varied wildly, from accusations that* Crash *celebrated violence and pornography to claims that it was a serious study of sex and violence in the entertainment culture and the probably sinister effects they can have on the public imagination. At the Cannes Film Festival the picture won the special Jury Prize for 'originality, daring and audacity'. This is the story that started the furore, all the more remarkable because it was written a quarter of a century ago, in 1973.*

James Graham Ballard (1930–) was a figurehead of the 'new wave' of science fiction writers in Britain in the late Sixties and has probably been the genre's most controversial writer ever since. Born in Shanghai, he read medicine at Cambridge, but left the university without taking a degree and found his metier writing experimental sf. Long fascinated with automobiles, he staged an exhibition at the Arts Lab in London in 1969, entitled 'Crashed Cars', which featured three genuine wrecks. The astonishing effect this had on viewers inspired him to write Crash. *The car accidents which killed Jayne Mansfield and James Dean, and the motorcade assassination of President Kennedy, have all featured in his stories, while his novel* Concrete Island *(1974) revolves around a driver marooned on a traffic island between motorway embankments. As a matter of record, Ballard has revealed that he was once in a car crash on the Chiswick Bridge, 'but it never did anything for my libido'.*

*   *   *

Vaughan died yesterday in his last car-crash. During our friendship he had rehearsed his death in many crashes, but this was his only true accident. Driven on a collision course towards the limousine of the film actress, his car jumped the rails of the London Airport flyover and plunged through the roof of a bus filled with airline passengers. The crushed bodies of package tourists, like a haemorrhage of the sun, still lay across the vinyl seats when I pushed my way through the police engineers an hour later. Holding the arm of her chauffeur, the film actress Elizabeth Taylor, with whom Vaughan had dreamed of dying for so many months, stood alone under the revolving ambulance lights. As I knelt over Vaughan's body she placed a gloved hand to her throat.

Could she see, in Vaughan's posture, the formula of the death which he had devised for her? During the last weeks of his life Vaughan thought of nothing else but her death, a coronation of wounds he had staged with the devotion of an Earl Marshal. The walls of his apartment near the film studios at Shepperton were covered with the photographs he had taken through his zoom lens each morning as she left her hotel in London, from the pedestrian bridges above the westbound motorways, and from the roof of the multi-storey car park at the studios. The magnified details of her knees and hands, of the inner surface of her thighs and the left apex of her mouth, I uneasily prepared for Vaughan on the copying machine in my office, handing him the packages of prints as if they were the instalments of a death warrant. At his apartment I watched him matching the details of her body with the photographs of grotesque wounds in a textbook of plastic surgery.

In his vision of a car-crash with the actress, Vaughan was obsessed by many wounds and impacts—by the dying chromium and collapsing bulkheads of their two cars meeting head-on in complex collisions endlessly repeated in slow-motion films, by the identical wounds inflicted on their bodies, by the image of windshield glass frosting around her face as she broke its tinted surface like a death-born aphrodite, by the compound fractures of their thighs impacted against their handbrake mountings, and above all by the wounds to their genitalia, her uterus pierced by the heraldic beak of the manufacturer's medallion, his semen emptying across the luminescent dials that registered for ever the last temperature and fuel level of the engine.

It was only at these times, as he described this last crash to me, that Vaughan was calm. He talked of these wounds and collisions with the erotic tenderness of a long-separated lover. Searching through the photographs in his apartment, he half turned towards me, so that his heavy groin quietened me with its profile of an almost erect penis. He knew that as long as he provoked me with his own sex, which he used casually as if he might discard it for ever at any moment, I would never leave him.

Ten days ago, as he stole my car from the garage of my apartment house, Vaughan hurtled up the concrete ramp, an ugly machine sprung from a trap. Yesterday his body lay under the police arc-lights at the foot of the flyover, veiled by a delicate lacework of blood. The broken postures of his legs and arms, the bloody geometry of his face, seemed to parody the photographs of crash injuries that covered the walls of his apartment. I looked down for the last time at his huge groin, engorged with blood. Twenty yards away, illuminated by the revolving lamps, the actress hovered on the arm of her chauffeur. Vaughan had dreamed of dying at the moment of her orgasm.

Before his death Vaughan had taken part in many crashes. As I think of Vaughan I see him in the stolen cars he drove and damaged, the surfaces of deformed metal and plastic that for ever embraced him. Two months earlier I found him on the lower deck of the airport flyover after the first rehearsal of his own death. A taxi driver helped two shaken hair hostesses from a small car into which Vaughan had collided as he lurched from the mouth of a concealed access road. As I ran across to Vaughan I saw him through the fractured windshield of the white convertible he had taken from the car park of the Oceanic Terminal. His exhausted face, with its scarred mouth, was lit by broken rainbows. I pulled the dented passenger door from its frame. Vaughan sat on the glass-covered seat, studying his own posture with a complacent gaze. His hands, palms upwards at his sides, were covered with blood from his injured knee-caps. He examined the vomit staining the lapels of his leather jacket, and reached forward to touch the globes of semen clinging to the instrument binnacle. I tried to lift him from the car, but his tight buttocks were clamped together as if they had seized while forcing the last drops of fluid from his seminal vesicles. On the seat beside him were the torn photographs of the film actress which I had reproduced for him that morning at my office. Magnified sections of lip and eyebrow, elbow and cleavage formed a broken mosaic.

For Vaughan the car-crash and his own sexuality had made their final marriage. I remember him at night with nervous young women in the crushed rear compartments of abandoned cars in breakers' yards, and their photographs in the postures of uneasy sex acts. Their tight faces and strained thighs were lit by his Polaroid flash, like startled survivors of a submarine disaster. These aspiring whores, whom Vaughan met in the all-night cafés and supermarkets of London Airport, were the first cousins of the patients illustrated in his surgical textbooks. During his studied courtship of injured women, Vaughan was obsessed with the buboes of gas bacillus infections, by facial injuries and genital wounds.

Through Vaughan I discovered the true significance of the automobile crash, the meaning of whiplash injuries and roll-over, the ecstasies of head-on collisions. Together we visited the Road Research Laboratory twenty miles to the west of London, and watched the calibrated vehicles crashing into the concrete target blocks. Later, in his apartment, Vaughan screened slow-motion films of test collisions that he had photographed with his ciné-camera. Sitting in the darkness on the floor cushions, we watched the silent impacts flicker on the wall above our heads. The repeated sequences of crashing cars first calmed and then aroused me. Cruising alone on the motorway under the yellow glare of the sodium lights, I thought of myself at the controls of these impacting vehicles.

During the months that followed, Vaughan and I spent many hours driving along the express highways on the northern perimeter of the airport. On the calm summer evenings these fast boulevards became a zone of nightmare collisions. Listening to the police broadcasts on Vaughan's radio, we moved from one accident to the next. Often we stopped under arc-lights that flared over the sites of major collisions, watching while firemen and police engineers worked with acetylene torches and lifting tackle to free unconscious wives trapped beside their dead husbands, or waited as a passing doctor fumbled with a dying man pinned below an inverted truck. Sometimes Vaughan was pulled back by the other spectators, and fought for his cameras with the ambulance attendants. Above all, Vaughan waited for head-on collisions with the concrete pillars of the motorway overpasses, the melancholy conjunction formed by a crushed vehicle abandoned on the grass verge and the serene motion sculpture of the concrete.

Once we were the first to reach the crashed car of an injured woman driver. A middle-aged cashier at the airport's duty-free liquor store, she sat unsteadily in the crushed compartment, fragments of the tinted windshield set in her forehead like jewels. As a police car approached, its emergency beacon pulsing along the overhead motorway, Vaughan ran back for his camera and flash equipment. Taking off my tie, I searched helplessly for the woman's wounds. She stared at me without speaking, and lay on her side across the seat. I watched the blood irrigate her white blouse. When Vaughan had taken the last of his pictures he knelt down inside the car and held her face carefully in his hands, whispering into her ear. Together we helped to lift her on to the ambulance trolley.

On our way to Vaughan's apartment he recognised an airport whore waiting in the forecourt of a motorway restaurant, a part-time cinema usherette for ever worrying about her small son's defective hearing-aid. As they sat behind me she complained to Vaughan about my nervous driving, but he was watching her movements with an abstracted gaze, almost encouraging her to gesture with her hands and knees. On the deserted roof of a Northolt multi-storey car park I waited by the balustrade. In the rear seat of the car Vaughan arranged her limbs in the posture of the dying cashier. His strong body, crouched across her in the reflected light of passing headlamps, assumed a series of stylised positions.

Vaughan unfolded for me all his obsessions with the mysterious eroticism of wounds: the perverse logic of blood-soaked instrument panels, seat-belts smeared with excrement, sun-visors lined with brain tissue. For Vaughan each crashed car set off a tremor of excitement, in the complex geometries of a dented fender, in the unexpected variations of crushed radiator grilles, in the grotesque overhang of an instrument panel forced on to a driver's crotch as if in some calibrated act of machine fellatio. The intimate time and space of a single human being had been fossilised for ever in this web of chromium knives and frosted glass.

A week after the funeral of the woman cashier, as we drove at night along the western perimeter of the airport, Vaughan swerved on to the verge and struck a large mongrel dog. The impact of its body, like a padded hammer, and the shower of glass as the animal was carried over the roof, convinced me that we were about to die in a crash. Vaughan never stopped. I watched him accelerate away, his scarred face held close to the punctured windshield, angrily brushing the beads of frosted glass from his cheeks. Already his acts of violence had become so random that I was no more than a captive spectator. Yet the next morning on the roof of the airport car park where we abandoned the car, Vaughan calmly pointed out to me the deep dents in the bonnet and roof. He stared at an airliner filled with tourists lifting into the western sky, his sallow face puckering like a wistful child's. The long triangular grooves on the car had been formed within the death of an unknown creature, its vanished identity abstracted in terms of the geometry of his vehicle. How much more mysterious would be our own deaths, and those of the famous and powerful?

Even this first death seemed timid compared with the others in which Vaughan took part, and with those imaginary deaths that filled his mind. Trying to exhaust himself, Vaughan devised a terrifying almanac of imaginary automobile disasters and insane wounds—the lungs of elderly men punctured by door handles, the chests of young women impaled by steering-columns, the cheeks of handsome youths pierced by the chromium latches of quarter-lights. For him these wounds were the keys to a new sexuality born from a perverse technology. The images of these wounds hung in the gallery of his mind like exhibits in the museum of a slaughterhouse.

Thinking of Vaughan now, drowning in his own blood under the police arc-lights, I remember the countless imaginary disasters he described as we cruised together along the airport expressways. He dreamed of ambassadorial limousines crashing into jack-knifing butane tankers, of taxis filled with celebrating children colliding head-on below the bright display windows of deserted supermarkets. He dreamed of alienated brothers and sisters, by chance meeting each other on collision courses on the access roads of petrochemical plants, their unconscious incest made explicit in this colliding metal, in the haemorrhages of their brain tissue flowering beneath the aluminised compression chambers and reaction vessels. Vaughan devised the massive rear-end collisions of sworn enemies, hate-deaths celebrated in the engine fuel burning in wayside ditches, paintwork boiling through the dull afternoon sunlight of provincial towns. He visualised the specialised crashes of escaping criminals, of off-duty hotel receptionists trapped between their steering wheels and the laps of their lovers whom they were masturbating. He thought of the crashes of honeymoon couples, seated together after their impacts with the rear suspension units of runaway sugar-tankers. He thought of the crashes of automobile stylists, the most abstract of all possible deaths, wounded in their cars with promiscuous laboratory technicians.

Vaughan elaborated endless variations on these collisions, thinking first of a repetition of head-on collisions: a child-molester and an overworked doctor re-enacting their deaths first in head-on collisions and then in roll-over; the retired prostitute crashing into a concrete motorway parapet, her overweight body propelled through the fractured windshield, menopausal loins torn on the chromium bonnet mascot. Her blood would cross the over-white concrete of the evening embankment, haunting for ever the mind of a police mechanic who carried the pieces of her body in a yellow plastic shroud. Alternatively, Vaughan saw her hit by a reversing truck in a motorway fuelling area, crushed against the nearside door of her car as she bent down to loosen her right shoe, the contours of her body buried within the bloody mould of the door panel. He saw her hurtling through the rails of the flyover and dying as Vaughan himself would later die, plunging through the roof of an airline coach, its cargo of complacent destinations multiplied by the death of this myopic middle-aged woman. He saw her hit by a speeding taxi as she stepped out of her car to relieve herself in a wayside latrine, her body whirled a hundred feet away in a spray of urine and blood.

I think now of the other crashes we visualised, absurd deaths of the wounded, maimed and distraught. I think of the crashes of psychopaths, implausible accidents carried out with venom and self-disgust, vicious multiple collisions contrived in stolen cars on evening freeways among tired office workers. I think of the absurd crashes of neurasthenic housewives returning from the VD clinics, hitting parked cars in suburban high streets. I think of the crashes of excited schizophrenics colliding head-on into stalled laundry vans in one-way streets; of manic-depressives crushed while making pointless U-turns on motorway access roads; of luckless paranoids driving at full speed into the brick walls at the ends of known culs-de-sac; of sadistic charge nurses decapitated in inverted crashes on complex interchanges; of lesbian supermarket manageresses burning to death in the collapsed frames of their midget cars before the stoical eyes of middle-aged firemen; of autistic children crushed in rear-end collisions, their eyes less wounded in death; of buses filled with mental defectives drowning together stoically in roadside industrial canals.

Long before Vaughan died I had begun to think of my own death. With whom would I die, and in what role—psychopath, neurasthenic, absconding criminal? Vaughan dreamed endlessly of the deaths of the famous, inventing imaginary crashes for them. Around the deaths of James Dean and Albert Camus, Jayne Mansfield and John Kennedy he had woven elaborate fantasies. His imagination was a target gallery of screen actresses, politicians, business tycoons and television executives. Vaughan followed them everywhere with his camera, zoom lens watching from the observation platform of the Oceanic Terminal at the airport, from hotel mezzanine balconies and studio car parks. For each of them Vaughan devised an optimum auto-death. Onassis and his wife would die in a recreation of the Dealey Plaza assassination. He saw Reagan in a complex rear-end collision, dying a stylised death that expressed Vaughan's obsession with Reagan's genital organs, like his obsession with the exquisite transits of the screen actress's pubis across the vinyl seat covers of hired limousines.

After his last attempt to kill my wife Catherine, I knew that Vaughan had retired finally into his own skull. In this overlit realm ruled by violence and technology he was now driving for ever at a hundred miles an hour along an empty motorway, past deserted filling stations on the edges of wide fields, waiting for a single oncoming car. In his mind Vaughan saw the whole world dying in a simultaneous automobile disaster, millions of vehicles hurled together in a terminal congress of spurting loins and engine coolant.

I remember my first minor collision in a deserted hotel car park. Disturbed by a police patrol, we had forced ourselves through a hurried sex-act. Reversing out of the park, I struck an unmarked tree. Catherine vomited over my seat. This pool of vomit with its clots of blood like liquid rubies, as viscous and discreet as everything produced by Catherine, still contains for me the essence of the erotic delirium of the car-crash, more exciting than her own rectal and vaginal mucus, as refined as the excrement of a fairy queen, or the minuscule globes of liquid that formed beside the bubbles of her contact lenses. In this magic pool, lifting from her throat like a rare discharge of fluid from the mouth of a remote and mysterious shrine, I saw my own reflection, a mirror of blood, semen and vomit, distilled from a mouth whose contours only a few minutes before had drawn steadily against my penis.

Now that Vaughan has died, we will leave with the others who gathered around him, like a crowd drawn to an injured cripple whose deformed postures reveal the secret formulas of their minds and lives. All of us who knew Vaughan accept the perverse eroticism of the car-crash, as painful as the drawing of an exposed organ through the aperture of a surgical wound. I have watched copulating couples moving along darkened freeways at night, men and women on the verge of orgasm, the cars speeding in a series of inviting trajectories towards the flashing headlamps of the oncoming traffic stream. Young men alone behind the wheels of their first cars, near-wrecks picked up in scrap-yards, masturbate as they move on worn tyres to aimless destinations. After a near collision at a traffic intersection semen jolts across a cracked speedometer dial. Later, the dried residues of that same semen are brushed by the lacquered hair of the first young woman who lies across his lap with her mouth over his penis, one hand on the wheel hurtling the car through the darkness towards a multilevel interchange, the swerving brakes drawing the semen from him as he grazes the tailgate of an articulated truck loaded with colour television sets, his left hand vibrating her clitoris towards orgasm as the headlamps of the truck flare warningly in his rear-view mirror. Later still, he watches as a friend takes a teenage girl in the rear seat. Heavy mechanic's hands expose her buttocks to the advertisement hoardings that hurl past them. The wet highways flash by in the glare of head-lamps and the scream of brake-pads. The shaft of his penis glistens above the girl as he strikes at the frayed plastic roof of the car, marking the yellow fabric with his smegma.

The last ambulance had left. An hour earlier the film actress had been steered towards her limousine. In the evening light the white concrete of the collision corridor below the flyover resembled a secret airstrip from which mysterious machines would take off into a metallised sky. Vaughan's glass aeroplane flew somewhere above the heads of the bored spectators moving back to their cars, above the tired policemen gathering together the crushed suitcases and handbags of the airline tourists. I thought of Vaughan's body, colder now, its rectal temperature following the same downward gradients as those of the other victims of the crash. Across the night air these gradients fell like streamers from the office towers and apartment houses of the city, and from the warm mucosa of the film actress in her hotel suite.

I drove back towards the airport. The lights along Western Avenue illuminated the speeding cars, moving together towards their celebration of wounds.

THREE

CHROME KILLERS

The Future Autogeddon

THE RACER

Ib Melchior

What does the future hold for the automobile? The ever-increasing reliability, comfort and speed of today's vehicles are countered by the sheer weight of their numbers, which ultimately threatens to bring the highways to a standstill. For a number of years, writers of science fiction and fantasy have been making their own grim predictions about the autogeddon which faces mankind, and Part Three of this book offers some of the very best of their contributions. Their stories range from dark fantasies just around the corner to technofantasies of the far future. Several movies have also utilised this theme—from The Car *(1977), about a driverless vehicle which mindlessly runs over people in a small American town, to Roger Corman's cult classic,* Death Race 2000 *(1975), based on this short story, 'The Racer', by Ib Melchior.*

Ib Melchior (1917–) was born and educated in Denmark, but joined a British theatrical company, The English Players, which toured Europe until the outbreak of World War Two. He volunteered for active service and served as a CIC agent in Europe, an experience which was to provide inspiration for a number of his later best-selling novels such as V3 *(1985) and* Code Name: Grand Guignol *(1987). After the war he settled in America and became involved in films, scripting several movies including* Reptilicus *(1963) and* The Time Travellers *(1964) which he also directed. His television work included such popular series as* The Outer Limits, *and he won a number of awards for television and documentary films.*

His short stories are notable for their ingenuity and authenticity, and 'The Racer', published in 1956, was actually inspired by a real event. Not long after settling in the USA, Melchior's interest in motor racing took him to the Indianapolis Speedway where he was eyewitness to a horrifying crash in which one of the drivers was killed. He then watched, appalled, as people all around him began to scramble to get a closer look at the mangled body in the burning wreck. Sitting next to him was the driver's wife, and the shock on her face haunted him for years until he finally turned the incident into this story of an endurance race which, he says, 'is a protest against the mindless fascination that society has with violence'. In 1975 Roger Corman filmed the story as Death Race 2000, *kick-starting the career of a young actor named Sylvester Stallone and producing a box office hit that has since inspired not only a whole series of imitations, but also two controversial computer games,* Carmageddon *and* Carpocalypse, *in which players have to destroy other motorists' vehicles and green-blooded, monster pedestrians.*

*   *   *

Willie felt the familiar intoxicating excitement. His mouth was dry; his heart beat faster, all his senses seemed more aware than ever. It was a few minutes before 0800 hours—his time to start.

This was the day. From all the Long Island Starting Fields the Racers were taking off at 15-minute intervals. The sputter and roar of cars warming up were everywhere. The smell of oil and fuel fumes permeated the air. The hubbub of the great crowd was a steady din. This was the biggest race of the year—New York to Los Angeles—100,000 bucks to the winner! Willie was determined to better his winning record of last year: 33 hours, 27 minutes, 12 seconds in Time. And although it was becoming increasingly difficult he'd do his damnedest to better his Score too!

He took a last walk of inspection around his car. Sleek, low-slung, dark brown, the practically indestructible plastiglass top looking deceptively fragile, like a soap bubble. Not bad for an old-fashioned diesel job. He kicked the solid plastirubber tyres in the time-honoured fashion of all drivers. Hank was giving a last-minute shine to the needle-sharp durasteel horns protruding from the front fenders. Willie's car wasn't nicknamed 'The Bull' without reason. The front of the car was built like a streamlined bull's head complete with bloodshot, evil-looking eyes, iron ring through flaring nostrils—and the horns. Although most of the racing cars were built to look like tigers, or sharks, or eagles, there *were* a few bulls—but Willie's horns were unequalled.

'Car 79 ready for Start in five minutes,' the loudspeaker blared. 'Car 79. Willie Connors, driver. Hank Morowski, mechanic. Ready your car for Start in five minutes.'

Willie and Hank took their places in 'The Bull'. At a touch by Willie on the starter the powerful diesel engine began a low purr. They drove slowly to the starting line.

'Last Check!' said Willie.

'Right,' came Hank's answer.

'Oil and Fuel?'

'40 hours.'

'Cooling Fluid?'

'Sealed.'

'No-Sleeps?'

'Check.'

'Energene Tabs?'

'Check.'

'Thermo Drink?'

'Check.'

The Starter held the chequered flag high over his head. The crowds packing the grandstands were on their feet. Hushed. Waiting.

'Here we go!' whispered Willie.

The flag fell. A tremendous cry rose from the crowd. But Willie hardly heard it. Accelerating furiously he pushed his car to its top speed of 190 miles an hour within seconds—shooting like a bullet along the straightaway towards Manhattan. He was elated; exhilarated. He was a Racer. And full of tricks!

Willie shot through the Tunnel directly to Jersey.

'Well?' grumbled Hank. 'Can you tell me now?'

'Toledo,' said Willie. 'Toledo, Ohio. On the Thruway. We should make it in under three hours.'

He felt a slight annoyance with Hank. There was no reason for the man to be touchy. He knew a driver didn't tell *anyone* the racing route he'd selected. News like that had a habit of getting around. It could cost a Racer his Score.

'There's not much chance of anything coming up until after we hit Toledo,' Willie said, 'but keep your eyes peeled. You never know.'

Hank merely grunted.

It was exactly 1048 hours when 'The Bull' streaked into the deserted streets of Toledo.

'OK—what now?' asked Hank.

'Grand Rapids, Michigan,' said Willie laconically.

'Grand Rapids! But that's—that's an easy 300 miles detour!'

'I know.'

'Are you crazy? It'll cost us a couple of hours.'

'So Grand Rapids is all the way up between the Lakes. So who'll be expecting us up there?'

'Oh! Oh, yeah, I see,' said Hank.

'The *Time* isn't everything, my friend. Whoever said the shortest distance between two points is a straight line? The *Score* counts too. And here's where we pick up *our* Score!'

The first Tragi-Acc never even knew the Racer had arrived. 'The Bull' struck him squarely, threw him up in the air and let him slide off its plastiglass back, leaving a red smear behind and somewhat to the left of Willie—all in a split second . . .

Near Calvin College an imprudent coed found herself too far from cover when the Racer suddenly came streaking down the campus. Frantically she sprinted for safety, but she didn't have a chance with a driver like Willie behind the wheel. The razor-sharp horn on the right fender sliced through her spine so cleanly that the jar wasn't even felt inside the car.

Leaving town the Racer was in luck again. An elderly woman had left the sanctuary of her stone-walled garden to rescue a straying cat. She was so easy to hit that Willie felt a little cheated.

At 1232 hours they were on the speedway headed for Kansas City.

Hank looked in awe at Willie. 'Three!' he murmured dreamily, 'a Score of three already. And all of them Kills—for sure. You *really* know how to drive!'

Hank settled back contentedly as if he could already feel his 25,000 dollar cut in his pocket. He began to whistle *The Racers Are Roaring* off key.

Even after his good Score it annoyed Willie. And for some reason he kept remembering the belatedly pleading look in the old woman's eyes as he struck her. Funny *that* should stay with him . . .

He estimated they'd hit Kansas City at around 1815 hours, CST. Hank turned on the radio. Peoria, Illinois, was warning its citizens of the approach of a Racer. All spectators should watch from safety places. Willie grinned. That would be him. Well— he wasn't looking for any Score in Peoria.

Dayton, Ohio, told of a Racer having made a Tragic Accident Score of one, and Fort Wayne, Indiana, was crowing over the fact that three Racers had passed through without scoring once.

From what he heard it seemed to Willie he had a comfortable lead, both in Time and Score.

They were receiving Kansas City now. An oily-voiced announcer was filling in the time between Racing Scores with what appeared to be a brief history of Racing.

'. . . and the most popular spectator sports of the latter half of the twentieth century were such mildly exciting pursuits as boxing and wrestling. Of course the spectators enjoyed seeing the combatants trying to maim each other, and there was always the chance of the hoped-for fatal accident.

'Motor Racing, however, gave a much greater opportunity for the Tragic Accidents so exciting to the spectator. One of the most famed old speedways, Indianapolis, where many drivers and spectators alike ended as bloody Tragi-Accs, is today the nation's racing shrine. Motor Racing was already then held all over the world, sometimes with Scores reaching the hundred mark, and long-distance races were popular.

'The modern Race makes it possible for the entire population to . . .'

Willie switched off the radio. Why did they always have to stress the *Score*? *Time* was important too. The *speed*—and the *endurance*. That was part of an Ace Racer as well as his scoring ability. He took an Energene Tab. They were entering Kansas City.

The check point officials told Willie that there were three Racers with better Time than he, and one had tied his Score. 'The Bull' stayed just long enough in the check point pit for Hank to make a quick engine inspection—then they took off again. It was 1818 hours, CST, when they left the city limits behind. They'd been driving over nine hours.

About 50 miles along the Thruway to Denver, just after passing through a little town called Lawrence, Willie suddenly slowed down. Hank, who'd been dozing, sat up in alarm.

'What's the matter?' he cried, 'what's wrong?'

'Nothing's wrong,' Willie said irritably. 'Relax. You seem to be good at that.'

'But why are you slowing down?'

'You heard the check point record. Our Score's already been tied. We've got to better it,' Willie answered grimly.

The plastirubber tyres screeched on the concrete speedway as Willie turned down an exit leading to a Class II road.

'Why down here?' asked Hank. 'You can only go about 80 mph.'

A large lumi-sign appeared on the side of the road ahead—

LONE STAR
11 MILES

it announced.

Willie pointed. 'That's why,' he said curtly.

In a few minutes Lone Star came into view. It was a small village. Willie was travelling as fast as he could on the secondary road. He ploughed through a flock of chickens, hurtled over a little mongrel dog, which crawled yelping towards the safety of a house and the waiting arms of a little girl, and managed to graze the leg of a husky youth who vaulted a high wooden fence—then they were through Lone Star.

Hank activated the little dashboard screen which gave them a rear view.

'That's not going to do much for our Score,' he remarked sourly.

'Oh, shut up!' Willie exploded, surprising both himself and Hank.

What was the *matter* with him? He couldn't be getting tired already. He swallowed a No-Sleep. That'd help.

Hank was quiet as they sped through Topeka and took the Thruway to Oklahoma City, but out of the corner of his eyes he was looking speculatively at Willie, hunched over the wheel.

It was getting dusk. Willie switched on his powerful head-beams. They had a faint reddish tint because of the colouring of 'The Bull's' eyes. They had just whizzed through a little burg named Perry, when there was a series of sharp cracks. Willie started.

'There they go again!' chortled Hank. 'Those dumb hinterland hicks will never learn they can't hurt us with their fly-poppers.' He knocked the plastiglass dome affectionately. 'Takes atomic pellets to get through this baby.'

Of course! He *must* be on edge to be taken by surprise like that. He'd run into the Anti-Racers before. Just a handful of malcontents. The Racing Commission had already declared them illegal. Still—at every race they took pot shots at the Racers; a sort of pathetic defiance. Why should anyone want to do away with Racing?

They were entering the outskirts of Oklahoma City. Willie killed his headbeams. No need to advertise.

Suddenly Hank grabbed his arm. Wordlessly he pointed. There—garish and gaudy—gleamed the neon sign of a theatre . . .

Willie slowed to a crawl. He pulled over to the kerb and the dark car melted into the shadows. He glanced at the clock. 2203 hours. Perhaps . . .

Down the street a man cautiously stuck his head out from the theatre entrance. Warily he emerged completely, looking up and down the street carefully. He did not see 'The Bull'. Presently he ventured out into the centre of the roadway. He stood still listening for a moment. Then he turned and beckoned towards the theatre. Immediately a small group of people emerged at a run.

Now!

The acceleration slammed the Racers back in their seats. 'The Bull' shot forward and bore down on the little knot of petrified people with appalling speed.

This time there was no mistaking the hits. A quick succession of pars had Willie calling upon all his driving skill to keep from losing control. Hank pressed the Clean-Spray button to wash the blood off the front of the dome. He sat with eyes glued to the rear view screen.

'Man, oh man,' he murmured. 'What a record! What a score!' He turned to Willie. 'Please,' he said, 'please stop. Let's get out. I know it's against regulations, but I've just gotta see how we did. It won't take long. We can afford a couple of minutes' Time now!'

Suddenly Willie felt he had to get out too. This was the biggest Tragi-Acc he'd ever had. He had a vague feeling there was something he wanted to do. He brought the car to a stop. They stepped out.

Within seconds the deserted street was swarming with people. Now the Racers were out of their car they felt safe. And curious. A few of them pressed forward to take a look at Willie. Naturally he was recognised. His photo had been seen in one way or another by everyone.

Willie was gratified by this obvious adulation. He looked about him. There were many people in the street now. But—but they were not all fawning and beaming upon him. Willie frowned. Most of them looked grim—even hostile. Why? What was wrong? Wasn't he one of their greatest Racers? And hadn't he just made a record Score? Given them a Tragi-Acc they wouldn't soon forget? What was the matter with those hicks?

Suddenly the crowd parted. Slowly a young girl walked up to Willie. She was beautiful—even with the terrible anger burning on her face. In her arms she held the still body of a child. She looked straight at Willie with loathing in her eyes. Her voice was low but steady when she said:

'Butcher!'

Someone in the crowd called: 'Careful, Muriel!' but she paid no heed. Turning from him she walked on through the crowd, parting for her.

Willie was stunned.

'Come on, let's get out of here,' Hank said anxiously.

Willie didn't answer. He was looking back through the crowd to the scene of his Tragi-Acc. Never before had he stopped. Never before had he been this close. He could hear the moaning and sobbing of the Maims over the low murmur of the crowd. It made him uneasy. Back there they worked hurriedly to get the Tragi-Accs off the street. *There were so many of them* ... Butcher ... ?

All at once he was conscious of Hank pulling at him.

'Let's get roaring! Let's go!'

Quickly he turned and entered the car. Almost at once the street was empty. He turned on his headbeams and started up. Faster—and faster. The street was dead—empty ...

No! There! Someone! Holding a ...

It was butcher—no, *Muriel*. She stood rooted to the spot in the middle of the street holding the child in her arms. In the glaring headlights her face was white, her eyes terrible, burning, dark ...

Willie did not let up. The car hurtled down upon the lone figure—and passed ...

They'd lost 13 minutes. Now they were on their way to El Paso, Texas. The nagging headache Willie'd suffered the whole week of planning before the race had returned. He reached for a No-Sleep, hesitated a second, then took another.

Hank glanced at him, worriedly. 'Easy, boy!'

Willie didn't answer.

'That Anti-Racer get under your skin?' Hank suggested. 'Don't let it bother you.'

'Butcher,' she'd said. 'Butcher!'

Willie was staring through the plastiglass dome at the racing pool of light from the headbeams. 'The Bull' was tearing along the Thruway at almost 180 mph.

What was that? There—in the light? It was a face—terrible, dark eyes—getting larger—larger—*Muriel*! It was a butcher—no, Muriel! No—it was a Racer—a Racing Car with Muriel's face, shrieking down upon him—closer—closer . . .

He threw his arms in front of his face. Dimly he heard Hank shout 'Willie!' He felt the car lurch. Automatically he tightened his grip on the wheel. They had careened close to the shoulder of the speedway. Willie sat up. Ahead of him the road was clear—and empty.

It was still dark when they hit El Paso. The radio told them their Oklahoma Score. Five and eight. Five Kills—eight Maims! Hank was delighted. They were close to setting a record. He'd already begun to spend his $25,000.

Willie was uneasy. His headache was worse. His hands were clammy. He kept hearing Muriel's voice saying: 'Butcher'—'Butcher'—'Butcher . . . !'

But he was *not* a butcher. He was a Racer! He'd show them. He'd win this race.

El Paso was a disappointment. Not a soul in sight. Phoenix next.

The clock said 0658 hours, MST, when they roared into Phoenix. The streets were clear. Willie had to slow down to take a corner. As he sped into the new street he saw her. She was running to cross the roadway. Hank whooped.

'Go, Willie! Go!'

The girl looked up an instant in terror.

Her face!

It was the old woman with the cat! No!—it was Muriel. Muriel with the big, dark eyes . . .

In the last split second Willie touched the power steering. 'The Bull' responded immediately, and shot past the girl as she scampered to safety.

'What the hell is the matter with you?' Hank roared at Willie. 'You could've scored! Are you out of your head?'

'We don't need her. We'll win without her. I—I—'

Yes, why hadn't he scored? It wasn't Muriel. Muriel was back in butcher—in—Oklahoma City. Damn this headache!

'Maybe so,' said Hank angrily. 'But I wanna be sure. And what about the bonus for setting a record? Ten thousand apiece. And we're close.' He looked slyly at Willie. 'Or—maybe you've lost your nerve. Wonder what the Commission will say to that?'

'I've got plenty of nerve,' Willie snapped.

'Prove it!' said Hank quickly. He pointed to the dashboard map slowly tracing their progress. 'There. See that village? With the screwy name? *Wikieup!* Off the Thruway. Let's see you score there!'

Willie said nothing. He hadn't lost his nerve, he knew that. He was the best of the Racers. No one could drive like he could; constant top speed, and the stamina it took, the split-second timing, the unerring judgement—

'Well?'

'All right,' Willie agreed.

They hadn't even reached Wikieup when they spotted the farmer. He didn't have a chance. 'The Bull' came charging down upon him. But in the last moment the car veered slightly. One of the horns ripped the man's hip open. In the rear view screen Willie saw him get up and hobble off the road.

'You could've made it a Kill,' Hank growled accusingly. 'Why didn't you?'

'Bad road,' Willie said. 'The wheel slipped on a stone.'

That's what must have happened, he thought. He didn't consciously veer away from the man. He was a good Racer. He couldn't help a bad road.

Needles was left behind at 1045 hours, PST. No one had been out. Hank turned on the radio to a Needles station:

'. . . has just left the city going West. No other Racer is reported within twenty minutes of the city. We repeat: A Racer has just left . . .'

Hank clicked it off. 'Hear that?' he said excitedly. 'Twenty minutes. They don't expect anyone for twenty minutes!' He took hold of Wilie's arm. 'Turn around! Here's where we can get ourselves that Record Score. Turn around, Willie!'

'We don't need it.'

'I do! *I want that bonus!*'

Willie made no answer.

'Listen to me, you two-bit Racer!' Hank's tone was menacing. 'You or nobody else is going to cheat me out of that bonus. You've been acting mighty peculiar. More like an Anti-Racer! Ever since you stopped at that Tragi-Acc back there. Yeah! That girl—that Anti-Racer who called you a—a butcher. Listen! You

get that Record Score, or I'll report you to the Commission for
having snooped around a Tragi-Acc. You'll never race again!'

Never race again! Willie's brain was whirling. But he *was* a
Racer. Not a butcher. *A Racer.* Record Score? Yes—that's what
he had to do. Set a record. Be the best damned Racer of them
all.

Without a word he turned the car. In minutes they were back at
the Needles suburbs. That building. A school house. And there—
marching orderly in two rows with their teacher, a class, a whole
class of children . . .

'The Bull' came charging down the street. Only a couple of
hundred feet now to that Record Score . . .

But what was that—it was . . . they were *Muriel*—they were
all Muriel. Terrible, dark eyes. No!—they were children—the
child in Muriel's arms. *They were all the child in Muriel's arms!*
Were they already moaning and screaming? Butcher! *Butcher!*
No! He couldn't butcher them—he was a *Racer*—not a *butcher.*
Not a butcher! Deliberately he swung the car to the empty side
of the street.

Suddenly he felt Hank's hands up on the wheel. 'You—dirty—
lousy—Anti-Racer!' the mechanic snarled as he struggled for the
wheel.

The car lurched. The two men fought savagely for control.
They were only yards from the fleeing children.

With a violent wrench Willie turned the wheel sharply. The
car was going 165 miles an hour when it struck the school house
and crashed through the wall into the empty building.

The voices came to Willie through thick wads of cotton—and
they kept fading in and out.

'. . . *dead instantaneously. But the Racer is still* . . .'

It sounded like the voice of Muriel. Muriel . . .

'. . . *keeps calling for* . . .'

Willie tried to open his eyes. Everything was milky white. Why
was there so much fog? A face was bending over him. Muriel?
No—it was not Muriel. He lost consciousness again.

When he opened his eyes once more he knew he was not alone.
He turned his head. A girl was sitting at his bedside. Muriel . . .

It *was* Muriel.

He tried to sit up.

'It's you! But—but, how . . . ?'

The girl put her hand on his arm.

'The radio. They said you kept calling for "Muriel". I knew. Never mind that now.'

She looked steadily at him. Her eyes were not terrible—not burning—only dark, and puzzled.

'Why did you call for *me*?' she asked earnestly.

Willie struggled to sit up.

'I wanted to tell you,' he said, 'to tell you—I—I am not a butcher!'

The girl looked at him for a long moment. Then she leaned down and whispered to him:

'Nor a Racer!'

ALONG THE SCENIC ROUTE

Harlan Ellison

*As long ago as the 1960s, American science fiction writers were pre-
dicting the motoring holocaust they believed awaited mankind. Foremost
among them were Frank Herbert, Harry Harrison, Fritz Leiber and
Harlan Ellison, and their stories of clogged highways, sinister cars and
vicious, renegade drivers helped to create a mini-genre of its own. 'Along
the Scenic Route' by Harlan Ellison is typical of them. In it he forecasts
that the antagonism felt by motorists who believe their masculinity is
threatened by other drivers will be channelled into legally sanctioned
duels on motorways, death or glory being the ultimate prize. So when
a blood-red Mercury with a youngster at the wheel cuts up George on
Route 101, what is a real man to do but take up the challenge — even
if he is driving the family car with his wife as passenger?*

  *Harlan Ellison (1934–) has become one of the most controversial
and highly regarded writers in American science fiction. A mercurial,
prolific and strongly opinionated man, the tenor of his extraordinary
career was struck when he moved from Ohio to New York as a young
man and became a member of a street gang in Brooklyn. From this
experience came a series of books about the violence of city life, including*
Rumble *(1958) and* The Juvies *(1961). He followed these with stories
in a variety of genres, as well as writing scripts for several TV shows
including* Route 66 *(1960–3) and* The Untouchables *(1959–62). At
this time, he began producing the sf short stories that have made his
reputation, in collections such as* The Beast that Shouted Love at
the Heart of the World *(1969),* Deathbird Stories *(1975) and others.
He also edited the legendary 'New-Wave' anthologies,* Dangerous
Visions *(1969–73), which are notorious for his highly idiosyncratic
introductions. Few other writers in the genre have made more pertinent
and angry statements about the human condition — elements that are
powerfully evident in 'Along the Scenic Route' (also known as 'Dogfight*

on 101') which he wrote for Amazing Stories *in 1969. Ellison has also added a typically acerbic Afterword about the story's creation — and its prophetic theme.*

*   *   *

The blood-red Mercury with the twin-mounted 7.6 mm Spandaus cut George off as he was shifting lanes. The Merc cut out sharply, three cars behind George, and the driver decked it. The boom of his gas-turbine engine got through George's baffling system without difficulty, like a fist in the ear. The Merc sprayed JP-4 gook and water in a wide fan from its jet nozzle and cut back in, a matter of inches in front of George's Chevy Piranha.

George slapped the selector control on the dash, lighting YOU STUPID BASTARD, WHAT DO YOU THINK YOU'RE DOING and I HOPE YOU CRASH & BURN, YOU SON OF A BITCH. Jessica moaned softly with uncontrolled fear, but George could not hear her: he was screaming obscenities.

George kicked it into Overplunge and depressed the selector button extending the rotating buzzsaws. Dallas razors, they were called, in the repair shoppes. But the crimson Merc pulled away doing an easy 115.

'I'll get you, you beaver-sucker!' he howled.

The Piranha jumped, surged forward. But the Merc was already two dozen car-lengths down the Freeway. Adrenaline pumped through George's system. Beside him, Jessica put a hand on his arm. 'Oh, forget it, George; it's just some young snot,' she said. Always conciliatory.

'My masculinity's threatened,' he murmured, and hunched over the wheel. Jessica looked towards heaven, wishing a bolt of lightning had come from that location many months past, striking Dr Yasimir directly in his Freud, long before George could have picked up psychiatric justifications for his awful temper.

'Get me Collision Control!' George snarled at her.

Jessica shrugged, as if to say *here we go again*, and dialled CC on the peek. The smiling face of a fusco, the Freeway Sector Control Operator, blurred green and yellow, then came into sharp focus. 'Your request, sir?'

'Clearance for duel, Highway 101, northbound.'

'Your licence number, sir?'

'XUPD 88321,' George said. He was scanning the Freeway, keeping the blood-red Mercury in sight, obstinately refusing to stud on the tracking sights.

'Your proposed opponent, sir?'

'Red Mercury GT. '88 model.'

'Licence, sir.'

'Just a second.' George pressed the stud for the instant replay and the last ten miles rewound on the Sony Backtracker. He ran it forward again till he caught the instant the Merc had passed him, froze the frame, and got the number. 'MFCS 90909.'

'One moment, sir.'

George fretted behind the wheel. '*Now* what the hell's holding her up? Whenever you want service, they've got problems. But boy, when it comes tax time—'

The fusco came back and smiled. 'I've checked our master Sector grid, sir, and I find authorisation may be permitted, but I am required by law to inform you that your proposed opponent is more heavily armed than yourself.'

George licked his lips. 'What's he running?'

'Our records indicate 7.6 mm Spandau equipment, bulletproof screens and coded optionals.'

George sat silently. His speed dropped. The tachometer fluttered, settled.

'Let him go, George,' Jessica said. 'You know he'd take you.'

Two blotches of anger spread on George's cheeks. 'Oh, yeah!?!' He howled at the fusco, 'Get me a confirm on that Mercury, Fusco!'

She blurred off, and George decked the Piranha: it leaped forward. Jessica sighed with resignation and pulled the drawer out from beneath her bucket. She unfolded the g-suit and began stretching into it. She said nothing, but continued to shake her head.

'We'll *see*!' George said.

'Oh, George, when will you ever grow up?'

He did not answer, but his nostrils flared with barely restrained anger.

The fusco smeared back and said, 'Opponent confirms, sir. Freeway Underwriters have already cross-filed you as mutual beneficiaries. Please observe standard traffic regulations, and good luck, sir.'

She vanished, and George set the Piranha on sleepwalker as he donned his own g-suit. He overrode the sleeper and was back on manual in moments.

'Now, you stuffer, *now* let's see!' 100. 110. 120.

He was gaining rapidly on the Merc now. As the Chevy hit 120, the mastercomp flashed red and suggested crossover. George punched the selector and the telescoping arms of the buzzsaws retracted into the axles, even as the buzzsaws stopped whirling. In a moment—drawn back in, now merely fancy decorations in the hubcaps. The wheels retracted into the underbody of the Chevy and the air-cushion took over. Now the Chevy skimmed along, two inches above the roadbed of the Freeway.

Ahead, George could see the Merc also crossing over to air-cushion. 120. 135. 150.

'George, this is crazy!' Jessica said, her face in that characteristic shrike expression. 'You're no hot-rodder, George. You're a family man, and this is the family car!'

George chuckled nastily. 'I've had it with these fuzzfaces. Last year . . . you remember last year . . . ? you remember when that punk stuffer ran us into the abutment? I swore I'd never put up with that kind of thing again. Why'd'you think I had all the optionals installed?'

Jessica opened the tambour doors of the glove compartment and slid out the service tray. She unplugged the jar of anti-flash salve and began spreading it on her face and hands. 'I *knew* I shouldn't have let you put that laser thing in this car!' George chuckled again. Fuzzfaces, punks, rodders!

George felt the Piranha surge forward, the big reliable Stirling engine recycling the hot air for more and more efficient thrust. Unlike the Merc's inefficient kerosene system, there was no exhaust emission from the nuclear power plant, the external combustion engine almost noiseless, the big radiator tailfin in the rear dissipating the tremendous heat, stabilising the car as it swooshed along, two inches off the roadbed.

George knew he would catch the blood-red Mercury. Then one smartarse punk was going to learn he couldn't flout law and order by running decent citizens off the Freeways!

'Get me my gun,' George said.

Jessica shook her head with exasperation, reached under George's bucket, pulled out his drawer and handed him the bulky .45 automatic in its breakaway upside-down shoulder rig. George studded in the sleeper, worked his arms into the rig, tested the oiled leather of the holster, and when he was satisfied, returned the Piranha to manual.

'Oh, God,' Jessica said, 'John Dillinger rides again.'

'Listen!' George shouted, getting more furious with each stupidity she offered. 'If you can't be of some help to me, just shut your damned mouth. I'd put you out and come back for you, but I'm in a duel ... can you understand that? I'm in a duel!' She murmured a yes, George, and fell silent.

There was a transmission queep from the transceiver. George studded it on. No picture. Just vocal. It had to be the driver of the Mercury, up ahead of them. Beaming directly at one another's antennae, using a tightbeam directional, they could keep in touch: it was a standard trick used by rods to rattle their opponents.

'Hey, Boze, you not really gonna custer me, are you? Back'm, Boze. No bad trips, true. The kid'll drop back, hang a couple of biggies on ya, just to teach ya a little lesson, letcha swimaway.' The voice of the driver was hard, mirthless, the ugly sound of a driver used to being challenged.

'Listen, you young snot,' George said, grating his words, trying to sound more menacing than he felt, 'I'm going to teach *you* the lesson!'

The Merc's driver laughed raucously.

'Boze, you *de*-mote me, true!'

'And stop calling me a bozo, you lousy little degenerate!'

'Ooooo-weeee, got me a thrasher this time out. Okay, Boze, you be custer an' I'll play arrow. Good shells, baby Boze!'

The finalising queep sounded, and George gripped the wheel with hands that went knuckle-white. The Merc suddenly shot away from him. He had been steadily gaining, but now as though it had been springloaded, the Mercury burst forward, spraying gook and water on both sides of the forty-foot lanes they were using. 'Cut in his afterburner,' George snarled. The driver of the Mercury had injected water into the exhaust for added thrust through the jet nozzle. The boom of the Merc's big, noisy engine hit him, and George studded in the rear-mounted propellers to give him more speed. 175. 185. 195.

He was crawling up the line towards the Merc. Gaining, gaining. Jessica pulled out her drawer and unfolded her crash-suit. It went on over the g-suit, and she let George know what she thought of his turning their Sunday Drive into a kamikaze duel.

He told her to stuff it, and did a sleeper, donned his own crash-suit, applied flash salve, and lowered the bangup helmet onto his head.

Back on manual he crawled, crawled, till he was only fifty yards behind the Mercury, the gas-turbine vehicle sharp in his tinted windshield. 'Put on your goggles ... I'm going to show that punk who's a bozo ...'

He pressed the stud to open the laser louvres. The needle-nosed glass tube peered out from its bay in the Chevy's hood. George read the power drain on his dash. The MHD power generator used to drive the laser was charging. He remembered what the salesman at Chick Williams Chevrolet had told him, pridefully, about the laser gun, when George had inquired about the optional.

Dynamite feature, Mr Jackson. Absolutely sensational. Works off a magneto hydro dynamic power generator. Latest thing in defence armament. You know, to achieve sufficient potency from a CO_2 laser, you'd need a glass tube a mile long. Well, sir, we both know that's impractical, to say the least, so the project engineers at Chevy's big Bombay plant developed the 'stack' method. Glass rods baffled with mirrors—360 feet of stack, the length of a football field ... plus end-zones. Use it three ways. Punch a hole right through their tyres at any speed under a hundred and twenty. If they're running a GT, you can put that hole right into the kerosene fuel tank, blow them off the road. Or, if they're running a Stirling, just heat the radiator. When the radiator gets hotter than the engine, the whole works shuts down. Dynamite. Also ... and this is with proper CC authorisation, you can go straight for the old jugular. Use the beam on the driver. Makes a neat hole. Dynamite!

'I'll take it,' George murmured.

'What did you say?' Jessica asked.

'Nothing.'

'George, you're a family man, not a rodder!'

'Stuff it!'

Then he was sorry he'd said it. She meant well. It was simply that ... well, a man had to work hard to keep his balls. He looked sideways at her. Wearing the Armadillo crash-suit, with its over-lapping discs of ceramic material, she looked like a ferryflight pilot. The bangup hat hid her face. He wanted to apologise, but the moment had arrived. He locked the laser on the Merc, depressed the fire stud, and a beam of blinding light flashed from the hood of the Piranha. With the Merc on air-cushion, he had gone straight for the fuel tank.

But the Merc suddenly wasn't in front of him. Even as he had fired, the driver had sheered left into the next forty-foot-wide lane, and cut speed drastically. The Merc dropped back past them as the Piranha swooshed ahead.

'He's on my back!' George shouted.

The next moment Spandau slugs tore at the hide of the Chevy. George slapped the studs, and the bulletproof screens went up. But not before pingholes had appeared in the beryllium hide of the Chevy, exposing the boron fibre filaments that gave the car its lightweight manoeuvrability. 'Stuffer!' George breathed, terribly frightened. The driver was on his back, could ride him into the ground.

He swerved, dropping flaps and skimming the Piranha back and forth in wide arcs, across the two lanes. The Merc hung on. The Spandaus chattered heavily. The screens would hold, but what else was the driver running? What were the 'coded optionals' the CC fusco had mentioned?

'Now see what you've gotten us into!'

'Jess, shut up, shut up!'

The transceiver queeped. He studded it on, still swerving. This time the driver of the Merc was sending via microwave video. The face blurred in.

He was a young boy. In his teens. Acne.

'Punk! Stinking punk!' George screamed, trying to swerve, drop back, accelerate. Nothing. The blood-red Merc hung on his tailfin, pounding at him. If one of those bullets struck the radiator tailfin, ricocheted, pierced to the engine, got through the lead shielding around the reactor. Jessica was crying, huddled inside her Armadillo.

He was silently glad she was in the g-suit. He would try something illegal in a moment.

'Hey, Boze. What's your slit look like? If she's creamy'n'nice I might letcha drop her at the next getty, and come back for her later. With your insurance, baby, and my pickle, I can keep her creamy'n'nice.'

'Fuzzfaced punk! I'll see you dead first!'

'You're a real thrasher, old dad. Wish you well, but it's soon over. Say bye-bye to the nice rodder. You gonna die, old dad!'

George was shrieking inarticulately.

The boy laughed wildly. He was up on something. Ferro-coke, perhaps. Or D4. Or merryloo. His eyes glistened blue and young and deadly as a snake.

'Just wanted you to know the name of your piledriver, old dad. *You* can call me Billy . . .'

And he was gone. The Merc slipped forward, closer, and George had only a moment to realise that this Billy could not possibly have the money to equip his car with a laser, and that was a godsend. But the Spandaus were hacking away at the bulletproof screens. They weren't meant for extended punishment like this. Damn that Detroit iron!

He had to make the illegal move *now*.

Thank God for the g-suits. A tight turn, across the lanes, in direct contravention of the authorisation. And in a tight turn, without the g-suits, doing—he checked the speedometer and tach—250 mph, the blood slams up against one side of the body. The g-suits would squeeze the side of the body where the blood tried to pool up. They would live. If . . .

He spun the wheel hard, slamming down the accelerator. The Merc slewed sideways and caught the turn. He never had a chance. He pulled out of the illegal turn, and their positions were the same. But the Merc had dropped back several car-lengths. Then from the transceiver there was a queep and he did not even stud in as the Police Copter overhead tightbeamed him in an authoritative voice:

'XUPD 88321. Warning! You will be in contravention of your duelling authorisation if you try another manoeuvre of that sort! You are warned to keep to your lanes and the standard rules of road courtesy!'

Then it was queeped, and George felt the universe settling like silt over him. He was being killed by the system.

He'd have to eject. The seat would save him and Jessica. He tried to tell her, but she had fainted.

How did I get into this? he pleaded with himself. *Dear God, I swear if you get me out of this alive I'll never never go mad like this again. Please God.*

Then the Merc was up on him again, pulling up *alongside*!

The window went down on the passenger side of the Mercury, and George whipped a glance across to see Billy with his lips skinned back from his teeth under the windblast and acceleration, aiming a .45 at him. Barely thinking, George studded the bumpers.

The super-conducting magnetic bumpers took hold, sucked Billy into his magnetic field, and they collided with a crash that shook the .45 out of the rodder's hand. In the instant of collision, George realised he had made his chance, and dropped back. In a moment he was riding the Merc's tail again.

Naked barbarism took hold. He wanted to kill now. Not crash the other, not wound the other, not stop the other—*kill the other!* Messages to God were forgotten.

He locked-in the laser and aimed for the windshield bubble. His sights caught the rear of the bubble, fastened to the outline of Billy's head, and George fired.

As the bolt of light struck the bubble, a black spot appeared, and remained for the seconds the laser touched. When the light cut off the black spot vanished. George cursed, screamed, cried, in fear and helplessness.

The Merc was equipped with a frequency-sensitive laserproof windshield. Chemicals in the windshield would 'go black', opaque at certain frequencies, momentarily, anywhere a laser light touched them. He should have known. A duellist like this Billy, trained in weaponry, equipped for whatever might chance down a Freeway. Another coded optional. George found he was crying, piteously, within the cavern of his bangup hat.

Then the Merc was swerving again, executing a roll and dip that George could not understand, could not predict. Then the Merc dropped speed suddenly, and George found himself almost running up the jet nozzle of the blood-red vehicle.

He spun out and around, and Billy was behind him once more, closing in for the kill. He sent the propellers to full spin and reached for eternity. 270. 280. 290.

Then he heard the sizzling, and jerked his head around to see the back wall of the car rippling. *Oh my God*, he thought, in terror, *he can't afford a laser, but he's got an inductor beam!*

The beam was setting up strong local eddy currents in the beryllium hide of the Chevy. He'd rip a hole in the skin, the air would whip through, the car would go out of control.

George knew he was dead.

And Jessica.

And all because of this punk, this rodder fuzzface!

The Merc closed in confidently.

George thought wildly. There was no time for anything but the blind plunging panic of random thought. The speedometer and the tach agreed. They were doing 300 mph.

Riding on air-cushions.

The thought slipped through his panic.

It was the only possibility. He ripped off his bangup hat, and fumbled Jessica's loose. He hugged them in his lap with his free hand, and managed to stud down the window on the driver's side. Instantly, a blast of wind and accelerated air skinned back his lips, plastered his cheeks hollowly, made a death's head of Jessica's features. He fought to keep the Chevy stable, gyro'd.

Then, holding the bangup hats by their straps, he forced them around the edge of the window where the force of his speed jammed them against the side of the Chevy. Then he let go. And studded up the window. And braked sharply.

The bulky bangup hats dropped away, hit the roadbed, rolled directly into the path of the Merc. They disappeared underneath the blood-red car, and instantly the vehicle hit the Freeway. George swerved out of the way, dropping speed quickly.

The Merc hit with a crash, bounced, hit again, bounced and hit, bounced and hit. As it went past the Piranha, George saw Billy caroming off the insides of the car.

He watched the vehicle skid, wheelless, for a quarter of a mile down the Freeway before it caught the inner breakwall of the Jersey Barrier, shot high in the air, and came down turning over. It landed on the bubble, which burst, and exploded in a flash of fire and smoke that rocked the Chevy.

At three hundred miles per hour, two inches above the Freeway, riding on air, anything that broke up the air bubble would be a lethal weapon. He had won the duel. That Billy was dead.

George pulled in at the next getty, and sat in the lot. Jessica came round finally. He was slumped over the wheel, shaking, unable to speak.

She looked over at him, then reached out a trembling hand to touch his shoulder. He jumped at the infinitesimal pressure, felt through the g- and crash-suits. She started to speak, but the peek queeped, and she studded it on.

'Sector Control, sir.' The fusco smiled.

He did not look up.

'Congratulations, sir. Despite one possible infraction, your duel has been logged as legal and binding. You'll be pleased to know that the occupant of the car you challenged was rated number one in the entire Central and Western Freeway circuits. Now that Mr Bonney has been finalised, we are entering your name on the duelling records. Underwriters have asked us to inform you that a check will be in the mails to you within twenty-four hours.

'Again, sir, congratulations.'

The peek went dead, and George tried to focus on the parking lot of the neon-and-silver getty. It had been a terrible experience. He never wanted to use a car that way again. It had been some other George, certainly not him.

'I'm a family man,' he repeated Jessica's words. 'And this is just a family car . . . I . . .'

She was smiling gently at him. Then they were in each other's arms, and he was crying, and she was saying that's all right, George, you had to do it, it's all right.

And the peek queeped.

She studded it on and the face of the fusco smiled back at her. 'Congratulations, sir, you'll be pleased to know that Sector Control already has fifteen duel challenges for you.

'Mr Ronnie Lee Hauptman of Dallas has asked for first challenge, and is, at this moment, speeding towards you with an ETA of 6:15 this evening. In the event Mr Hauptman does not survive, you have waiting challenges from Mr Fred Bull of Chatsworth, California . . . Mr Leo Fowler of Philadelphia . . . Mr Emil Zalenko of . . .'

George did not hear the list. He was trying desperately, with clubbed fingers, to extricate himself from the strangling folds of g- and crash-suits. But he knew it was no good. He would have to fight.

In the world of the Freeway, there was no place for a walking man.

AFTERWORD

When I arrived in Los Angeles on New Year's Day 1962, I discovered a city more wonderful than I had ever imagined. It had all the verve and passion of New York during its last really vibrant period—'54–'57—coupled with the insouciance of New Orleans before it became aware of itself as The Big Easy. It had the charm of small-town America and the urbanity of Big Town USA.

All that is gone, today. The demon of 'Progress' as worshipped by ex-Governor Reagan and all the clone-idiots who have followed him in office since he singlehandedly destroyed the California educational system, has turned LA into yet another sprawling, choking, murderous, inconvenient, imbecile paradise for realtors, rampant builders, illiterate gangs of slaughtering arseholes, weirdos of every stripe, and that great American icon, OJ Simpson, may his dick fall off in his soup.

Nonetheless, I am an Angeleno. I've lived here longer than anywhere else in my peripatetic life, and I cannot think of a better place to reside, for all its drawbacks. (No, I'm not nuts about the earthquakes, but you've got the equivalent crap where you are—twister, flood, smog. Fundamentalists—so that part's a tradeoff).

I wrote this story at least ten years, maybe more, before actual drive-by shootings became common throughout the US, but commencing with LA at the cutting edge. I wrote it on the subject of middle-class conformity, mediocrity, and the utter stupidity of *Macho* behaviour. The idea that such a wild and improbable social escapade could become commonplace in less than a decade, never occurred to me. When the first freeway 'duels' began out here, I was contacted by the AP, the UP, the INS, and a dozen newspapers. How they had made the liaison between my little fable and the new reality, I never found out. Maybe someone working the *NY Times* night desk had read the story. They all asked me how I felt about 'predicting' this phenomenon, and wasn't this another classic example of how insightful 'sci-fi' was supposed to be? I didn't have the heart to tell them that if you've got hundreds of writers all wildly predicting anything they can think of, that eventually there will be a few hits (but in fact, sf has as lousy a hit-to-miss ratio on prediction and extrapolation as the most bogus fortune-teller found in the tabloids). Didn't have the heart—particularly after they pointed out that I'd coined the term 'fax' in the same story—and decided to accept the mantle of Nostradamus.

All bullshit, of course, but how else are we clowns to stay in business? You can fool some of the people some of the time, and some of the people some of the time, but you can't fool some of the people some of the time. I think I've got that right.

AUTO-DA-FE

Roger Zelazny

Imagine a public arena baked by the sun. In the ring, two adversaries circle one another, searching for a weakness and the opportunity to kill. The scene might be that of a bullfight: instead, in the arena of the future, the duel is between a man and an automobile. We are about to witness the great El mechador *confront his moment of truth with a cunning red Pontiac . . . It seems appropriate that this story should follow Harlan Ellison's tale of a motorway duel because it was actually written for his* Dangerous Visions *anthology and is certainly one of the best tales in the book.*

Roger Zelazny (1937–95) was a close friend of Harlan Ellison and, like him, dedicated to pushing the frontiers of science fiction even further. It was an interest in Elizabethan drama, especially its dark intricacies, that inspired Zelazny's early stories which he wrote while employed in the Social Security Administration in Cleveland, Ohio. His unique imagination was soon recognised in collections such as The Doors of His Face, the Lamps of His Mouth *(1971) and the series of fantasy novels known as* The Chronicles of Amber *which freed him to write full time. These books continued to appear at regular intervals until his premature death. Another of Zelazny's books,* Damnation Alley *(1969), was filmed in 1977, with George Peppard and Jan-Michael Vincent as members of a group of men who travel across a post-holocaust America in landmobiles. 'Auto-da-Fé' looks to the same uncertain future and is, in the words of Harlan Ellison's original introduction, 'A penetrating extrapolation of our "mobile culture".'*

*   *   *

Still do I remember the hot sun upon the sands of the Plaza de Autos, the cries of the soft-drink hawkers, the tiers of humanity stacked across from me on the sunny side of the arena, sunglasses like cavities in their gleaming faces.

Still do I remember the smells and the colours: the reds and the blues and the yellows, the ever present tang of petroleum fumes upon the air.

Still do I remember that day, that day with its sun in the middle of the sky and the sign of Aries, burning in the blooming of the year. I recall the mincing steps of the pumpers, heads thrown back, arms waving, the white dazzles of their teeth framed with smiling lips, cloths like colourful tails protruding from the rear pockets of their overalls; and the horns—I remember the blare of a thousand horns over the loudspeakers, on and off, off and on, over and over, and again, and then one shimmering, final note, sustained, to break the ear and the heart with its infinite power, its pathos.

Then there was silence.

I see it now as I did on that day so long ago . . .

He entered the arena, and the cry that went up shook blue heaven upon its pillars of white marble.

'Viva! El mechador! Viva! El mechador!'

I remember his face, dark and sad and wise.

Long of jaw and nose was he, and his laughter was as the roaring of the wind, and his movements were as the music of the theramin and the drum. His overalls were blue and silk and tight and stitched with thread of gold and broidered all about with black braid. His jacket was beaded and there were flashing scales upon his breast, his shoulders, his back.

His lips curled into the smile of a man who has known much glory and has hold upon the power that will bring him into more.

He moved, turning in a circle, not shielding his eyes against the sun.

He was above the sun. He was Manolo Stillete Dos Muerots, the mightiest *mechador* the world had ever seen, black boots upon his feet, pistons in his thighs, fingers with the discretion of micrometers, halo of dark locks about his head and the angel of death in his right arm, there, in the centre of the grease-stained circle of truth.

He waved, and a cry went up once more.

'Manolo! Manolo! Dos Muertos! Dos Muertos!'

After two years' absence from the ring, he had chosen this, the anniversary of his death and retirement, to return—for there was gasoline and methyl in his blood and his heart was a burnished pump ringed 'bout with desire and courage. He had died twice within the ring, and twice had the medics restored him. After his second death, he had retired, and some said that it was because he had known fear. This could not be true.

He waved his hand and his name rolled back upon him.

The horns sounded once more: three long blasts.

Then again there was silence, and a pumper wearing red and yellow brought him the cape, removed his jacket.

The tinfoil backing of the cape flashed in the sun as Dos Muertos swirled it.

Then there came the final, beeping notes.

The big door rolled upward and back into the wall.

He draped his cape over his arm and faced the gateway.

The light above was red and from within the darkness there came the sound of an engine.

The light turned yellow, then green, and there was the sound of cautiously engaged gears.

The car moved slowly into the ring, paused, crept forward, paused again.

It was a red Pontiac, its hood stripped away, its engine like a nest of snakes, coiling and engendering behind the circular shimmer of its invisible fan. The wings of its aerial spun round and round, then fixed upon Manolo and his cape.

He had chosen a heavy one for his first, slow on turning, to give him a chance to limber up.

The drums of its brain, which had never before recorded a man, were spinning.

Then the consciousness of its kind swept over it, and it moved forward.

Manolo swirled his cape and kicked its fender as it roared past.

The door of the great garage closed.

When it reached the opposite side of the ring the car stopped, parked.

Cries of disgust, booing and hissing arose from the crowd.

Still the Pontiac remained parked.

Two pumpers, bearing buckets, emerged from behind the fence and threw mud upon its windshield.

It roared then and pursued the nearest, banging into the fence. Then it turned suddenly, sighted Dos Muertos and charged.

His *veronica* transformed him into a statue with a skirt of silver. The enthusiasm of the crowd was mighty.

It turned and charged once more, and I wondered at Manolo's skill, for it would seem that his buttons had scraped cherry paint from the side panels.

Then it paused, spun its wheels, ran in a circle about the ring. The crowd roared as it moved past him and recircled.

Then it stopped again, perhaps fifty feet away.

Manolo turned his back upon it and waved to the crowd.

—Again, the cheering and the calling of his name.

He gestured to someone behind the fence.

A pumper emerged and bore to him, upon a velvet cushion, his chrome-plated monkey wrench.

He turned then again to the Pontiac and strode towards it.

It stood there shivering and he knocked off its radiator cap.

A jet of steaming water shot into the air and the crowd bellowed. Then he struck the front of the radiator and banged upon each fender.

He turned his back upon it again and stood there.

When he heard the engagement of the gears he turned once more, and with one clean pass it was by him, but not before he had banged twice upon the trunk with his wrench.

It moved to the other end of the ring and parked.

Manolo raised his hand to the pumper behind the fence.

The man with the cushion emerged and bore to him the long-handled screwdriver and the short cape. He took the monkey wrench away with him, as well as the long cape.

Another silence came over the Plaza del Autos.

The Pontiac, as if sensing all this, turned once more and blew its horn twice. Then it charged.

There were dark spots upon the sand from where its radiator had leaked water. Its exhaust arose like a ghost behind it. It bore down upon him at a terrible speed.

Dos Muertos raised the cape before him and rested the blade of the screwdriver upon his left forearm.

When it seemed he would surely be run down, his hand shot forward, so fast the eye could barely follow it, and he stepped to the side as the engine began to cough.

Still the Pontiac continued on with a deadly momentum, turned sharply without braking, rolled over, slid into the fence, and began to burn. Its engine coughed and died.

The Plaza shook with the cheering. They awarded Dos Muertos both headlights and the tailpipe. He held them high and moved in slow promenade about the perimeter of the ring. The horns sounded. A lady threw him a plastic flower and he sent for a pumper to bear her the tailpipe and ask her to dine with him. The crowd cheered more loudly, for he was known to be a great layer of women, and it was not such an unusual thing in the days of my youth as it is now.

The next was the blue Chevrolet, and he played with it as a child plays with a kitten, tormenting it into striking, then stopping it forever. He received both headlights. The sky had clouded over by then and there was a tentative mumbling of thunder.

The third was a black Jaguar XKE, which calls for the highest skill possible and makes for a very brief moment of truth. There was blood as well as gasoline upon the sand before he dispatched it, for its side mirror extended further than one would think, and there was a red furrow across his rib cage before he had done with it. But he tore out its ignition system with such grace and artistry that the crowd boiled over into the ring, and the guards were called forth to beat them with clubs and herd them with cattle prods back into their seats.

Surely, after all of this, none could say that Dos Muertos had ever known fear.

A cool breeze arose and I bought a soft drink and waited for the last.

His final car sped forth while the light was still yellow. It was a mustard-coloured Ford convertible. As it went past him the first time, it blew its horn and turned on its windshield wipers. Everyone cheered, for they could see it had spirit.

Then it came to a dead halt, shifted into reverse, and backed towards him at about forty miles an hour.

He got out of the way, sacrificing grace to expediency, and it braked sharply, shifted into low gear, and sped forward again.

He waved the cape and it was torn from his hands. If he had not thrown himself over backward, he would have been struck.

Then someone cried: 'It's out of alignment!'

But he got to his feet, recovered his cape and faced it once more.

They still tell of those five passes that followed. Never has there been such a flirting with bumper and grille! Never in all of the Earth has there been such an encounter between *mechador* and machine! The convertible roared like ten centuries of stream-lined death, and the spirit of St Detroit sat in its driver's seat, grinning, while Dos Muertos faced it with his tinfoil cape, cowed it and called for his wrench. It nursed its overheated engine and rolled its windows up and down, up and down, clearing its muffler the while with lavatory noises and much black smoke.

By then it was raining, softly, gently, and the thunder still came about us. I finished my soft drink.

Dos Muertos had never used his monkey wrench on the engine before, only upon the body. But this time he threw it. Some experts say he was aiming at the distributor; others say he was trying to break its fuel pump.

The crowd booed him.

Something gooey was dripping from the Ford onto the sand. The red streak brightened on Manolo's stomach. The rain came down.

He did not look at the crowd. He did not take his eyes from the car. He held out his right hand, palm upward, and waited.

A panting pumper placed the screwdriver in his hand and ran back towards the fence.

Manolo moved to the side and waited.

It leaped at him and he struck.

There was more booing.

He had missed the kill.

No one left, though. The Ford swept around him in a tight circle, smoke now emerging from its engine. Manolo rubbed his arm and picked up the screwdriver and cape he had dropped. There was more booing as he did so.

By the time the car was upon him, flames were leaping forth from its engine.

Now some say that he struck and missed again, going off balance. Others say that he began to strike, grew afraid and drew back. Still others say that, perhaps for an instant, he knew a fatal pity for his spirited adversary, and that this had stayed his hand. I say that the smoke was too thick for any of them to say for certain what had happened.

But it swerved and he fell forward, and he was borne upon that engine, blazing like a god's catafalque, to meet with his third death as they crashed into the fence together and went up in flames.

There was much dispute over the final *corrida*, but what

remained of the tailpipe and both headlights were buried with what remained of him, beneath the sands of the Plaza, and there was much weeping among the women he had known. I say that he could not have been afraid or known pity, for his strength was as a river of rockets, his thighs were pistons and the fingers of his hands had the discretion of micrometers; his hair was a black halo and the angel of death rode on his right arm. Such a man, a man who has known truth, is mightier than any machine. Such a man is above anything but the holding of power and the wearing of glory.

Now he is dead though, this one, for the third and final time. He is as dead as all the dead who have ever died before the bumper, under the grille, beneath the wheels. It is well that he cannot rise again, for I say that his final car was his apotheosis, and anything else would be anticlimactic. Once I saw a blade of grass growing up between the metal sheets of the world in a place where they had become loose, and I destroyed it because I felt it must be lonesome. Often have I regretted doing this thing, for I took away the glory of its aloneness. Thus does life the machine, I feel, consider man, sternly, then with regret, and the heavens do weep upon him through eyes that grief has opened in the sky.

All the way home I thought of this thing, and the hoofs of my mount clicked upon the floor of the city as I rode through the rain towards evening, that spring.

AFTERWORD

This is the first time I've had a chance to address the readers of one of my stories directly, rather than through the mimesis game we play. While I go along with the notion that a writer should hold a mirror up to reality, I don't necessarily feel that it should be the kind you look into when you shave or tweeze your eyebrows, or both as the case may be. If I'm going to carry a mirror around, holding it up to reality whenever I notice any, I might as well enjoy the burden as much as I can. My means of doing this is to tote around one of those mirrors you used to see in fun houses, back when you still had fun houses. Of course, not anything you reflect looks either as attractive or as grimly visaged as it may stand before the naked eyeball. Sometimes it looks more attractive, or more grimly visaged. You just don't really know, until you've tried the warping glass. And it's awfully hard to hold the slippery warping glass. And it's awfully hard to hold the slippery thing steady. Blink and—who knows?—you're two feet tall. Sneeze, and May the Good Lord Smile Upon You. I live in deathly fear of dropping the thing. I don't know what I'd do without it. Carouse more, probably. I love my cold and shiny burden, that's why. And I won't say anything about the preceding story, because if it didn't say everything it was supposed to say all by itself, then that's its own fault and I'm not going to dignify it with any more words. Any error is always attributable to the mirror—either to the way I'm holding it, or to the way you're looking into it—so don't blame me. I just work here. But ... If anything *does* seem amiss with visions of this sort, keep on looking into the glass and take a couple of quick steps backwards. Who knows? Maybe you'll turn into the powder room ...

VIOLATION

William F. Nolan

The concept of the machine-like traffic officer, famously seen on the cinema screen in the two Robocop *movies in 1987 and 1990, is actually part of a much older tradition in science fiction. Over the years there have been a number of stories of metal enforcers as the answer to the worst depredations of the motor car and those who drive them without thought for others. The following story, set in a not too distant future, offers perhaps the last word on the idea — in every sense of the word.*

William F. Nolan (1928–) is best known for the novel Logan's Run *(1967), made into a film in 1976, which he co-wrote with George Clayton Johnston, about a future in which law enforcers are charged with putting to death everyone once they reach the age of 21. However, his early life as a racing car driver and biographer of several of the 'kings of speed' is less well known, although in the context of this story rather important. Nolan is proud of the fact that he once earned a trophy competing in an Austin-Healey in a 100-mile race at Le Mans and later put his inside knowledge of racing sports cars to good use when he wrote* Omnibus of Speed *(1958) and the biographies of two US champion drivers, Barney Oldfield and Phil Hill. His love of speed also inspired him to write our next story, as he has explained: 'The truth is I sometimes drove as fast off the track as I did on it. As a result, I collected a hatful of traffic tickets. I didn't lose my licence, but I certainly deserved to lose it. Traffic cops were The Enemy. I began to think of myself as their personal victim — and since I could do nothing to ease the frustration of being stopped and ticketed I sat down one afternoon and decided to take out my frustration at the typewriter. I wrote "Violation".'*

* * *

It is 2 a.m. and he waits. In the cool morning stillness of a side street, under the soft screen of trees, the rider waits quietly—at ease upon the wide leather seat of his cycle, gloved fingers resting idly on the bars, goggles up, eyes palely reflecting the leaf-filtered glow of the moon.

Helmeted. Uniformed. Waiting.

In the breathing dark, the cycle metal cools: the motor is silent, a power contained.

The faint stirrings of a still-sleeping city reach him at his vigil. But he is not concerned with these; he mentally dismisses them. He is concerned only with the broad river of smooth concrete facing him through the trees, and the great winking red eye suspended, icicle-like, above it.

He waits.

And tenses at a sound upon the river—an engine sound, mosquito-dim with distance, rising to a hum. A rushing sound under the stars.

The rider's hands contract like the claws of a bird. He rises slowly on the bucket seat, right foot poised near the starter. A coiled spring. Waiting.

Twin pencil-beams of light move towards him, towards the street on which he waits hidden. Closer.

The hum builds in volume; the lights are very close now, flaring chalk-white along the concrete boulevard.

The rider's goggles are down and he is ready to move out, move onto the river. Another second, perhaps two . . .

But no. The vehicle slows, makes a full stop. A service truck with two men inside, laughing, joking. The rider listens to them, mouth set, eyes hard. The vehicle begins to move once more. The sound is eaten by the night.

There is no violation.

Now . . . the relaxing, the easing back. The ebb tide of tension receding. Gone. The rider quiet again under the moon.

Waiting.

The red eye winking at the empty boulevard.

'How much farther, Dave?' asks the girl.

'Ten miles, maybe. Once we hit Westwood, it's a quick run to my place. Relax. You're nervous.'

'We should have stayed on the gridway. Used the grid. I don't *like* these surface streets. A grid would have taken us in.'

The man smiles, looping an arm around her.

'There's nothing to be afraid of as long as you're careful,' he says. 'I used to drive surface streets all the time when I was a boy. Lots of people did.'

The girl swallows, touches her hair nervously. 'But they don't any more. People use the grids. I didn't even know cars still *came* equipped for manual driving.'

'They don't. I had this set up special by a mechanic I know. He does jobs like this for road buffs. It's still legal, driving your own car—it's just that most people have lost the habit.'

The girl peers out the window into the silent street, shakes her head. 'It's . . . not *natural*. Look out there. Nobody! Not another car for miles. I feel as if we're trespassing.'

The man is annoyed. 'That's damn nonsense. I have friends who do this all the time. Just relax and enjoy it. And don't talk like an idiot.'

'I want out,' says the girl. 'I'll take a walkway back to the grid.'

'The hell you will,' flares the man. 'You're with *me* tonight. We're going to my place.'

She resists, strikes at his face; the man grapples to subdue her. He does not see the blinking light. The car passes under it swiftly.

'Chrisdam!' snaps the man. 'I went through that light! You made me miss the stop. I've broken one of the surface laws!' He says this humbly.

'What does that mean?' the girls asks. 'What could happen?'

'Never mind. Nothing will happen. Never mind about what could happen.'

The girl peers out into the darkness. 'I want to leave this car.'

'Just shut up,' the man says, and keeps driving.

Something in the sound tells the rider that this one will not stop, that it will continue to move along the river of stone despite the blinking eye.

He smiles in the darkness, lips stretched back, silently. Poised there on the cycle, with the hum steady and rising on the river, he feels the power within him about to be released.

The car is almost upon the light, moving swiftly; there is no hint of slackened speed.

The rider watches intently. Man and girl inside, struggling. Fighting with one another.

The car passes under the light.

Violation.
Now!
He spurs the cycle to metal life. The motor crackles, roars,
explodes the black machine into motion, and the rider is away,
rolling in muted thunder along the street. Around the corner,
swaying onto the long, moon-painted river of the boulevard.

The rider feels the wind in his face, feels the throb and power-
pulse of the metal thing he rides, feels the smooth concrete rushing backward under his wheels.

Ahead, the firefly glow of tail-lights.

And now his cycle cries out after them, a siren moan through
the still spaces of the city. A voice which rises and falls in spirals
of sound. His cycle-eyes, mounted left and right, are blinking
crimson, red as blood in their wake.

The car will stop. The man will see him, hear him. The eyes
and the voice will reach the violator.

And he will stop.

'Bitch!' the man says. 'We've picked up a rider at that light.'

'*You* picked him up, I didn't,' says the girl. 'It's your problem.'

'But I've never been stopped on a surface street,' the man says,
a desperate note in his voice. 'In all these years—never once!'

The girl glares at him. 'Dave, you make me sick! Look at you—
shaking, sweating. You're a damn poor excuse for a man!'

He does not react to her words. He speaks in a numbed monotone. 'I can talk my way out. I know I can. He'll listen to me. I
have my rights as a citizen of the city.'

'He's catching up fast. You'd better pull over.'

His eyes harden as he brakes the car. 'I'll do the talking. All
of it. You just keep quiet. I'll handle this.'

The rider sees that the car is slowing, braking, pulling to the
kerb.

He cuts the siren voice, lets it die, glides the cycle in behind
the car. Cuts the engine. Sits there for a long moment on the
leather seat, pulling off his gloves. Slowly.

He sees the car door slide open. A man steps out, comes
towards him. The rider swings a booted leg over the cycle and
steps free, advancing to meet this law-breaker, fitting the gloves
carefully into his black leather belt.

They face one another, the man smaller, paunchy, balding, face flushed. The rider's polite smile eases the man's tenseness.

'You in a hurry, sir?'

'Me? No, I'm not in a hurry. Not at all. It was just . . . I didn't *see* the light up there until . . . I was past it. The high trees and all. I swear to you. I didn't see it. I'd never knowingly break a surface law, Officer. You have my sworn word.'

Nervous. Shaken and nervous, this man. The rider can feel the man's guilt, a physical force. He extends a hand.

'May I see your operator's licence, please?'

The man fumbles in his coat. 'I have it right here. It's all in order, up to date and all.'

'Just let me see it, please.'

The man continues to talk.

'Been driving for years, Officer, and this is my first violation. Perfect record up to now. I'm a responsible citizen. I obey the laws. After all, I'm not a fool.'

The rider says nothing; he examines the man's licence, taps it thoughtfully against his wrist. The rider's goggles are opaque. The man cannot see his eyes. He studies the face of the violator.

'The woman in the car . . . is she your wife?'

'No. No, sir. She's . . . a friend. Just a friend.'

'Then why were you fighting? I saw the two of you fighting inside the car when it passed the light. That isn't friendly, is it?'

The man attempts to smile. 'Personal. We had a small personal disagreement. It's all over now, believe me.'

The rider walks to the car, leans to peer in at the woman. She is pale, as nervous as the man.

'You having trouble?' the rider asks.

She hesitates, shakes her head mutely. The rider leaves her and returns to the man, who is resting a hand against the cycle.

'Don't touch that,' says the rider coldly, and the man draws back his hand, mumbles an apology.

'I have no further use for this,' says the rider, handing back the man's licence. 'You are guilty of a surface-street violation.'

The man quakes; his hands tremble. 'But it was not *deliberate*. I know the law. You're empowered to make exceptions if a violation is not deliberate. The full penalty is not invoked in such cases. You are allowed to—'

The rider cuts into the flow of words. 'You forfeited your Citizen's Right of Exception when you allowed a primary emotion—

anger, in this instance—to affect your control of a surface vehicle. Thus, my duty is clear and prescribed.'

The man's eyes widen in shock as the rider brings up a belt-weapon. 'You can't possibly—'

'Under authorisation of Citystate Overpopulation Statute 4452663, I am hereby executing . . .

The man begins to run.

'. . . sentence.'

He presses the trigger. Three long, probing blue jets of star-hot flame leap from the weapon in the rider's hand.

The man is gone.

The car is gone.

The street is empty and silent. A charred smell of distant suns lingers in the morning air.

The rider stands by his cycle, unmoving for a long moment. Then he carefully holsters the weapon, pulls on his leather gloves. He mounts the cycle and it pulses to life under his foot.

With the sky in motion above him, he is again upon the moon-flowing boulevard, gliding back towards the blinking red eye.

The rider reaches his station on the small, tree-shadowed side street and thinks, *How stupid they are! To be subject to indecision, to quarrels and erratic behaviour—weak, all of them. Soft and weak.*

He smiles into the darkness.

The eye blinks over the river.

And now it is 4 a.m., now 6 and 8 and 10 and 1 p.m. . . . the hours turning like wheels, the days spinning away.

And he waits. Through nights without sleep, days without food—a flawless metal enforcer at his vigil, sure of himself and of his duty.

Waiting.

THY BLOOD LIKE MILK

Ian Watson

The final story in this book is set on a terribly polluted Earth of the far future, when the sun is rarely seen by its inhabitants. It is a world of superhighways full of automated slave traffic. Among these vehicles are sometimes to be found renegade drivers at the wheels of their sun buggies — almost the ultimate form of automobile — competing with one another along the highways. The story of one of these men, Considine, and his quest is perhaps the most profound and unsettling prediction of Autogeddon that has so far been written.

Ian Watson (1943–) has been described by The Encyclopedia of Science Fiction *(1993) as a 'natural successor to H. G. Wells', and during his career, now spanning thirty years, he has moved as effortlessly through the genres of sf, fantasy and prophecy as did his great predecessor. A teacher and lecturer in Tanzania, Japan and England before becoming a full-time author, Watson has received a number of prizes for his short stories and novels such as* The Jonah Kit *(1975) which won the 1978 British Science Fiction Award. His series about a strange, divided world of the future, the* Black Current *trilogy published in the Eighties, is also very highly regarded by readers and critics alike.*

The constant variety and range of Ian Watson's work has made him one of the most important sf writers of his generation — a fact that was already becoming evident when he wrote 'Thy Blood Like Milk' in 1973 for New Worlds. *It is an extraordinary tour de force combining worship of the ancient sun gods with the far future of motoring.*

*   *   *

This tale is for the sun god, Tezcatlipoca, with my curses, and for you Marina — whom I never knew enough to love — with apologies and blessings, somewhat tardy . . .

Have you ever screamed at your nurse to go away—to leave you in peace—and hated her, as bitterly as you've ever hated anybody? And begged her, as you never begged anyone in your proud life before?

Ten of us lay in the ward in plastic webbing imprisoning us, yet only three of us really counted, Shanahan, Grocholski, and me, for we were the only presidents. Yet a big haul for them, indeed, three presidents! How cleverly the hospital distinguished between us and the ordinary runners: the extra dose of nerve sensitiser in the syringe, the absence of any opiates. We hung on the raw edge of pain, gritting our teeth as the taps were spun and at times—when your bloodstreams burned like second nervous systems on fire in our bodies, and it seemed we were being roasted on a gridiron, from our insides outwards—at such times we let go and screamed. Whereas when the runners were being drained they moaned but did not need to scream. Mixed in with their quarter-pint soup of drugs (anti-shock, anti-coagulant, vitamins, iron) they received the opiates that let them still catch the idea of pain, but be somewhat glassed off from it—while we three were locked up in bright tin boxes with the howl of a thumb-nail on slate a thousand times amplified. The nerve sensitiser wasn't merely sadistic, but meant to aid the nurse monitoring the effects of the milking on our bodies; the opiates were supposed to block off the worst of the sensations arising. I might say that according to the compensation laws we should have all had opiates. But that's how they ran a punishment ward. Idiot thinking. Shanahan, Grocholski, and I—we didn't hold each other's occasional screams and pleas against each other. The pain just happened to be unbearable. As simple as that. In the eyes of the runners our agony confirmed our presidencies. The Aztec priests were tortured by the Spaniards before their congregations. So the Aztec priests screamed and begged, when their turn came? The congregations still believed in them.

'You scum of the earth!' Marina hissed as she jabbed our tethered buttocks with that cruel syringe, an Ahab tormenting her own private whale over and over again. (But I did not know her, did not know *you* as Marina yet.) 'Do you know what will happen

to you today? We're going to take so much out of you and for
so long that your brain will starve for oxygen, you'll be half way
to an idiot, a drooling vegetable.'

'You know that's illegal, you bitch,' I snarled as you tickled
my bare flesh with the syringe anticipatorily making my nerves
try to crawl away.

'Anyone may make mistakes,' her eyes gleamed.

Only a scare, a put-on. Panic. She wouldn't dare.

'You must be a pretty girl under that mask. Why do you hate
us so bitter?'

'Why give you the satisfaction of knowing?'

'You gave me the satisfaction of knowing just then—there's
something to know.'

And the syringe hit my flesh hard, at that, and dug in.

The hot acid gruel washed into me. My veins now lavaflows
cursed with a consciousness of their own heat and motion. The
exquisite agony of being emptied out. The pain of my tortured
body racing to make more and more blood as the metabolic drugs
goaded it on.

And under and around this pain, the fear that as life-blood
flowed out through the taps, my brain was starving and impoverished, on the brink of becoming the brain of an animal, a toad,
a stone—

'Bitch!' I screamed.

Out through one set of pipes flowed my rich blood, in through
another the miserable substitute fluid that my body raced to build
upon. And Marina (whom I did not know as Marina yet) danced
the empty syringe before my eyes, to conduct the music of my
torment—keeping an eye on the dials and gauges but pretending
not to. Why did she hate us so bitter? Well, I hated her just as
bitter! Why ask why. I knew it when I rode for the sun, I might
end up here if they found one single excuse to lay their hands
on me.

Then the pain got too bad to think about anything else.

No windows in the ward. What was there to look out on? We
were outside any Fuller dome, in this hospital. The pollution
crawling up and down the sides of the building, dark grey to
pitch black. A general turbidity over the land: over the great
plains where the braves of another age and world hunted buffalo;
on the treeless hills, where it had long since snuffed out the pines;

pressing soft on the Great Dead Lakes, and, further out, pressing soft on the dark cesspool of the North Atlantic. Pressing upon the superhighways where mostly automatic traffic crawled and where we had hunted in our packs for that rare bird of paradise, that dark orchid, the patch of clear sun—the 'sunspot' that blooms mysteriously amid the murk, shafts of gold piercing a funnel of light down to earth whereby the clear sky could be briefly glimpsed and worshipped. Were not the deaths we caused on the highways only petty sacrifices to ensure the coming of the sun?

And the murk lay thickly on this hospital, Superhighway 31 Crash Hospital, Prison Wing, in whose ward we swooned in pain as we gave up our lifeblood to recompense the beneficiaries of this murk, authors of the forever eclipse of the sun . . .

When did I set out upon the sun trail? When did I drive down my own superhighway of the spirit, choosing my own side of the split world, the zone of blood and the sun? Oh these years of hunting for the sun—down ten times a thousand miles of gloomy darkness, oily globules crawling on our windshields, eyes glazed by the green gleaming radar screens of our sun buggies as we swung them, steering blind, through the rivers of automated slave cars, slave trucks riding their guide lines! Brains blazing with the data stream from Meteorology Central—the temperature gradients, the shifting chemistry of the pollutants, the swirling shapes of air turbidity, the cat's cradle of contrails spied upon by the satellite stations high above! (Have you seen a picture of the Earth from satellite? The masked globe, in its gossamer spidery web of contrails, a mud of many shades of brown ochre grey stirred slowly, punctured in several magic shifting locations by the white walls of sunspots drilling their way to the barren ground or the dead seas or the great photophobic anaerobic algae beds (where, perversely, the light kills them) or the dots of Fuller domes where the wasp world lives out its memories of middle class existence). Grabbing the data with our minds to make a gestalt of it that will lead us to the sun! These years of hunting for the sun—and finding it! Being first to reach those clear fresh zones of radiance, where the flash harvests green and bronze the earth, and tiny flowers rage and seed and die within the span of thirty minutes. Being the only men to see it. To know that nature was still fleetingly alive, in an accelerated abbreviated panic form, still mistress of a panic beauty. These years of discovering the sun and duelling for it on the highways, and ever in the back of our minds somewhere awareness of the Compensation Laws—the blood-debt to be settled.

'Hey,' called Shanahan, as Marina came to him next in line with the syringe primed and loaded, a little bit of machismo on his part. 'Why not come for a ride in my sun buggy after I get out of here? I'll drive you into the deep dark countryside and we won't hunt for no sunspots either. What we've got to do, we can do in the dark! Hey—but come to think of it—why not just come on a sun hunt with me? Put a blush of real genuine sunburn on those delicate white limbs of yours. Or could it be that you're just a wasp that buzzes about a sundome for her holidays, and never flies out?'

'Yes I'm a wasp, this is my sting.'

And she stung Shanahan's quivering buttocks with the syringe, putting an abrupt end to his taunts. He hung in the white plastic webbing, twitching with pain, fat fly in a spider's web that he couldn't break out of. Marina spun the taps, spiderlike sucked him dry, until he howled.

Till he screamed like ice, like thumbnails on slate.

And Marina—with what grim delight you watched him writhing.

With as much magic and mysticism in the hunt for the sun as there was meteorology, remember how we met together to plot strategies, when our own sun club—Smoking Mirror—first coalesced (later to be known as Considine's Commandos)? And the Indian runner, Marti, who said that his great great grandaddy had been an Indian magician, who stayed with Smoking Mirror till one black afternoon he pushed his buggy too fast, too wildly for a mere machine, down a highway crowded with slave traffic, perceptions throbbing with input, idea associations swarming, sense of time and space distraught—for he'd taken a peyotl pill to commune with his magical ancestry. Marti, who knew all the sun myths of all the Indians, South and North, of the Americas. Marti, who said the name we should call ourselves by—Smoking Mirror—alias of the savage wealthy treacherous Aztec sun god, Tezcatlipoca. Marti who wore the obsidian knife round his neck on a leather thong. The same knife (stolen from a museum case) that the Aztec priests used to tear out the palpitating hearts of the prisoners sacrificed to Tezcatlipoca.

When we reached his smashed buggy and went out to it in our oxygen masks (we had a few minutes before the patrols arrived from the nearest emergency point, with their Compensation Laws to enforce on us, for the flanks of the highway were strewn with the wreckage of the slave cars Marti had collided with) we found the obsidian knife had turned, by a freak, as Marti struck the steering wheel, and driven itself into his chest.

I pulled it out and hung it in my buggy and never washed the blood off the blade. We met the sun that day, the next day, and for three days after—blazing sun spots drilling their way through the smog as we charted our crazy sad, angry course of mourning and celebration of Marti's spirit, across the continent, till even Meteorology Central sat up and took notice of the wild unstatistical improbability of our successes (a first sighting of a sunspot is a kind of scalp, see? a new brave's feather in our headdress) and the sun hordes came tracking us from all over the land to batten on us, converging, duelling, crashing towards us, driving our luck away—Tezcatlipoca would only reveal himself to us, to praise Marti who had named us in his honour.

Only after that when Marti had become history (though the dark-stained knife still hung in my buggy) the new name Considine's Commandos became known, and we settled down to a long period of reasonable successes, but never so successful as that one wild week after Marti died, sacrificed to the sun.

We duelled on the highways with the other clubs, skittering through the slave convoys where the wasps sat back in waspish disbelief with their windows blanked, lapping up video reruns and playing Scrabble, hearing occasionally the scream of tyres from the impossible Outside, brief nightmare intrusion on their security, banshees, werewolves, spooks haunting the wide open Darks between the Fuller domes.

One club that even called themselves the Banshees we tangled with on the southern highways, knowing them only by their radar blips, sneers and taunts over the radio, till one day—or night, where's the difference?—we all of us happened into the same bar at the same time, and I was carrying Marti's obsidian knife, beneath my shirt, or I would never have walked out of that bar to drive again. This time Marti had saved me, but the knife had other enemy blood on it now; and Marti's spirit seemed to disappear. At the cost of losing us the sun, he saved me. For weeks we hunted. For months. And nothing. We got to loathe the midnight roundup of the sunspot sightings from Met Central. Things were beginning to fall apart. Would have done, maybe, if we hadn't been cracked wide open, by the day that brought the Compensation Laws down on all our heads.

'You know what I'd do to that bitch if we were out of these plastic cocoons,' Grocholski growled. 'That bitch' was around the corner preparing our meals. 'I'd rip off her sweet white mask and sweet white uniform, hook her up to this marvel of medical science and drain her whole damn bloodstream while I raped her as cool and clinical as you like, and put no liquid back in her but my seed—what's one fluid ounce to eight pints of the red stuff?—and I'd leave her hanging here in the web for her friends to find like veal in a slaughterhouse.'

Vicious sentiments, Grocholski. But Grocholski had performed just as nasty at that—as cool and clinical, I had heard, though I hadn't met the man before the hospital threw us together here in the ward. He had pulled a girl's teeth out with pliers, one by one, for trying to walk out on him . . .

Vicious enough to bring Marina out, so genuinely distraught that she ripped off her white gauze mask and let us take a look at her full face for the first time—beautiful, I thought, amazed, though I hardly dared let myself admit it—not Barbi-dolly or Bambi-cute, but strong with a warp somewhere in it, maybe in the twist of the lips, that gave her the stamp of authenticity— being unlike the million other stereotypes from the same mould. And her green eyes blazed, till they boiled with tears that evaporated almost as she shed them, so hotly angry was she.

'I don't believe in any heaven. For you vicious beasts killed my man. My heaven was here on Earth! But now I believe in hell. And I know how to make a hell for you. Nobody will get any opiates from now on. Nobody. Thanks to your politeness.'

'Hey,' protested a runner from his white webbing. 'You don't have the right to deprive us—that's illegal!'

'Isn't your people's philosophy outside the Law?'

I tried to tell her then, because suddenly I wanted her to know.

'We do have a code to follow, the same as you—it's a different code, is all . . .'

You didn't hear me, Marina, or you didn't seem to. For Shanahan was shouting:

'They always used the Indian women as torturers! The girls made the best!'

So he'd noticed, too, how high your cheek bones were, though masked and hidden partly by your rounded cheeks, the skin not pulled so tight—sealskin over a canoe frame—the way it had been with some Indian girls I'd known, riding for the sun with us, recognising—and that was what I wanted you to understand, Marina—how we were the new buffalo hunters of the darkness, the new braves and warriors of the polluted darkened highways.

Then things got noisy in the ward. The act of freeing your mouth from the mask's embrace had freed all of our mouths too—but not so much for taunts and obscenities, for a while, till it turned ugly again, but for pointed remarks directed at a real and sexy—if hostile—woman.

With the mask off you became more real, and though we still hated you, we couldn't dismiss you as a perfect plastic wasp girl any more. At least I couldn't. You'd graduated to the status of an enemy.

Marina stared round the ward hotly, at the devils hanging in hell in their plastic wrappings, waiting helplessly to repay their debts to society—and made no move to put her mask back on.

She even answered a question.

'Why do I do this? I volunteered. It's not a popular job, dealing with your people. I volunteered, so I could hurt some of you the way that I've been hurt.'

'How have you been hurt, Princess?' yawned Grocholski.

'Didn't you hear her saying we'd killed her man, Gr'olski?'

You gazed at me bitterly, yet in your unmasked gaze was a kind of salutation.

'How did it happen?'

'How do you think you kill good men? You ran him down in the dark, deliberately, while he was tending at an accident.'

'Did you see it yourself?'

'Wasps can't see to fly in the dark,' jeered Grocholski, carrying machismo further into the zone of his own personal viciousness.

'That's how I know,' Marina told me icily, ignoring Grocholski who was thrashing about in his web simulating laughter. 'Talk like that. Attitudes like that. Oh, he could see you coming on the radar screen before he stepped out of the ambulance. He could see. But he stayed out on the road to rescue a woman caught in a burning car. He was still foaming it down when you ran him over. You dragged him half a mile. They wouldn't let me see him, he was so smashed.'

'Wouldn't *let* you see him?' Grocholski caught out of what she said—but he didn't press the point.

And I wanted her to know—to really understand, inside herself—what we people had, when we weren't being vicious beasts—how we were the real authentic people of our times, facing up to the dirt and dark outside instead of hiding in Fuller domes, hunting down the last glimpses of the natural world—the sun, the sky! How we were the last braves, the last hunters—how could I get that through to the Indian in you smothered in the plastic waspish flesh?

'The ambulance man saw it all on radar—how you changed course at the last moment, to hit him, out there on the road.'

'Ambulance man probably hated us anyway—tell any sort of lie.'

'Do you,' in that frozen voice that I yearned to melt, 'deny you run men down just for kicks?'

'You're not so kind yourself, are you? Why not ask yourself deep down what you're doing here torturing us—whether you aren't enjoying it? Revenge? A long revenge, hey! Something you're specialising in?' (Dared I say it yet—and expect you to accept at least a little bit of it—if not immediately, then later maybe when you were alone, lying awake in bed and worried because something had gone astray in your scheme of things?) 'You're interested in us beasts. You took this job to be near us. Like a zoo visitor watches the tigers. Smell our musk, our fear, our reality.'

Marina's hand cracked across my face, so hard my whole body rocked in its white cocoon.

I swallowed the taste of blood in my mouth and stared hard at her, whispered:

'True, it's true, think about it.'

A look of horror came into her eyes, as she quickly pulled the gauze mask over nose and mouth again.

I suppose the Compensation Laws worked our way too. How else could it be, in a split society?

They bought our tacit support for the maintenance of 'civilised' life—the deceits that otherwise we'd have done our best to explode, us sunclubbers, saboteurs, ghettopeople, all of us outlaws (whom it's plain ridiculous to call outlaw when full fifty per cent of the people live outside of wasp society). And the wasp world could only blast us out of existence by turning its own massive nuclear artillery upon itself—so, in return for the relative security of its slave superhighways, our own relative freedom to roam them. If the wasp world put too many feet wrong, explosives would go off in its highway tunnels, gatherings of the tribes pull down a Fuller dome, a satellite shuttle plane blasting off be met by a home-made missile with a home-made warhead on it. And if we put too many feet wrong (taking wasp lives with our sun buggies was one way) and if they caught us, there would be a blood debt to pay, hooked up to their milking machines, where we were not supposed to be hurt *too* much, or die, or get brain damage, but just *repay, repay* society. For they need red blood like vampires need it.

So I began working on your mind, Marina.

As for the others, well, Grocholski's thoughts were of tearing his enemies' teeth out with pincers, he knew nothing about minds. A king—but a stupid king, like many kings who must have triumphed over the stupidity of their subjects by a greater and crueller stupidity.

Shanahan was a subtler sort of president, had some idea what we stood for, could put it some way into words. Yet he couldn't see his way clear, as I could, into this woman's soul with all its possibilities.

And you worked on my body, Marina.

Neglected your promised cruelties to the others. Still treated Shanahan and Grocholski like dirt, but carelessly, indifferently, reserving your finest moments for me.

And I tried to grit my teeth through the pain and not scream out meaningless noises or empty curses, but always something that would drill the hole deeper and deeper into you—as the sun drills through the smog—till the protective layers were undercut and the egg of myself could be laid in your heart.

'Milkmaid with buckets of blood in your yoke, why not believe me?' I winced, as Marina thrust the gruel of drugs into the tender parts of my body. 'We're hunting for something real in a dirty world—the dirt you wasps have spread around, till there's such a pile you have to hide yourselves away from it.'

She drained the blood from me till I fainted, green eyes boring into me, doting on my pain . . .

The Myth of the Five Suns—how brightly Marti told it one day after a long fruitless race for the sun that took us near five hundred miles across the plains, till we pulled in tired and restless at a service area run by ghettopeople with their hair like headdresses, like black coronas around eclipsed suns.

'Five worlds there were,' said Marti, the pupils of his eyes dilated to black marbles, his tight brown skin over small sharp bones like a rabbit sucked dry by ants, wizened by the desert sunshine that he had smarted under in his dreams. 'In the First World men swam about like fishes under a Sun of Jewels. This world perished in a flamestorm brought about by the rising of the second sun, the Sun of Fire. The fishes changed into chickens and dogs that raced about in the great heat, unwilling to pause for their feet were burning. But this Sun of Fire died down in turn, gave way to the Sun of Darkness, whose people fed on pitch and resin. They in their turn were swallowed up by an earthquake and a Sun of Wind arose. The few survivors of the Sun of Darkness became airy dancing monkeys that lived on fruit. But the fifth sun was the Sun of Light—the one the ancient Mexicans knew. Which sun are we under now, can you riddle me that?'

'Sun of Darkness,' answered one of the ghettopeople. 'Here's your pitch and resin to eat.' Dumping our plates of hamburgers, which may have been made from oil sludge or algae—so perhaps he was right in a way.

Then Snowflake—of the snub nose and blonde pigtails, with her worry beads of rock-hard dried chestnuts on a silver chain—who was riding with Marco in his buggy—wanted to tell a story herself, and Marti let her go ahead while we were consuming the burgers.

'There was this waspman, see, whose slave car broke down on the highway miles from town, and quite by chance in the midst of a sunspot. He'd lost all sense of time on the journey, watching video, so when the car stopped he thought he'd reached his destination—especially when he opened the car door and saw the sun shining and a blue sky overhead, like at home in

the Fuller dome. He got out of the car, too busy with his briefcase
to notice that under that sun and that blue sky the land stretched
out black and devastated, a couple inches deep in sludge. An
area where some light-hating plants had taken over, see, which
had the trick of dissolving if the sun came out . . .'

'What?' cried Marco, indignant.

'Shut up, this is a story! At that moment the power came on
in his car again and away it whisked leaving him standing there
on the road. Other cars zipped by on either side. He waved his
arms at them and held his briefcase up but all the passengers
were watching video and had their windows opaqued. He got
scared and leapt off the road into the sludge. However the sunspot was coming to a close now. The blue sky misted over and
soon he was all alone in the darkness with cars zipping by on
one side and a hand clutching down his throat for his lungs as
the pollution flowed back, his eyes watering onion tears. And in
the darkness, doubly blinded by tears, he wandered further and
further away from the road into the sludge. Even the noise of
the cars seemed to be coming four ways at once to him. But now
it was dark again the sludge was coming together, shaping itself
into fungi two feet high, and amoeba things as big as his foot,
and wet mucous tendrils like snots ten feet long that coiled and
writhed about . . . and all kinds of nameless nightmares were
there in the darkness squelching and slobbering about him . . .
So he went mad, I guess. Or maybe he was mad to start with.'

A few runners, a few of the ghettopeople applauded, but Marco
looked disgusted at her butting in—though our mouths had been
full while she was doing the talking—and Marti expressed his
annoyance at what he thought of as her sloppy nursery horror-
comic world, preferring his horror neat like raw spirit, and
religious and classical—and as we drank off our tart metallic
beer (solution of iron filings) to wash the burgers down, he dwelt
on the how and when of the Aztec sacrifices to the sun.

'Oh handsome was the prisoner they taught to play the flute
and smoke in a neat and elegant fashion and sing like Caruso.
After a year of smoking and singing and playing the flute, four
virgins were given to him to make love to. Ten days after that
they took him out onto the last terrace of the temple. They opened
his chest with one single slash of a knife. This knife.' (He whirled
the obsidian blade on the thong from around his neck, where

he'd hung it when he left the buggy, flashed it at us.) 'Unzipped him, tore out his heart!'

How strange, and remarkable, that the heartblood of the Aztecs' prisoner flowing for the sun should become our own heartblood pumped into storage bottles and refrigerated with glycerol at this hospital! A sacrifice of ice against a sacrifice of fire—both harshly painful—the one lasting as long as an iceberg melting, the other over and done with in a flash of time!

Waking up weak-headed but set in my purpose, growing sharper with each hour, I shouted for you to come to my web-side, as Shanahan and Grocholski stared at me bemused and grumbled to one another about this perversion of machismo.

'Nurse!'

And you drifted to my side, green eyes agleam, hate crystals in your Indian skull.

'What is it, Considine?'

'Mightn't you hurt me a bit more if I knew you were a person with a name? A nameless torturer never had much fun. Wouldn't you love to be begged for mercy by name—the way *he* called you by name, with emotion—the emotions of fear and anguish, if not of love? The victim begs to know his tormentor's name.'

'So you're a victim are you?'

'We're all victims of this dirty world.'

'No, you're not victims, not you people. You're here to pay because you made victims of other people. So that the lives of your future victims may be saved, by your own life-blood.'

Almost as an afterthought, you added softly:

'My name's Marina, Considine.'

'Ah.'

Then I could let my forced attention unfocus and disperse into the foggy wool of fading pain . . .

And when she came again to plunge the bitter drugs into my body and spin the taps that recommenced the sacrifice of blood, she murmured, eyes agleam with the taunting of me:

'Your blood has saved two lives already, Considine—that must please you.'

'Marina,' I hissed before she had a chance to stick the syringe in me, 'Marina, it's only a role in *our* game that you're playing, don't you realise? In our Sunhunter's game! For sure it's our game, *ours*, not *yours*!'

She held the syringe back, letting me see the cruel needle.

'You know the name of the game, Marina? No, of course you don't, in your white sterile uniform and your plastic waspish life, how could you ever know? But if you've really got Indian blood in your veins, that might help you understand . . .'

'What's there to understand, Considine? I see nothing to understand except you're scared of a little pain.'

'Not scared,' I lied. 'The pain, the savagery—has to be. You have to hurt me, it's your destiny. Day by day you sacrifice me to the sun, my priestess!'

While she still hung back from me, listening in spite of herself, I told her something of Tezcatlipoca—of the giant in an ashen veil carrying his head in his hand, of the pouncing jaguar, of the dreadful shadow, of the bear with brilliant eyes. Of how he brought riches and death. Of the blood sacrifices on the last terrace of the temple. I told how Marti's knife had turned against his own bosom and how the sun had greeted us in splendour every day for a week thereafter. She went on listening, puzzled and angry, till the anger overcame the puzzlement in her, and she thrust the syringe home . . .

But of Tezcatlipoca the trickster I hadn't told her—nor of his deadly practical jokes.

How he arrived at a festival and sang a song (the song the prisoners were taught to sing) so entrancing that all the villagers followed him out of town, where he lured them onto a flimsy bridge, which collapsed, tossing hundreds of them down into the rocky gorge. How he walked into a village with a magic puppet dancing in his hand (the dance the prisoners were taught to dance) that lured the villagers closer and closer in their dumb amazement, till scores of them suffocated in the crush. How he pretended to be sorry, told the angry survivors that he couldn't guarantee his conduct, that they had better stone him to death to prevent more innocent victims succumbing to his tricks. And stone him to death they did. But his body stank so vilely, that many more people sickened and died before they could dispose of it.

As I lay there racked with pain, these stories spun through my head in vivid bloodstained pictures, and my mind sang the song that led the sun's victims onto the bridge, and my body danced the twitching dance that suffocated the survivors, and my sweat glands and my excrement stank them to death.

How would I, Considine, sun's Messenger, lead and dance and stink Marina out of this bright-lit ward, into the darkness that was my home?

When a doctor made his rounds of the blood dairy, he remarked how roughly I was being treated.

'Don't kill the goose that lays the golden egg!' he twinkled, to Marina. No doubt nurses had broken down on this hateful job before.

I smiled at her when he said that, for after a time assuredly the victim and the torturer became accomplices, and when that happens their roles are fast becoming interchangeable. I grinned the death-grin of Tezcatlipoca as he lay dead in the village and stank the villagers into vulture fodder for a joke . . .

So the Doctor thought she might try to assassinate me, snuff me out! Surely the least likely outcome of our duel, by now.

The sacrifice was always preceded by a period of great sensual *indulgence*—a recompense for the pain to be suffered. Yet this victim here, myself, was tied down, bound in white plastic thongs, while his tormentor hung over him day by day replaying a feeble mimic spearthrust into his body, spilling his blood but replacing it again. Day by day it hurt rackingly, yet death never came. What could come? Only freedom—reversal of the sacrifice—overwhelming pleasure—triumph—and the sun! My pain-racked grin glowed confident, drove wild anguished discords through Marina's heart.

'Be careful, Nurse—this one's metabolic rate is far too high. He's burning himself up.'

'Yes, yes,' murmured Marina, distractedly, fleeing from me across the dark plateaux of her heart . . .

And, when more days had passed and I felt invincible in my agony, I commanded:

'Come to me, Marina.'

Does the male spider command the female spider to come to him with her ruthless jaws? Does the male mantis command the female mantis who will wrench his head off with her sawblade elbows?

'Marina.'

She came to my side, under the bemused gaze of Shanahan

and Grocholski, who had given up trying to understand, and, unblessed by the presence of Tezcatlipoca in their skulls, were glad enough to lie back in their plastic webs relaxing from those first few days of machismo, happy enough that the heat was off them. They kept quiet and watched me wonderingly as I suffered and commanded.

'Marina.'

'Yes, Considine?'

'The time's approaching, Marina.'

'Time, Considine?'

'There has to be a climax. What climax can there be? Think!'

'I . . .'

'I'll make it easier for you. You can't drain me dry. Can't . . . terminate me. What satisfaction would there be in that? Who would you turn to then? To Shanahan? Grocholski? Look at them. Lying like slugs in their beds—great torpid bullies. What satisfaction would there be? Sure, Grocholski is a bastard, he'd pull your teeth out one by one with a pair of pliers. But has he any . . . spirit? Has the sun god whispered in his ear?'

Marina turned, watching the two presidents lolling in their white webs, shook her head—as though she understood the question.

Turning, she whispered:

'What climax, Considine?'

'I'll tell you tomorrow, Marina—unless you can tell me before then. Sleep on it, Marina, sleep on it . . .'

She came to me in the night like a sleepwalker—Lady with a Pencil Torch, whose beam she played over the webbing till she located the release tag, and there she rested her hand but didn't pull it yet-a-while.'

As she knelt there bereft of her mask, hr face level with mine, I gazed at her, not as avenging fury and priestess, but briefly as another human being passing in the dark. She knelt poised at the mid-point of a transformation in her role, for a brief time quietly happy in the lightening of the burden, the falling away of the robe of one office before the assumption of the next.

This pause must have lasted you an eternity, Marina.

I watched the long high planes of your cheeks in the back-wash of light off the plastic webbing, the hilltops of your cheekbones, sharper now in the contrast of dark and bright—and your eyes dark pools beyond the cheekbones, in shadow—and kept my peace.

Tezcatlipoca took the form of an ashen-veiled giant carrying his head in his hand and searched for the sunspot where he could be himself, the sun. The sight of him in the dark made nervous people fall dead with fear, the way the wasps in their slave cars shivered at our banshee wail as we passed them by on the highways, invisible, vindictive, reckless. Yet one brave man seized hold of the giant and held on to him—bound him in white plastic webbing, in spite of his screams and curses. Held him hour after hour till near morning when it was time for the sun to rise. Then the ashen giant began promising the brave man wealth and even omnipotence to let him go. At the promise of omnipotence the brave man agreed and tore out the giant's heart as a pledge before he let him go. Wrapping the heart up in his handkerchief, took it home with him. When he opened it up to look at the heart, however, there was nothing but ashes in it. For the sun had already risen, and in his new omnipotence broke his promise and burned his pledge.

Take heed, Marina, hand on the release tag—take heed of the sun when he is free. You hold my heart now in your handkerchief, blood drips into your bottles through the mesh, safely. The heart is not yet ashes.

Her hand touching the webbing, her Indian face divided by a watershed of light ... at this brief pause in time could I have afforded a little pity, a little affection ... ?

'Is it time ... ?'

She whispered into the darkness from which the sun must rise—for the sun is time itself (or so I thought then) so far as our twenty-four hour clocks knew, so far as the circadian rhythms of our body are aware.

What else is time, but the sun in the sky? But this is the Age Without Time—for the travellers over the blackened prairies, for the wasp refugees in the Fuller domes!

At the end of every fifty-two years, the fires were all quenched throughout Mexico, and a fresh fire kindled on a living prisoner's chest—to keep time on the move. What fire shall be kindled in whose chest, to bring Time back into the world today?

'Yes, it's time to kindle the sun.'

Marina's breast rose and fell convulsively as she pulled the tag.

Plastic thongs slid off my limbs in four directions at once like frightened snakes and I slipped to the floor, free of the pain hammock, knocking aside the sanitary facilities which she'd forgotten to remove, with a noisy clatter that alerted Shanahan. He craned his head against the tension of the web, as I sat massaging life into my limbs.

'Considine,' he called softly. A worried Marina flashed the pencil of light across his face, and he blinked blindly at us.

'Considine, get me out of here—please!'

'Put him back to sleep, Marina.' (Quietly.) 'It's not his time for release—Tezcatlipoca isn't with him.' My feet prickling intolerably with thawing-out frostbite.

She crept towards Shanahan, dazzling him with her pencil of light; injected him with something, while he imagined his web was being undone. By the time my legs were fit to stand on, he was calm again.

She gripped my arm to steady me, helped me dress.

'Your car's in the ambulance sheds.'

'Buggy,' said I angrily. 'Sun buggy.'

'There's so much I have to learn.'

'There isn't much,' I assured her—and this, alas, was honest—as we slipped out of the ward towards the darkness of freedom.

'What is the sun really like?'

'A ball of incandescent gas . . .'

Of course Marina hadn't seen the sun. Except as a baby, long time ago, forgotten, maybe. Models of the sun were all. Hot yellow lamps hanging from the eggshells of the Fuller domes, switched on in the morning, switched off again at night. If a sunspot had ever bathed the hospital, she wouldn't have seen it through the solid walls.

As we crept into the ambulance sheds, she began to cough, grating explosive little coughs that she did her best to stifle with her hand.

A dull orange glow from standby lighting pervaded the gloom of the sheds, where half a dozen of the great sleek snubnosed ambulances were parked and a number of impounded buggies—beyond, light spilling from a window in the crew room door and the sound of muffled voices.

We climbed into my buggy—the key was in the lock—and I ran my hands gently over the controls, reuniting myself with them.

Tezcatlipoca's jaguar stencilled on my seat radiated confidence strength suppleness and savagery through my body . . .

Marina sat limply in the passenger seat looking around my world, stifling her cough—but the air was cleaner in my buggy, would get even cleaner once we were on the move.

'Who opens the doors?'

'We have to wait for an ambulance to leave, then chase it out. How soon till we see the sun, Considine?'

'Sooner than you think.'

'How do you *know*?'

'What is the sun, Marina? A blazing yellow ball of gas radiating timelessly and forever at six thousand degrees Centigrade, too bright to look upon. A bear with bells on his ankles, striped face, blazing eyes. A magician with a puppet dancing in his hand. A smoking mirror. A giant in an ashen veil with his head in his hand. A G-type star out on the edge of the galaxy around which planets and other debris revolve. Your choice.'

'I've seen movies of the sun—maybe it's no big thing after all.'

'Oh it's big, Marina—it's the climax.'

Then a siren went off in the shed, shockingly loud, and the lights came up full.

The ambulance crew spilled from their room, zipping their gear and fixing their masks as they ran. They took an ambulance two along the line from us.

Its monobeam flared out ahead, splashing a hole bright as the sun's disc on the door. Its turbines roared.

And the door flowed smoothly, swiftly, up into the roof.

As I started the buggy's engine a look of fear and terrible understanding came over Marina's face—sleepwalker wakening on the high cliff edge. She tore at the door handle. But naturally it was locked and she couldn't tell where to unlock it.

'Marina!' Using the voice that cuts through flesh to the bone. 'Quit it!' A voice I'd never used to beg or plead with in the hospital. Authority voice of the Sun Priest. Obsidian voice. Voice that cuts flesh. Black, volcanic, harsh.

Her hand fell back upon the seat.

The ambulance, blinding the smog with its monobeam, sped through the doors—and us after it, before the doors dropped again.

Great Tezcatlipoca, Who Bringeth Wealth and War, Sunshine
and Death, Sterility and Harvest! For Whom Blood Floweth Like
Milk, That Milk May Flow!

The smog so thick outside. Even the great eye of the ambulance
saw little. Undoubtedly they were relying on radar already, as I
was—and wondering, doubtless, what the tiny blip behind their
great blip represented, Remora riding on a shark . . . I dropped
back, not to worry them.

When we got to the highway entry point, I took the other
direction.

Whichever way I took, I knew it led to the sun.

Two hours down the highway, Marina sleeping on my shoulder, bored with the monotonous environment of the sun buggy
(green radar no substitute for video), radio crackling out data
from Met Central revealing total disarray among the air currents,
turbid gas blowing everywhichways, absurd peaks and dips in
the nitrogen oxides, crazy chemical transformations—a scene in
disarray awaiting my touch, and what I brought it was the body
of Marina, magnet to the iron filings of the everywhichways
polluted sky.

Two hours down the highway, piloting with ever-greater cer-
tainty, careless of pursuit, I picked the radiophone up, tuned to
the Sun Club waveband . . .

Nearby, voices of some charioteers of the sun.

'Considine calling you. Considine's Commandos. Smokey
Mirror Sun Club. I'm heading straight for the sun. Anyone caring
to join me is welcome. Vector in on my call sign . . .'

My voice woke Marina up, to the babble of voices answering
over the radiophone.

'Considine?'

'How did you get out?'

'How do you *know*? Man?'

Who had ever dared call a hunt into being among sunrunners
other than his own? How great the risk he ran, of shame, revenge,
contempt!

How did I know, indeed!

'Where are we?' yawned Marina. 'What's going on?'

'We're hunting for the sun—I've cried fox and I'm calling the
hounds in.'

'Whose voices are those?'

'It hasn't been done before, what I'm doing. Those voices—
the cry of the hounds.'

'Considine, I'm hungry. Is there anything to eat in the car?'

'Hush—I've told you, *buggy* is the name. No eating now—it's
time to fast. This is a religious moment.'

A louder challenging voice that I recognised broke in on the
waveband. The Magnificent Amberson's.

'Considine? This is Amberson. Congratulations on your break-
out—how did you do it?'

'Thanks, Amberson. I got a nurse to spring me.'

'A nurse?'

'She's with me now—she's part of it.'

'Hope you know what you're doing, Considine. You really
meaning to call a general hunt?'

'A gathering of the tribes. That's it, Amberson.'

'Sure your head isn't screwed up by loss of blood? The weather
data is chaos. Sure you haven't bought your way out of there by
offering something in return—say, a gathering of the tribes in a
certain location?'

'Screw you, Amberson—I'll settle with you for that slander
after I've greeted the sun. Sun hounds, you coming chasing
me?'

And a rabble of voices, from far and near, jammed the
waveband.

Marina clutched my arm.

'It frightens me, Considine—who are they all? Where do they
come from?'

'Some of the other half of the people in this land, Marina—
just some of the other half of the people. The ones who stayed
outside in the dark. The ones that weren't wasps. The Indians
your ancestors would have understood. Spirit voices they are—
gods of the land.'

'Indians my ancestors?'

'Yes.'

Green blips swam by me on the radar screen—slave cars that
I sped by effortlessly. I paid no heed to the weather data. My
gestalt, my mind-doll, was fully formed. Its embodiment
hunched by me in the passenger seat, the curves and planes of
Marina's body were the fronts and isobars and isohets of the
surrounding dirt-darkened land. A message, she had been placed
in the hospital for me to find, with pain the trigger to waken me

to her meaning. So many forms a true message can take—a circle of giant stones of the megalith builders, a bunch of knotted strings of different lengths and colours (the *quipu* archives of the Incas)— a human body if need be. If the human body becomes a world unto the lover or the torturer, may not the world itself with its dales and hillocks, its caves and coverts and cliffs, be a body? Marina, my chart, on whom I read my destination!

'Now you must take your clothes off, Marina, for you'll soon be bathing in the sun—we'll soon be lovers.'

'My clothes?'

'Do so.'

I used the Voice of the Sun, the Voice from the Sky. And dazed she began to fumble at her nurse's uniform.

Her nudity clarified my mind—I knew exactly where to turn off now, on to which decrepit smaller road.

'Sun hounds!' I sang. 'Don't miss the turning.'

Goosebumps marched across Marina's flesh and her nipples stood out in the mental cold of her life's climax—the dawning awareness that she had been inserted into life long ago and grown into precisely this, and this, shape, as hidden marker for the greatest future sunspot, burning spot of all burning spots that might start the clouds of darkness rolling back across the land at last, burning away the poisoned blackened soup from the Earth's bowl in a flame-oven of renewal.

'Sun hounds!' I sang. 'The Sun of Darkness is about to set. The Sun of Fire comes next in turn. The men of this creation are to be destroyed by a rain of fire, changed into hopping chickens and dogs.'

'Are you mad, Considine?' came Amberson's voice, nearer now. 'Look, I'm sorry I said what I did. I apologise. But, man— are you mad!'

Now that I'd turned off to the east I was driving slower, yet the buggy rocked and jolted over the broken-backed minor road, tossing us about like fish in a scaling drum.

'It bruises me!' cried Marina, shipwrecked, clinging to her seat.

Your white nudity, Marina—and the Earth's dark nudity to be explored, revealed!

'I give you the sun, you hounds and runners and presidents of this land!' I hurled the words into the babbling radiophone. And even Met Central was starting to show excitement, for they were listening too, and beginning to feed out data rapidly that vectored in on me and my position.

As I stared through the windshield, the greyness ahead slowly lightened to a misty white that spiralled higher and higher into the upper air. We could see fifty yards, a hundred yards ahead. A great light bubble was forming in the dark. In wonder and gratitude, I slackened speed.

We stopped.

'Thank God for that,' muttered Marina.

'Considine here, you sun-hounds—you'd better come up fast, for I'm in the light-bubble now, it's rising, spiralling above, five minutes off the sun at most I'd say. It's *big*, this one.'

'Is that the truth, Considine?' Amberson demanded.

'The truth? Who's nearest?' I called to the sun runners in general. And looked around. My buggy stood on a smashed stretch of road bandaging the blackened ground, at the base of a great funnel of strengthening light . . .

'Maybe I am.' (Very loud, and breathlessly—as though running ahead of his buggy to catch me up.) 'Harry Zammitt of Helios Hunters. I'm . . . coming into the fringes of it now. I see your buggy, Considine. The white whirlpool. Up and up! It's all true. Considine—I don't know how to say it. What you've done. Busting out, hunting down the sun in a matter of hours!'

As that first buggy bumped into the intensifying bubble of light, I piloted my own machine off the road onto the black ground.

We sat, watching the first rays of the sun burn through in golden shafts as the last mist melted.

And suddenly the day was on fire around us.

I squinted up through dark glasses and my windshield at a sun that seemed greater and brighter, a different colour even, from any I'd ever seen before, steely whiter—as if there was less separating me from the sun, that day.

'Out,' I ordered Marina, leaning over her bare legs to flip the door-lock open.

She stepped out obediently into the sunshine, while I gathered the obsidian knife up by the thong from under my seat, dropped it in my pocket.

'But it hurts,' she cried in surprise—the hopping chicken with burnt feet, exactly! 'It's too hot.'

'Naturally the sun is hot.'

Yes it was hot, so very hot. The hard hot rays burning at my skin the moment I stepped outside, hot as a grill, a furnace.

Harry Zammitt moved closer in his buggy, and other buggies were rolling into the sunspot now.

'Marina—you must stand against the buggy—no, better bend your body back, sprawl backwards over the hood, lie on it—but keep your eyes closed or you'll be blinded.'

'You can't make love to me across a car,' she whined feebly, moving in a daze, wincing as her body touched the heating metal. 'It hurts.'

'It's a buggy,' said I. 'Lie back, damn you, lover. Across the hood of my buggy.'

'You animal, you primitive animal,' she mumbled doing just as I said, spreading herself across the hood with her eyes screwed shut. For her this was the climax that confirmed all her fears and lusts for such scum as myself. Oh Marina!

For me the climax was different.

(Had I ever tried to warn you—had I? Who was I now, Considine the human being, or Considine the Priest of the Sun? Liar Considine, how you enjoyed being possessed—how you enjoyed the sanctification of your torture, in order to achieve the torture of sanctity—Marina!)

I, Considine, Priest of the Sun, snatched the obsidian knife from my pocket and brought it slashing down into your chest.

A pretty mess I made of you. The Aztecs must have had dozens of prisoners to practise on. At one blow! Monkey's maybe. Maybe they executed monkeys in the dark rooms under the temple pyramids. By the time I had hacked through the chaos of smashed ribs, torn breast muscle, flesh, that had been your body and my guide—by the time I had trapped the palpitating blood-sodden rag of your heart in my fist and wrenched it free—by that time I was vomiting onto the black soil.

(Soil that showed no signs of the flash harvest of grass and tiny blooms we all looked for, though it had been sprinkled with blood—as was I.)

My mouth putrid with bile, I turned, held your heart, Marina, high, dripping, to the blazing hurtful sun that blistered my skin raw as a flayed criminal's.

'What are you doing, Considine!' screamed the Magnificent Amberson, plunging towards me across the black earth—for he had finally got here, in the wake of some of his followers—sheltering himself under a sheet of metal.

'Sacrificing,' said I. 'As the sun god requires.'

'Sun god?' he snarled.

'Tezcatlipoca has been reborn in the sky—surely you see?'

'Bloodthirsty maniac—I don't care about that—I can't see anything up there! Where has the ozone cover gone?'

I turned to Amberson then blankly, still clutching the wet heart. 'What?'

'The ozone layer in the upper air, don't you realise it's gone? Met Central is shouting murder about it. The hard radiation is getting through. You're burning to death if you stay out here. That's why there's no harvest, you fool. Scattering blood around isn't going to help!'

I dropped the heart on the ground, where it lay bubbling gently, tiny bubbles of blood, into the unresponsive warming soil.

Amberson snatched at me, maybe to drag me under the metal sheet with him, but I shook him off and jumped into my buggy, locking the doors, opaqued the windows.

And sat trembling there with the obsidian blade freshly blooded in my lap.

'Considine!' cried voices over the radiophone.

'Considine?' Amberson's voice—he was back in his sun buggy. 'Yes, I'm here.'

'Now hear me, sun runners all, Considine led you here, and I admit I don't know how. But now maybe he'd like to explain why we can't go outside without being burnt, and where the harvest is?'

I said nothing.

'No? I'll tell you. Anyway, it's coming over Met Central. The ozone layer in the upper air has finally broken down—the pollution has got to it and changed it—and as the ozone layer just happens to be what filters out of the hard radiation from the sun, we had better get the hell out of here. Reflecting—as we do—on the demise of the honourable sport of the sun hunt. From now on anyone who spots the sun is going to wish himself a hundred miles away. So get going sun runners. And bugger you Considine. Let's all know this as Considine's Sunspot—the last sunspot anyone ever hunted for. A nice curse to remember a bloodthirsty fool by!'

*

Tezcatlipoca, why had you cheated me? Did her blood not flow like milk to your satisfaction? Was it because I botched the sacrifice so clumsily? Where the Aztec priest used one swift blow of the knife to unsheath the heart, I used twenty . . .

One thing Amberson was wrong about. The biggest thing of all. The thing that has given me my present role, more hated than Amberson could ever have dreamed as he uttered his curse upon me.

For Considine's Sunspot was not going to close up, ever. It carried on expanding, taking in more acres hour by hour.

Far more than the ozonosphere had altered in those chemical mutations of the past few hours. The pall of dirt that had blanketed the Earth so many years was swift to change, whatever new catalyst it was that had found a home in the smog; now, starting at one point and spreading outward, the catalyst preceding (swimming like a living thing—Snowflake's 'childish' nightmare!) on a wave front from the point of light, the changed smog yielded to the hard radiations of the naked sun.

I was right—which is the horror of it—I was right. Tezcatlipoca is alive again, but no friend to man. Nor was he ever friend to man, but cheated and betrayed him systematically with his magic and his song, and his stink. Tezcatlipoca, vicious bear, hideous giant coming head in hand, bounding jaguar, using me as focus for his flames, as plainly as he used Marina (my lost love!) for his map.

Considine's Sunspot spreads rapidly from one day to the next, gathering strength, sterilising further areas of the country, burning the earth clean. Algae beds consumed faster than they can be covered over. Fuller domes shrivelling, flimsy-fabriced. Buildings in flames, so brittle. The asphalt motorways blazing fifty-mile-long tinder strips.

So let me be Priest of the Burning World then, since it is what I foretold and since, strangely (is it so strangely in these fear-crazed times?), the cult of Tezcatlipoca has revived, at least its ceremonies have, blood sacrifices carried out in the polluted zones beyond the encroaching flame front, in vain hopes of stemming it—oh, they only add fuel to the sun's fire!—with their cockerels and bullocks stolen from the zoo sheds . . . and people too, captive and volunteer—beating hearts torn out by far more expert hands than mine, tossed blindly at where the sun burns its way towards them. And, what no one will volunteer for, the flame kindled in

the darkness on someone's writhing scream-torn body, to impress
the god of fire—Xiuhtecuhtli—oh yes, modern scholarship is on
our side! And after further scholarly researches (did not witch-
craft almost win a World War?) babies are cooked alive, eaten
in honour of Tlaloc, god of rains and springs, who waters the
earth. Outlaws and inlaws, bandits and wasps—we are all in this
together, now.

My fate, Wandering Jew of the burning roads, is to lurk outward and ever outward, casting around the perimeter of Sunspot
Considine, buggy rationed and fuelled free of charge, with
hatred, meeting up with my worshippers, torturers, meteorol-
ogists (has not meteorology absorbed all the other sciences?),
time and again overcome by a craze of words bubbling from
Tezcatlipoca's lips—taunts, demands, tricks and curses fluttering
through my mouth from elsewhere, like captive birds set free,
like the souls of his victims escaping into the sky.

And I ask:

Why *me*?

And:

Why you, Marina?

How I love you, in retrospect, having held your beating heart
within my palm!

And the sunspot that bears my name, great tract of flame-land
seared into the world, pre-Cambrian zone of sun-scarred earth
sterile except for the bacteria lying in waiting for some million-
year-to-come event—do you realise that logically the whole
world will bear my name one day, if the sunspot expands to
embrace it, though no one will be here to use the name—of
Considine's Planet (as it may be known to the ghosts upon it)—
why am I not allowed to drive in there and die? But the mad
sun god will not allow it, while yet he holds me dangling on a
string, jerking my vocal cords as it amuses him. Since I plucked
her heart out I am his creature utterly. As she was mine, and
earlier still as I was hers. So it rolls around.

Once I was a free man, sun hater, outlaw. Now a potential
planet—and a slave. The empty gift of omnipotence! Considine's
world—naked pre-Cambrian of some future society of insects,
perhaps!

Marina.

Whose heart I felt flutter in my hand.

Thy blood like milk for me has flowed, hot as iron pouring from a furnace!

Marina and Considine.

Eve and Adam of the world's end, our non-love brought life to its close, victim and executioner of the vanishing smog-scape—which we all long for nowadays, passionately, and would sacrifice anything, or anyone to bring it back to us.

This tale is for the sun god, Tezcatlipoca, with my curses, and for you, Marina . . .

ACKNOWLEDGEMENTS

The Editor and Publishers are grateful to the following authors, agents and publishers for permission to include copyright stories in this collection:

'Trucks' by Stephen King. First published in *Cavalier* magazine, June 1973. Copyright © by Stephen King. Reproduced by permission of Hodder & Stoughton Limited.

'The Dust Cloud' by E. F. Benson. Reproduced by permission of A. P. Watt Ltd on behalf of the Executors of the Estate of K. S. P. MacDowall.

'Second Chance' by Jack Finney. Copyright © 1956 by the Hearst Corporation, renewed 1984 by Jack Finney. Reproduced by permission of Abner Stein.

'Used Car' by H. Russell Wakefield. Reproduced with permission of Curtis Brown Ltd, London, on behalf of the Estate of H. Russell Wakefield. Copyright H. Russell Wakefield.

'Duel' by Richard Matheson. Copyright © 1971 by Richard Matheson. Reproduced by permission of Abner Stein.

'Who's Been Sitting in My Car?' by Antonia Fraser. Reproduced with permission of Curtis Brown Ltd, London. Copyright © Antonia Fraser.

'Not From Detroit' by Joe R. Lansdale. First published in *Midnight Graffiti* magazine, 1988. Copyright © Joe R. Lansdale, 1999. Reproduced by permission of the author.

'Never Stop on the Motorway' by Jeffrey Archer. Published in *Twelve Red Herrings* by Jeffrey Archer and reproduced by permission of HarperCollins Publishers Ltd.

'The Death Car' by Peter Haining. Copyright © 1999 by Seventh Zenith Ltd and reproduced by permission of the author.

'Night Court' by Mary Elizabeth Counselman. Published in *Half in Shadow* by Mary Elizabeth Counselman and reproduced by permission of Forrest J. Ackerman, 2495, Glendower Avenue, Hollywood, CA 90027.

'Accident Zone' by Ramsey Campbell. Copyright © Ramsey Campbell and reproduced by permission of the author.

'The Last Run' by Alan Dean Foster. First published in *Fantasy & Science Fiction* magazine July 1982. Reproduced by permission of MBA Literary Agents.

'The Hitch-Hiker' by Roald Dahl. Reproduced from *The Wonderful World of Henry Sugar* by Roald Dahl, by permission of David Higham Associates Ltd.

Extract from *Crash* by J. G. Ballard published by Vintage/ Random House, London. Copyright © 1973 by J. G. Ballard and reproduced by permission of the author c/o Margaret Hanbury, 27, Walcot Square, London SE11 4UB.

'The Racer' by Ib Melchior. Copyright © 1952 by Dee Publications, renewed 1980 by Ib Melchior, reprinted by arrangement with Forrest J. Ackerman.

'Along the Scenic Route' by Harlan Ellison. Copyright © 1969 by Harlan Ellison. Renewed copyright © 1997 by Harlan Ellison. Reprinted by arrangement with, and permission of, the author and the author's agent, Richard Curtis Associates Inc., New York.

'Auto-da-Fé' by Roger Zelazny. Copyright © 1967 by Roger Zelazny. Published by permission of the Amber Corporation c/o Ralph M. Vicinanza ltd.

'Violation' by William F. Nolan. First published in *Future City*, 1973. Copyright © 1999 by William F. Nolan and reproduced by permission of the author.

'Thy Blood Like Milk' by Ian Watson. Copyright © Ian Watson 1973. First published in *New Worlds 6* edited by Michael Moorcock and Charles Platt, 1973. Reproduced by permission of the author.